"...IT?"

The cut in Jenny's hand wasn't as bad as Gabe first thought. But his heart lurched when he got a good look at her face. Her lower lip began to tremble, and her eyes watered up.

She nodded like a little girl. "In the kitchen," she said.

"C'mon, I need to take a better look at your hand." Gabe applied antiseptic ointment to the gash on her palm and finished tying off the ends of a bandage. And then, for reasons he didn't wish to examine too closely, he lowered his head and pressed a small kiss to her palm.

She gasped. And desire swept through him like a coastal hurricane. He raised his head and looked into her face. "Did I hurt you?"

"No." She breathed the word.

He cradled her hands in both of his. "You saved my life tonight." Of this he was entirely certain.

"You're crazy, Mr. Raintree—"

He pressed his finger across her lips. "Perhaps I am crazy. And the name is Gabe."

"Gabe," she whispered when he removed his finger. He caught his own name on her lips as he leaned in for one, short kiss.

"A captivating tale." —RomRevToday.com

"Amazing … These lovely folks filled with Southern charm [and] gossip were such fun to get to know … This story spoke to me on so many levels about faith, strength, courage, and choices … If you're looking for a good Christmas story with a few angels, then *Last Chance Christmas* is a must-read. For fans of Susan Wigg."

—TheSeasonforRomance.com

"Visiting Last Chance is always a joy, but Hope Ramsay has outdone herself this time. She took a difficult hero, a wounded heroine, familiar characters, added a little Christmas magic, and—voila!—gave us a story sure to touch the Scroogiest of hearts … It draws us back to a painful time when tensions—and prejudices—ran deep, compels us to remember and forgive, and reminds us that healing, redemption, and love are the true gifts of Christmas."

—RubySlipperedSisterhood.com

Last Chance Beauty Queen

"4½ stars! Get ready for a story to remember when Ramsay spins this spirited contemporary tale. If the y'alls don't enchant you, the fast-paced, easy read will. The third installment in the Last Chance series is filled with characters that define eccentric, off the wall, and bonkers, but most of all they're enchantingly funny and heart-warmingly charming." —*RT Book Reviews*

"Hope Ramsay has penned an irresistible tale in *Last Chance Beauty Queen* with its unforgettable characters and laugh out loud scenes … Watch how an opposites-attract couple find their way to each other … and a possible future. Grab this today and get ready for a rollicking read." —RomRevToday.com

"A little Bridget Jones meets *Sweet Home Alabama*."
—GrafWV.com

Home At Last Chance

"4 stars! Nicely told."   —*RT Book Reviews*

"Entertaining ... Readers will feel once again the warm 'Welcome to Last Chance' by the quirky Ladies' Auxiliary crew ... Contemporary fans will enjoy the homespun regional race to the finish line."
—GenreGoRoundReviews.blogspot.com

"An enjoyable ride that will capture interest and hold it to the very end."   —RomRevToday.blogspot.com

"Full of small town charm and southern hospitality ... You will want to grab a copy of *Welcome to Last Chance* as well."   —TopRomanceNovels.com

Welcome to Last Chance

"Ramsay's delicious contemporary debut introduces the town of Last Chance, SC, and its warmhearted inhabitants ... [she] strikes an excellent balance between tension and humor as she spins a fine yarn."
—*Publishers Weekly* (starred review)

"[A] charming series, featuring quirky characters you won't soon forget."
—Barbara Freethy, *New York Times* bestselling author of *At Hidden Falls*

NN *at* LAST
CHANCE

HOPE RAMSAY

FOREVER

NEW YORK   BOSTON

Copyright © 2014 by Robin Lanier

Forever
Hachette Book Group
237 Park Avenue
New York, NY 10017

www.HachetteBookGroup.com

Printed in the United States of America

First Edition: April 2014
10 9 8 7 6 5 4 3 2 1

OPM

Forever is an imprint of Grand Central Publishing.
The Forever name and logo are trademarks of Hachette Book Group, Inc.

The Hachette Speakers Bureau provides a wide range of authors for speaking events. To find out more, go to www.hachettespeakersbureau.com or call (866) 376-6591.

The publisher is not responsible for websites (or their content) that are not owned by the publisher.

ATTENTION CORPORATIONS AND ORGANIZATIONS:
Most HACHETTE BOOK GROUP books are available at quantity discounts with bulk purchase for educational, business, or sales promotional use. For information, please call or write:

**Special Markets Department, Hachette Book Group
237 Park Avenue, New York, NY 10017
Telephone: 1-800-222-6747 Fax: 1-800-477-5925**

To Annie and Frances

Acknowledgments

Every author has a few people who make writing a book possible. I would like to give my deepest thanks to my writer friends who are always at the ready with suggestions when I get stuck. In particular, many thanks to the Ruby Slippered Sisterhood, who provided many wonderful ideas for ghostly mischief involving an author, a minister, a dinner party, and a china cabinet. I'd like to give a nod to singer-songwriter David Wilcox for his song "Hard Part," with its amazing lyrics about the deepest kind of love. And of course, Charlotte Brontë for writing *Jane Eyre* and giving the world (and me) the wonderful characters of Jane and Rochester. As always, I could not get through writing a book without my dear husband, Bryan, my steady agent, Elaine English, and my talented editor, Alex Logan.

CHAPTER 1

The bitter January wind had blown in a cold front. The clouds hung heavy and somber over the swamp. There would be rain. Possibly ice.

Jenny Carpenter wrapped a hand-knit shawl around her shoulders and gazed through the kitchen window of the house she'd bought last August. The tops of the Carolina pines bent in the wind. The weatherman said it was going to be quite a storm, and Allenberg County had already had one ice storm this year—on Christmas Eve. It was now just two weeks past New Year's Day.

She turned away from the window toward the heart of her house. Her kitchen restoration was nearly finished. Yellow subway tiles marched up the backsplash behind the Vulcan stove. An antique pie safe occupied the far wall. The curtains were gingham. Everything about this room was bright and cheerful, in sharp contrast with the weather outside.

Jenny closed her eyes and imagined the smell of apple pie cooking in her professional baker's oven. This kitchen would rival the one Savannah Randall had installed at the old movie theater in town. She smiled. Savannah's strudel was good, but Jenny's apple pie had still won the blue ribbon at the Watermelon Festival last summer. She could almost hear Mother sermonizing about pride, and her smile faded. She turned back toward the window.

She couldn't remember a colder January. And Jenny hated even the mild winters that usually visited South Carolina. Today she had good reason to hate the season. Winter was getting the best of her.

She'd hired a crew to cut back the overgrowth on either side of the driveway, but they had called to say that they wouldn't be out today, and probably not tomorrow. The movers weren't going to show up today either, which meant Mother's antique furniture would spend yet another night in the commercial storage space where it had been sitting for five years. Without furniture Jenny would have to postpone her plans to move in at the end of the week. Finally, Wilma Riley, the chair of the Methodist Women's Sewing Circle, had called five minutes ago all atwitter because there was ice in the forecast.

The sewing circle had graciously volunteered to help Jenny sew curtains for the bedrooms and sitting room. The fabric bolts—all traditional Low Country floral designs— were stacked in the room that would soon be the dining room. But as Wilma pointed out, the gals were not coming all the way out to the swamp on a stormy day in January. So today, Jenny might be the only one sitting out here sewing.

It wasn't just the weather that had her second-guessing herself. She'd taken a huge risk buying The Jonquil House. The old place wasn't anywhere near downtown. If she'd been able to buy Charlotte Wolfe's house, her bed-and-breakfast would have been located near the middle of things. And she would probably already be in business, since Charlotte's house was in perfect condition.

But Charlotte had changed her mind about selling. She'd returned from California with her son, Simon. And Simon had married Molly Canaday, and they were all living happily in Charlotte's beautiful house.

So Jenny had bought The Jonquil House, which was way out on Bluff Road, near the public boat launch on the Edisto River—a prime location for fishing and hunting. And you couldn't beat the view from the porch on a summer's day. She hoped to attract business from fishermen and hunters and eco-tourists anxious to canoe the Edisto or bird-watch in the swamp.

The Jonquil House had the additional benefit of being dirt-cheap, since it had been abandoned for years. But Jenny had to spend a lot of cash to shore up the foundation, replace the roof, and update the plumbing and electrical. Not to mention installing her state-of-the-art kitchen. Still, the purchase price had been so ridiculously low that, on balance, Jenny was financially ahead of where she would have been if she'd bought Charlotte's house.

And if all went well, The Jonquil House would be open for business by March first, just in time for the jonquils to be in full bloom. There were hundreds of them naturalized in the woods surrounding the house. No doubt they had been planted by the Raintree family, who had built the house more than a hundred years ago as a hunting camp and summer getaway.

Those jonquils were the reason she'd chosen yellow for her kitchen walls. She couldn't wait to take pictures of her beautiful white house against the backdrop of the dark Carolina woods, gray Spanish moss, and bright yellow daffodils.

That photo would be posted right on the home page of the inn's website, which was still under construction, too.

She was thinking about her breakfast menu when there came a sudden pounding at her front door. Her new brass knocker had yet to be installed, but that didn't seem to bother whoever had come to call.

In fact, it sounded like someone was trying to knock the darn door down.

She hurried down the center hall, enjoying the rich patina of the restored wood floors and the simple country feeling of the white lath walls. Maybe the movers had changed their minds, and she'd be able to get Mother's furniture set up in the bedrooms after all.

She pulled open the door.

"It's about damn time; it's freezing out here." A man wearing a rain-spattered leather jacket, a soggy gray wool hat, and a steely scowl attempted to walk into her hallway. Jenny wasn't about to let this biker dude intimidate her, even if he was a head taller than she was.

His features were stern, and his nose a tad broad, as if it had been broken once. Several days' growth of slightly salt-and-pepper stubble shadowed his cheeks, and his eyebrows glowered above eyes so dark they might have been black. If he'd been handsome or heroic looking, she might have been afraid of him or lost her nerve. Handsome men always made Jenny nervous. But big guys with leather jackets and attitudes had never bothered her in the least. She always assumed that men like that were hiding a few deep insecurities.

"Can I help you?" she said in her most polite, future-innkeeper voice.

"You damn well can. I want a room."

"Um, I'm sorry but the inn isn't open."

"Of course it's open. You're here. The lights are on. There's heat."

"We're not open for business."

He leaned into the door frame. Jenny held her ground. "Do you have any idea who I am?"

She was tempted to tell him he was an ass, but she didn't use language like that. Mother had beaten that tendency out of her. It didn't stop her from thinking it, though.

When she didn't reply, he said, "I'm the man who sold you this house. I would like, very much, to come in out of the rain."

"The man who—"

"The name's Gabriel Raintree. My family built this house. Now let me in."

She studied his face. Gabriel Raintree was a *New York Times* bestselling author of at least twenty books, several of which had been made into blockbuster horror films. His books were not on her reading list. And she wasn't much of a moviegoer.

She'd never met Mr. Raintree. The sale of The Jonquil House had been undertaken by his business manager and attorney. So she had no idea if this guy was the real Gabriel Raintree or some poser. Either way she wasn't going to let him come in. Besides, the house was not ready for guests. The furniture had not even arrived.

"I'm sorry. The inn isn't open."

His black eyebrows lowered even farther, and his mouth kind of curled up at the corner in something like a sneer. He looked angry, and it occurred to Jenny that maybe she needed to bend a little. The minute that thought crossed her mind, she rejected it. She had inherited a steel backbone from Mother, and this was a good time to employ it. She wouldn't get very far as an innkeeper if she allowed herself to be a doormat.

"I need a place to stay," he said, "for at least three months. I'm behind on my deadline."

Three months. Good Lord, she wasn't running a boardinghouse. But then, she supposed that if anyone could afford three months' lodging at a B and B it would be someone like Gabriel Raintree.

The income would be nice. But she wasn't ready for any guests.

"I'm very sorry. The inn won't be open until March. If you need to stay in Last Chance, there's always the Peach Blossom Motor Court. Or you could see if Miriam Randall will take you in. She sometimes takes in boarders."

"Damn it all, woman, this is my house." He pushed against the door, and Jenny pushed back.

"Not anymore," she said.

He stopped pushing and stepped back from the threshold. By the deep furrows on his brow, she could only surmise that he was surprised anyone would stand in his way. She slammed the door on him to punctuate her point. Then she twisted the bolt lock and took a couple of steps back from it, her heart hammering in her chest.

Gabe stood on the porch breathing hard, trying to control his anger and a dozen other emotions he didn't want to feel, chief among them a deep, gnawing loneliness.

The hollow feeling had been with him for a long time—even before his breakup with Delilah years ago. And now, this place and the memories it raised made the loneliness feel deep and wide, like a gaping chasm. There was something dark and frightening down in the depths of that empty place. Something monstrous.

He leaned on the porch railing and looked around at the familiar scene. His younger self had been happy and carefree here. Christ, it had been a long, long time since he'd felt that way.

And The Jonquil House was perfect for what he needed right now, a quiet place almost entirely off the grid where he could wrestle with his writer's block and escape from his mistakes. Hiding out here in the middle of nowhere seemed like a good idea. He'd have solitude. He could be alone with his demons.

But a tiny little innkeeper stood between him and what he needed. It was worse than that—she hadn't even recognized him.

He let go of a short bark of laughter. He should be happy. In Charleston, he couldn't walk down a street without someone, usually dressed like a Goth, accosting him and wanting a piece of him.

He stared at the closed door. He was an idiot if he let that woman bruise his ego. Besides, he'd come here to hide out. And she'd just convinced him it was the perfect place for that singular activity.

He surveyed the overgrown drive, memories filling his head. Twenty-five years ago he would have been greeted by Zeph Gibbs, the hunting guide and caretaker. Lottie Easley would be back in the kitchen cooking up hoppin'-john and corn bread and fried okra. He could almost taste Lottie's cooking.

And he longed to see their faces. But they were ghosts now. Especially Luke, the brother he'd lost twenty-five years ago in a hunting accident.

Ten-year-old Gabe had been there the day Luke died, but Gabe had no memory of what had happened that awful day. Those memories were locked behind a barrier as high and thick as Hadrian's Wall.

His heartbeat echoed inside his empty chest. He had worshiped his older brother, and Luke's death had changed everything.

He moved down onto the porch step and let the rain fall on his head and shoulders. It was quiet here. Peaceful. Precisely the kind of place he needed to get back in touch with his muse. The kind of place he needed to write the damn book that had been eluding him for almost a year. The kind of place where a lonely man could simply be left alone.

The muscles of his neck and shoulders tensed in frustration. If the inn wasn't going to open until March, he'd have to come up with another plan.

But he didn't want a Plan B. He wanted to come back here. Something in his gut told him that this was precisely the right place to be.

The rain was picking up, and sleet was beginning to mix with it. The roads were going to get bad before too much longer.

Either way, he'd have to stay the night at the seedy motel in town. But tomorrow, when the storm had passed, he'd come back out here and negotiate. The little innkeeper had her price. Everyone did.

Tomorrow he'd buy back The Jonquil House.

The wipers smeared the light from the motel's sign as Gabe pulled his Lexus SUV into the parking lot. Peach blossoms blinked on and off, like opening flowers, but the neon was burned out in a few places, so that the sign read "each Bosom Moo," which Gabe found vaguely hilarious, given the motel's reputation.

He remembered the motel from his boyhood. It hadn't looked nearly so run-down twenty-five years ago.

He sat in his car for a long moment, the wipers thumping a syncopated counterpoint to the recording of Bach's Brandenburg Concerto Number 1 coming from his top-of-the-line sound system.

Maybe he should turn around and head toward Columbia. Columbia might be a sleepy southern capital, but they had hotels there. Nice ones, with room service. He might be able to hide out in Columbia. Of course, he'd have to be careful not to go out to eat or walk the streets or any of those things. There were a lot of people in Columbia, and some of them were sure to recognize him. Someone would tweet about him. And his editor would come looking for him. And his crazy fans would find him and hound him.

But here, he was just one of the Raintree boys, come back to town after a long hiatus. If he wanted to be a hermit living out at The Jonquil House, the people here would let him be. Last Chance was full up to the brim with eccentric people and no one thought anything about it.

Besides, the fishing was better here.

He almost smiled at the thought, and then he remembered that it was the dead of winter and he'd pretty much freeze his ass off if he went fishing. And of course, he hadn't been fishing in years. But if he lived here, he might take it up again.

He weighed his options as he watched the icy rain splatter on his windshield. In the end, the sleet made the decision for him. The Lexus might have four-wheel drive, but that was next to useless on black ice.

He checked in, took one brief look at the run-down furniture in the room, and then headed back out into the weather. There had to be a café or something where he could get himself some dinner.

It occurred to him that he'd almost never eaten out when he'd come to visit this place as a boy. Lottie had done the cooking. He'd have to find himself a cook, once he bought The Jonquil House back.

Just thinking about Lottie's corn bread had his stomach growling. He hadn't eaten since this morning, and he was feeling a bit light-headed. His blood sugar was low.

He reached for the roll of LifeSavers he always carried and popped one into his mouth. It was cherry-flavored.

He stood on the concrete pad under the roof overhang that protected his room door from the rain. It wasn't a long walk from here into the heart of downtown Last Chance, but the ice was building on the sidewalks fast. The road, on the other hand, had been treated with sand and salt.

So he took a chance and drove the SUV slowly back into downtown. He found a parking spot in front of The Kismet movie theater. The old movie palace looked pretty good, especially compared with the run-down motel.

Looking up at the marquee, it finally hit him that it had been a quarter century since he'd set foot in this little town. *Lethal Weapon* had been the last movie he and Luke had seen in this old movie theater. Luke died three days later, on the Saturday before Easter.

The memory caught him unaware. He tried not to think too much about Luke.

Maybe that was the missing puzzle piece. Maybe that was why he'd awakened yesterday and knew that he had to return here. Who knew.

He climbed out of his car and stood for a long time under the marquee. It wasn't a first-run theater anymore, and that hardly surprised him. The signs on the front door said it was only open on Friday and Saturday nights. These days the movies came with dinner attached.

A light was burning in the theater's lobby. He took a step toward the glass doors and peered in. The place was much as he'd remembered. A gifted carpenter had created a masterpiece when he'd set his hand to The Kismet's lobby. It was awash with Moroccan motifs and Moorish archways. Gabe cocked his head to get an angle on the ceiling, but it was too dark. Once upon a time, the ceiling had been painted like a night sky with twinkling stars.

The theater was worthy of historic registry status, and it warmed him in some odd way to know that it hadn't been left to molder.

A moving shadow just beyond the candy counter momentarily startled him, until he remembered that the owner of The Kismet had always kept a cat—a black one. The shadow danced again, casting itself eerily against the walls. Gabe cupped his hands around his face to get a better look.

A black man with gray hair, wearing a pair of faded overalls and carrying a toolbox, stood up from behind the candy counter.

Gabe took a step back, his heart pounding. He would know that man anywhere. That face was from out of the distant past. Why had he assumed that Zeph Gibbs was dead and gone?

The hairs on the back of Gabe's neck rose, and the icy night got a little more frigid—cold enough to freeze him right where he stood while something hot and evil writhed in his gut.

The door opened. Zeph stepped out of the theater and stopped in his tracks. Time seemed to slow down as their gazes met and clashed.

"Gabe?" Zeph cocked his head.

"It's me."

"Lord a'mighty, what are you doin' here?"

It wasn't exactly a hearty welcome, but that didn't surprise Gabe for some reason he couldn't exactly articulate. Zeph had been a big part of his boyhood. This man had taught him to shoot a BB gun and bait a hook and walk quietly in the woods. And yet seeing him once again after a quarter century brought no joy.

"Hello, Zeph." There seemed to be a torrent of words locked up inside him, but the simple greeting was all he could manage. Christ on a crutch, he had some strange feelings about Zeph.

Gabe had turned Zeph into a villain named Zebulon Stroud in the novel titled *Black Water*. And *Black Water* had taken Gabe to the top of the *New York Times* bestseller list. *Black Water* was also the first of Gabe's novels to be made into a feature-length motion picture. Danny Glover had won an Oscar for his portrayal of the villain. Zeb Stroud was one of those characters people remembered, like Hannibal Lecter.

"You need to leave," Zeph said.

"That's going to be hard with all this ice."

"Tomorrow then, when it melts."

"Look, Zeph, about the character in *Black Water*, I sure don't want you to take it—"

"This has nothing to do with that story. I'm not mad at you for that. But you can't stay here."

"I can't stay here? Why not? I know The Jonquil

House has been sold, but I can certainly book a room at the motel. In fact, I have."

"Why are you here?"

"I was thinking about buying The Jonquil House back from that little woman who owns it now."

"You can't. You have no business being in this town. Not now. Not ever."

This confused him. "Why not?"

"You know good and well why it's a bad idea to come back here." Zeph turned and locked the theater door.

Gabe couldn't think of one good reason why he shouldn't stay. But he understood why Zeph wouldn't be happy about him being here. After all, Zeph was responsible for Luke's death. The man probably didn't want Gabe hanging around reminding him of that tragedy all the time. Granddad had never forgiven Zeph.

But Gabe could.

"Look, Zeph, I'm not my grandfather. I don't blame you for what happened. I'm not here to rub your nose in it."

Zeph turned around. He didn't say a word, but he pressed his lips together as if he was trying damn hard not to say something ugly.

Gabe stuck out his hand. "I forgive you."

Zeph stood there staring at Gabe's outstretched hand as if he had been speaking in tongues or something. "What are you talking about, boy? You and I both know that's not why I want you to go."

"Then why?" He lowered his hand.

Zeph's eyes unfocused for a moment. It made him look a little wild-eyed and crazy, like Zebulon Stroud. Staring into those black eyes was more than unsettling. The bad guy in *Black Water* had been a psychopathic killer.

But of course Zeph wasn't like that at all. Luke's death was an accident.

"You don't remember, do you?" Zeph said.

"I don't remember what?"

Zeph shook his head. "Lord have mercy," he said, then blew out a long breath that created a cloud of steam.

"You mean about Luke?" Gabe said. "No I don't remember exactly what happened. Afterward, you know, I went to see a therapist, and she told Granddad that it was just as well that I didn't remember. But now I'm starting to think maybe that was bad advice. What happened, Zeph? You're the only one who can tell me."

"You should go back to Charleston. Don't come here turning over rocks. You might not like what you find underneath."

And with that, the man who'd once been Granddad's hunting and fishing guide turned on his well-worn boot and strode off into the storm.

CHAPTER 2

By the time Jenny finished one curtain panel, the ice had grown so thick on the driveway that leaving The Jonquil House was no longer an option. She wasn't all that troubled.

She had sandwich fixings and potato salad in her new Sub-Zero refrigerator, enough to feed the entire Methodist sewing circle. There was a pile of firewood stacked out back for a nice fire, which she could build in the front room, or better yet in the back bedroom with the iron bed.

The bed belonged to the house. She had found it rusting and broken in that little back bedroom. She'd brought it back to life with some paint and a new mattress. The curtains and bedspread for that room were not yet sewn, but Jenny had brought a couple of throw blankets in case someone got cold on this dreary day. There was also an emergency blanket in her car.

Tonight would be a good time to crawl under the covers and catch up on her reading. She was way behind on the current book club book, *The Haunting of Hill House* by Shirley Jackson.

It was odd to be reading a ghost story in January instead of October, when the book club usually tried to read something creepy. But the group had put together a list of classic genre novels and had been methodically working down the list regardless of month or season.

Not that Jenny was a huge fan of creepy stories. But she did love to read.

She was laying out the fire in the back bedroom when her cell phone rang. She checked the number. It was Maryanne, Jenny's long-lost cousin who had turned up on her doorstep three weeks ago, on Christmas morning.

Right now, Maryanne and her baby son, Joshua, were living in one of the spare bedrooms in the house in town that Jenny had leased for years. The lease on the house was up at the end of January, and the plans were for Maryanne to move into the apartment above the beauty shop in town, where she'd be able to walk to her new job at the Methodist day care center.

"Hey, Maryanne," Jenny said into her cell phone.

"Oh, thank goodness," Maryanne said, her voice definitely strained on the other end of the line. "Daniel said the roads are just terrible. I was worried about you. You aren't driving in this stuff, are you?"

"I'm fine. I decided to stay out here. I've got food. I'm going to try out the iron bed in the back bedroom. I'm sorry I didn't call. I'm not used to having someone worrying about me."

"Oh. I...Uh..."

If it were possible for Jenny's heart to smile, it would have right at that moment. Mother had died three years ago, and Jenny believed that she was alone in the world until Maryanne had shown up on her doorstep. "It's all right, Maryanne. I'm glad someone cares enough to worry about me." Her throat tensed with the sudden emotion. "I only wish I had called to let you know what my plans were. I'm sorry."

"Oh, don't. We both need to get used to having each other. So did the movers come?"

"No, they didn't. And neither did the landscapers or the sewing circle. And to top it all off, I had a run-in with someone claiming to be Gabriel Raintree who pounded on the door and demanded a room. I sent him packing. But other than that, it's been quiet out here."

"Gabriel Raintree the author?"

"Gabriel Raintree the former owner of The Jonquil House. Or so he claimed. He looked kind of like a wild man to me, if you want to know. I think it's time to get that dog I've always wanted."

"What did he want?" Maryanne's voice sounded strained.

"You're worried about me, aren't you?"

"I am. I just found you, and I've wanted a real family for so long that I'm hanging on really tight. Maybe I should send Daniel out to pick you up. I don't like the idea of big, wild men pounding on your front door. The Jonquil House is out there in the middle of nowhere."

"So Daniel drove down from Atlanta? In the middle of the week?"

"Yeah, he did. He's quit his job, and he's moving back here. He's going to join Eugene Hanks's law practice as a junior partner."

Wow. Things between Maryanne and Daniel were moving quickly. Jenny hoped they weren't moving too quickly. Jenny knew how it could be when you were first in the throes of love. She had once had her own whirlwind love affair a decade ago—with a married man. Of course she hadn't known he was married, so when reality hit, it hit with a gigantic crash that sent her reeling.

At least Maryanne knew Daniel wasn't married. He'd divorced a few years ago. But Jenny wondered if Daniel loved Maryanne as much as he loved her little boy. And she was worried that the answer might be no.

Or maybe she was a tiny bit jealous. Romance seemed to be finding everyone in Last Chance these days. Except Jenny.

And when Reverend Bill Ellis ran off with Hettie Marshall last year, Jenny had been knocked for another serious loop—which had clarified everything for her.

She was not ever going to marry.

She was never going to have a child of her own.

She could either let that ruin the rest of her life or she could adjust her thinking. She opted for the attitude adjustment and decided she would embrace her single status and create a life worth living on her own. So she had written up a business plan, submitted it to Angel Development, secured a loan, and resigned from her job as a math teacher at the high school. And when March came, she would have her own business—one that she'd created for her own self.

She was thirty-six years old and in command of herself and her life. And the Lord had seen fit to send her Maryanne and Joshua this Christmas, so she wasn't even alone anymore. What more did she need?

"Don't send Daniel out into this storm," she said into the phone. "I'll be fine. I have a good book and firewood and food. And I'm used to being alone. So stop worrying about me, okay?"

"Okay," Maryanne replied. "Sleep well. It's your first night in the new house. You should have some champagne or something."

"I'm not much of a wine drinker, but I've made myself a nice cup of hot tea."

"That's not very exciting. I'll get Daniel to buy you some champagne, and we'll toast to The Jonquil House when your furniture is installed."

"All right," Jenny said, although she would just as soon make a toast with something like ginger ale. She ended the call and lit her fire.

The chimney drew well, and soon the back bedroom was warm and cozy. She climbed on the new mattress, bundled herself up in one of the throw blankets, and folded the other to make a pillow.

She opened her book and began to read.

The wallpaper is yellow with delicate jonquils twining around green wreaths. She brushes on the wallpaper paste, places the sheet, and matches the pattern. She is happy. She is whistling a tune that her father used to hum when he walked through his peach orchard in the springtime.

What is that tune?

"I hate jonquils," the voice says behind her.

She turns.

No one is there, just the little room with the iron bed. The jonquil paper will look perfect above the white lath. She turns back to her task.

But the paper disintegrates and the daffodils dance away from her in a gyrating, seductive way. They jump off the wall and twirl their way out the window in the back.

She follows them through the window onto the porch and then into the yard.

"Flowers belong in the yard," the voice says behind her. "Or on a grave."

She turns. Still no one. The sun shines in pools of gold all around her. The jonquils are waving in the soft spring wind.

"It was daffodil time," the voice says.

She looks up at the dogwood tree, its buds about to pop open. "Where are you?" she asks.

"Nowhere. Everywhere. You need a cat."

"A cat? No. I need a dog. I want a dog. I've wanted one for a long time. Since the farm burned." Her voice is emphatic. She still misses Brutus, her granddaddy's long-dead dog. Mother hated dogs, but Mother is gone, and she can do what she wants now. "I want a big dog. The bigger the better."

"Hmmm. I don't think so. A spinster should have a cat."

"I don't like cats."

"But you are a spinster."

It is true. She's not afraid of being a spinster. Being a spinster should not stand in the way of her having a dog, though. "Don't give me stereotypes," she says to the voice as she turns away, intent on enjoying the jonquils.

But the flowers wilt, turning brown and dead as if caught by a sudden spring freeze.

She is cold. Very cold. And alone. Her bones feel brittle. Her life feels brittle.

She is walking in the woods by the river. Someone, a shadow, is walking with her.

"It was springtime," the voice says. She tries to see the shadow out of the corner of her eye, but it's no use.

If she tries to look, whoever is walking beside her melts into thin air.

"Who are you?"

"No one in particular."

She is standing in a clearing holding a gun. She wants to put it down. She doesn't like guns. But her hands are stiff and they don't work. She is paralyzed.

And then the gun goes off.

Jenny struggled to move her hands. They didn't want to move, and she panicked. And then, all at once, they came up off the bed with a jerk, as if they moved in spirit before her body caught up. She opened her eyes and blinked into darkness. She was lying on her back on the iron bed.

What had happened to the overhead light? What had happened to the fire? What had happened to the springtime?

No, that wasn't right. She'd been dreaming of the spring. She'd been dreaming of creepy wallpaper that came alive and marched around the yard. No doubt that dream had been suggested by the book she'd been reading when she fell asleep.

But the book didn't explain the sudden loss of light.

She wrapped herself in the throw and padded across the cold wooden floor to the light switch. She rocked it back and forth a few times. Nothing.

It would appear that the ice had taken its toll on the power lines.

Still, that didn't explain why the window was wide open. The icy rain soaked her turtleneck, even though the window was protected by the back porch. The wind must be howling out there.

She wrestled with the sash. It didn't want to close,

which was odd because the window was brand new. She'd replaced every single window in The Jonquil House. None of them should have opened on their own, or gotten stuck.

After a few freezing minutes of trying to close the window, she gave up. She gathered her two throw blankets and left the back bedroom. She was halfway down the hallway to the front room when the door behind her slammed closed.

The noise startled her. She gasped right out loud like a ninny. And then she realized that the open window had merely created a draft that closed the door. Old houses were like that.

She made her way down the hallway without further mishap, even though it was pitch black.

She didn't have a flashlight in the house, but she had laid a fire in the main parlor's fireplace. She'd also left a tube of long safety matches right on the hearth. So it didn't take long to get the fire going.

She wrapped up in her throw and settled down on the hard floor for a long night of catnapping.

A whining dog came to Zeph's cabin door an hour before dawn and pulled him from his restless sleep.

Another stray had come to him.

But he was almost knocked over by surprise when he opened the door and found a not-quite-full-grown mastiff. Black as night, with a little bit of brown on his face, the dog was like some haunt come back from the long dead. He looked exactly like Bear, Luke's dog.

Poor Bear had been abandoned by the Raintrees when Luke died. That old boy had become Zeph's constant companion for the next ten years until he was blind and lame and had to be put down.

Lord have mercy, Zeph still missed Bear. He still missed Luke. And telling Gabe to leave this evening had been one of the hardest things he'd ever done. He was glad Gabe didn't remember what had happened, but the boy still needed to leave here and quick, before the ghost decided to haunt him.

It was no fun being haunted. No fun at all. And Zeph wasn't going to let it happen to Gabe. Not if he could help it.

The dog standing out in the cold whined again, and Zeph realized that the critter wasn't some dream born of Gabe Raintree's sudden and unexpected return.

The critter was pitifully thin and dirty. Like every stray that came to Zeph, this dog was desperately in need of love. Helping the strays was Zeph's penance. And so he took every one of them in with an easy heart.

He stepped into his boots, pulled on his heavy winter coat, and ventured out into the cold.

He had expected the dog to come to him, like all of them did. As if they knew he was there to help them. But this dog was different.

When Zeph got close, the creature growled and backed away. And then it turned tail and ran off a little ways. But it stopped and looked back. It sat down and waited.

The message was clear. The dog wanted Zeph to follow. So he went back inside and got himself a flashlight and his shotgun.

The ice hung heavy on the woods, and the footing was treacherous, but the rain had stopped and the moon had come out. It glowed blue and cold on the trees, making the icy Spanish moss look jewel-encrusted.

The dog headed straight to The Jonquil House, as if he

were Bear come back from the dead. Zeph's skin prickled with more than cold.

What was he supposed to do? He wanted Miz Jenny to leave the house, too, before she got caught up in the ghost's web. But nothing was moving that woman. She was as determined as any steel magnolia he'd ever had the chance to know.

And now the dog was heading her way, because the ghost wanted to give Miz Jenny a dog. If she had a big dog like that, she'd need to stay out here. A big dog like that wouldn't be happy in some small house in town.

The ghost made all the decisions when it came to strays. But this wasn't right. Zeph didn't want Miz Jenny to be haunted, any more than he wanted Gabe poking around, remembering things that were best forgotten.

He needed to stop this disaster before it happened.

But how? He had to do his penance. The ghost reminded him of that every waking day. And how in the heck was he supposed to get Miz Jenny to give up her house, or Mr. Gabe to leave town?

The dawn was just breaking when Zeph and the dog reached their destination. The dog scooted into a thick clump of rhododendrons planted at the corner of the house and went to ground, like that big black critter knew exactly what was expected of him.

The ghost was behind Zeph now, even though he couldn't see it. He wasn't surprised. He was bound to the ghost by a lie.

Zeph was supposed to stay here to see that the dog was delivered to Miz Jenny. The dog was exactly what Miz Jenny wanted. Hadn't she told just about everyone in town that she was going to get herself a big dog just as soon as she moved into the inn. And tonight was the first night she'd spent out at the house.

And now, if she got a dog, she'd be putting down roots real strong.

He wanted to run up those porch steps and warn her, pure and simple, but if he did that, they'd be coming to get him and put him in some VA hospital in the crazy ward. People gave lip service to their belief in ghosts. But he knew darn well that folks would be looking at him sideways if he started telling the truth.

Gabe startled awake with a strangled cry. He opened his eyes onto the dingy yellow wallpaper in his motel room. It took a moment to get his bearings and remember where he was. Sweat trickled down his face. His damp sheets were twisted around his torso.

He sat up, trying to catch the fading threads of the dream that had so disturbed him. There had been a dog. He'd been walking through the woods feeling happy and complete. And then the dream morphed into the familiar nightmare that always ended with him standing in a clearing with a gun in his hand.

He pushed away the unpleasant part and focused on the dog. It took a moment before he remembered. The dog was Bear, Luke's old dog.

Christ. Gabe hadn't thought about Bear in decades. The dog had disappeared from his life along with his older brother. What had happened to Bear?

The question seemed urgent. Had the poor dog died in the accident, too? Or had he merely been abandoned?

The dog occupied Gabe's thoughts as he showered, dressed, and took his daily meds. By the time he left his motel room, the sun was coming up, and the temperature was rising enough for him to attempt a slow stroll into town.

He walked north on Palmetto Avenue, past Christ Episcopal and the First Methodist Church, up to the old Coca-Cola bottling plant. Twenty-five years ago, he'd watched the bottling process from the front windows. But it looked as if the building hadn't been used for bottling in quite some time. It was under renovation, with a big sign on its front saying that it was the future home of the Last Chance Artists' League.

The restoration of the downtown area seemed to be well under way. He passed a number of shops that seemed to be thriving. He crossed Chancellor Street and headed into the Kountry Kitchen.

Entering the café was like walking into the past. The place was awash in red vinyl and 1950s chrome. He took a seat at the counter.

"Hey there, stranger." A busty waitress in a pink uniform strolled down the counter, bearing a Bunn coffeepot in her hand. "Coffee?"

He nodded and noted the name monogrammed above her pocket. Flo.

It was such a stereotype he almost laughed. If he'd put a waitress named Flo into one of his books, his editor would have run him out of town. He smiled as she poured her magic elixir into a heavy white crockery mug.

"So," she said, leaning her hip into the counter. "You get stranded by the storm last night?"

"Yes." Maybe if he gave her monosyllabic responses she would get tired and leave him alone. He wasn't the kind of guy who chatted up waitresses.

He was the kind of guy who liked being alone.

"Staying at the Peach Blossom?"

"Yes."

"Brave. But I reckon you didn't have much choice. So where you from and where're you going?"

He looked up. "Flo, honey, I'd like a couple of eggs sunny-side up and some bacon on the side with wheat toast and some grits. And I'd like that served with a little bit of peace and quiet, if you don't mind."

The waitress's eyes grew round, but she was smart enough to get the message. She turned away with a small "I declare" muttered under her breath.

For the next five minutes, he was able to sip his excellent coffee in blessed solitude as he stared out the front windows, watching Last Chance, South Carolina, roll out its morning sidewalks.

His eggs arrived about the same time that a couple of blue-haired ladies showed up and occupied the booth right behind him. He wanted to tune them out, but their conversation about the new Methodist minister in town was so loud it was impossible not to listen.

When one of them said, "I think he'd be perfect for Jenny," his ears pricked. He wanted to know if the Jenny in the conversation was the same tiny woman with the hazel eyes and the big glasses who was now the owner of The Jonquil House.

For some reason, he disliked the idea of the church ladies trying to match the innkeeper up with someone like a preacher. She didn't exactly strike him as minister's wife material. He didn't know why. She certainly dressed like a preacher's wife.

He was reaching for his wallet when one of the ladies behind him raised her voice. "Excuse me, young man, but aren't you Gabriel Raintree?"

Christ. Was there no place to hide anonymously?

He swiveled toward the ladies. The woman who had spoken had cottony white hair plaited into a couple of crown braids. Her glasses fit right in with the 1950s motif of the café. They tilted up at the corners and were festooned with rhinestones.

She was wearing a purple pantsuit.

"You *are* Gabe Raintree, aren't you?" she said. "I remember you from when you were just a little boy. I remember your granddaddy, too. I heard he passed a few years ago."

"Yes, ma'am," he said putting on his Charleston good manners. There were folks all over the state who remembered Governor George Raintree. Which should have been enough for the old man. But no, Granddad had wanted to build a political dynasty, first with his son, Colin Raintree, Gabe's father. And then, when Mom and Dad died in a boating accident, Granddad had put all of his dynastic eggs into Luke's basket. Death had robbed Granddad of his beloved son and grandson, and he'd taken his bitterness out on Gabe, who had never really measured up.

The little old lady studied Gabe through her trifocals. "I can't say as I ever voted for your granddaddy. But you look a lot like him."

"I do?" No one had ever said that to him. Not ever. Granddad had been a strikingly handsome man. Everyone said so. Gabe wasn't handsome to start with, and he'd broken his nose three times during his college wrestling career, which hadn't helped one bit.

The old lady snorted a goofy-sounding laugh. "You're the spitting image of him. So what brings you back?"

"Excuse me, but do I know you?"

"Oh, I'm so sorry. I'm Miriam Randall. I've lived in this town my whole life."

"Oh. You're the lady who sometimes takes in boarders, aren't you?"

"I used to, but I'm out of the boardinghouse business. My nephew has my house all torn up with renovations. Why do you ask? Are you looking for a place to stay?"

"I spent last night at the Peach Blossom Motor Court."

"Ah, I see."

"I had been hoping to stay at The Jonquil House."

The little old lady flashed her dentures at him. "I'm sure you know the way. When you get out there, you tell Jenny hey for me. Tell her I'll be out one of these days to see what she's done with the old place. I've heard she's brought it back from the grave."

A cold shiver touched Gabe's spine. The Raintrees had been responsible for letting the house go to ruin. He didn't like feeling responsible for that.

"Miss Carpenter told me yesterday that the inn won't be open until March," he said.

"Oh, I'll bet you could sweet-talk Jenny into giving you a room. That girl has a big heart inside of her, but she rarely gets to use it."

"Actually I was thinking about trying to buy the house back from her."

The half smile on the old lady's face faded. "Son, you take my advice. Don't you ask Jenny to sell that place. It's her pride and joy. I reckon it's kind of sad that a woman like Jenny has to love a house, but then she's given it a chance, despite its creepy reputation and disreputable condition. And you have to love a woman who sees the worth in something that everyone else says is better off left alone."

CHAPTER 3

Jenny was up at dawn and drawn to the window in the living room. A pale version of the sun, partially obscured by high cirrus clouds, sparked on ice-caked branches.

The power was still off, and the house was cold. She needed to build another fire, but first she needed to deal with the window she'd left open. She headed off to the back bedroom, only to discover the window closed and locked—precisely the way it had been last night before she drifted off to sleep.

Had the open window been part of a dream? It had seemed so real last night, and yet there could be no other logical explanation.

She had dreamed the whole thing, probably because she'd fallen asleep reading that creepy story written by Shirley Jackson. Jenny crossed the room and picked up the offending book from the bed where she'd left it. Jenny was thinking the unthinkable—she might stop reading *The Haunting of Hill House*.

Wouldn't the book club be surprised? She'd been the

only one who'd actually read all thousand pages of *Atlas Shrugged*. *The Haunting of Hill House* wasn't much more than a novella, but she didn't want to finish it.

Shivers racked her body, but whether they were from the scary scenes in the book or the bitter cold seeping into her house, she couldn't say. Thank goodness her new stove ran on gas. She put a kettle on for tea, then bundled into her puffy winter coat and headed out to the woodpile behind the house for some more firewood.

The backyard was ringed by densely overgrown woods. In the spring, it would come alive with a carpet of daffodils, and then later the wild azaleas and dogwoods would bloom. A small corner of the yard was thick with blackberries, and come autumn she'd pick them and bake them into pies for her guests. She loved this backyard, even now, when all was withered, brown, solitary, and iced over as if God, the ultimate baker, had given the world a sugar glaze.

She hadn't taken more than four mincing steps over the frozen ground before a rude noise broke the serenity. A car came up the gravel driveway around in front, its engine growling like some beast in the cold quiet, its tires crunching on the ice.

She turned and made her way back to the wraparound porch and the front of the house. She hoped the vehicle in her drive was her furniture delivery or the landscapers, but she knew it was neither. No one but a fool or a power company worker would be out on an icy morning like this.

All at once the cold morning chill invaded, finding its way through her winter coat, wool sweater, and cotton turtleneck right down to her flesh and bones. Her neck hairs prickled in a way that had little to do with the cold.

A big, black Lexus had just pulled into her parking lot, but before she could ascertain who this unfamiliar car belonged to, the rhododendrons along the front of the house rustled and out glided a great big dog, as black as the car. Jenny had never seen a dog quite like this one, with long hair and a huge head that made it look almost like a miniature lion.

Its ribs were clearly visible, and she knew right then that this dog was hers to take care of. It was the strongest sensation. A feeling of connection and even love that warmed her from the middle out.

She had dreamed of this dog last night. And here he was like a gift from the heavens, ready-made to love and to feed. And feeding people was, more or less, her calling in life. Not that a dog was a person, exactly, but this dog needed feeding in the worst way.

She forgot all about the strange car and hurried to her porch steps. "Here boy," she called to the dog. "Come on, don't be scared. I'll take care of you."

The dog took two or three steps in her direction, his big brown eyes looking sad and lonely. She connected with his expression. And she felt something deep down give way. Here was a friend for life.

But everything changed an instant later when the driver of the Lexus emerged. It was the same guy who'd darkened her door yesterday claiming to be Gabriel Raintree and demanding a room. He looked about as shaggy as the dog, with uncombed hair, unshaved chin, and attitude radiating from his piercing black eyes.

The pricey Lexus seemed a bit out of character somehow. She'd expected him to have a black-and-chrome Harley stashed someplace. But then it was an icy morning, and this must be his alternative form of transportation.

The dog looked over his shoulder and then stopped in

his tracks. He turned and then shot forward, barking as if he knew he was supposed to be a watchdog, or perhaps he was just auditioning for the post.

In any case, the dog was effective. The man backed up a step and then promptly lost his footing on the ice.

Down he went with a curse. The dog came to stand directly over him, barking until the frozen swamp echoed with the noise.

Uh-oh. Visions of personal injury lawsuits danced in Jenny's head. Maybe taking in a stray was a bad idea. The guy had been kind of unpleasant yesterday, but she didn't want to see anyone hurt.

She carefully moved down the porch steps. "Here boy," she said in a calm voice.

The dog turned his back on the prostrate man and bounded up to her. She flinched, even though she knew somewhere in her mind that showing fear was absolutely the wrong thing to do. This stray was large with a capital L, and he'd already knocked one person down. Obviously he was going to need the full dog obedience course once she fattened him up so his ribs weren't so prominent.

The dog continued barking, but his big brown eyes didn't look crazy or feral or anything like that. "It's okay," she said in a soothing voice. "You're going to be okay now. You're home." The dog finally sat down, and she gave him a tentative pat on his lion-like head.

The dog whimpered a little. As if he wasn't entirely sure she was going to be kind. Jenny's heart melted a little more. The poor guy had clearly been mistreated by someone. And obviously half starved.

While she was soothing the dog, she asked the man, "Are you okay?"

He didn't answer right away because he was too busy swearing.

"Is there something I can help you with?" she said in her best innkeeper voice. The man rose to his knees and then to his feet. He tested his weight on his left foot and let forth a manly grunt of pain. He limped over to the porch step and sat down.

"You're hurt?" Jenny asked.

"You need to keep that animal in check."

The man stared daggers at the dog. After a moment, the dog lowered himself and made a little whining noise while looking up at the guy. Jenny didn't know what to think about this. Obviously the dog had passive-aggressive tendencies.

"Don't you feed him? He looks half starved," the man said.

Jenny decided not to rise to the accusation in his voice. "Why are you here?" she asked calmly. "I told you yesterday that the inn isn't open for business."

"I'm here to make you an offer on the house."

"What?"

He reached down and rubbed his ankle. "Ow!"

"You need to get some ice on that."

"Are you going to invite me in?"

"Are you really Gabriel Raintree?"

He cocked his head and looked up at her. "Of course I am. Do you want to see my ID?"

"As a matter of fact, I do." She folded her arms across her chest, which was kind of hard to do because her winter coat was big and puffy. But she felt like she needed the whole arm-folding thing. She needed to look serious and in charge. Because this guy looked like the kind who would seize control of any situation if given half a chance.

One of his black eyebrows arched, and his lips pressed into a grim line. But he also reached into his back pocket, pulled out his wallet, and opened it up to his driver's license. He held the wallet out to her.

She minced her way across the frozen ground, the dog following her movements with a wary eye. She plucked the wallet from the man's outstretched hand.

He was, indeed, Gabriel Raintree.

She handed the wallet back. He managed a somewhat ironic smile and said, "Have trust issues, do you?"

She didn't dignify his comment with a response. "Why are you here?"

"To buy back the house."

"It's not for sale."

"Of course it is. We just need to negotiate a price. Everything is for sale . . . Jennifer?"

"I'm Jenny Carpenter. And I'm cold. Come on inside. I'll get some ice for your ankle and call Doc Cooper for you."

Gabe sat on the porch step eyeing the dog. There was no question about it, he'd had a dream about this dog last night. It looked like a purebred mastiff, exactly like Bear, only starved to death.

He glanced up at the woman. She didn't look like the kind of person who would abuse a dog, but Gabe had learned that the world was full of people who didn't look like what they truly were.

All people had the capacity to do monstrous things. He knew this as an undisputed fact of life. It was the bedrock upon which he based every single one of his stories.

People sometimes said that he wrote paranormal fiction, but that wasn't true at all. He never used any paranormal phenomena in his stories. He didn't need do. His villains were all human beings.

He flexed his foot, and the pain shot up his leg.

Damn it all to hell and back again. His ankle felt like someone had branded it with a hot poker. He tried to stand up, but when he put weight on the joint, he almost collapsed again onto the icy drive.

"You *are* hurt. Oh, dear," Jenny Carpenter said. She stood there in one of those brown, puffy winter coats that looked like a cocoon. She had her brown hair piled up on top of her head in a messy bun, and her glasses made her look vaguely owl-like.

And yet, for all she was trying to look like a plain Jane, she was anything but. Her face had a classic Greek quality to it, with a bow mouth and a long nose—not exactly the modern standard for beauty, but beautiful nevertheless. Her complexion was like fine bone china. And something almost ethereal emanated from her, like a warm fire on a cold day.

How could a person like her starve a dog? But then the scariest monsters were the beautiful ones.

He gestured toward his left ankle. "I think I've sprained it or something. I don't think I can make it inside without some help."

"Oh." An uncertain look crossed the woman's face, as if she was still trying to decide if he was a scoundrel or something.

"Will you come here? Please?" He was losing his patience—mostly with the hot pain radiating up his shin.

"Oh." She picked her way across the icy ground.

"I'm going to have to use you like an old man uses a

cane," he said. Then he laid his hand on her tiny shoulder. It seemed impossible that a woman this small, this compact and thin, could hold him up. But she put her shoulder into it, and he draped his arm across her back. Together they limped across the ice, up the steps, and into the house.

The house wasn't much warmer than the outside. Off in the kitchen, a kettle was whistling briskly.

"That's my tea," she said. "And I'm sorry it's so cold in here. We don't have any heat because the power's off. I'll build a fire and warm things up. For now, the only place I can put you is in the back bedroom. It's down the—"

"I know where it is," he said.

"Oh, of course you do."

"That was Luke's room," he said, and a frigid wariness slithered down his back. He didn't want to visit Luke's bedroom. When he'd come here yesterday looking for a room, he'd assumed he could have his old one back. His room had been upstairs with a view of the backyard and the river beyond.

The woman paused a moment, as if she, too, was feeling the same uneasiness. "There are people in town who say that Luke haunts the house," she said.

"Do you believe in ghosts?" he asked.

"No. But I imagine you do."

"No, actually, I don't. I've never written a single story about a ghost. I think they're trash. People can be evil enough without inventing ghosts."

"That's a bright view of the world, isn't it?"

He said nothing in response as they made their way down the hall. Jenny Carpenter might be tiny, but she was warm and sturdy. She smelled like something floral and spring-like. She wasn't a monster. No one could smell that good and be evil. It was impossible.

The place felt strange. Something was off, and Gabe couldn't put his finger on exactly what. The rooms were bare, the floor too shiny, the air cold. Bone-numbing cold.

But when he arrived at the threshold of Luke's room, the house seemed to change its mind about him. Warmth flooded through him. And not only because he became aware of Jenny's body next to his. Stepping into Luke's bedroom was like coming home.

Luke's iron bed was still there in the same place he'd left it. The room was empty of Luke's things, of course. Still, there was something of Luke that haunted the place.

He wanted the house back now more than ever. The fact that it came with these memories and a black dog made the need that much more urgent.

The woman at his side helped him onto the bed, then she bustled off like a good innkeeper and came back with a blanket, a cup of tea, and a ziplock bag of ice for his rapidly swelling ankle.

"I've called Doc Cooper. It's going to be a while before I can take you to town for an X-ray."

"Why is that?"

"You may have been crazy enough to come driving on icy roads but I'm not insane, Mr. Raintree. The sun is up, and the ice is melting. And you will survive. Would you like some ibuprofen for the pain?" She held out a bottle of pills.

"Are you a nurse? You have nurse-like qualities."

She cocked her head and gave him the tiniest of unintentional smiles. She managed to look utterly adorable in

a shabby-sweater, turtleneck-girl way. "Are you suggesting that I'm thinking about chopping you into little pieces
like that nurse character did to the author in *Misery*?"

"So you're a fan of horror stories then?"

"I read *Misery* because it was a book club selection
one October a few years back. It was a hard book for me
to finish. And no, I'm not a fan of horror or, quite frankly,
any of your works."

"You belong to a book club?"

"I do. Do you want these pills or not?"

"No, I'm okay."

So she belonged to a book club. She gave all the
appearances of one of those unmarried women who
spent most of their free time with their noses poked in
a book. People who rocked on the front porch while
simultaneously visiting all kinds of places and lives. All
vicariously.

He loved readers.

But this particular reader had possession of his house,
and he wanted it back.

"Miss Carpenter," he said, "you can keep your pills.
What I want is my house."

"I'm sorry, Mr. Raintree, but The Jonquil House is no
longer yours, and it's not for sale."

"I'm prepared to offer a lot of money to get it back." He
mentioned a sales price that was easily three times what
The Jonquil House was worth.

Her eyes widened. Clearly the number had shocked
her. He was on his way to feeling smug when she shook
her head. "I'm not selling the house. I've dreamed of
opening a bed-and-breakfast for years and years. I've put
all of my heart and soul into restoring this house, not to

mention all of my life's savings. I've come to love this place. And I'm not about to sell it back to the man who neglected it to the point that it was almost falling down.

"No, Mr. Raintree, you cannot have it back. Not for any price."

Why on earth would Gabriel Raintree sell her a house and then try to buy it back at an inflated price?

Her vivid imagination began to spin all kinds of scenarios. Was there treasure in the crawl space? Had Blackbeard's pirates buried something out in the backyard where the jonquils grew? Was there a floorboard loose somewhere concealing a secret hidey-hole with a cache of jewels?

She shook her head. What was she thinking? Obviously her imagination was running wild. There were no secret passages or pirate treasure or hidey-holes. Just the house. So his actions made no rational sense.

She sliced up some of the ham that she'd intended to feed to the sewing circle. She put it on a paper plate and headed back to the front of the house, where she found the dog sitting right by the porch steps as if he were waiting on someone.

He was one big puppy, and by the size of his paws he wasn't fully grown yet. Once he'd put on weight, he would probably outweigh Jenny.

Getting him into her tiny Ford Fiesta to take him to the vet was going to be a challenge. But then she'd been thinking that an innkeeper needed a bigger car for hauling groceries and whatnot. Maybe it was time to get herself something new. She'd had her Fiesta for twelve years, and it hadn't been new when she bought it.

"Here boy," she said in her most soothing voice as she

offered the ham to the dog. The dog stood up and lowered his head, as if he was uncertain about this relationship.

So she spoke soothing words, and the dog inched forward. And with every inch, Jenny's heart melted, just like the ice on the drive now that the sun had arrived.

The dog got close enough to sniff the ham and then took it gently from the paper plate. At least he had some manners.

Jenny let herself laugh. "You are some lion, aren't you? Pretty ferocious, huh? Maybe I'll name you Aslan, like the lion in the C. S. Lewis story." She scratched him behind his ears, and the dog's eyes squinted in pleasure. "You're what I've been hoping for," she whispered as the dog sat down at her feet. "We're going to be great friends, you and I."

Mr. Raintree chose that moment of bonding to make a further nuisance of himself. "Jeeennnnyyyyy!" His shout echoed all the way from the back of the house.

The dog jumped and backed away, lowering his head again and then giving a few whiny-sounding barks.

"Great," Jenny muttered as she stood up. "What now?"

She turned and headed back inside, but this time the dog followed her through the door. Before she could do anything to stop the beast, he'd bounded down the hallway and right into the back bedroom, where Mr. Raintree was hollering like a farmhand calling the pigs for dinner.

Jenny hurried after the dog, arriving in the back room just as he rose up and put his filthy front paws on her brand-new mattress.The dog wagged his tail, and it looked like he was smiling at the idiot man occupying the only bed in the establishment.

Despite his earlier aggression, Aslan didn't look like he was in attack mode this time. And Mr. Raintree, who ought to have been frightened of the dog, seeing as Aslan had knocked him down, didn't seem at all fazed by his appearance at the bedside.

This was a positive development, wasn't it? After all, if Mr. Raintree really wanted his house back, he could probably threaten to sue her for personal injury or something. She should feel relieved.

But instead the scenario ticked her off. She didn't want to lose the dog. She was always losing the ones she loved. And suddenly she was more than merely angry. She was a little bit scared that Mr. Raintree might find a way to take his house back, and he might take the dog, too.

She swallowed back those silly fears and managed a small, insincere smile. "What do you need?" she asked.

"Those pills you were talking about. And another cup of tea. It's freezing in here." Mr. Raintree's words were more of a command than a request.

"Right away," she said with a bob of her head and a slow grinding of her teeth. She hurried to the kitchen and put together a tray with another cup of tea, a few cookies that had been intended for the sewing circle, and, of course, her bottle of ibuprofen.

When she came back, the dog was up on the bed, cuddled up beside the man, with his big head resting in the guy's lap. Her mattress was dirty, and she prayed that it wasn't now flea-infested.

Clearly, the dog had made his choice, and there wasn't a darn thing Jenny could do about it. It was the story of her life. Maybe she should heed the warning of that dream she'd had last night. She might want a dog, but perhaps a cat was what she needed. With a cat, you didn't expect much in the way of loyalty.

She pasted another smile on her face, because that's what she always did when stuff like this happened. But her smile must have looked phony because Mr. Raintree looked up at her and said, "Don't worry, I'll pay for a new mattress. And I'll take the dog off your hands, too. You have no business having a dog if this is the way you take care of it."

She thought about correcting his misapprehension and decided that it wasn't worth the breath it would take. She gave him his tray, then turned on her heel and headed out to the backyard, intent on finishing the chore that she'd started half an hour ago, before her heart had been broken by a stray dog with a fickle heart.

She didn't make it far across the backyard before Zeph Gibbs materialized from out of the big stand of rhododendrons. He was carrying a shotgun, and he sneaked up on her.

"God almighty, Zeph, you just scared me half to death."

He nodded and brought his hand to the brim of his Atlanta Braves ball cap. "Ma'am."

Jenny wasn't exactly happy to see Zeph. The man had been a pain in the neck for the last few months as her contractors had restored the house. Zeph often came to the work site and would stand in the yard and watch without moving. It was kind of creepy.

At first she thought maybe he wanted a job. After all, Savannah said he'd done incredible work restoring The Kismet's lobby. But when Jenny had offered him a position as a carpenter, he'd shaken his head and told her that resurrecting this house was a big, big mistake.

And a few weeks ago, Zeph had even stopped her right

outside the library on book club night and pleaded with her to find another place for an inn. He told her that she would regret opening an inn out in the swamp. Jenny still wasn't sure if that was a warning or a threat. Zeph owned a shack of some kind deep in the woods not more than a quarter mile away. She was beginning to think that having Zeph as a neighbor was going to be a problem.

Jenny clamped down further on the turmoil roiling inside her. "Mr. Gibbs," she said in the voice she used when addressing the parents of troublemaking students, "I would be much obliged if you wouldn't go sneaking up on people. Especially carrying a gun. You're going to scare my customers just like you scared me. And that's not good for business. Now, what can I do for you?"

He cocked his head. "Ma'am, people coming out here are going to get scared no matter what I do. Is Mr. Gabe all right?"

Well, that was just creepy. How did he know that Mr. Raintree was here and that he'd fallen on the ice? There was only one way: He'd been spying on her. Her stomach clenched. She had always regarded Zeph as an eccentric, but never as a person she might have to fear. All that changed in the blink of an eye. "Uh, no, he fell on the ice."

Zeph nodded as if he already knew. "He hurt his ankle?"

Obviously he *had* been spying. "Yes, I think he may have broken something. It's pretty swollen." She kept her voice neutral, but her heart was pounding in her chest. What was he up to?

"Have you called the doctor?"

"Of course I have. But I can't drive him to the clinic.

My Fiesta doesn't handle icy streets well. I need to wait until the roads improve."

"No need, Miz Jenny. I'll bring around my truck. I'll take him to town for you."

She hesitated a moment. Should she trust him with Mr. Raintree? "You used to work out here, didn't you?"

"Yes, ma'am, I remember Mr. Gabe when he was just a young 'un."

She was being silly and skittish. She needed to find her courage and buck up. Zeph wasn't here to cause any trouble. He was merely lending a helping hand.

"What you come out here for, boy?" Zeph asked in that voice that took Gabe back to his childhood. Zeph never minced words. Gabe had forgotten that. He'd also forgotten how much he'd wanted to please Zeph back when he'd been a little boy.

Gabe carefully readjusted the position of his damaged foot. It hurt like a sonofabitch. He might have been more comfortable in the crew cab seat behind the driver, but the dog was occupying that space—all of it.

"I came out here to buy the house back."

Zeph's big hands tightened on the wheel. "Why you want to do that?"

Gabe shrugged. He didn't want to tell Zeph the true reason.

"I'm waiting," Zeph said.

"Because I got homesick."

"Homesick? You haven't been back in twenty-five years. Why now? After you already sold the house to Miz Jenny."

"Because I had second thoughts, okay?"

"I reckon that's a good reason. I sure do wish you hadn't sold that house. It was best left the way it was."

That was a surprise. Gabe turned and studied Zeph. He'd gotten much older. His hair was the color and texture of cotton, and there were dark freckles on his cheeks that hadn't been there before. But he looked fit.

Zeph gave him a little glance and then spoke again as he trained his eyes on the road. "I just think The Jonquil House shouldn't be turned into a bed-and-breakfast."

"Why's that?"

"It's too far from town. And the swamp can get scary at night sometimes."

It could have been dialogue from one of Gabe's novels. "Scary how?"

This time Zeph shrugged. "Just scary."

"I'm an expert on scary. Are we talking swamp things that walk at night, or ghosts, or psychopathic murderers who use Hoodoo? I mean, scary comes in lots of flavors, Zeph."

The man pressed his lips together. "There are things scarier than the critters who live in the swamp. There are things that can get into a man's head, you know? And make him do things he never would do. Things not of this world."

"So you believe in ghosts, then."

Zeph tightened his grip on the steering wheel. "Don't you?"

Gabe turned away to watch the scenery flashing by. The ice was melting, leaving behind endless fields of brown stubble where corn and soybeans had grown the season before. "There are far worldlier things to be frightened of."

Just then the dog poked his cold, wet nose into the corner of Gabe's neck and gave him a sloppy kiss. The kiss made him laugh in a way that he hadn't in a long, long time. "Hey, you big bear," he said. "I think I'm going to keep you." It was crazy, but the dog seemed to have filled up part of that cavernous hollow place inside him.

"Bear is what Luke called his dog," Zeph said.

"And this dog looks exactly like Bear, doesn't he? It's kind of amazing, but I feel like he belongs to me."

"You took that dog from Miz Jenny. He's her dog. And there will be consequences for what you've done."

"She didn't take care of him very well. Look at him. He's starving."

"Son, Miz Jenny didn't set eyes on that dog until this morning, same time as you did. And the first thing she did was feed him some ham. When it comes to feeding people, Miz Jenny isn't stingy."

"If he's a stray, then he's not her dog, is he? You can't have it both ways."

"No, I reckon not." There was a hard, angry quality to Zeph's voice.

"Why are you so pissed off at me?" Gabe asked.

"I'm not pissed off. I just want you to leave."

Gabe knew better than to follow this circular line of questions. He was getting nowhere with the old guy. So he changed his tack. "What happened to Bear?" he asked.

"Your granny didn't want him. She didn't want to be reminded of your brother. She was going to have your granddad put him down. Can you imagine? Luke would have been furious. So I stepped in. I took him. But I told your grandparents that I thought you needed the dog. They thought otherwise. I'm surprised you don't remember any of this."

He said nothing because his heart was twisting in

his chest. Now that Zeph mentioned it, he remembered Granddad walking out the front door with his rifle and the dog. He remembered knowing what Granddad planned to do and being entirely unable to stop him. He remembered he was weeping like a girl because Granddad had smacked him across the face for pleading Bear's case.

Shit. He didn't want to remember this crap. But hell, it wasn't as if he didn't already know that Granddad could be cruel. He certainly hadn't forgotten that.

CHAPTER 4

Jenny waited in the cold for the power to be restored. But it didn't happen, and according to Maryanne, who had called several times with news updates, the county didn't expect all the power to be restored for a few days.

So the sewing circle wasn't coming again, and she couldn't even sew on her own since her sewing machine wasn't the kind that worked with a treadle.

Her day unraveled even further when the moving company called with the news that they wouldn't be able to deliver her furniture until the following Monday because of downed power lines and other mayhem caused by the storm.

She was stuck with nothing to do but brood about the puppy who had abandoned her. And since she didn't like to brood about anything, she picked up *The Haunting of Hill House*, even though she had sworn that she wasn't going to finish it. But it was the only book she had out here at the house. And tonight was book club night.

She finished the book, but the ending was so creepy she wondered why she had bothered. She was still feeling unsettled and grumpy later that evening when she walked into the Last Chance branch of the Allenberg Library for the bi-weekly meeting of the Last Chance Book Club.

It was Molly Wolfe's turn to bring refreshments, so of course there were a couple of boxes of store-bought cupcakes. Molly wasn't much of a cook, and besides she was about six weeks short of her delivery date and not dealing well with being pregnant. So everyone was happy enough with the cupcakes.

Jenny bypassed the sweets and poured herself a cup of coffee from the urn. She was heading toward an empty seat at the table when Nita Wills, the librarian, grabbed her by the arm.

"Jenny, what's this I hear about Gabriel Raintree buying back The Jonquil House?"

Boy, the gossip mill in Last Chance moved fast, and no doubt Mr. Raintree knew exactly how to feed it. After all, he was a famous author and had plenty of experience controlling public relations.

"I am not selling the house, Nita." She practically growled the words.

"But I heard directly from Annie Jasper that he's planning on moving back in. Annie said Zeph drove him into the clinic this morning, and he has a broken ankle that he got out at The Jonquil House. Honey, if this is true, it's a godsend."

Great, Jenny needed this gossip like she needed a root canal. But what could she do? Annie Jasper was a wonderful nurse, and also the source of medical news for every busybody in town.

"Nita, it wasn't a godsend for Gabriel Raintree to slip on the ice and break his ankle."

"Oh, no, I didn't mean his breaking his ankle. I meant his buying back The Jonquil House."

"But—"

"Didn't Gabriel Raintree just sell The Jonquil House to you?" Savannah Randall joined the conversation and interrupted Jenny in one fell swoop. Savannah was the proprietor of The Kismet dinner theater and an excellent baker. Jenny noted that Savannah had also bypassed the inferior cupcakes.

"Yes, he sold me the house," Jenny said. "And yes, he's offered a lot of money to buy it back. But I'm not selling."

"How much did he offer?" Lola May wanted to know.

"A lot."

"How much is a lot? I mean, what if he offered you a million dollars? Honey, everyone has their price." Lola May had a pretty pessimistic view of life.

"That's exactly what he said. But he didn't offer me a million. And even if he did, the fact is that *I'm* not for sale." Jenny lost control of her voice. It came out in a harsh tone that Mother would have called unladylike. Jenny took a gulp of air and tried to control herself.

"No one's talking about you selling yourself, honey," Savannah said. "We're just talking real estate. And if he wanted to give you an inflated price, you might think twice about turning him down. I mean, you can make a lot of money flipping houses, you know."

"Yes, but I'm not in the house-flipping business." Her blood pressure climbed. "And I don't want to sell to that...that...obnoxious, self-important idiot."

"Wow," Savannah said, giving Jenny the strangest look, "you really don't like him, do you?"

"Not one bit. He stole my dog." These words were spoken more softly, but they were still a bit hard-edged.

"You have a dog? Since when?" Lola May asked.

"Since this morning." Jenny's face heated. It was totally ridiculous to blame Gabriel Raintree for stealing her dog when the dog was a stray and had decided that he liked Mr. Raintree better than he liked her. You would think that a dog would follow the hand that fed him, but in Jenny's life, that old adage was proving to be unreliable conventional wisdom. Sort of like the old one about the way to a man's heart being through his stomach.

She folded her arms across her chest and waited for the onslaught of questions that the book club members were sure to fire at her.

But the questions didn't come. Instead, Savannah draped her arm around Jenny's shoulders and gave her a little half hug. "Cheer up, Jenny I have a feeling the dog isn't gone forever."

Having Savannah give her a hug was something new and different. They were bake-off rivals and belonged to different churches.

They also had some difficult history to get over. Jenny had been insanely jealous of Savannah for a while last year when it looked as if Reverend Bill Ellis would choose her strudel over Jenny's pie. But Bill had fooled everyone by running off with Hettie Marshall, who was, without question, the worst cook in Allenberg County.

Still, the entire Bill Ellis fiasco rankled. And all the more so because everyone in town, including Jenny herself, had believed that Bill was interested in her. But he wasn't. It was just her apple pie that he liked.

"I heard from Annie that Mr. Raintree's ankle isn't badly injured," Nita said, "just a little bone chip or something. And he's staying at the Peach Blossom Motor Court with an animal that must be your dog, because you won't give him a place to stay. But I heard that Garnet Willoughby isn't all that happy about having a dog staying at the Peach Blossom."

Lola May snorted. "Like Garnet has any standards. The Peach Blossom already has fleas and bedbugs, too, I'll bet. So who cares if someone wants to keep a dog there? That place is only fit for dogs, if you ask me."

"Aslan deserves better," Jenny said in a small emotional voice. Darn, why was she so fixated on that dog? It was like she'd dreamed him into existence, and somehow knew in her deepest places that they belonged together.

"Aslan?" Nita said. "Like the character in *The Lion, the Witch and the Wardrobe*?"

Jenny nodded. "I found the dog this morning in my rhododendrons. And the truth is, the dog knocked Mr. Raintree over, so I don't even understand why he and the dog bonded the way they did." Her voice wobbled, and Savannah actually patted her back as if she understood how Jenny felt.

"Maybe Mr. Raintree has just taken Aslan hostage, you know," Lola May said. "Maybe he's going to try to make a trade with you—the dog for the house."

"Well," Nita said with some urgency, "whatever you do, don't upset him. We need him."

"We need him? For what?"

"To save the library."

Before Nita's words could fully sink in, the librarian turned away and called all the members of the club to gather around the table. Everyone sat down, and Nita folded her hands together in front of her, a serious look on her face.

"Ladies, and gent"—she nodded toward Angel Menendez, the only male member of the club—"I have some disturbing news. I just heard from the Allenberg County executive's office that they plan to shut down the Last Chance branch of the Allenberg County library system at the end of this fiscal quarter, which is March thirty-first. Budgets are tight, and I was told that the county doesn't believe they can afford to keep on two librarians. So, in essence, I've gotten my pink slip, and we're losing our meeting place."

"But they can't do that," Rocky deBracy said. "Last Chance is contributing more to the tax base of this county than Allenberg is, and I would guess that Last Chance is now bigger, population-wise."

"Doesn't matter. Allenberg is the county seat."

"But my husband's plant is contributing plenty. And more people are moving in here all the time. We need a library. We need the after-school programs. We need you."

Nita shrugged. "Apparently, County Executive Hayden seems to think that I'm a prime example of wasteful government spending."

"Ha!" Rocky replied. "That's only because he's thinking about running for Congress and these days you have to run to the right of Attila the Hun to win a Republican primary." Rocky, who had once worked for Senator Rupert Warren, spoke with authority. She knew exactly how politics worked.

Savannah leaned forward and took Nita's hand. "This is about Kamaria, isn't it? Hayden is coming after you because your daughter is thinking about running for Congress, too."

"I can't prove that's the case, Savannah. But Dennis

Hayden is dreaming if he thinks Kamaria will capitulate to this kind of blackmail. And I wouldn't want her to do something like that. So I'm afraid that the doors will be closed at the end of March unless we can find some money to keep them open."

"We can always organize bake sales," Hettie Ellis said. Hettie was a heck of a fund-raiser. She'd single-handedly raised the money to restore Golfing for God, the Bible-themed miniature golf course outside of town. And she'd chaired the Christ Church building fund committee for years, even before she was actually married to the pastor of the church.

"You don't even need a bake sale. Dash will make a hefty contribution," Savannah said, speaking of her ex-professional-ballplayer husband who had more money than God. Savannah folded her arms across her chest. "I can't believe anyone would close our library."

"Hugh will contribute, too. And don't forget Tulane. He and Sarah may be on the NASCAR circuit most of the time, but they have done so much to restore the town. Don't you worry, Nita. We'll find the funding," Rocky said.

"Funding a library isn't our only problem, Rocky," Nita said. "We have to find a way to get the county government to acknowledge that having a *publicly funded* library is important to the people who live here."

"What do you have in mind?" Hettie asked.

"Something that will get a lot of people out to support the library and send a message to the county government and Dennis Hayden in particular. So when I heard that Gabriel Raintree had come back to town, I thought maybe we could get him involved in some way. I mean, if we had a bestselling author living right here in Last Chance, and he put his name behind library programs, the county would have to pay attention. Wouldn't they?"

"You think?" Savannah asked.

Nita shrugged. "It's a thought. I know we can raise money. I know Dash and Tulane and Hugh will make generous donations. But don't you see? If all we do is secure large donations from a few of the wealthier members of the community, then we'll end up with a private library. In fact, I think Dennis Hayden would be overjoyed to privatize our library. And once that happens, all the books here will go back to the Allenberg branch. So I just think we need something to get people involved and interested, like a rally or something."

"Oh, I've got an idea," Savannah said. "I've been planning to show *Black Water* at The Kismet one of these weekends. Why don't we invite Mr. Raintree to give a talk about his book and then we could show the movie? Having an event would get people in one place, and we could talk about why we need a public library. Maybe we could get people to sign petitions at the same time or something. And if we *do* have to start over and create a private library, we'll have a nice mailing list of potential ongoing supporters."

"That's a fabulous idea," Hettie said. "And if we got a big turnout, we'd at least send Dennis Hayden a message that there are a lot of voters here who care about our library."

Nita turned her dark eyes on Jenny. "This won't work if we don't do something about Mr. Raintree's living arrangements. I mean, the poor man's broken his ankle, and he's staying at the Peach Blossom Motor Court all by his lonesome. I feel as if we haven't shown him much in the way of southern hospitality."

Nita could have been Jenny's mother in that instant, reminding her that a southern woman was always hospitable. At least in public.

She looked at the faces around the table. They were going to judge her if she didn't do something to support this effort.

"I didn't give Mr. Raintree a room at the inn because we don't have any furniture in any of the guest rooms. But if y'all insist, I'll let him stay in the back bedroom. It's not really furnished, but it does have an old iron bed. Also, I don't think he wants to stay out there right at the moment because I don't have power or heat. So after the lights are back on, I'll offer him a place to stay. For free."

"Thank you," Nita said on a big breath. "And you'll ask him to do a book signing or a book talk or something?"

She doubted that Mr. Raintree would agree to this, but she nodded.

"Thank you, Jenny, that's all we need. Now, before we move on to a discussion of *The Haunting of Hill House*, I was thinking that it might be fun to read one of Mr. Raintree's books for next time. How many of y'all have read *Black Water*?"

Most of the hands in the group came up. "I saw the movie, too," Savannah said.

"I see we have some Raintree fans here," Nita said. "But even though a lot of you have already read the book, I still think we should read *Black Water* for the next time."

"No." Jenny's voice was firm.

"No?" Nita looked at her as if she'd just arrived from another planet.

"No. I don't think we should read two scary books right in a row, especially if so many of us have read *Black Water* already. I, for one, do not like reading books like *The Haunting of Hill House*. And I certainly don't want to read a horror story that was written about our swamp. I think we should return to the list of classics that Cathy put together for us. What's the next one on that list?"

"*Jane Eyre*," Cathy said with a little grin. "And if you ask me, I'm with Jenny. *The Haunting of Hill House* gave me the heebie-jeebies."

"But if we're going to—" Nita began before Cathy interrupted her.

"You know, we've asked Jenny to go out on a limb for us, and she's agreed. The least we can do is read something she wants to read this next time. I mean, almost all of us have already read *Black Water*. It was a mega-bestseller a couple of years ago. How many people have read *Jane Eyre*?"

A few hands came up, but definitely a smaller number of readers had actually read the classic.

"My point is made," Cathy said.

Everyone looked down the table at Hettie Ellis, who in addition to being married to the pastor of Christ Church was also the CEO of Country Pride Chicken, the second largest employer in the county. What Hettie said usually passed for law at the book club, even though Nita was supposed to be in charge.

"I think Cathy has a point," Hettie said with a smile toward Jenny. "Some of us may want to re-read *Black Water*, but I think our group should let Jenny make the choice for next time."

"I pick *Jane Eyre*," Jenny said in a voice that sounded decidedly grumpy even to her own ears. It was a small victory, considering that she'd have to give Mr. Raintree a set of keys to The Jonquil House and give him the first-floor bedroom until she could get some furniture delivered.

She'd feel a whole lot better about having him move in if she could understand why he suddenly wanted to live there so badly.

The wind had a mind to blow Jenny over on Thursday morning as she got out of her Fiesta. She had never set foot in the parking lot of the Peach Blossom Motor Court before, not even on prom night all those years ago when so many of her girlfriends had gone off with the boys they eventually married.

She hadn't had a boyfriend in high school. She hadn't gone to the prom. And now eighteen years later, it wasn't a warm May night but a biting-cold January morning.

She hunkered down in her big, puffy winter coat and examined the seedy establishment. The long, single-story building was wrapped in 1940s-vintage faux stone that was as tacky as it was shabby.

About twenty room doors opened onto a concrete walkway with an awning that was held up by ugly steel posts. The columns and the doors had been painted a garish shade of pale orange, no doubt because someone, long ago, thought peach blossoms were the same color as orange sherbet.

Jenny knew better because she owned a peach orchard that she'd inherited from her grandfather. Of course, peach-blossom pink doors and posts wouldn't have been an improvement.

It took only a moment's conversation with Garnet Willoughby in his shabby office to discover Mr. Raintree's room number and to learn that Garnet was in a big, hot hurry to get rid of the difficult Mr. Raintree and his "noisy dog."

Now Jenny stood before the room in question feeling a range of emotions she didn't want to show. She rolled her head on her neck and shrugged her shoulders a few times, willing herself to relax. Then she exhaled, trying to blow out the tension.

It sort of worked.

She steeled herself and knocked on the door.

A low, impatient voice sounded from beyond the peeling orange paint. "Who the hell is it?"

Before she could answer, the dog started barking, but another sharp word from Mr. Raintree and Aslan stopped.

"It's Jenny Carpenter."

She heard movement within the room, but it took almost a minute before Mr. Raintree opened the door.

He didn't look well. His eyes were bloodshot, and the stubble on his face seemed to have a bit more gray in it than she remembered. The collar of his white T-shirt was misshapen enough to show a little bit of collarbone, and the tiniest swirl of chest hair. He looked as if he'd slept in his jeans. He braced himself with an aluminum cane in his right hand, his left ankle encased in a plastic walking cast.

Aslan stood on his left side. A studded, black leather collar encircled the dog's neck, giving Mr. Raintree a means for keeping him from bolting out the door, which Aslan seemed to want to do the moment he set his beautiful brown eyes on Jenny.

And Jenny had to stop herself from dropping to her knees and giving the dog a great big hug. She was, truly, infatuated with the animal. But she wasn't about to show that to Mr. Raintree. Not right at this moment anyway.

But she did end up staring at Mr. Raintree's left hand, which was wrapped around the dog's collar. His skin was brown, as if he'd been off to Bermuda in the middle of winter. His fingers were blunt and powerful. A tracery of veins traveled like a road map across his knuckles and up his arm.

"What do you want?" he asked, drawing her attention back to his unshaven face with its dark eyes and tousled hair that fell over his forehead. He sounded as gruff as he looked, and a little bit of her hard heart melted. He was hurt, and he seemed to need as much care as the dog.

She dug into the pocket of her big coat and pulled out a jump ring with the set of shiny brass keys she'd had made at Lovett's Hardware.

"These are the keys to The Jonquil House. I'm prepared to give you a room at the inn on two conditions. First, the house is not yet ready for guests and won't be for a while, so you'll be temporarily housed in the back bedroom—Luke's room. When my furniture is delivered, I'll move you to a better room upstairs.

"And second, I need to ask you a big favor."

Aslan sat down and leaned into Mr. Raintree's bad leg, but he didn't seem to mind. Man and dog looked as if they were both listing a little to the right. "How much are you asking for this room?" he said.

Any fool could see that the dog was bonding to the man. Jenny's heart gave a lurch in her chest. She was so irked by this state of affairs that she forgot all about the library and Nita's looming unemployment and spoke her mind. "For starters, you can give me back my dog."

The corner of Mr. Raintree's mouth twitched. She couldn't decide if that little tic betrayed his annoyance or amusement. He studied her for a moment, saying nothing, while his black eyes focused on her in an almost preternatural way.

"He's not your dog," he finally said. "Zeph told me he's a stray. I've taken him to the vet and gotten him all his shots. So he's mine now. And his name is Bear."

"Bear? He doesn't look like a bear. He looks like a lion. I was thinking of calling him Aslan."

"No. He's Bear. He looks just like—" He bit off the words, and something in those black eyes changed. There was a much more vulnerable person behind the mask he usually wore.

And it occurred to her that maybe Mr. Raintree needed the dog more than she did. Which was something, because Jenny needed a companion in the worst way.

She stared up into Mr. Raintree's sad eyes and decided that she would get herself a cat. "Look, I'm very sorry. I didn't realize that you'd taken him to the vet. So let me start over. I don't want the dog back."

"Then what?"

How on earth was she supposed to tell this self-absorbed man that the book club was hoping to enlist his help in saving the local library?

It was absurd.

Then again, the insides of the Peach Blossom Motor Court, which she could see just beyond his big shoulders, gave new meaning to the word "seedy." He might jump at the chance to help the local librarian if it meant he could sleep in a nice, clean room with a fireplace.

She cleared her throat. "Mr. Raintree, I'm here as a spokesperson for the Last Chance Book Club. We meet every other week at the Last Chance branch of the Allenberg Library. We just learned that the county wants to shut down our library. And our librarian, Nita Wills, is about to lose her job. So, anyway, the group wanted to ask you if you would be willing to help us with a fund-raiser to save the library and the librarian."

It was a long speech, and she'd kind of rushed through it. As she spoke, his dark eyebrows arched with a look of utter amazement.

"So they sent *you* to convince me? *You*, who have already admitted that you aren't one of my fans? Interesting choice." His right hand tightened on his cane.

"Well, you see, it's that—"

"Miss Carpenter, are you blackmailing me?"

"Blackmail?" Of all the words he might have used to describe this deal she was trying to make, "blackmail" was not one of them. "Uh, no, I'm trying to strike a bargain."

She cocked her head and made a show of looking past him into the shabby room. "The Jonquil House might not be finished, but it is much cleaner and nicer than the room you're staying in right at the moment. And there's space for the dog to exercise."

"Is the power back on?"

"Yes, and I'm taking steps to get a generator."

"Good thinking, since it's out there in the swamp."

"Mr. Raintree, a day ago you offered to buy the house at a ridiculous price and now—"

"Are you willing to sell?"

"No, but I'm willing to let you stay there even though we are not open for business yet."

"And what would this library group require of me?"

"A lecture at The Kismet, followed by a showing of *Black Water*."

"You're asking a lot."

She wasn't surprised that he didn't want any part of her bargain. She got the feeling that he preferred being alone. She could almost understand how he might feel that way. If you were alone for long enough, it became a way of life.

"I'm sorry, then," she said, and turned away toward the parking lot. She made a show of putting the keys in her pocket.

"Wait," he shouted after her. "How much rent are you charging?"

She turned, the wind whipping her hair across her face. "Mr. Raintree, I said I would *give* you a room at the inn. I don't plan to charge you any rent, especially seeing as you slipped in my drive. It's the least I can do."

"I can afford to pay rent."

"I'm not asking for any. Just your help with the library."

His mouth twitched at the corner. "You're a book lover, aren't you?"

"I am."

He nodded. "Then I'll accept your bargain."

CHAPTER 5

The front door of The Jonquil House was locked when Gabe arrived later in the afternoon. He was about to slip the key into the lock when Bear turned and started to bark.

"Hush," Gabe said as he turned to look over his shoulder.

Zeph Gibbs stood in the middle of the circular drive, cradling a shotgun. How many times had he seen Zeph standing exactly like that? The man was like still water. You couldn't read what was going on inside him just by examining the surface.

Boyhood memories tumbled through Gabe's mind. Once, Gabe had deeply admired Zeph's ability to move through the woods without making any kind of sound. Zeph used to say that he learned that trick as a boy growing up in a shack not a stone's throw from the river. He'd grown up hunting and fishing—not because it was a fun thing to do, but because catfish and possum might be all his family had to eat. He'd once told Gabe and Luke that being quiet in the woods and good with a gun had saved his life a time or two in Vietnam.

Gabe turned all the way around, leaning on his cane. He gave Bear's lead a little tug, and the dog sat.

"Zeph," Gabe said, "what can I do for you?"

"I heard something about you renting the house."

"No, Miss Carpenter is letting me stay here for a while. In Luke's old room. I promised to help the library with its problem."

Zeph frowned. "The library has a problem?"

"I gather budget cuts are threatening the local library and its librarian. I promised to help with some fund-raising. I happen to love libraries, and I'm deeply worried that they might be going the way of bookstores."

Zeph stilled even further. Where did this enmity come from?

"What is it, Zeph? Spit it out."

"I just want to know if you're all right, sleeping in Luke's old room."

The question took him aback. "Of course I'm okay. It's a damn sight better than the Peach Blossom Motor Court. Now, if you don't mind, my ankle is killing me, and I'd like to get it propped up in that bed."

"You need to go, Mr. Gabe. Staying here in this house is a bad idea. A really bad idea."

"You've told me that at least a dozen times, but you haven't told me why."

"It's better that you don't remember what happened here."

"I know what happened here. My brother got shot, and it soured my grandfather, and literally sent my grandmother to her deathbed. But life goes on."

Zeph said nothing. He kept staring with those dark eyes of his. Zeph could be pretty unnerving when he set his mind to it.

"Look, I'm not leaving. This is a good place for me right now, and you just need to quit worrying about me, okay?"

"I won't be responsible for what happens this time. Do you understand?" Zeph said in a low, hard voice that sent wary shivers rippling up Gabe's back.

Gabe didn't remember Zeph being this menacing, but he must have been. Otherwise where had Gabe come up with Zebulon Stroud, the crazy killer in *Black Water*? For the first time, Gabe wondered if maybe his book had hit closer to the mark than intended.

"What do you mean—responsible *this time*?" he asked in a quiet voice.

"Don't be a fool. This ain't no place for you anymore. You should just leave the dog and get in your fancy car and drive away."

"I'm not leaving the dog, and I'm not leaving town. Don't ask me again."

"Mr. Gabe, please. You'll be happier if you leave."

He barked a laugh that made Zeph flinch. "Happy? I can't remember the last time I was happy. I'm not interested in pursuing happiness. It's highly overrated. I just want some peace and quiet, and another bestseller."

Gabe turned away and slipped the key into the lock, but he was uncomfortably aware of Zeph as he stepped through the threshold. The man's stare seemed to burn a hole in the middle of his back.

He hobbled down the hall and turned left into the room that had belonged to Luke.

Someone, probably Jenny Carpenter herself, had made up the bed with plain white linens and a pale blue microfiber blanket that looked brand new.

There were no curtains at the windows, no furniture except the bed. The wainscoting and plaster was painted white. All in all, the room looked like an empty canvas.

That suited Gabe fine. Having a sterile room to work in would minimize distractions.

He left the dog in the room and returned down the hall, intent on bringing in his luggage. But when he got to the front door, he found all his luggage and his groceries sitting up on the porch laid out bizarrely end-to-end in a straight line. The positioning was almost creepy. And how the hell had Zeph gotten into the locked trunk of his car? More important, how had he moved all this stuff to the porch so quickly?

He looked around, but he could find no sign of Zeph. The old man had dematerialized back into the woods.

The skin on Gabe's neck prickled as he stared at his luggage and pushed back the unwanted feeling that he'd become trapped in one of his own novels.

His disquiet lasted only a moment before he shook it off with a private little smile. No, this wasn't anything except the reemergence of his imagination. He had nothing to fear here. In fact, he was certain The Jonquil House would be the perfect place to write.

Which is exactly what he spent the rest of his day doing. He climbed up into the bed, propped his laptop on his knees, and settled down to work for the first time in months. His mind was clear. He wasn't looking over his shoulder. And the phone wasn't ringing constantly.

He could think here, even though it was incredibly cold.

He got about a thousand words down then took a break. He and Bear headed out the back door to the woodpile, where he found plenty of wood to keep a fire going in the fireplace.

He and the dog made several trips, stacking the wood in the corner by the hearth. He also found a card table and folding chair in the living room. There was a sewing machine on the table, but he didn't give a darn. He moved the machine to the floor and hauled the table into his bedroom.

It was easier to write at a desk. He worked until his eyes felt sandy, and the day had faded into night. He saved his file to the hard drive, took the dog out for a walk, fell into the bed, and slept like he hadn't slept in a long, long time.

Sometime in the middle of the night, the dog woke him up. The room had been utterly dark when he'd gone to sleep. But now, his laptop was open and powered on, with the screen open to his file manager.

The coals still glowed in the fireplace, but the room was bitterly cold.

"What the f—" He climbed out of bed and limped over to his improvised desk. He sat down, blinking at the screen as his mind slowly awakened.

"Shit, where the hell is my book?" he asked to no one in particular. But the dog let out a little whine.

He began frantically searching through his files and folders. Everything seemed to be in order, except that the file containing the first three thousand words of his novel had been completely deleted from his laptop.

He turned on the light, squinting as he headed through the bedroom door and out into the hallway. Bear followed at his heels. Gabe went into the kitchen first and tried the door.

Damn it. It was unlocked. Great. And he couldn't even blame his landlady, because the last one through the back door had been himself and the dog. How could he have been so stupid? Easy, he'd been deep into the book at that moment and only left the keyboard because Bear needed to go.

The door didn't have a dead bolt, which was worrisome, but he set the snap lock and then headed off to the front door to check it as well. Thankfully that door was locked.

He was wide awake now and angry at himself. He couldn't be too careful, even here in Last Chance, South Carolina.

Now that Gabe Raintree had taken residence in the back bedroom at The Jonquil House, there was no space for Jenny. So on Thursday night, Jenny slept at the rented town house that she'd shared with her late mother for the last five years. Friday morning, she awakened in the wee hours and baked hot cross muffins in her old stove.

Then she shared a cup of coffee with Cousin Maryanne. After a nice cup and some time with the baby, Maryanne bundled herself and Joshua out the door to go to their new situation at the Methodist day care center. Maryanne's new job didn't pay much but it allowed her to earn some income and be with her child.

Jenny hadn't said anything, but once the inn got going, she planned to offer Maryanne a job as her helper. For now, though, the day care center was a perfect fit for the young mother.

After Maryanne and Joshua had left, Jenny threw on her raggedy work clothes, wrapped up the remainder of the morning muffins, and headed out to The Jonquil House.

Mr. Raintree had posted a yellow sticky note on his bedroom door that said "Do Not Disturb" in big block letters. Jenny chose to ignore it.

She knocked briefly.

"Are you illiterate?" came the snarling voice from the other side of the door.

"No, but I come bearing muffins. And dog food. I've made a pot of coffee and the muffins are on the counter in the kitchen. The dog food is in a bowl by the back door. Help yourself, Mr. Raintree. And also, please let me know if you need linens."

"I need quiet," he shouted. Bear punctuated this by barking.

"Then I suggest you stop shouting," Jenny said.

She refrained from grinding her teeth as she ascended the stairs. All the stress was giving her an ache in her jaw.

For the rest of the morning, she threw all her energy into hanging wallpaper in the big back bedroom. She gave Mr. Raintree not a single thought until she heard the kitchen door open. She peeked through the window to see what he was up to.

He'd let the dog out without a leash, which seemed pretty cavalier, seeing as Bear was a stray and probably liked to wander. At the moment, though, the dog seemed happy to be marking his territory on every rhododendron in sight.

Mr. Raintree, dressed today in jeans and a tattered Harvard sweatshirt, was limping his way toward the woodpile with clear intent.

"Oh, good Lord," Jenny said aloud.

She headed down the stairs at breakneck speed and into the backyard in time to see Mr. Raintree attempting to balance several pieces of wood while simultaneously walking with a cane.

She hurried across the yard and right up to him. "Here,

let me carry that. You have no business being up on that ankle."

He gazed down at her, his face looking much less gloomy today than it had on Thursday. There was the tiniest smile at the corner of his mouth, and something changeable in the depths of his great, dark eyes. She knew he was a hard, self-absorbed man, and yet his eyes didn't convey that right at this moment. They shone with kindness. But of course, she was imagining things. She had a terrible tendency to want to believe the best about people.

"You don't look big enough to carry wood. I wouldn't make you do that for me," he said.

If there was one thing that annoyed her, it was men who thought women were helpless. "You'd be surprised how tough I am," she snarled, reaching for the wood in his arms. But he turned away and started walking toward the back door. Short of tackling him, which would be rude for an innkeeper, she was going to have to let him haul wood.

Of course, the paltry number of logs in his arms wouldn't last very long, so Jenny headed off to the woodpile for a load of her own. She wanted to prove that she wasn't a shrinking violet of a woman. Besides, it was her *job* to haul wood.

Bear came over to woof at her briefly, but it was only in play. He looked cleaner and healthier than he had on Thursday morning. Mr. Raintree was obviously kind to the dog, and she wasn't imagining that.

She carried her load of wood back to the house with the dog trotting beside her. As she passed through the kitchen, she noticed that her muffins hadn't been touched.

When she got to the threshold of Mr. Raintree's door, she paused for a moment. He'd only been there a day, but the room looked occupied. Several suitcases were open. Dirty clothes littered the floor.

He'd borrowed her folding table and chair from the living room, where she'd set up her sewing machine. The card table now held a laptop computer and a messy pile of papers torn from a yellow legal pad. Coals already glowed from the fireplace, so he must have been making a lot of trips to the woodpile.

"This room is drafty as crap," he said as he dropped a log onto the fire. He picked up the fireplace poker, which, like the bed, had been left behind when the Raintrees had abandoned the house a quarter century ago. "I don't think your baseboard heating is working in here," he continued. "And I really don't like muffins in the morning. So don't put yourself out on my account."

Maybe he wasn't all that kind. Or maybe he was in pain from his ankle. She stacked her logs beside the fireplace. "Did you try one of the muffins?" she asked.

"No."

"Maybe you should." She turned to go, but he called her back before she could reach the door.

"Did you bake them?"

"I did."

"Don't take it personally. I don't usually eat sweet things. I bought some milk and cereal, and some sandwich makings. I hope you don't mind my using the refrigerator."

"Of course not."

The coals in his fireplace must have been hot because the wood he'd stacked on the andirons had already caught fire. He looked down and poked the log a few times. The fire's glow lit up his stony features, softening them in a way that made the breath catch in Jenny's throat.

Just then, he looked up at her across the bare, almost sterile room. "You're staring at me. What is it? Are you checking me out? Please don't tell me that you think I'm handsome."

"No," she said without thought.

He chuckled. And the sound seemed to warm the room by degrees. "You're a piece of work, Jenny Carpenter. You look exactly like the kind of conventional woman who hands out platitudes. And yet every time I speak with you, you surprise me. Don't you know that southern women never speak their minds directly?"

The room suddenly felt tropical. Her mother had scolded her dozens of times for speaking her mind. She needed to watch it, now that she was an innkeeper. "I'm sorry," she said. "I was too blunt. I should have said something about how what's on the outside doesn't matter much."

He snorted a laugh. "I'm glad you didn't. I like honesty. The truth is I'm not even remotely handsome. I never have been. Unlike..." His voice faded away, and he turned to look at an empty corner of the room.

"Unlike who?"

He shrugged. "No one." He turned back to the fire, and the muscle along his jaw flexed. "I need to get back to work."

His landlady turned around and scooted out of the room like a rabbit with a dog on her tail. She was a funny little thing dressed in oversized painter pants and a gray-and-garnet University of South Carolina sweatshirt. She'd swept her hair up into a messy bun. Tendrils of gleaming brown hair had come loose, framing her face, making it softer somehow. The pile of hair on top of her head bounced as she hightailed it out of Gabe's room, and he found himself wishing that all the hairpins would fall out.

She looked like a little sparrow. So tiny and yet so determined. She had not one bit of artifice about her. She'd lived a simple life cloistered here in East Nowhere, and it showed. Jenny Carpenter was not a worldly woman.

He smiled at the thought as he collapsed into the hard metal folding chair that he'd purloined from the front room. He propped his bad foot up on an open suitcase and stared into the blank screen of his computer. The cursor blinked, awaiting his brilliance. Or at least a few words, even crappy ones.

But he had nothing, except the fading image of Jenny Carpenter looking him straight in the eye and telling him she didn't think he was much to look at.

He stared at the screen for a moment, then put his fingers on the keys and began to type.

She wore a shapeless dress, her hair pulled into a loose knot at the top of her head. Her glasses perched low on the bridge of her nose, and she stared at me with a pair of bewitching hazel eyes. "Welcome to the Fairfax Hotel," she said . . .

He got that far and could go no further. But he sat there poised for inspiration that never came.

When his ankle started throbbing, he popped a pain pill and took a nap. He woke up some time later with a slight headache and a growling stomach. It was almost dusk, and the house was quiet. Jenny had probably left for the day. He needed to get up and make himself a sandwich or something. Then he'd return to the computer and put in a few more hours.

He rolled out of bed and limped to the card table determined to delete every blessed word he'd written. He clicked his mouse to wake up his laptop. He expected the computer to display the double-spaced document containing the two or three paragraphs he'd managed. But when the screen lit up there were only two words in his document, typed in forty-eight-point type so they filled the entirety of his screen.

GHOSTS EXIST.

Gabe went cold from the inside out. He had no recollection of deleting his story or typing those words. Someone was playing tricks on him.

There were only two logical explanations for how those words got there: Either he'd had a break with reality, which might be possible since he'd taken a painkiller. Or his landlady was not what she appeared to be.

And that, right there, was a much better story than some stupid tale about a ghost haunting a hotel. What if the sweet, innocent, frumpy owner of the hotel was some kind of psychopath? He got all kinds of excited for a moment before he remembered that Alfred Hitchcock had already written the definitive tale about a psychopathic hotel owner.

And besides, why the heck would Jenny Carpenter want to mess with his head? It didn't make any sense. Jenny was a sweet, innocent woman who wanted his help with library fund-raising, nothing more.

And then it occurred to him that there was one additional explanation. Zeph Gibbs could stalk anything without making a noise. He could move through the woods, or a room, as silent as a breath of air. And Zeph most definitely wanted him to leave town.

CHAPTER 6

On Saturday morning, the Methodist Ladies Sewing Circle arrived at the front door of The Jonquil House carrying card tables, folding chairs, and sewing machines. They set up the cutting area in the dining room and lined up the card tables with sewing machines in the living room. But before they got to sewing, they descended on the plate of muffins Jenny had set out in her new kitchen. They gobbled them up, reassuring Jenny that the muffins had a place on her future breakfast menu, regardless of what the dour Mr. Raintree thought of sweets in the morning.

Sabina Grey, the co-owner of the antiques mall in town, pulled Jenny's thoughts away from her boarder when she said, "Oh, my goodness, ladies, have you met the new pastor? Because if you haven't, be prepared to die when you see him the first time."

"I don't want to die," Jenny said. "I'm too young."

"I wasn't being literal," Sabina replied, her blue eyes dancing with mischief.

"I know. I'm sorry. It's been a rough few days. So what's wrong with our new minister?" Jenny asked.

"Wrong? Oh, no, there is not one blessed thing wrong with that man." This came from Elsie Campbell, who, as chair of the Methodist Altar Guild, had the responsibility of organizing a crew every Friday to polish the cross and arrange the flowers on the altar. She had probably met the new minister yesterday. "I believe he has a halo that follows him around," Elsie continued. "Or maybe it's just because he's so handsome, it's practically blinding."

"And he's not married," Sabina said with a smirk.

Elsie giggled. "Honey, when you see him, you are going to forget all about Reverend Ellis."

Wilma Riley, the chair of the sewing club, snorted. "I hope y'all don't get into a catfight over him. That would be so silly, especially since both of you know good and well that you're better off without a man. Marriage is overrated."

"And how would you know?" Sabina asked. "I mean, you've never been married."

Wilma gave Sabina the stink eye, which was pretty darn intimidating because Wilma had mastered the stink eye. She was also the closest thing that Last Chance had to a feminist, even if she was chair of the sewing circle. She had the long, lean look of a fashion model, even now in her golden years. Today she was wearing a quilted jacket with a turquoise-and-navy floral pattern and three-quarter-length sleeves. Her white T-shirt featured a matching floral applique. Wilma was one heck of a seamstress and had even worked for a long time in the fashion industry in New York.

The fact that she was a walking contradiction never

bothered her in the least. She always turned herself out to the nines, but she made it a point to let everyone know that she dressed to please herself (and show off her skills as a seamstress), not to please some man. Even worse, she was likely to quote Betty Friedan at the slightest provocation, and usually at precisely the wrong time.

"Jenny, honey, now would be a poor time for you to become romantically involved. You do know this, right?" Wilma said.

Jenny nodded and managed a little smile. "I do."

"Good. You take my advice and stay the heck away from Reverend Lake. If Sabina wants to chase him, you just let her do it, you hear?"

The ladies began talking at once, the way they usually did when Wilma took a stand no one agreed with. Jenny refrained from saying a single word. In truth, she didn't know what to say that any of her friends would want to hear.

She was on Wilma's side. She didn't want to be courted by another preacher. She didn't want to be courted *period*. She was tired of waiting for somebody to show up on some nebulous someday. All she had was *today*, and if she didn't make today worthwhile, then she was wasting her life.

She was proud of what she'd accomplished in the last few months. She had channeled all her energies into the inn, and it showed. Now she would be utterly content with a regular stream of guests and maybe a cat…or two. She'd decided to give up on the whole dog scenario. Maybe once Mr. Raintree moved out and took Bear with him, she would think about a dog.

She was making another pot of coffee and thinking about

the dog she'd let get away and her likely future as a crazy cat lady innkeeper when the door to Mr. Raintree's room opened. Bear came bounding out, heading straight for the kitchen and his food bowl and not in the least deterred by Wilma, who was blocking his path. He had no trouble knocking the chair-woman of the sewing circle right off her feet.

Which explained why Wilma's introduction to Mr. Raintree—who appeared at the kitchen door wearing a pair of rumpled jeans, a three-day beard, and a T-shirt that had once been white—was not entirely auspicious.

Mr. Raintree didn't even seem to notice that Wilma was sprawled on her butt. He scowled at the women in the kitchen and bellowed, "Would you ladies please shut up?" Bear punctuated this directive with a couple of loud woofs. The ladies stopped talking, which was practically a miracle.

Of course Wilma was only quiet because she'd been stunned into silence. And she was not likely to stay silent for very long. She scrambled to her feet and stood toe-to-toe with Mr. Raintree and poked her well-manicured finger right into the middle of his chest. "It's a toss-up as who has worse manners, you or your dog."

Wilma was a huge dog lover. She had at least three poodles at home and worked tirelessly with Charlene Polk down at the veterinary clinic on spay and neuter programs. Wilma never blamed any four-legged creature for bad behavior. In her view, all doggie problems were caused by humans.

Wilma gave Mr. Raintree another poke with her finger. "And, quite frankly, not a one of us is going to shut up. The bill of rights applies to us just as it does to you."

Jenny needed to head this one off at the pass because Mr. Raintree's dark eyes were starting to spark with anger and his brows were lowering right into a masculine scowl that was surprisingly becoming to him. She inserted herself between Wilma and her boarder. "Y'all meet Mr. Gabriel Raintree. He's a famous author, and he's staying out here for a little bit while he works on his next book."

"Well, I don't care if he's the king of England. He needs to keep his dog in check."

"It's not my dog," Mr. Raintree said. "Bear belongs to Jenny."

The sewing circle looked at Jenny, while Jenny looked at Mr. Raintree, her mouth dropping open in surprise. Jenny was on the cusp of saying something very unladylike, but she was saved from that embarrassment when someone opened the front door and hollered, "Hello, is anyone home?"

"Good Lord," Elsie said. "Is that Miriam Randall? What's she doing crashing our party?"

Jenny closed her mouth and gave Mr. Raintree her own version of the stink eye, which was inferior to Wilma's but would have to do. Then she headed off to the front foyer. This required her to brush past her infuriating boarder. And wouldn't you know it? Despite his scruffy appearance, the man smelled good enough to eat. Which was sort of strange because, while Jenny loved to cook for everyone and anyone, she was a picky eater herself.

She hurried down the center hall and found Miriam Randall and her niece, Savannah, standing in the foyer, each of them dressed in heavy winter coats.

"Hey, y'all, this is a surprise. I've got the sewing circle here and we're just having some muffins and coffee. Y'all want to come on back and see my new kitchen?"

Of course Savannah was here to check out Jenny's

kitchen. They'd been one-upping each other at book club meetings for months with their tales of industrial kitchen remodeling. Savannah's sudden, unannounced visit had to be filed under the heading of kitchen espionage.

Savannah smiled and held out a Tupperware container. "I know you probably have baked goods out the wazoo, but I brought you a little housewarming gift. It's a strudel, and I thought with you having a guest out here and all, that it might come in handy."

Of course it was a strudel. Savannah wouldn't have sent anything less.

"Savannah's here to talk to your boarder about this book club fund-raiser y'all are planning. I'm just tagging along," Miriam said with a twinkle behind her thick 1950s-style trifocals. "And coffee would be wonderful. I don't suppose you have any of those muffins you make every year for the Easter breakfast, do you?"

"A few."

"Wonderful." And with that Miriam Randall took off her coat and headed down the hallway without so much as a by-your-leave.

"I'm sorry," Savannah whispered as she and Jenny followed the old lady. "Miriam's had a bee in her bonnet for a couple of days. She insisted that we come out here to visit, unannounced. I have no idea what she's up to, honestly, besides wanting to get another look at your boarder. She saw him the other day at the Kountry Kitchen. And she's fibbing when she says I came out here to talk to Mr. Raintree. Nita asked Hettie to chair the library fund-raising committee, not me. She called and asked me to be a member, that's all."

"Yeah, she called me too," Jenny said. "She wants to

have a meeting with Mr. Raintree, and I think he told her next Thursday would be okay. Out here at the house."

"Good. I'm sorry about Miriam, but she's gotten a little strange in the last few months."

"It's all right. I've already got the sewing club here. What's a few more people?"

They reached the kitchen. And luckily Bear and Mr. Raintree had left the scene of their various crimes.

"I can't believe you're letting that man stay here," Wilma said the moment Jenny returned. Wilma was so upset with Mr. Raintree that she didn't even say hi to Savannah and Miriam.

"He's a..." Wilma pressed her lips together, no doubt because Miriam was in the room. If Miriam hadn't been there, Wilma might have really spoken her mind in language that was probably bluer than the deep blue sea. Instead she took a deep breath and said, "You should evict him."

"I can't do that, Wilma," Jenny said. "I don't have to like every person who stays here."

"And besides," Savannah said, "we need him for the library fund-raiser. And y'all should know that Hettie Ellis is chairing the effort and could use some volunteers. Y'all have heard about the library being closed, haven't you?"

"You're letting him stay here in order to save the library?" Wilma said, aghast. "Honey, you are never going to succeed in business if you let a man like that take advantage of you. Please tell me you are charging him for staying here."

"Well, er, ah...the truth is I'm letting him stay for free right at the moment, as a goodwill gesture because he's agreed to help with the library and the house is not ready for guests. And he used to own the house, Wilma, that should count for something. And he broke his ankle out in my driveway. I couldn't let him stay at the Peach Blossom Motor Court."

"You're letting him stay for free?" Wilma's eyes rolled. "Jenny Carpenter, you are not in business to please obnoxious members of the opposite sex. You are a businesswoman. You need to remember that."

"Yes, ma'am," Jenny said, nodding. It was the best way to get Wilma off her high horse. And in truth, Wilma had a point, but Jenny had already decided not to charge Mr. Raintree, and she wasn't going back on that decision. She gave Wilma a smile that was intended to disarm her, then put Savannah's strudel down on the counter. "Ladies, Savannah has just brought one of her delicious strudels. Who wants a piece?"

Thank goodness for Savannah's strudel. It immediately changed the tone of the gathering. Jenny got out some more paper plates, and Savannah started slicing. Elsie got a couple of folding chairs from the front room, and suddenly the sewing circle meeting had turned into an interfaith coffee klatch.

"So," Miriam said as she wandered over to the back window, "where *is* Mr. Raintree?"

"He went out the back with the dog," Wilma said.

"Ah, so he did." Miriam stood at the window obviously taking the measure of Jenny's famous guest. "I caught a glimpse of him at the Kountry Kitchen the other day. He's quite impressive, isn't he?"

"Who, Mr. Raintree or the dog?" Wilma asked.

Miriam laughed and turned away from the window. "I think they're a matched set."

Wilma nodded. "I knew it. I knew that dog wasn't really yours, Jenny."

Jenny sighed. "The dog is a stray. He turned up here a few days ago. Mr. Raintree has named him Bear and taken him to the vet, so I suppose he's taken ownership. But I wouldn't say he has title free and clear."

"Hmm, that's interesting," Miriam said.

"What is?"

"He named the dog Bear? I believe his brother once had a dog named Bear. Poor thing got left behind when Luke was killed. I think Zeph Gibbs ended up taking care of the dog. He lived a long time, as I recall, always following Zeph like a shadow everywhere he went." The old lady turned and peered through the window for a long moment. "It's uncanny how much Gabe looks like his grandfather. Governor Raintree was also a very impressive man. But kind of hard, if you know what I mean. Well, at least he became hard after his son died in that boating accident. George was grooming his son to become president of the United States. And I reckon when his son died, he put all his energies into his grandsons."

Miriam finally gave up staring through the window. She turned and sat down in one of the folding chairs Elsie had just brought in. Then she accepted a plate of strudel as if she were royalty.

Which was almost true. Miriam Randall was the matchmaker in Last Chance, and legend had it that her marital forecasts never went awry. Those whom Miriam matched stayed matched for life. So naturally she was a true celebrity in Allenberg County. For just about everyone except Wilma Riley.

Savannah took her aunt's place at the back window, but when she peered through the pane, she let go of an audible gasp as if she'd just seen a snake or a gator or something. She took two quick steps back from the window.

"What is it? You look like you've just seen a ghost," Jenny said.

Savannah turned away from the window with a patently phony smile plastered on her face. "Nothing at all. Gabriel Raintree just isn't what I was expecting."

"Me neither," Miriam said. "He's grown some since I last set eyes on him. But enough about your guest. The truth is, Jenny, I was curious about him, but I really came here to talk with you about something."

The air in the kitchen suddenly became almost too thick to breathe. Allenberg's most famous matchmaker had taken time out of her Saturday routine to visit Jenny?

And she'd come when Wilma was visiting. Oh, boy.

"Honey," Miriam said, without further preamble. "I know Bill Ellis was a huge disappointment. But you need to understand that you and he were never meant to be."

"Yes, ma'am. I know that." This was incredibly embarrassing.

"She's well rid of him," Wilma said, planting her fists on her boy-slim hips.

"Well, I wouldn't put it that way," Miriam said. "But it would have been a mistake if she and Bill had ended up together." Miriam turned away from Wilma. "Jenny, honey, you need to be patient. One day, a handsome man is going to come into your life, and you'll understand why Bill was not the man for you."

"Oh, my goodness," Sabina said in a voice that sounded much too young for her thirty-five years. "It's an omen, I know it is. It means you and Timothy Lake were made for each other."

"Timothy Lake?" Savannah asked.

"Our new preacher now that Pastor Mike has gone off to Charleston," Elsie said.

"And he's to-die-for handsome," Sabina added.

Miriam said, "Well, isn't that nice," while Wilma looked daggers at the old lady and muttered, "Oh, brother, here we go again."

Gabe watched Bear as he marked his territory along the boundaries of the backyard. He was feeling a little guilty for having disavowed the dog. He couldn't even explain why he'd done it, except that the woman poking his chest had annoyed him.

That, and he wanted to see Jenny's reaction. He had to admit that the little innkeeper was adorable when she got angry. The outrage on her face was practically delicious. Jenny had opened her mouth and was about to say something profane. He had a feeling it would be entertaining, especially if she'd unleashed a torrent of cuss words in front of her friends. Too bad Miriam Randall interrupted, because Jenny was at her best when she spoke her mind.

He turned his face toward the sun and soaked up the warmth. He'd been cold for days. But out here, the cold had broken. The ice had melted, leaving behind mud and puddles. Bear was enjoying the thaw with his big nose glued to the ground. He'd need a bath by the time he was done scenting out all the interesting things in the yard.

Gabe watched the dog for a long moment, enjoying his company, when, quite abruptly, Bear sat down, cocked his head, and gave a little half bark, behaving as if someone unseen had commanded him to sit. The dog sat at attention, his gaze focused on one particularly large rhododendron.

Gabe hobbled across the yard toward the dog. "What is it, boy?"

The dog made no response to his question. He didn't even look in Gabe's direction, which was odd. Gabe followed the dog's gaze, sure he'd find Zeph lurking in the bushes. But if Zeph was hiding in there, he was doing a masterful job of it.

Gabe was thinking about limping over to the rhododendron and having a closer look when the hinges on the back door squealed. The noise must have flushed whatever critter Bear had been staring at because he took off like a rocket, disappearing quickly into the rhododendrons' dark, shiny foliage.

"Wait, Bear," Gabe called, as he tried to run after the dog. He managed two awkward, painful steps before he realized the futility of trying to follow.

"You let him out without a leash?"

Gabe looked over his shoulder. Jenny stood there with arms akimbo, her navy blue cardigan buttoned all the way up her front. She wore a pair of baggy khakis and an utterly adorable scowl on her face.

"Of course I did. We've been fine up to now. In fact, Bear and I have made countless trips to the woodpile over the last few days because your heating system is on the fritz. He's never run away before."

"Oh, my God. He's a stray. Of course he's run away before. Otherwise how did he get to be a stray in the first place? I mean, he looks like a purebred mastiff. He must have belonged to someone before he came here."

"Probably someone who abused or neglected him. How do I know it wasn't you?" He said the last bit just to get her goat.

"Don't. You know good and well that I didn't even know Bear existed until Wednesday, when he knocked you down. I'm sorry he did that, but it wasn't my fault. Clearly we're going to have to teach him some manners if you plan to stay here for the next three months. Knocking people over has become something of a habit. Wilma is furious. And I want to avoid lawsuits if at all possible."

"*We* need to teach him?" Somehow he found that particular pronoun both surprising and thrilling.

She startled as if he'd slapped her across the face. Color crept up her cheeks. "What I should have said is that *I* need to teach him, since you just told the world that Bear belongs to me."

"I didn't tell the world. Just a group of annoyingly loud females."

"Mr. Raintree, those annoyingly loud females are members of the Methodist and Episcopalian congregations in this town. And Wilma is a card-carrying member of the ASPCA. If you say something to those women, it's like broadcasting it on CNN."

She paused a moment and eyed his cast, then looked out at the woods' undergrowth. "Bear," she called, "come here, boy."

"He's long gone, I'm afraid," Gabe said.

"Great, my day has just come unraveled because of you. The minute I tell Wilma what's happened she's going to want to organize the entire sewing circle into a doggie search-and-rescue operation. Which means my curtains will *never* get done."

She turned on her heel. She was utterly breathtaking in her fury.

"So don't tell her," Gabe suggested in a calm voice.

Jenny whirled around. "Don't tell her? You mean just let Bear wander in the woods by his lonesome?"

"He'll come back. We've got the food, and he's perpetually hungry."

"That's a terrible attitude, you know?"

He shrugged. "It's a realistic attitude. Your sewing club ladies have no business tracking him through the swamp."

"You're probably right about that. But someone's got to look for him. You think you could manage?"

"Not in a cast."

She smiled. For some reason, it seemed to delight her that there was something he couldn't quite manage for himself. She was a funny, interesting woman.

"I'm sorry about Bear," he said. "But before you run off looking for him, I need to ask you a question about something. This is a hard question. I'm not sure how to ask it without sounding like a crazy wacko."

She gave him a direct, no-bull kind of look. It had been a long time since he'd met *anyone* who didn't try to suck up to him, or get on his good side, or ask him for an introduction to his editor. "Mr. Raintree, I've read one of your books, and as far as I'm concerned you *are* a crazy wacko. What is it that you want? And make it quick. I need to go after the dog."

"Have you ever had any odd experiences here at The Jonquil House? Anything you couldn't quite explain?"

"Are you looking for plot suggestions? Honestly..." She turned.

"No, wait. This has nothing to do with my book. And how did you know I was thinking about writing a haunted house story?"

She turned back toward him. "I didn't know. I just

thought, well...I mean there are all kinds of rumors about The Jonquil House, you know. About how it's haunted."

"And you believe them?"

"Of course not. But surely..."

"I asked you about strange happenings not because I think the place is haunted, but because I'm concerned. Or maybe I'm paranoid. I think someone is playing tricks on me."

"Tricks? How so?"

"Someone is coming into my room and deleting files on my computer while I'm asleep. To be honest, I haven't entirely ruled you out as the culprit. On Thursday night, I lost three thousand words."

"I did not sneak into your room and delete your files."

"I didn't say you did. I only said you were the most likely suspect. But there could be others."

"I'm finding this hard to believe, Mr. Raintree."

"The first night—Thursday—I inadvertently left the back door unlocked. But last night I double-checked to make sure everything was locked up tight, *including* my own bedroom door. And the same thing happened. So I'm wondering, does someone other than you have keys to the house?"

"No. Just you and me. And I can't imagine anyone sneaking in here with Bear. He barks at strangers. So I hope you'll forgive me if I ask you how much pain medication you've been taking."

"I've stopped taking meds, and I'm trying to sort out whether this is someone who has it out for me or someone who is unhappy with you. Have you had anything odd happen?"

She blinked at him from behind her owlish glasses. Her face had grown pale. "Actually, something strange did happen. But I thought it was a dream."

"What?"

"On the night of the ice storm, I was reading in bed and I fell asleep and had a strange dream. When I woke up, the window was open, and rain was coming in. That was strange, because I could have sworn the window was locked from the inside. I tried to close it, but I couldn't make it budge even though it's a brand-new window that shouldn't be sticking. I finally gave up and went to the front room, started a fire, and slept the rest of the night on the floor. But in the morning when I went into the bedroom, the window was closed and locked from the inside, and there wasn't any sign that it had rained into the house. I'm pretty sure I dreamed the whole thing, if you must know."

"Are you sure no one else has keys to the house? Someone like maybe Zeph Gibbs?" he said, one worry replacing another. If she had intruders in the house *before* he moved in, then this wasn't a case where his problems had followed him to Last Chance. But the unknown dangers were always more frightening than the ones you'd grown accustomed to.

"I think someone is messing with us," he said.

"What? No. What are you suggesting?"

"I don't know. But it's possible that Zeph came into the house and closed the window for you."

"In the middle of the storm? But how did the window get open in the first place? And he doesn't have keys."

"I can think of a lot of ways he might have gotten in. You don't have dead bolts on the doors."

"I don't need dead bolts. This is Last Chance, South Carolina, not some big city. And Zeph Gibbs is a little odd, but I don't think he's—"

"Did anyone lose this critter?" The voice interrupted

Jenny before she could finish her thought. And just like that Zeph Gibbs materialized from out of the same bushes where, a moment ago, the dog had vanished. As usual, Zeph was carrying a shotgun. But this time he was also leading Bear on a short red leash.

Jenny and Gabe turned in unison as Zeph crossed the yard. He led the dog past Gabe and placed the leash into Jenny's slender hand. "Miz Jenny, you need to keep this dog on a leash when he's outside. I think he's got a wandering soul, if you know what I mean."

Gabe didn't know Jenny all that well, but he was certain she didn't trust the old man, even though she'd spoken up in his defense.

Zeph turned toward him and gave him a hard stare. "Boy," he said in that voice that used to make him jump when he was a child, "I'm going to tell you one more time. You need to get out of here. It's not safe for you to stay here. You may not believe in ghosts but that don't mean nothing if they believe in you."

And with that, Zeph nodded toward Jenny then turned and glided back into the woods on a pair of surprisingly quiet boots.

"I would not trust that man," Gabe said. "He's trying to make us think there's a real ghost living in this house, and we both know that ghosts aren't real. Promise me you'll get the locks changed."

"All right. I'll call the locksmith right away. I knew he didn't want the house renovated, but I've never thought he was dangerous. You think I should talk to Sheriff Rhodes about him?"

"If I were you, I'd talk to the sheriff right away."

CHAPTER 7

The sun set early this time of year, but Zeph wasn't much troubled by the darkness. He never had been for some reason. In Vietnam the darkness could be terrifying, but it could also be a friend.

He stood in the deep shadows of a thirty-foot magnolia tree, his hands jammed into the pockets of his coat, his collar turned up against the cold. He studied the front door of the house on Maple Street. The sight was more than familiar. Coming here was like a compulsion. It was something he fought with all his willpower. But sometimes, when the loneliness of his life overwhelmed him, he would come right here and watch until she turned off her lights and settled down for the night. And sometimes he even stood here in the darkness.

But tonight was different. Tonight he needed to do more than stand in the shadows. He needed to act.

Lives hung in the balance.

He walked with a measured pace up the front porch steps and stood at the door, his heart racing, his stomach doing backflips, his hands slightly sweaty even on this cold night.

He knocked. He waited. The door opened.

"Why, Zeph Gibbs, what brings you to my door?" Nita's voice was library-soft, the way it always was.

"Ma'am," he managed before his throat closed up.

"C'mon in, Zeph, it's freezing out there. Can I get you a cup of coffee or something? I've got some cookies I just made for the grandchildren."

He hauled in a deep breath. The chocolate aroma coming from her door was as seductive as anything Zeph could imagine. How long had it been since he'd eaten a home-baked cookie? A long time. He wanted one. But he knew he couldn't take one.

"Uh, no, ma'am, I just needed to stop by and ask you, please, not to encourage Gabe to stay in Last Chance."

"Gabe? You mean Mr. Raintree?"

He nodded. "Yes, ma'am."

"Oh, for goodness' sake, Zeph, I've told you a million times not to call me ma'am. It makes me feel old. And maybe just a bit uppity if you want to know the truth. Now you come inside and you call me by name."

He shook his head, but the next thing he knew, Nita had grabbed him by the arm and was hauling him over her threshold. He was a weak man when it came to Nita. He should have resisted, but he didn't. He ended up on the wrong side of her door.

And then he made it worse by following her down a long hall into her kitchen and sitting down at a little table covered with a red-and-white-checked cloth. There was a plate of cookies right in the middle of that table, and another batch cooling on a rack on the counter. A radio somewhere was tuned to a soul station, and Ray Charles was singing about Georgia. The room was so warm he had to take off his coat.

Nita put a cup of coffee in front of him. "Now help yourself to a cookie."

She sat in the facing chair just as her cat, Jasmine, materialized from out of nowhere, floated right up into his lap, and settled there like she was a long-lost friend.

Which she was. He'd given Nita this cat last spring, and Nita was obviously doing a good job feeding her. Jasmine was a little bit fat.

"So how have you been?" Nita asked. "I saw the work you did on the lobby of The Kismet. Honestly, I don't think anyone in town, except maybe Dash Randall, had any idea you were such a gifted carpenter."

"Thank you, ma'—uh, Nita."

She gave him one of her wide, toothy smiles. Oh, man, she'd always had a smile as big as all of creation. When Nita smiled, it was like God singing.

He caught his breath and spoke again. "Uh, I know you're about to lose your job, and I think that's just terrible. But I'm asking you please to give up on this idea of using Gabe to help raise money for the library. Gabe needs to leave town as soon as possible."

Nita didn't react the way he had expected her to. He'd figured she would argue with him. But instead, she stared at him for a long, uncomfortable moment, her gaze kind of pinning him to his chair. He'd never had a feeling that someone was looking right through him until right this moment.

Then she gathered herself up and spoke in her always soft voice. "Zeph, honey, a while ago I heard something from Molly Wolfe—something her husband told her—about the day Luke Raintree died. And I have a feeling your request has something to do with that, doesn't it?"

"What did you hear?" His heart was pounding so hard he·could hear it inside his skull.

"I heard that it wasn't you holding the gun when it went off and killed Luke."

He stopped stroking the cat and put both his hands palms-down on the tablecloth. Then he stopped moving entirely, except for his racing heart. Lord have mercy, he wished his heart *would* stop. Because he'd dedicated twenty-five years to keeping Gabe's secret. And it wasn't easy to hear that his secret was known to someone other than himself, Gabe, and Simon Wolfe, Molly's husband. The three of them were the only people who knew the truth.

But he should have figured, now that Simon had returned to Last Chance, that he would tell his wife what had happened. Molly Wolfe wasn't what anyone would call a gossip, but obviously she'd said something to Nita, so now Zeph didn't know who in town knew the truth and who didn't.

Nita leaned forward and covered his hand with her own. The touch made everything inside him get all jumbled up together. He'd been thinking about holding Nita's hand since he was a boy of fifteen. It sure had taken a long time for it to happen. And he'd never thought that it would happen like this. He gazed down at her long, manicured fingers as they draped themselves over his own dark, hard, callused ones.

"Zeph. I haven't told a soul. And I don't think Molly or Simon has told anyone, either. It's not the kind of gossip the Wolfes would want spread around. And to tell you the truth, when I found out, I said to myself, *Well, isn't that just like Zeph Gibbs, taking the blame to protect a ten-year-old boy.* And here you are, trying to protect him again, even though he's thirty-five now. Honey, Gabe Raintree can take care of himself."

"But you don't understand. I made that decision because his grandfather was a hard, hard man who didn't like Gabe very much to begin with. If he'd known the truth, well, I don't know what would have become of Gabe."

"But, honey, George Raintree died a long time ago."

"I know that. But see, Gabe doesn't remember what happened." Zeph looked up into Nita's soft brown eyes. "I ran into him the night of the ice storm, and it was clear that he believes the lie I told all those years ago."

Her face softened. "Then there's no reason to worry. Let him believe the lie. And if you want, I'll have a word with Molly about it. I'll bet Simon would just as soon drop the matter. It's time to move on, Zeph. Luke died twenty-five years ago."

Everything Nita Wills said made perfect sense, except for one thing. She didn't know about the ghost. And the ghost sure as shooting wasn't at all interested in letting Gabe get away scot-free. In fact, the ghost had gotten real interested in haunting Gabe, only Gabe had no idea he was being haunted.

What would Nita think if he told her the truth? She'd think he was crazy. Just like most everyone in town.

She wasn't going to help him. There wasn't any reason to stay here, even though it would be so easy to drink the coffee and eat a cookie and listen to Ray Charles on the radio.

But he didn't belong here. He never would.

He stood up. "Miz Nita, thank you for listening and telling me what you know. I surely do wish you would give up trying to use Gabe to save the library. It's the only reason Miz Jenny gave him a room out at The Jonquil House. If you decided not to use him, Miz Jenny would evict him, which is what she wants to do. Lord have mercy, those two don't get along. Now, if you don't mind, I need to be going."

He picked up his coat and headed for the door lickety-split, before the grace shining in Nita's eyes sucked him in. Before he ate one bite of the heavenly manna she was offering in the form of coffee and cookies.

He needed to keep his head straight. Gabe's life might depend on it.

"Oh, my goodness, Reverend Lake is headed this way," Sabina said in a breathless, goofy voice that reminded Jenny of the legions of silly teenagers she'd spent most of her adult life teaching.

She glowered at her friend. "Stop being ridiculous. He's just a man."

"But he's a gorgeous man."

Jenny had to agree. If Timothy Lake were a statue, he would rival Michelangelo's *David*. He had to be six foot two or taller with a runner's body and a face like a Greek god—quite literally. He had a sensuous mouth, a long, straight, aquiline nose, and a square chin with a prominent cleft. His piercing blue eyes pinned her right where she stood. He needed a haircut, but it didn't matter. His tousled locks could only be described as golden, and they fell over his forehead just so. They absolutely gave him the appearance of having a halo.

Beside her, Sabina let go of a deep, yearning sigh while

Jenny sipped her coffee, completely unimpressed by the pastor's good looks. She needed the coffee bad. She hadn't slept well last night. Her conversation with Mr. Raintree yesterday had unsettled her. She didn't fully believe him, but she had to admit that Zeph Gibbs gave her a little case of the heebie-jeebies.

She had decided not to call the sheriff. After all, she had no real evidence that Zeph was guilty of anything except eccentricity. But she had made an appointment with the locksmith to have all the locks changed, just to be safe.

Jenny watched the preacher advance. He was carrying a paper plate with a half-eaten muffin on it. No doubt he planned to praise her baking skills. He appeared to be enjoying the muffin; there was a crumb at the corner of his mouth.

"Now, just be nice, Jenny," Sabina said. "Let him do the talking. You were kind of abrupt to him at the end of the services."

She had been abrupt. She'd shaken his hand, welcomed him to the congregation, and beat a hasty retreat down to the basement to help the altar guild set up the after-service refreshments. She hadn't even introduced herself.

And if she could remain anonymous, she would. Her plan was to spend as little time in his company as possible so as to discourage the gossip and speculation that had run through Last Chance like a wildfire in just twenty-four hours. After the sewing circle left The Jonquil House last evening, it took exactly twenty minutes before her phone started ringing.

She didn't have the heart to tell her friends and neighbors that she'd entered the post-husband-envy phase of her life. They meant well. But if she could have one wish, it would be that Elsie and Sabina would be more like Wilma. Wilma was the only one who seemed to understand that some people were beyond romance. And it was all right for them to be that way.

The minister stopped in front of her and held out his hand, which was almost as beautiful as his face. She found herself comparing that pretty, manicured hand to Mr. Raintree's much rougher and less well-kept hands. It struck her, then, that Mr. Raintree and Reverend Lake couldn't be less alike if they tried.

"Elsie told me you're the person who made the muffins. I'm blown away. This may be the best muffin I've ever tasted."

Of course his compliment made her face flame. Of course he noticed. And like day follows night, he smiled, revealing perfect teeth. "I'm Tim," he said, holding out his hand for her to shake.

Beside her Sabina sighed.

Jenny took his hand, intending to give him a quick, business-like shake, but he held on to her. And his palms were dry, and warm, and perfect, and scary as hell. Men like Reverend Lake were so far out of Jenny's league as to be another species entirely. She had no idea what to say to him. And really, she didn't want to talk to him at all. She would be happy to scurry back into the kitchen and make another pot of coffee.

"I'm Jenny," she managed to say.

And then Sabina took over. Because Sabina knew how shy Jenny could be when confronted by situations like this. "Jenny is about to open a bed-and-breakfast out on Bluff Road," she said. "And don't you believe what any of the Episcopalians say about Savannah Randall—Jenny is the best cook in Allenberg County. She always wins the blue ribbon for her peach pie. And we've been enjoying Jenny's muffins for years here." This was where Sabina leaned in and said in a near whisper, "And she's been known to cook supper for bachelor ministers."

Maybe if Jenny were lucky, the earth would swallow her up right now, just the way Reverend Lake had suggested that hell swallows sinners in his sermon. Come to think about it, in addition to being boring as sin, the preacher's sermon was a tiny bit heavy on the hellfire and damnation to suit Jenny.

Timothy Lake smiled, but somehow his smile didn't reach all the way to his eyes. "I'll look forward to an invitation," he said. His voice was as deep and resonant as Grant Trumbull's, the announcer for the local FM radio station. But it made sense for him to have a strong voice. He was a preacher. All preachers had deep, resonant voices.

"Why don't you invite him out to The Jonquil House next week?" Sabina said. "I mean, you'll have dining room furniture by tomorrow night, and I know how you're looking forward to using that new stove." Sabina was on a roll now. Once she started talking, it was pretty hard to shut her up. She turned toward the minister. "You have to see what she's done with that old house. I mean it's really beautiful. She has a gift for decorating and cooking. Lord knows, she's also got a good eye for antiques."

"Uh, well," Jenny stammered, "I'm sure that Reverend Lake has other social engagements next week. I—"

"I'd love to come see the inn. I've heard a lot about it, and you. I'm trying to get to know everyone in the congregation. So dinner next week could be very nice."

"Oh." She ran out of words.

"How about Wednesday?"

"Uh, Wednesday?"

"Is that a good day? Will you have furniture by then?"

"Uh, yeah, the furniture is being delivered tomorrow."

"Wednesday, then."

"Uh, okay."

And with that, the minister smiled and turned and headed off to have a conversation with Bernadette Oscar, who organized the Sunday School and all of the church's youth programs.

Meanwhile Sabina let out a little squeal that Jenny was sure the minister heard. "Oh, I'm so happy. Honey, he's going to be perfect for you. And you just need to relax because, really, if Miriam Randall says that Pastor Tim is the one for you, then he's the one for you."

CHAPTER 8

Monday was a busy day. The service providers who had bailed on Jenny the previous week showed up all at once. So by eleven in the morning, six burly movers were hauling pieces of furniture into various rooms, an equal number of landscapers were running trimmers and chain saws in the front and back yards, her electrician was poking around in the heating system seeing if he could figure out why the baseboard heating was so finicky in the back bedroom, and the locksmith was changing the locks on all the doors.

Jenny had finished wallpapering all of the upstairs bedrooms. The curtains had been sewn and hung, and now she hovered in the hallway, watching the movers haul the big bedroom pieces into place.

There were two bedroom suits. Mother had bought one of them when she set up housekeeping as a young bride. The other had once belonged to Grandma Nelson, who had bequeathed it upon her death about fifteen years ago. Both bedroom sets were made of walnut and came with marble-topped vanities. The larger suit had a four-poster bed, a beautiful mirror with a Gothic arch, and a lot of racetrack molding. The smaller bed came with a matching chifferobe, which was handy because the middle bedroom didn't have a real closet.

The furniture was dusty from its long sojourn in storage, but the moment the men finished putting together the bed frames, Jenny knew that guests were going to be blown away by the Iris and the Rose Rooms. The reproduction furniture for the Daisy Room was on order and would arrive whenever it arrived. Jenny had given up trying to get a hard answer from the company she'd purchased it from. She fervently prayed it would be here before March first.

Jenny was equally pleased by the transformation of her dining room. Mother's walnut dining room set with its claw-and-ball footings and the matching china cabinet brought the room to life. The honey-colored wood contrasted with the magnolia-blossom wallpaper she'd chosen for the area above the chair rail. And the moss green damask-rose upholstery on the chairs matched the wallpaper's background perfectly, even though Jenny had selected the wallpaper with just the memory of the upholstery to go by. The chair backs and cushions were in remarkably good shape, and since they matched, she concluded that she could put off reupholstering them for a couple of years.

Once the furniture men left, she spent the rest of her day with a rag and furniture polish. By sunset, the house smelled pleasantly of lemon and beeswax. She was finishing the dining room table, her mind completely occupied by the prospect of serving breakfasts and the occasional dinner to guests in this beautiful room, when Mr. Rain-tree burst her bubble.

"What the hell is that?" he asked.

She looked up to find him leaning in the doorway to the kitchen. He appeared as disheveled as ever in a black T-shirt, jeans, biker boots, and walking cast. She wondered if he had shaved even once since he'd arrived in town. He looked completely badass.

She blushed at the thought. And then wondered if the flush was because she'd never, ever say the word "ass" in public, or whether she was titillated by the idea that Mr. Raintree was, in fact, the original bad boy, with a bad-boy attitude to go with his bad-boy looks. And starting tomorrow, the two of them would be sharing the house.

She faced him and squared her shoulders. "It's a table," she said slowly.

His stare never wavered. "I know it's a table, but it's an ugly table." He cast his gaze over the magnolia wallpaper. "Flowers? Really? The house looks like it was decorated by a seventy-year-old spinster."

The comment hit perilously close to the mark. It hurt, especially since she was beginning to find the man lounging in her door frame just the tiniest bit attractive. And it shouldn't have hurt. Hadn't she decided to embrace her spinsterhood?

She tore her gaze away and started babbling. "The house is called The Jonquil House and so I decided to dedicate each room to a specific flower. This room, as you can see, is dedicated to magnolias. Upstairs you'll find the Rose, Iris, and Daisy Rooms. The Rose and Iris Rooms are now furnished, not quite completely but good enough for you to move into one of them, which I'd like you to do as—"

"You want me to sleep in a room called the Rose Room?" The indignation in his voice sounded like an alarm bell.

"You'll be more comfortable upstairs. The beds are bigger. And besides, the upper floors are warmer. The Iris Room has a fireplace, too."

"You mean Granddad's room."

"It's the Iris Room now."

"Well, you can call it what you want, but the room with the fireplace belonged to Grandma and Granddad. And they sure didn't have any flowered wallpaper. When I was growing up, this house was a *hunting* lodge. We hung fishing rods and hunting trophies on the wall for decoration. We had comfortable furniture." He turned around and strode off in the direction of the foyer and the stairs, no doubt looking for more outrages. Goodness gracious, Mr. Raintree was moody. One minute he was smiling, and the next he was as grumpy as a bear coming out of hibernation.

In the last few days, she'd gotten a little better at reading his moods. If he came out and limped around the house, it was because the writing wasn't going well. If he stayed in his room with the door closed, it was because he was making progress.

But there were times when he would emerge from his room and go into the yard to play with the dog. Somehow, when he was interacting with the dog, he seemed more relaxed. More himself.

Right at the moment, though, Bear was in the kitchen scarfing down the dog food that Jenny had put down for him. Mr. Raintree often forgot to feed the dog, so of course Jenny had taken on that responsibility.

And since the dog wasn't with him, the broody version of Mr. Raintree was now stomping through the upstairs bedrooms, his uneven gait quite distinct even through the soundproofing that she'd had installed in all the walls and ceilings.

She didn't fully understand him, but she did sympathize with his situation. It had to be difficult for him to watch her change the house he remembered from his childhood.

If the roles were reversed and he was changing Grandpa's farmhouse, she would be upset, too. Before the fire destroyed it, Grandpa's farmhouse had been where her family had gathered for every holiday and special occasion. The farm had been the family's home place. Maybe The Jonquil House was like that for Mr. Raintree.

His footsteps sounded down the stairway, punctuated every third step or so by a muttered profanity. When he got to the bottom of the stairs and turned into the living room, the cursing stopped.

"This is more like it," he said. And then Jenny heard the sound of the recliner being activated.

She headed off to the living room to see what he was up to. The room was in pitiful shape. The furniture the movers had just installed was about as plain and ugly as furniture could get. It consisted of a blue velour recliner, a dilapidated sofa, and a couple of cheap end tables with ugly 1970s-style lamps.

For years, Mother had talked about how she would one day inherit Granny Carpenter's living room furniture—and the beautiful Victorian farmhouse. But then the furniture and the house burned up, and Granddaddy came to live with them for a while, and then Mother got MS and started her long, slow decline.

So Mother's dreams burned up, but Jenny would make

good on them. With Lucy and Sabina's help, she'd contacted several antiques dealers in Charleston with a list of antebellum items she was looking for, including a camel-backed sofa, matching side chairs, and a marble-topped coffee table.

But for now, her living room looked like a set for *That '70s Show*. She entered the room to find Mr. Raintree sprawled in the recliner, his injured foot elevated. Something wicked sparkled in those great dark eyes of his. He followed her with his gaze, and his regard set her heart to thumping in her chest. Why on earth would he look at her like that? He had already identified her as a plain Jane spinster.

"Do you have a remote for the TV?" he asked.

"No, I'm sorry, I don't."

"Jenny, don't be sorry."

"I . . . Uh . . ." She didn't really know how to respond, so she closed her mouth and turned on the television.

Gray static filled the small-format screen.

"Wiggle the rabbit ears," Mr. Raintree commanded.

She did as she was told and even changed the channels a few times. But nothing was coming through, except for the waves of masculine displeasure emanating from her guest. Or was it something other than displeasure? She couldn't tell.

So she apologized again. "I'm sorry. This television is very old, and we're not going to get much with the rabbit ears. I'm going to get satellite installed in a day or two, but in the meantime, if you're desperate for entertainment, there's a box in the corner with some ancient video game equipment. I found it in the attic. I have no idea if it still works, but I suppose it once belonged to you. So if you want to hook it up to the television, be my guest."

"Is it a Nintendo system?" He turned his gaze on the dusty box as if it might be a snake coiling in the corner.

"I have no idea what kind. It's old, though. And please, don't get too comfortable with this furniture because it has to be replaced with something before March first. I've got several antiques dealers looking for pieces that might be right. But if they fail me, I'll have to buy reproductions."

"You're getting rid of the recliner?" He seemed unusually put out.

"That recliner is about twenty-five years old and threadbare. I can't have guests coming in and seeing furniture like that. Besides I want furniture that will complement the dining room."

"Complement the dining room? Jesus, don't tell me you're planning to put some god-awful, prissy velvet sofa in here."

"Well, I was looking for a camel-backed sofa. Something antebellum."

He groaned and shook his head. "When that happens, please move the recliner into my bedroom."

"Mr. Raintree, there is no room for a recliner in any of the bedrooms. And speaking of bedrooms, which of the upstairs ones would you like to move into? I'll help you move your things tomorrow."

"I don't want to move upstairs."

"I thought you were unhappy about the heat in the back room."

"It's been warmer the last few days."

"Oh, well, I'm glad to hear that. My electrician was out today, and he said there wasn't anything wrong with the baseboard heat.", She wondered if Mr. Raintree had been teasing her about the heat. "Oh, and I've had all the locks changed. I put your new keys on the kitchen counter.

"I think it would be best if you moved upstairs," she continued. "I'm planning to move in tomorrow, and the back bedroom is going to be mine. It's close to the kitchen, and I—"

"I'm not moving out of that room. And I'm certainly not letting *you* sleep back there."

"What do you mean?"

"I mean that something very odd is going on in this house, and it seems to be happening mostly in the back bedroom. To be honest, I don't think you should move in at all."

"Mr. Raintree, I've humored your suspicions by changing the locks on the exterior doors. But I'm not going to allow you to scare me into giving you the house back, or selling it to you, or whatever your game might be. I know people say this house is haunted, but I don't believe in ghosts. Do you?"

His mouth twitched, but he said nothing. Was he playing her for a fool?

"So please pick one of the rooms upstairs, and we'll get you moved in tomorrow." She turned toward the dining room door.

"No," he said to her back. "I'll take the ground-floor bedroom. And not because of any ghosts, but because I like that room. Besides, you don't want me having to negotiate the stairs every day, what with my bum ankle and all."

She gave him another glance and was surprised to discover he was smiling at her. Damn that man. He was manipulating her, and she was going to let him get away with it.

Wilma Riley would be so disappointed in her.

• • •

Jenny turned and bustled from the room. There was no other word to describe exactly how she moved. She was alive and animated. Her energy infused the house in some way Gabe couldn't quite describe.

When she was here, the place seemed warm and happy. When she left, the old place seemed lost and alone.

Or maybe he was projecting his own feelings on the house. In truth, he looked forward to her arrival in the mornings, and he'd been quite put out when she'd been so late getting here yesterday.

He had forgotten that everyone in this neck of the woods went to church on Sunday. He'd actually paced his room waiting for the sound of her little Fiesta crunching up the drive.

And yet, for all that, he was worried about her moving into the house. Someone was playing tricks. Were they trying to make him crazy? Or was this more sinister and aimed at everyone in the house?

He didn't know. But he sure knew that he didn't want Jenny to be harmed. He'd become strangely protective of her. And he always seemed to know exactly where she was at any given moment.

In truth, Jenny Carpenter was a huge distraction that he didn't want or need. His only focus right now needed to be writing the book and making sure that his past mistakes didn't catch up with him.

He was brooding over this when Bear came bounding into the living room, gave the new furniture a glancing look, and then found a comfy spot right by the recliner. He settled down and let go of a deep, satisfied sigh. No doubt, Jenny had put out some food for him. The way she fed the dog, Bear would be as big as a grizzly pretty soon.

Jenny's calling in life seemed to be feeding people and pets. Every morning, she left pastries for him and a can of dog food for Bear. Bear had already succumbed to this bribery.

But Gabe was resisting the temptation, sticking to his Cheerios every morning like a good boy. He had almost slipped on Sunday when she'd fired up her oven and baked chocolate chip cookies. The aroma had invaded his room and driven him crazy.

He gazed down at the dog. "She's gotten to us right in our most vulnerable spots," he said.

Bear gave him a doggie eye roll and a halfhearted tail wag before he dropped his big head between his paws, closed his eyes, and went off to his dog dreams.

Gabe sat there thinking about the little innkeeper until he heard the engine of Jenny's car turn over and the sound of her tires on the gravel drive. He was alone now. The house was measurably colder.

He hauled himself out of the recliner, limped across the room, and opened the dusty cardboard box sitting in the corner. He recoiled from the contents the moment he flipped back the lid. The box contained a Nintendo Entertainment System, circa 1986.

He remembered it.

Which was saying something, because pre-hunting-accident memories were hazy and incomplete. He hadn't thought about the game system since he was ten, but now the memories were right there in the front of his mind. He and Luke were forever bickering over video games. Gabe wanted to play The Legend of Zelda, and Luke was obsessed with Final Fantasy.

He stared down at the mass of tangled wires and controllers. This system had once been attached to an old TV, which was shoved into the corner next to Grandma's spinet piano.

He turned to examine the front windows. That's what was wrong with the room. The piano was missing. And the TV was in the wrong place.

He couldn't do anything about the piano, but Jenny's TV was on a fake-wood stand with big plastic casters. He pushed the television into the right place, and just like that the room seemed better, as if he'd corrected its feng shui or something.

Still, he missed the piano. His fingers suddenly itched for a keyboard where he could practice his scales, like he'd done as a boy.

To distract himself, he pulled over a somewhat threadbare ottoman, sat down beside the TV, and started hooking up the Nintendo system. To his surprise, once he got all the wires connected and plugs plugged, the old video game system awakened. The TV screen came to life with the opening scene for Final Fantasy. The game system asked if he wanted to load the last saved game, which belonged to the player with the initials LER.

Lucas Edward Raintree.

He stared at the initials for a long time. A heavy sense of loss percolated deep in his gut. He had bickered with his older brother, but he had also adored him. Luke had been everything Gabe was not. He'd been athletic, and graceful, and handsome, and a great student. And in some ways, he'd been like a parent after Mother and Daddy died. Gabe had been so young he didn't remember his parents.

Everyone had loved Luke. And Granddad had had such high expectations for him. Gabe, not so much. Gabe had been the disappointment. He had been fat and awkward and lacked all of Luke's social graces. He'd never been one of the popular kids at school. And Granddad, who wanted both of his grandsons to have careers in public service, hated that one fact most of all. Granddad was forever harping on the fact that a politician had to be likable to be elected.

For a while, after Luke died, Grandma had been Gabe's refuge. Gabe didn't have to earn his grandmother's love. She had simply always been there for him. But she'd passed away a year after Luke.

That's when Granddad decided to take all of his disappointments out on his one remaining, unworthy grandson. Gabe was required to flawlessly execute Granddad's long list of expectations. And since he could never fully meet those demands, he was constantly criticized and bullied and abused in ways that didn't show on the outside.

Gabe grew up knowing he wasn't loved. But then love was overrated in his experience. It was better to be alone.

The dog stretched and gave an audible yawn. And suddenly Gabe remembered something he'd forgotten about his brother.

Luke had a soft spot for animals. He was forever adopting stray cats and injured birds. It was the one thing about Luke that drove Granddad crazy. Luke hated hunting and fishing, and Granddad lived for those sports.

Gabe closed his eyes. He could almost conjure up the old living room on the day of the accident. He and Luke had been sitting here in this room playing video games. Or, more correctly, Luke had been playing Final

Fantasy, while Gabe watched and whined for a turn. No doubt Gabe's whining had irritated Granddad, who was in one of his grumpy moods. He'd come down from his study and had bawled them out for sitting inside on such a beautiful spring day. Then he'd pulled Luke's new rifle out of the gun case and told Luke to go practice his target shooting.

Gabe could almost see Granddad scolding Luke about the gun in his mind's eye, and Luke reluctantly saving his game and heading out the door. Zeph had been out in the garden doing a little weeding. The jonquils were in bloom. It was Easter break.

Granddad had scolded Gabe, too, which wasn't anything new. He had been told to get off his fat behind and go help Zeph in the garden. But by the time Gabe left the house, Luke had talked Zeph into coming along with him to the field where they used to practice shooting.

Since Zeph wasn't weeding anymore, Gabe took that as permission to tag along. He got his air gun and followed his older brother to the grassy field where they set up targets. Gabe remembered that he was jealous of Luke and his rifle. Gabe wanted a rifle, too, but he was too little for one, according to Granddad. He had to be twelve, and he had to go to the shooting range for mandatory NRA safety training before he would be allowed to practice with real ammunition. Until then he was limited to his air gun and BBs.

Of course all of that changed after Luke died. Granddad sold all his hunting rifles and never went to a shooting range again. So Gabe never got that rifle he had wanted so badly. Instead his dreams were filled with nightmares about guns.

He tried to remember what happened after he'd tagged along, but it was all a blur. Obviously something terrible occurred, because Luke ended up shot in the chest. But Gabe couldn't remember, and everyone said it was a blessing.

Gabe wasn't all that sure about that. He had a feeling the empty place inside him might not feel so cavernous if he could just remember.

He opened his eyes, not even surprised to discover that tears smeared his vision and his hands were shaking. He studied the opening screen of Final Fantasy.

The game system had been waiting twenty-five years for Luke to come back and finish his game.

CHAPTER 9

Jenny arrived at The Jonquil House early Tuesday morning as part of a convoy that consisted of one ancient Fiesta (hers) and two pickup trucks belonging to Sheriff Rhodes and Kyle Connors. The sheriff was not driving his truck; his "little" brother Clay was behind the wheel. Kyle and Clay were members of the Wild Horses country and western band that played a few nights a week down at Dot's Spot.

The two men had been roped into helping Jenny by Jane Rhodes, the manicurist at the Cut 'n Curl, a member of the book club, and Clay's wife. At a book club meeting a month ago, Jenny had complained about the high cost of hiring a moving company, and that was the end of that. Before the meeting was over, Jane had volunteered Clay to round up the requisite number of pickups for the job.

There being a large number of trucks in Allenberg County, and Clay being a co-owner of the hardware store, he probably could have commandeered dozens of pickups if it were necessary. Clay was the original good neighbor

Sam. He went around doing good deeds and on any given day, half the county owed him a favor.

As it turned out, she only needed two pickup trucks, which was almost pitiful, seeing as she'd been alive for thirty-six years.

She killed the Fiesta's engine and hopped up the front porch. "Y'all are a godsend, both of you," she said to her helpers with a big smile. She was feeling as light as a balloon today. And the day had dawned perfect. The cold weather had vanished, and a January thaw had settled in. It was a great day to move into the house of her dreams.

The two big men smiled at her and nodded, then started picking up boxes. Jenny slipped her key into the new front door lock and propped the door open for them.

She took two steps into the foyer, and her elation deflated a tiny bit. The house seemed bitterly cold again, colder than it was outside.

She was about to cuss the electrician when she heard the computer-generated music and sound effects wafting from the living room. She headed in that direction only to discover that the room's furniture had been rearranged. The TV was in the corner and the recliner had been pulled away from the wall so that Mr. Raintree could sprawl in it while simultaneously playing video games.

He was now fast asleep while the game seemed to be playing on without him. He looked a bit more disheveled today than he had yesterday. Meanwhile, Bear was sitting up, his big head cocked to one side as he watched the action on the TV screen.

Clay Rhodes came striding through the front door. "Hey, Jenny, where do you want this box marked linens?" he asked in a big voice.

Bear decided it was time to defend his territory, and like a good watchdog he charged at Clay and started barking.

Mr. Raintree startled awake, and at the same moment the game that had been progressing on the television seemed to reach a conclusion as well.

"Hush, Bear," Jenny directed, but the dog paid her no mind, and she had to snag him by the collar to keep him from knocking over Clay Rhodes. Although Clay was such a big man that Bear probably couldn't have actually knocked him over, but Jenny didn't want to risk it.

"Bear, be quiet," Mr. Raintree said as he folded the recliner. And, of course, Bear followed his orders without delay. He sat down and looked over at his master, awaiting his next command.

Clay was still standing in the threshold of the living room giving Mr. Raintree and Bear the once-over.

"Clay, those boxes of linens should go upstairs in the hallway. Just drop them there and I'll take care of the rest," Jenny said.

"Gabe?" Clay said, continuing to stare at the man. "I heard you were back."

Mr. Raintree blinked a couple of times. He still looked kind of sleepy. "Do I know you?"

Clay shrugged. "We used to play together when we were kids. You were a year younger than me, and I remember teaching you how to catch a bullfrog one time for the Easter frog jump."

Mr. Raintree shook his head. "I don't remember that."

Clay shrugged. "It doesn't matter. Welcome back." He turned toward Jenny. "Upstairs in the hall?"

She nodded, and Clay headed up the stairs, the sound of his footsteps thudding through the house.

Kyle came through the door carrying a box marked "Jenny's closet," and Bear started barking again.

"Bear, sit," Mr. Raintree commanded. The dog obeyed. And it occurred to Jenny that Mr. Raintree was used to having people obey his commands.

"Where does this go?" Kyle asked.

"Oh, that's my personal stuff. Take it down the hall to the back—"

"Upstairs," Mr. Raintree interrupted. He turned toward her with one of his half smiles. It looked kind of rough and ready in his sleep-wrinkled face. "Don't you remember, we decided last night that you were sleeping upstairs?"

She tried not to grind her teeth. She remembered him trying to use his ankle as an excuse. And she'd decided she wasn't going to let him get away with that. But now, looking at him, she realized that it would be a mistake to fight with him. She would lose. Besides, he was her guest, and the Rose Room was much nicer than the room right off the kitchen. So she should enjoy it for the time being.

She turned toward Kyle. "Put all the boxes marked personal up in the Rose Room. It's the bedroom in the back of the house, you'll know it by the wallpaper."

She turned back toward Mr. Raintree, intent on suggesting that, since he had won the fight over the first-floor bedroom, he should plan on sleeping there at night and not in the recliner. But she held her tongue when she found him staring at the TV as if he'd seen a ghost. His face had gone sheet white.

"What is it?" she asked.

"That's just not right."

"What?"

"I was playing Legend of Zelda last night when I fell

asleep. But the game cartridge in the machine right now is Final Fantasy. Did you change it?"

"No. I just walked in. You can ask Clay or Kyle. Maybe you forgot or changed the games in your sleep. Or maybe the system isn't working right, because when I first came into the room, it looked like it was on demo mode or something."

"Demo?"

"It seemed to be playing all by itself." She glanced at the TV, which now displayed the menu asking if the player wanted to load a saved game or start a new one.

Mr. Raintree picked up the controller and clicked through the menu. "That can't be," he muttered. His hands were trembling a little, and Jenny wondered if perhaps Mr. Raintree had been overdosing on his meds.

"What can't be?" she asked.

"Look at the date for the last save." He pointed a finger at the screen. "The game was saved just a few minutes ago."

A wariness prickled her backbone. "That's odd, isn't it? A few minutes ago you were fast asleep."

He gave her a laser-beam stare. "Exactly. But it's worse than that. Someone played my brother's last game. See the initials?"

"LER?"

"Lucas Edward Raintree. Last night when I hooked up the game and first turned it on, the save date for that game was twenty-five years ago. Luke played that game the morning he was shot. I took the game cartridge out of the system. I didn't want to touch Luke's last game. Last night, I played an entirely different game."

"What are you suggesting, Mr. Raintree?" Jenny said.

"Someone came in here and put the Final Fantasy cartridge in the game, loaded Luke's last game, and played it. Since it was saved just a few minutes ago, whoever did that has to be here in this house right now. And that person has to be someone Bear knows, otherwise he would have barked."

He looked up at her, his dark brow lowering into a troubled scowl.

"Mr. Raintree, I did nothing to your game. I just arrived. And if you don't believe me, you can ask Clay and Kyle."

"Both of them entered the house after you did. Bear barked at them."

He continued to stare for a long moment, then shook his head and looked down at the dog. "Come on, Bear, let's go take a walk." His voice sounded rusty and overlaid with some emotion that Jenny couldn't quite fathom. He snagged his cane from the floor and headed out the open front door in his uneven gait, the dog following obediently at his heel.

He was more than merely moody, she realized. Something deep and dark was troubling her boarder. He might be self-medicating, or hallucinating, or something strange. Yesterday she might have argued with him about his accusation, but not today. Today she realized that Gabriel Raintree was alone and troubled. He needed help and support, not an angry tongue.

She made up her mind, right then, that she'd stop fussing at him and dedicate herself to being the innkeeper she wanted to be. If she could take care of a grumpy, troubled person like Mr. Raintree, then she truly had a calling for this life she'd chosen.

And hadn't she decided to run an inn because she

wanted the company? Well, here he was. Her first guest. And he needed company maybe even more than she did.

Bear headed out into the big rhododendrons, sniffing around, marking his territory. While the dog took care of business, Gabe folded his arms against his chest and watched the big dudes moving Jenny's boxes into the house.

He was uneasy about her moving in. Something wasn't right. Someone was messing with him—someone Bear knew, someone local.

All the rational evidence suggested that it was Jenny. She was the only one who could have changed the game and saved it moments before he awakened. And she could have come into his room and deleted his files and written that message about ghosts. She and Zeph were the only two people who could get past Bear.

So she had every opportunity, but what possible motive did she have? Unless she was some kind of psycho, there wasn't one blessed reason for her to be playing with him. He did not, for one minute, believe she was a psycho.

But he'd been fooled before.

Bear returned to his side, and he buried his hand in the dog's mane. Bear leaned into him, giving him love without any conditions. If only people were more like Bear, the world would be a happier place.

He let go of a mournful sigh. He needed to take a shower and get back to work.

He and Bear headed back into the house, dodging the guys with the boxes. The dog knew that Jenny controlled the food, so Bear made a beeline into the kitchen where she was unpacking an incredible number of cartons.

Gabe watched for a moment as she spoke to the dog like a woman speaking to a baby. Bear soaked up the love, and then he gobbled up the bowl of kibble she put down for him.

She looked up from the dog and startled. "Oh, Mr. Raintree, I thought you'd gone back to your writing. I'm sorry about the noise, but Kyle and Clay will be finished shortly, and I promise I'll try to be as quiet as I can so you can work. But I need to get these things put away as quickly as possible."

"It's all right, and I wish you'd quit calling me Mr. Raintree. It's Gabe."

"Oh. All right then, Gabe." She seemed so awkward and maybe a little flustered. She pushed her big owl glasses up her nose. Her hair was up in its usual sloppy-looking bun, and tendrils of slightly curly hair framed her face. She was wearing one of her navy blue sweaters, a white turtleneck, and a pair of the baggiest jeans he'd ever seen.

She looked wholesome. She looked like a breath of spring air. There was not one thing sinister about her, or even remotely crazy. She seemed sane and stable and real in a way that so many people never managed to achieve.

He was ruling her out as a suspect. And if she was ruled out, the only other possibility was Zeph Gibbs. And Gabe had no trouble believing that Zeph was a few cards short of a full deck.

"Uh, I know you don't like sweets in the morning," Jenny said, breaking into his bleak thoughts, "but is there something I can make you for breakfast? I make a mean egg-and-cheese casserole."

He shook his head. "No, I like my Cheerios, thanks.

And don't trouble yourself. I can deal with cereal on my own. I'll try to stay out of your way."

"Oh, that's all right. I'm just working on recipes for when the inn is open. And it wouldn't be any trouble at all to cook—"

"I don't need you to cook for me." His voice sounded gruffer than he intended. He probably should tell her the truth about the diabetes, but that was something private— something he didn't share with people.

A truly fetching blush crawled up her cheeks. She looked rosy, and for a moment he glimpsed the passionate person who hid behind those horrible sweaters. "I'm sorry. I won't ask again," she said, looking away.

"I *like* Cheerios," he found himself saying.

"Oh."

"Really, it's a favorite." Could he be more inane? It was time to retreat, before he let her know the entire sordid story of how they'd discovered his disease a month after his grandmother died.

"I'm sure it is," she said with a nervous smile. "If you like Cheerios in the morning, that's just fine, Mr. Raintree. And I promise, I'll try to be extra quiet as I unpack. Oh, and I'm having a guest for dinner tomorrow night at about six-thirty. I would be pleased if you would join us for dinner. You don't have to sample the pie if you don't like sweets."

"A guest?"

She nodded. "Reverend Lake, the Methodist preacher. He's new in town."

She was having dinner with a preacher? Alone? He disliked that idea more than he wanted to admit. He recognized this feeling. He was getting possessive of her, and that wasn't a good sign at all. He'd felt that way once before, and it had proved to be the biggest mistake of his life.

For Jenny's sake, he ought to turn around and go back into his writing cave and stay there and not come out until spring.

But instead he found himself saying, "I'd be delighted to join you and the preacher for dinner."

CHAPTER
10

Sabina and Maryanne arrived at Jenny's door at precisely five-thirty on Wednesday afternoon, just as Jenny was popping the apple pie into her baker's oven. The roast chicken that she planned to serve was in the second oven, and Jenny was in Heaven over the fact that she had two ovens she could use at the same time.

The rest of her meal was staged and ready: Her macaroni-and-cheese casserole had been put together and only needed to be warmed. She had okra and stewed tomatoes simmering on the stove. The rice and corn bread would come last.

Out in the dining room, she'd unpacked all of Mother's Blue Willow china and her table was set with Mother's best linen tablecloth, the one with the lace insets that had been reserved for special occasions. Teri Summers, the new florist at Last Chance Bloomers, had sent up a beautiful arrangement of Japanese irises that sat in the middle of the table in a low cut-glass bowl, surrounded by three of the four Fostoria etched water goblets that Jenny had purchased at Sabina's antiques mall late last year.

She was ready for the preacher.

Or so she thought until Maryanne and Sabina marched themselves into her kitchen. Sabina carried a gigantic tote bag filled with what looked like a set of hot rollers. Maryanne carried little Joshua, who was all bundled up even though the temperature outside was pushing sixty. He looked red-cheeked and sleepy-eyed, as if he'd just awakened from a catnap in his car seat.

"Look at you, you're a hot, sweaty mess," Sabina said in a big voice that was sure to disturb Mr. Raintree—Gabe.

"Keep your voice down. Mr. Raintree is writing." She rolled her eyes toward the back bedroom that opened right off the kitchen. The yellow sticky note was still adhered to his door.

"Why is he in your room?" Maryanne asked as she peeled off Joshua's winter jacket.

"Mr. Raintree's ankle is injured. Letting him sleep downstairs seemed appropriate." Jenny decided that her cousin and friend didn't need to know how she'd shamefully argued with him about the room. She felt bad about that, suddenly.

"Oh," Sabina said, "that was nice of you."

"What are you doing here?" Jenny asked. "The preacher's due in an hour."

"Exactly," Maryanne said.

"Exactly what?"

Sabina gave a dramatic eye roll. "You aren't going to greet him wearing an old-lady apron, a floppy sweater, and jeans, are you?"

"Of course not."

"Okay, please don't tell me you're going to go take a shower and put your wet hair up in a bun and put on one of those shapeless April Cornell dresses that you love so much."

"What's wrong with April Cornell?"

"Nothing if you want to remain a spinster. C'mon, I'm taking you upstairs to help you get dressed. I enlisted Maryanne to keep an eye on your dinner, since Lucy has a big date tonight with Ross Gardiner. So it's not like I could stay home and watch her getting ready, you know?"

"Sabina, you need to move on," Jenny said. "I mean Ross is with your sister, you know? It's slightly icky for you to have a crush on him. And I know you love Lucy and wouldn't ever want to hurt her."

"Yeah, I know. But it was easier to come here and fix you up than to sit around listening to Lucy talking about how tonight's the night Ross is going to propose. So I enlisted Maryanne, and she agrees with me that you need to make a few changes."

"But—"

"It's okay," Maryanne said. "I'll make sure the pie comes out when the oven timer dings."

"And the chicken, too. I have two ovens." Jenny's voice sounded a tiny bit frantic to her own ears.

"Yeah, I got it. You want me to put in the mac and cheese?"

"No, I'll put it in. It shouldn't go in until six anyway."

"Maryanne," Sabina said with authority, "you are deputized to put the mac and cheese in the oven at six and start the rice at six-fifteen. Because Jenny, honey, it's going to take more than half an hour to get you ready for Timothy Lake."

Sabina reached into her tote bag and pulled out a bottle of wine. "Maryanne, you can also open this up and let it breathe."

"Wine?" Jenny's voice squeaked. "But I don't have any Fostoria wineglasses."

"Oh, my God, Jenny, just put out two of your everyday glasses. Honestly. He's a preacher. He's not going to judge you if your wineglasses don't match your water goblets. Just remember that no woman gets an orgasm from a shiny kitchen floor."

"Since when do you quote Betty Friedan?" Jenny said. "And besides, that quote, as Wilma will tell you, is all about how a woman needs to be herself. So you've made my point in spades."

Sabina let go of an exasperated sigh. "Jenny, have you ever had an orgasm?"

Her face flamed. She had experienced orgasms, and her pursuit of them as a young woman had been the biggest mistake of her life. "I'm not going to answer that."

"Right, so screw Betty Friedan and Wilma, too. I'm here to tell you that if you took half as much time on yourself as you lavish on your house and table settings..." Her voice trailed off when she finally found the wineglasses. She picked up two plain stems and started toward the door to the dining room. "...you'd be a happier person, and you might just know what you're missing in the orgasm department."

"I can't believe we're having this discussion," Jenny said, "and I need three wineglasses, not two."

"Three?" Sabina's eyebrows arched.

Jenny shrugged, her face flaming even hotter than it had when Sabina had asked that doozy about orgasms. "I, uh, invited Mr. Raintree for dinner."

"You what?"

"I invited Mr. Raintree."

"But this was supposed to be—"

"Look, he's a guest in the house, and I wasn't going to make a dinner and not invite him. Especially since he doesn't ever ask me to make him breakfast, and he's always going out to the woodpile and getting his own wood." *And he thinks I tampered with his Nintendo for some nefarious reason.*

"I thought you said he had an injured ankle," Maryanne said as she swayed back and forth, the baby resting his downy head on her shoulder. Maryanne hadn't known Jenny for more than a few weeks, but it was uncanny how the girl could see right through her BS.

"He limps to the woodpile," Jenny said. It was a completely idiotic thing to say. And it didn't help that her words elicited a little smile on Maryanne's face, and a mad-as-heck scowl on Sabina's.

"I don't believe this. I worked so hard to set this up and—"

"Wait just one moment." Jenny interrupted Sabina before she could say something Jenny didn't want to hear. "I know you mean well, but the thing is, Sabina, I've decided that being an unmarried woman is liberating. I don't have to worry about my hair or the dresses I wear or how I look. I can be free to invite people to dinner and just cook for them, without expecting anything in return. And if I want to lavish attention on the details of my table settings, it's only because I love doing that, not because I'm worried about what anyone will think of me.

"I'm tired of trying to cook my way into a man's heart. It doesn't work."

Sabina put the wineglasses on the counter, took Jenny by the shoulders, and looked her right in the face. "Honey,

I'm just here to help you out. You'd be so pretty if you did something with your hair and put on something other than a gunnysack."

"I'm not beautiful, Sabina. And I'm okay with that. Really. Now you can take your tote bag full of whatever back out to the car."

"Nope."

"Okay, you and Maryanne can keep an eye on dinner while I go up and change. I need a shower."

"Thank God for that. I was worried for a moment that you'd greet the preacher wearing flour in your hair, and I'm not talking about the kind of flour that blooms."

"Ha." Jenny turned and headed down the hall to the stairs. Sabina followed her, tote bag in hand. "You're not giving this up, are you? Even though I invited Mr. Raintree and this isn't anything like a dinner date for two?"

"Honey, I'm determined to be the helping hand that brings love into your life, and I'm convinced that Pastor Tim is the man for you."

"Why?"

"Because Miriam Randall says so. And I reckon that if Miriam says it's going to happen then it's going to happen, even if you invited a second man to the table. Heck, Pastor Tim might just be more interested if he thinks there's competition."

"Competition? From Mr. Raintree? Are you crazy?" She was protesting too much, and she knew it. Mr. Raintree intrigued her way more than Reverend Lake.

Sabina shrugged. "Honey, you invited him because you're afraid."

"What?"

"You're afraid of what Miriam said the other day.

You don't see yourself with a handsome man, do you? You don't think you deserve one. But I'm determined to change your mind."

"I'm not putting on any makeup," Jenny said on an exasperated breath as she headed up the stairs.

"But—"

"Sabina, if Pastor Tim is my soulmate, then I don't need makeup or wine, or pies, or any other thing. If it's meant to be it will happen."

"Okay, no makeup, but please let me do something with your hair."

Gabe strolled into the dining room, Bear at his side. He stood in the room for a full minute and a half, studying the little-old-lady wallpaper, the lace tablecloth, and the blue dishes. The room was a hundred times more formal than it had been when he was a boy. Jenny had turned it into the kind of upscale, fussy place that out-of-towners would probably love.

But not him. He wanted it back the way it used to be. In fact, the feeling was so strong that he had to stop himself from finding a seam in the wallpaper and picking at it. The compulsion to set the magnolias free was almost more than he could resist. He studied the cream-colored blossoms so intently that they seemed to move of their own accord—as if blown by some unseen wind.

He stepped into the hallway feeling light-headed. Damn, he hadn't eaten enough today.

He'd been busy starting something entirely new about a "haunted" inn that was remarkably like The Jonquil House. He'd outlined the story, and come up with a working synopsis that had all the usual haunted house tropes, like unexplained noises in the night, foul messages on foggy bathroom mirrors, flickering lights in the hallways, and walls that spontaneously generated flies. Only in his story there was a rational explanation for everything. His ghost story didn't have any ghosts at all, just a sweet and attractive little innkeeper who lured people in for nefarious purposes.

He wasn't exactly sure what his characters' motives were, but he had a feeling he would figure them out before too long.

A knock sounded at the front door, and Bear started barking.

"Coming," Jenny called from upstairs. "Mr. Raintree, please ask Bear to stop barking."

He hushed the dog just as Jenny came down the stairs on nimble feet that hardly made a noise.

She wasn't wearing a turtleneck. Or a sweater. Or baggy pants. Her blue dress had a high waistline and full skirt that came halfway down her calves. The bodice covered her from her neck to wrists, and the whole thing was made of a medium blue floral fabric that was as old-fashioned as the flowered paper Jenny had pasted on every wall in the house.

This particular fabric molded to Jenny's torso above the waistline and revealed her figure in a way that her baggy turtlenecks and sweaters could not. Her breasts were the perfect size, and he wished the neckline of her dress didn't button all the way up to her throat. Her legs—the part he could see—were shapely, and he wished the dress's hemline were about five inches shorter.

While the décolletage and hem of her dress were a tad disappointing, her hair brought a smile to his lips. Freed from its bun, it cascaded to her shoulders in soft waves the color of a sparrow's wing. She might be up to something nefarious, but Gabe wanted to touch her hair. He wanted to touch other parts of her, too.

What the hell was that woman doing to him? She was haunting him, in more ways than one. He ought to pack his bags and leave this place, except that might be precisely what she wanted of him. And by nature, he'd always been contrary.

She hurried to the door and admitted a tall man wearing a Roman collar and a face that ought to be in the movies.

Gabe went immediately on guard, every atom in his body reacting negatively to the man who walked in the front door. Strangely, the moment the preacher set foot in the foyer, The Jonquil House itself seemed to express its own displeasure. The temperature dropped, and the air became heavy and hard to breathe.

Jenny turned in Gabe's direction and introduced Reverend Timothy Lake.

"Mr. Raintree," the minister said in a voice that conveyed disapproval, even though he spoke with a smile on his face.

Gabe took the man's hand briefly. Then the minister turned and aimed a half-lidded gaze toward Jenny. The guy was admiring her hair and her legs, no doubt about it.

Gabe jammed his hands into his pockets and looked down at Bear, who was also studying the minister and whining a little, as if he, too, was unhappy about this turn of events.

"Mr. Raintree, I think it might be best if we closed Bear up in your room," Jenny said, eyeing the dog.

"Probably a wise idea," he said.

Gabe called the dog and headed down the hallway, trying to parse out the source of his sudden, intense animus toward Timothy Lake.

Was it possible for The Jonquil House to have feelings about the people inside it? He shook away that errant thought. He didn't believe in haunted houses. His immediate dislike of the preacher was much easier to explain: the green-eyed monster called jealousy.

Jenny ushered the two men into her dining room, where Maryanne had thoughtfully opened the bottle of wine before she and the meddling Sabina had beaten a hasty retreat ten minutes ago.

Jenny felt exposed. Her dress was old and a little tight through the bodice. Her hair seemed to be wild and out of control, sort of like her heartbeat.

And having an out-of-control heart was annoying. It wasn't as if Timothy Lake made her hormones go haywire. It was quite the opposite. The minister made her nervous and tongue-tied. He was just so *beautiful* she had trouble looking at him.

Having Mr. Raintree there didn't help in the least. Her boarder had shown up with his bad-boy flags flying. He'd shaved sometime this morning, but the dark stubble was already starting to shadow his square chin. His fitted black dress shirt with the tiny gray double stripe accentuated his broad shoulders. His dark pants fit him like a second skin. And he'd topped off the ensemble with a black leather suit jacket.

Reverend Lake and Mr. Raintree looked like an angel and a demon as they preceded her into the dining room.

Predictably, Mr. Raintree made a beeline for the wine and started pouring, beginning with Jenny's glass.

Jenny wasn't at all surprised when the preacher declined the wine. On the other hand, Jenny had to stifle the urge to snatch up her glass and down it in a single gulp. Instead, she excused herself and headed into the kitchen. She needed to get the corn bread out of the oven, decant the gravy, and get the food on the table.

She hadn't expected either of her guests to follow or offer help. In all the years she'd been cooking for potential suitors, no man had ever followed her into the kitchen. And if she had to imagine the man who would break that protocol, she would never, in a million years, predict that he'd look like Mr. Raintree.

But there he was. Limping without his cane. "What can I carry?" he asked.

She turned toward him, immediately flustered and off her guard. "I'm fine," she said.

He shook his head. "What can I carry?"

She glanced at the cast on his foot, and he gave her a smile. "I've been toting wood for days. I think I can manage a few dishes."

"But you're a guest here. You shouldn't have to carry *anything*."

Something changed in his stance. She wasn't quite sure how to read it, but her insides churned and flipped in reaction to it. His shoulders dropped a fraction, and the spark in his dark eyes dimmed. She'd hurt him in some way, and that bothered her. She had started out not liking him in the least, but she'd been wrong about him.

He was good for Bear. He was thoughtful in a lot of ways. He wasn't nearly as demanding as she thought he would be. He stood there, waiting, and she knew she would never get him to leave without something in his hands.

And then, all at once, she realized what was going on. It was as if someone whispered in her ear. "You used to help set the table when you were a boy staying here, didn't you?"

His shoulders straightened, and his mouth quirked up on one side. "We had a cook named Lottie, but Luke—" He bit off the last of the sentence.

Jenny understood. "I'm sorry. It's my job to make you feel like a guest, and I guess that's awkward for you sometimes. You have a much longer history with this house than I do."

He nodded.

She gave him a brief smile, picked up the tureen with the okra, and handed it to him. "Here, take this, and then the chicken. We'll carve it at the table." She pointed to the bird that had been resting for about half an hour. "The mac and cheese needs to be put on a trivet, and use a pot holder. I need to get the corn bread out of the oven."

He turned and limped away with the tureen while Jenny pulled two cast-iron corn bread pans from her baking oven and turned the muffins out into a basket lined with a blue-and-white-checked napkin. Then she poured the gravy into the old silver gravy boat that had belonged to her grandmother. By now, Mr. Raintree had enlisted the preacher's help, and her large kitchen suddenly felt crowded.

Among the three of them the food made it to the table quickly and, for Jenny's purposes, a bit chaotically.

Jenny stationed herself at the unset end of the table and

started carving the chicken, while the two men took their places facing one another. If she didn't know better, she'd think that Mr. Raintree and Reverend Lake were a couple of junkyard dogs circling each other, trying to figure out which one was going to be the leader of the pack.

The testosterone level in the room skyrocketed, just as the temperature started to drop. The lovely January thaw had been short-lived, and in the silence created by the men, Jenny could hear the swishing and sighing of the pines outside as the wind picked up.

"So, I understand you write horror novels," Reverend Lake said to Mr. Raintree, breaking the silence.

"Some people call them that. I like to think of them as thrillers." Mr. Raintree took a sip of wine.

Reverend Lake took a sip of water. "I see. Do you ever worry about how young people might react to your books? They are so violent, and largely bereft of positive Christian messages."

"No, I don't worry about the messages in my book. I'm writing them to entertain." Mr. Raintree put his wineglass down a lot harder than was necessary. The wine sloshed, and a drop of it stained Mother's pristine tablecloth.

Jenny bit back an oath. It was a small stain. She could probably lift it with some hydrogen peroxide and dish soap. She needed to learn how to be more flexible. And she also made a mental note to move up the delivery date for her first set of commercial linens.

She started carving the bird just as Reverend Lake resumed his decidedly one-sided conversation. "I understand that in one of your books, a character practices Voodoo."

"Have you ever read one of my books?"

"No, I haven't."

"Ah, well, let me correct you. Voodoo is a religion with its roots in West Africa. What my character in *Black Water* practices is a demented and twisted from of Hoodoo, which is a kind of folk magic that comes from Africa. Of course, my villain is a psychopath, and what he practices is neither Voodoo or Hoodoo."

"Voodoo is a religion? Really, Mr. Raintree, I don't see how—"

Just then, the fork, which Jenny was using to hold the bird steady while she carved up the white meat, developed a mind of its own. It almost felt as if someone had grabbed her by the wrist with icy fingers and forced her to literally throw the bird across the table. The chicken practically took flight and then landed on the table, shattering wineglasses before rolling right into Reverend Lake's lap. The only good thing about this was the fact that the flying chicken abridged whatever small-minded thing the preacher was about to say.

There were many bad things about this turn of events—chief among them the fact that any chance Jenny might have had of a courtship with Reverend Lake had just flown out the window. But on second thought, perhaps that was a blessing in disguise.

Nevertheless Jenny sprang into action. "Oh, my God, I'm so sorry. The fork just slipped," she cried and descended on the minister with a napkin. She retrieved the chicken, but there was grease all over the preacher's pants that she unadvisedly attempted to blot up. This, of course, immediately caused the minister to stand up, knocking his chair down in the process.

And that set off a chain reaction of mishaps, which

ended in disaster. The chair fell back against a potted plant. The plant flew out of its pot and smashed against the china cabinet, shattering several of the glass panes in its doors. And then the cabinet started to totter side-to-side in a manner that looked like someone was trying to push it away from the wall.

Jenny and the minister backed up a few steps, just as the cabinet teetered forward and tipped over, spilling Mother's Blue Willow china in all directions and aiming directly for Mr. Raintree's head.

Jenny stopped thinking. She grabbed Mr. Raintree by his leather jacket and hauled him back from the brink. He tripped and fell to the floor, taking Jenny with him.

She landed on top of him just as the china cabinet came crashing down onto the table, destroying Mother's china, tablecloth, and table in one horrifying moment.

And if that wasn't enough, the minister said a long string of truly profane words right before the lights went out.

CHAPTER 11

Jenny's first thought, as the lights went out, was not about Mother's furniture or china or any such thing. Her entire mind, in fact her entire being, was overtaken by a soul-deep *awareness* of Gabriel Raintree, who was pressed underneath her from toe to chest.

The room might be colder than a witch's teat, but Mr. Raintree's body was as hot as a furnace. Then he upped the temperature when he wrapped his arms around her. For one insane moment, Jenny thought he might kiss her. She decided not to fight it. She was, in fact, going to enjoy the heck out of it.

"This place is a madhouse." Reverend Lake's voice had the same effect as a bucket of cold water. Jenny put the brakes on her libido at the same time that Mr. Raintree released her. She scrambled to her feet, cutting her hand on a piece of broken china as she pushed off the floor. It was right at that moment that Bear started to bark as if the house was on fire.

Suddenly aware that she'd abandoned her boarder on the floor, she asked, "Are you all right, Mr. Raintree?"

"I'm fine," came his deep voice. "Thanks to you. You saved my life."

"I did no such thing," she said, but the moment the words left her mouth the full, horrible import of what had just happened came crashing down on her.

"Has anyone got a flashlight? A candle? Really, Jenny, if you're planning to open this house as an inn you should have some emergency power and emergency exit lighting." The minister sounded extremely put out.

"I plan to have all of that, but it hasn't been installed yet. The men are coming next week." She turned, trying to see Mr. Raintree in the darkness. "Do you need help getting up, Mr. Raintree?"

"I'm fine." She heard china shifting, and then his presence made itself known just behind her. He was still radiating heat, which was a good thing because the temperature in the room had plummeted even further.

"This place is a death trap," Reverend Lake said.

And with that pronouncement, Jenny's throat thickened, and it was all she could do to keep from sobbing. Reverend Lake would undoubtedly go blabbing his mouth in town, and people would wonder if she was competent. Or worse, they'd wonder if it was safe to stay here.

Just as this thought crossed her mind, Bear abruptly stopped barking. And then the front door opened with an eerie creak.

"What's that?" the minister asked. He sounded scared to death.

A bright white light shone down the hallway, and Reverend Lake made a girlie whimpering sound.

"Miz Jenny, you all right?" a voice called.

Zeph Gibbs. Jenny didn't know whether to be grateful or angry at her neighbor's sudden and unexplained appearance.

"How the hell did you get in here?" Mr. Raintree demanded before Jenny could open her mouth.

"I opened the door," Zeph said as he walked into the dining room and shined his light over the disaster. "Lord a'mighty," he whispered.

"You have that right," Reverend Lake said. "Something—" He snapped off his words the moment Zeph aimed the light toward the wall where the china cabinet had been standing a moment ago.

The wallpaper hung in shreds, as if some wild animal had run its gigantic claws over it.

"Dear Lord, save us from the demons in this house," Reverend Lake shouted, but he showed remarkably little faith in his Lord when he turned and ran from the dining room as if his hair were on fire. The lights came back the moment Reverend Lake started his car and peeled out of the parking lot.

"That's going to be a big problem," Zeph said under his breath as he turned off his flashlight.

"You think the preacher is a problem? What the hell is that?" Mr. Raintree pointed at the shredded wallpaper. "And how the hell did you get in here?"

"I told you, Mr. Gabe, I walked in through the front door. It wasn't locked."

"Mr. Raintree, I—" Jenny began.

Her boarder turned toward her, his dark eyes sparking with ire. "For God's sake, call me...Oh, my God, you're bleeding."

Mr. Raintree stooped and picked up a napkin from the broken china at his feet, and before she could tell him not to, he pressed it into the palm of her hand and applied pressure.

She watched the blood soak into the fibers of her mother's table linen, and her composure broke. Everything was destroyed: the china, the table, the linen, the dinner, and the handsome man she didn't care much about except in theory. A big, unwanted sob bubbled up from her insides. On a wave of sorrow she cried, "Oh, my beautiful dream."

The gash in Jenny's hand wasn't as bad as Gabe first thought. But his heart lurched when he got a good look at her face, flecked with scratches from flying debris. He knew now that he hadn't misplaced his trust. She wasn't laying traps for him. She wasn't some crazy who wanted to mess with his mind.

She was the victim here. Someone was messing with *her*.

Her lower lip began to tremble, and her eyes watered up. When the sob came, Gabe was ready.

She fell against his chest, and he closed his arms around her. She was so tiny, and she trembled as she cried, like a sparrow in a cage. He tucked her head under his chin and buried his nose in her lustrous hair.

She smelled like lavender, old-fashioned and sweet and flowery. He held her close and studied the gashes on the wall. Someone might have been able to rip that wallpaper and hide it with the cabinet. But Gabe couldn't explain the unnatural way the chicken had flown across the table. Or how a china cabinet that big could topple over without someone pushing it.

None of this was adding up to anything even remotely rational.

So he stopped trying to figure it out and just drank

in her scent, and let himself feel relief knowing that she was as good and kind and rational as he had hoped and believed.

When Jenny's sobs had dwindled to mere hiccups, he whispered, "Do you have a first-aid kit?"

She nodded like a little girl. "In the kitchen," she said against his shirt.

"C'mon, I need to take a better look at your hand."

She stepped away from him, her eyes puffy and her nose red. He draped his arm around her shoulders and helped guide her through the mess on the floor.

Zeph was waiting for them, sitting on one of the kitchen stools with Bear at his feet, fast asleep. Zeph must have rifled through her cabinets because he had Jenny's first-aid kit out and opened on the center island counter.

"Why are you here?" Gabe asked the moment Zeph rose from the stool and helped Jenny to sit down. "Were you spying on us?"

The old man took a little step back. "I reckon you might look at it that way. I was just keeping watch is all."

"Keeping watch for what?" Gabe demanded as he took hold of Jenny's hand and unwrapped the bloody napkin. Jenny's wound had pretty much stopped bleeding. It wasn't a bad cut, but Gabe felt responsible in some way he couldn't quite articulate.

"I was keeping an eye on the ghost. I was worried something like this might happen. He's got his moods, the ghost does."

Gabe and Jenny raised their gazes in near unison. "Ghost?"

"Mr. Gabe, I know you don't believe in haunts, but you're just going to have to amend your believing. And besides, the ghost has been haunting you for days. I thought you would have figured that out by now."

"I've been haunted?" Gabe broke open a packet of antiseptic to clean Jenny's wound.

"Of course you have."

"So you're trying to tell me that the deleted computer files and the unexplained change in the save date for Final Fantasy have all been the work of a ghost."

"I am. And what happened tonight, too. The thing is, the ghost is usually pretty quiet unless he takes a dislike to something. Then he lets you know. Sometimes in a big way."

"Like clawing the wallpaper from the wall? Like deleting my novel from my hard drive?"

"Yes, like that. I reckon he doesn't like your book very much. And he's pretty upset about the wallpaper."

Jenny suddenly straightened her shoulders and glared at Zeph. "What's wrong with the wallpaper?"

"Well, ma'am, the ghost thinks flowers belong in the garden."

Jenny blinked at Zeph for a full fifteen seconds, her hazel eyes growing bigger with each tick of the clock. "Oh, my goodness, he tried to tell me that the very first night."

"What?" Zeph and Gabe said in near unison.

"I had a dream. I told you about it. Well, I told you about part of it. But in the beginning of the dream, I was putting up wallpaper, and the flowers started to dance and they danced right out into the garden and I followed them. And there was a voice, and he sort of suggested that flowers belong in the yard and a big dog was coming my way, and then the next day Bear arrived."

"You didn't tell me about the wallpaper," Gabe said.

"I didn't think it was important. I thought the open window was important. And of course, I thought Bear belonged to me because of that dream. And that was just silly, because anyone can see that he belongs to you."

Gabe applied antiseptic ointment to the gash on her palm. He was trying hard not to notice her hands. They were long-fingered and nimble. The nails were plain and well-shaped. Truth to tell, he was trying to get that moment when she covered him with her body out of his mind, too. She was brave, his little sparrow.

"The ghost intended that dog for you, Miz Jenny," Zeph said, pulling Gabe away from his thoughts.

He looked up. Zeph had moved to the back door.

"How do you know the dog was meant for Jenny?" Gabe asked.

"Because he attracts strays."

"What? Who? The ghost?"

Zeph shrugged one shoulder and then started talking real fast. "I know what everyone says about animals and haunts, but this particular haunt doesn't scare the critters away. They come to him whenever they need help. And it's my penance to help them find new homes. The ghost tells me what to do. And the ghost intended that big ol' dog for Miz Jenny, not for you, Mr. Gabe. That might be why he's a little annoyed at you right now. I don't think he meant to hurt anyone tonight. He's just frustrated about the house and about . . . well, other things. He's not a vicious ghost. Really he's not."

"If he's not, then why the hell have you been trying to get Jenny and me to leave? You know how this looks, Zeph, don't you? It looks like you might have created the *appearance* of a ghost, just to scare us. That would be way more rational than believing in actual ghosts."

"I didn't do any such thing. And if you thought about it, Mr. Gabe, you'd realize that it's not me or Miz Jenny trying to fool you. It's just a ghost trying to get your attention.

"And as for wanting y'all to leave, well, it's just that I didn't want y'all to be haunted. It's not easy. It requires a lot of work. And you can't tell folks about it because, if you do, they'll think you're crazier than a loon, which is exactly what you're thinking about me right this minute, isn't it?"

Zeph stood still for half a minute staring at Gabe, and Gabe stared back. He had faced this situation before. Zeph was trying to make him believe that he was rational. And he wanted to believe Zeph, but he knew better.

Zeph must have known he'd lost the battle, because he turned on his boot heel and was halfway out the door. Jenny called him back. "Wait, Zeph, is the ghost Luke?"

Her words scorched Gabe right down to his soul. Was it possible that both of them were trying to drive him insane?

Zeph turned, his big, brown eyes wide. "Yes, ma'am. I'm sorry, Mr. Gabe, you should never have come back here." He turned and headed out into the darkness, where he dematerialized into the woods as if he were a ghost himself.

"You don't believe what he just said," Gabe said.

"I think I do. And that scares me. Because if I really have a malicious ghost then I'm not going to be able to open the inn. And I have everything invested in this place. I can't afford to fail."

"I'll buy back the house and the furnishings, Jenny. You don't—"

"No!" She folded her arms across her chest. "No, I'm not leaving." She looked up at the ceiling. "You hear that, ghost, I'm not going. And if you are the ghost of Luke Raintree, then I am so disappointed in you, young man. I won't tolerate temper tantrums in my house. Is that absolutely clear?"

"You sound like Mrs. Abernathy, my tenth-grade math teacher," Gabe said.

She turned her hazel eyes on him. "That makes perfect sense, because before I bought this house, I *was* a tenth-grade math teacher."

Gabe had to laugh. If she was trying to con him, then she was one heck of a good actor, because no one could fake that schoolteacher demeanor. And knowing that she'd been a teacher in a former life freed him in some strange way. The empty place inside seemed a tiny bit smaller for it.

He believed in Jenny. His belief in ghosts would have to await further evidence. Because there *was* a rational explanation for what had happened tonight.

"You don't believe there's a ghost, do you?" she said.

"No."

"If it isn't a ghost, then someone is playing tricks on us, and they aren't very nice tricks. The funny thing is that I'm less frightened by the idea of a ghost throwing a temper tantrum than I am by the alternative. Besides, how do you explain why I felt the touch of an ice-cold hand on my wrist while I was carving the chicken?"

"Someone touched you?"

"Not someone, something, some force. It threw the chicken across the table. I know that sounds nuts. And you'll probably choose to think that I threw the chicken at Reverend Lake because he was behaving like a total jerk. But I would never have done anything that would have destroyed Mother's china and furniture." Her voice wavered, and there wasn't anything fake about the emotion she was showing.

He finished tying off the ends of a bandage he'd wrapped around her hand. And then, for reasons he didn't wish to examine too closely, he lowered his head and pressed a small kiss to her palm.

She gasped. And desire swept through him like a coastal hurricane. He raised his head and looked into her face. "Did I hurt you?"

"No." She breathed the word.

He cradled her hands in both of his. "You saved my life tonight." Of this he was entirely certain.

"No, I didn't. I'm sure you would have been all right. If the ghost is your brother, surely he had no reason to hurt you. He just hated Mother's dining room set and the magnolia wallpaper." Her last words came out in a watery voice, and tears overflowed her eyes.

He brushed them from her cheek. "Whatever the reason, I am in your debt. It is one of the few debts that doesn't burden me in the least." He stopped, his voice becoming thick.

"You're crazy, Mr. Raintree, there is no—"

He pressed his finger across her lips. "Perhaps I am crazy, because I want to believe there is a ghost here. It would be so simple, so uncomplicated. And the name is Gabe."

"Gabe," she whispered when he removed his finger. He caught his own name on her lips as he leaned in for one, short kiss.

CHAPTER
12

That night Jenny dreamed she was in a canoe paddling on the Edisto River after a spring rain. The current was swift, and she was all alone in the canoe, trying to reach the riverbank where The Jonquil House stood. A man in black waited on the porch for her. Every now and again he would wave, and a feeling of pure joy filled her. But the current was too swift. The best she could manage by paddling with all her might was to stand still in the rushing water.

When she finally awoke from her fretful sleep, the sun was already well up in the sky. She'd overslept. She checked her bedside clock. It was nine o'clock.

She must have slept right through her alarm, which was unusual. She usually woke up before it sounded. She'd spent her life teaching high school, and classes started promptly at eight, and early-bird math tutoring at seven. So she'd been getting up at 0-dark-thirty for years. She'd lost the ability to sleep in.

She picked up the clock and quickly discovered that

the alarm had been reset to 11:00 a.m. She had no explanation for this, except that the ghost was a pain in the backside and ought to be taken out to the woodshed and disciplined the old-fashioned way. Not that she was a big fan of corporal punishment, but really, the ghost had destroyed Mother's china.

She knew it was completely insane to believe that a ghost was responsible for what had happened last night, but she had no other rational explanation. Mr. Raintree— Gabe—was ready to blame Zeph for everything, but Zeph hadn't been in the room when the chicken took flight. And Mr. Raintree hadn't felt the grip of that icy hand on his wrist.

Jenny was a math and science teacher. She was a skeptic of the highest order. But she truly believed there was something supernatural going on at The Jonquil House. Of course, she wasn't ready to call up the Travel Channel yet and make a play to have The Jonquil House on *Most Haunted USA*. She had a feeling that might attract exactly the wrong kind of customer.

Just then she remembered with a start that Nita, Rocky, and Savannah were scheduled to drop by at ten o'clock to talk about the library fund-raiser. She had foolishly offered to host the meeting and to make them muffins. She rolled out of bed and hit the shower at a dead run.

Ten minutes later, it occurred to her as she was pulling on a pair of jeans and a sweater that she not only didn't have muffins, but she didn't have a dining room table, either. She would have to entertain them in the living room.

And she was worried about the questions they were sure to ask about the events of the previous evening. It was nine o'clock in Last Chance, South Carolina, the gossip capital of the world. It was a surefire bet that everyone in town knew Reverend Lake had been attacked by a flying chicken.

In fact, it was kind of amazing that no one had called her yet to get all the juicy details. She picked up her cell phone and discovered that she was wrong. People had been calling since six in the morning. She had no less than ten messages from Sabina, alone, but somehow her phone had been put into silent mode. She had no recollection of having done that herself.

She looked up at the ceiling. "You owe me, ghost," she muttered. "I am not going to be turned out of this house. Not by you and not by—"

She didn't say his name. She feared Gabe more than the ghost. Gabe made her body sing. Gabe made her yearn for things she was supposed to be giving up because she could never have them.

She wasn't going to be a fool for love again.

Her dream last night was easy to interpret. She was going to drown in a flooding river if she let Gabe's little peck on the mouth run away with her imagination, or, God forbid, her heart.

She hurried downstairs, intent on making it to the kitchen and starting some coffee. She prayed that the Library Committee would be late, but she had a feeling that, with Nita Wills involved, they would be punctual.

Which meant she had exactly three minutes to get the coffee on. She rushed down the hallway but skidded to a stop when she got to the dining room archway.

Zeph and Gabe were working together, righting the china cabinet. It was banged and scratched, and its broken arch pediment was literally busted into three big pieces and a bunch of large splinters.

The men set the big cabinet back on its feet against the wall, hiding the torn wallpaper. The wood was scratched, but it looked as if it might be salvaged. The dining room table, not so much. There was an enormous dent in the wood at one end, and two of the legs had broken. It listed on its two good legs in the middle of the room. Several of the chairs had sustained damage as well. Jenny's throat tightened. She'd been dreaming of the day that she could entertain people in a room like this, and now it was an utter shambles.

She was so angry she wanted to cry and cuss at the same time. But she held her tongue and cleared her throat, and the two men turned toward her. "I'm glad the two of you have made peace. And Mr. Raintree, uh, Gabe, I see your ankle is feeling better."

He was wearing his Harvard sweatshirt and a pair of jeans that had to be at least ten years old. His dark hair looked as if he'd just rolled out of bed, and his five o'clock shadow had turned into a two-day stubble. He certainly didn't look like a man who was scheduled to meet with the committee. But then she doubted that he gave a rat's behind about the Library Committee. He'd probably forgotten all about it.

Which made his current actions in her dining room and his thoughtfulness last night all the more extraordinary. He'd carried dishes from the kitchen to the table. He'd cared for her hand last night. And now he was trying to fix the damage. Knowing he cared was kind of seductive, actually. She was also nonplussed at her reaction to this small bit of kindness.

She was a fool and an idiot. She needed to stop right now. "Miz Jenny," Zeph said, "I am so sorry about what happened last night. But your momma's table and cabinet can be fixed, and I'd be obliged if you let me work on them. I reckon you know I have a way with wood."

She did know that. Savannah had hired him to restore the lobby of The Kismet, and he'd done a remarkable job. She turned her gaze on Mr. Raintree, who was scowling a little bit. She knew his opinion. He didn't believe in the ghost, and he was ready to blame Zeph for everything.

Well, he was wrong. And she decided right then and there to believe Zeph's story about the ghost of Luke Raintree.

"Zeph, that's a very generous offer, but you know I can't let you work without paying you something."

"I guess I don't mind being paid, but I don't know what to charge. And I feel responsible for what happened. I reckon I should have told y'all about the ghost earlier."

Mr. Raintree rolled his eyes. Zeph saw the expression but chose to ignore it.

"The truth is you didn't make the chicken fly across the room, or the cabinet fall over. And I don't see why you should be taking responsibility for a ghost who chose to throw a temper tantrum."

Zeph actually smiled at this. "Ma'am, I've tried my hardest to keep him from throwing tantrums. Sometimes he's just like the teenager he used to be."

"How did you stop him from being obnoxious?"

"By paying attention to what he wants."

"That's just spoiling him. And that's no way to live. I've given this some thought, and we need to find someone who can send this ghost on his way. And in the meantime, I'll pay you whatever you think is fair to repair the furniture."

"Send him on his way?" Zeph said.

"To the other side, or to Heaven, or exterminate him

or whatever we need to get rid of him. I do not want him hanging around here breaking china for no good reason."

"But I—"

Zeph's argument was cut short by a knock on the door.

"Oh, good Lord, that's the Library Committee right on time, and I don't have any muffins."

"The Library Committee?" Zeph's black skin turned a shade paler. If Jenny didn't know better, she'd say that Zeph was more frightened of the committee than he was of ghosts. Which probably revealed more about the Library Committee than it did Zeph Gibbs.

"They're here for me," Gabe said. "I'll get the door, you get the coffee. Zeph, I'd be obliged if you could finish cleaning up the trash in here. Anyone asks, the cabinet fell over because the floor is not quite level. Got it?"

Jenny and Zeph both gave Gabe a look, which he chose to ignore as he strode off to the front door and opened it as if The Jonquil House was still his.

Jenny hurried off to the kitchen only to discover that the coffee was already on, and the pie she'd made for last night's dinner was sitting untouched right on the counter. Someone had gotten the pie server out of the drawer along with several everyday dessert plates. Jenny doubted that Zeph would have done something like that.

So obviously Mr. Raintree had not forgotten about the Library Committee.

Even more amazing, he'd resisted her pie. No one resisted her pies. Especially men.

Zeph had just finished dumping the last dustbin of broken china into a garbage bag when his worst nightmare wandered into the dining room.

"Oh, Zeph, I—" Nita Wills stopped talking as she took in the broken furniture. "Goodness, Zeph, what happened here?"

"A little accident. I reckon the floor isn't quite level, and the china cabinet fell over last night." He thanked his stars that the cabinet was hiding the ripped-up wallpaper. "Mr. Gabe called me this morning and asked if I'd help Miz Jenny get the room set to rights. And to see if the furniture could be repaired."

Of course, that wasn't the truth either. He'd knocked on the door early this morning and roused Gabe from his bed and offered to help with the cleanup. Gabe didn't trust him, which he supposed was only natural. Gabe hadn't yet accepted the fact that he was being haunted. But he'd come to it sooner or later.

The time to save Gabe from the ghost had come and gone. Zeph had failed.

Nita was staring at him as if she could read every one of these crazy thoughts. As if she knew he was lying. He often had this feeling when in her presence. He didn't know where to look, so he looked down at the floor.

"I was looking for the bathroom," she said.

"Oh, it's just down the hall off the kitchen."

She left the room, and he heaved a huge sigh.

But his relief was short-lived, because a moment later she strode into the room and began examining the floor like she was some kind of building inspector or something.

She looked up eventually with a worried frown on her pretty face. "Zeph Gibbs, you know as well as I do that the floor in here is level."

He didn't say a word as she strode across the room in his direction. She stopped when she was right in front of him, invading his personal space and making his hands go a little sweaty and his head go a little crazy. She was dressed in a tight brown tweed dress that hugged her body and made the spit dry in his mouth.

He ought not to be noticing the librarian's body. He was too old for that kind of thing. And besides, Nita was a well-educated woman. What use would she have for a man like him?

"Zeph, something funny is going on around here. Jenny's got all kinds of scratches on her face and a bandaged hand. You would tell me if Gabe Raintree is doing something evil to her."

"What?" He straightened up. "Gabe hasn't done one thing to hurt Miz Jenny. I swear it. I've been keeping an eye on them. The cabinet fell over on its own, and that's how she got hurt."

"Keeping an eye on them? How?"

"I just have."

"Like you keep an eye on me sometimes?"

"Ma'am?"

"Don't you ma'am me, Zeph Gibbs. I've seen you out there sometimes watching my house. And I've wondered about it because I don't think you're the kind of person who would hurt anyone. So have you been watching Jenny and Mr. Raintree?"

He'd been caught. He could hardly believe it. He was good at hiding in the shadows. And now that she knew he sometimes watched her house, he was going to have to give it up. Because her knowing changed everything. She was going to think he was some kind of crazy stalker or something. He wished with all his soul that he could just quit fibbing and tell her the whole, unadulterated truth.

But he knew that was crazy. He'd told the truth last night, and Mr. Gabe still didn't believe him.

Nita wouldn't believe him either.

"Speak up, have you been spying on Jenny?"

"No, ma'am, I have not been spying. I've just been keeping an eye on Mr. Gabe, just to make sure he doesn't have any trouble."

"What kind of trouble are you worried about?"

Zeph shrugged.

"Zeph, I know you feel some allegiance to Mr. Raintree. I mean, you knew him when he was little, and you've been taking the blame for something he did a long time ago. But I want you to stop doing that. I'm coming to believe that Mr. Raintree is a walking advertisement for trouble. And I wish I'd listened to you when you asked me to drop this idea of using him for the library. It's too late to stop that now, but I just want you to know that I wish I had listened to you."

"Ma'am?"

"You don't know, do you?"

"Know what?"

"As you can imagine, since I've asked him to help with the library project, and I knew there was this skeleton in his closet, so to speak, I decided I should do a little check on his background."

"Ma'am, what are you talking about?"

"I'm talking about Mr. Raintree's reputation. Apparently he's been in more than one public altercation. At least one of them was some kind of domestic dispute with a girlfriend, and it ended in an arrest, although no charges were brought. I'm beginning to think he might be a very violent man. He certainly writes very violent stories. And then there's what happened to his brother."

"He didn't intentionally hurt Luke. And just because he writes scary books doesn't make him violent. Have you read his books? He uses beautiful words. And his heroes are always decent human beings," Zeph said.

Nita cocked her head. "Zeph, that is not the first time that you've said something to me that suggests you're an avid reader."

"I am. I have a little library of my own at home, made up of secondhand books. It passes the time."

"When you're not standing outside my house or Jenny's house keeping an eye on things?"

He nodded, his whole body flushing hot with shame.

"I wonder if your loyalty to Mr. Raintree is misplaced."

"It's not."

She glanced at the china cabinet. "I have a hard time believing that a piece of furniture as big and heavy as that one just fell over for no reason. So I know you're not telling me the truth."

"It wasn't Mr. Gabe who turned it over. And if you don't believe me, you can talk to the Methodists' new preacher. He was here."

"And he's going to tell me the cabinet just fell over?"

"I don't know what he's going to tell you." But Zeph had a feeling it was going to be something about demons. And half the population of Last Chance would believe him because he was a preacher. And that was going to cause a lot of problems in this town. Of course, Nita wasn't going to believe any such thing. Nita was a woman of reason.

Which was why he wasn't ever going to tell her about the ghost.

"Zeph, if I find out that you aren't telling me the truth, I'm going to be so disappointed in you. I don't want my library program to be associated with someone who hurts people. Do you understand that?"

"I do, Miz Nita. But Mr. Gabe hasn't done any harm to Miz Jenny. You can trust me on that."

"Can I trust you on anything else?"

She didn't wait for him to say another word. She just turned and walked away from him, her backside swaying in that tight dress.

He swallowed hard in his dry mouth. It stung to know that Nita Wills thought he was a liar. And it was doubly hard to bear because it was true.

CHAPTER
13

On Saturday morning, three days after the china cabinet debacle, Jenny helped her cousin move into the small one-bedroom apartment above the Cut 'n Curl beauty shop. It didn't take all that long, because all of Maryanne's possessions fit perfectly into Jenny's old Fiesta and Maryanne's even older Honda Civic.

Of course, Ruby Rhodes, the proprietor of the beauty shop and Maryanne's new landlady, made things easy for Maryanne. The apartment was fully furnished with everything she would need, including dishes. And Ruby had gone one better by donating a porta-crib and an old changing table that had once belonged to her two older granddaughters. So Maryanne and Joshua had a home of their own, and the baby finally had a real place to sleep. For the last few weeks, he'd been sleeping in a makeshift bed that Maryanne had cobbled together out of a bureau drawer and some big cushions.

And bless her heart, she had steadfastly refused to take any help from her boyfriend, Daniel, who wanted to buy the boy a top-of-the-line crib, which would never have fit in the little apartment.

Ruby's donated porta-crib was the right size and the right price, and came from a source who didn't want anything in return. Ruby had to be one of the kindest souls in town. She was always letting people stay at her apartment above the beauty shop. And half the time she didn't even charge rent. Although Maryanne had insisted on paying her own way in that regard, too.

They were just putting away Maryanne's clothes in the closet and bureau when Sabina knocked on the door and invited herself in. She was carrying the most adorable little nursing rocker that Jenny had ever seen.

"Hey," she said, putting the rocking chair down in the middle of the small room. "Lucy was at an auction down in Bamberg on Thursday, and she got this gem for a song. I saw it yesterday, and I immediately decided that you and Joshua needed to have it. So it's my housewarming present."

Maryanne's eyes teared up. "Oh, my God, it's perfect." She sat down in the chair, and Jenny handed her the baby. "I can't believe it," she said, looking around the small apartment. "Everyone here has been so incredibly kind to me. Y'all don't know me from Adam."

Jenny gave her cousin's shoulder a squeeze. "Honey, you're my kin, and Carpenters have been living in Allenberg County for generations. That's all you need to know. No one thinks of you as a stranger."

"Besides," Sabina said, "there isn't anyone in town who hasn't noticed the change in Daniel Jessup. And people love Daniel. I ran into Thelma Hanks at the post office the other day, and she's overjoyed that Daniel is coming home and joining Eugene's practice. Thelma said Eugene works too hard. And now that Eugene's got a partner, Thelma's hoping she and Eugene will be able to sneak away for a cruise or a second honeymoon or something. When you have Thelma on your side, it counts for a lot. She's well liked by just about everyone in town."

Maryanne brushed a tear away from her cheek. "I never had a place where I belonged before."

"Well, you do now," Sabina said as she crossed the room and flopped down on the daybed. "All right, I've kept my mouth shut for three whole days, but I can't stand it a minute longer. Jenny, what the heck happened on Wednesday night?"

Jenny had been ducking Sabina's calls for several days because she didn't know whether to confide in her or not. And lying to her oldest girlfriend didn't seem right either.

"Honey, everyone's saying you threw a chicken at the preacher. That doesn't sound like you."

"I didn't throw any chickens, all right?"

"Of course you didn't. But how did it end up in his lap?"

"How did you know it ended up in his lap?"

"Because Reverend Lake apparently told Elsie all about how you threw the chicken at him, and it landed in his lap and then you...Well I won't repeat what Elsie said."

"Oh. My. God. Does she think I threw it just so I could touch his lap?"

Jenny started pacing. This was a disaster. Now that people were telling this tale it would be impossible to tell the truth. She couldn't explain about the ghost. It would sound so lame, like those guilty people who always got up and said it wasn't their fault because the devil made them do it. "Oh. My. God. What am I going to do?"

Maryanne snorted. "You don't have to *do* anything, hon. The minister regards you as some kind of brazen hussy."

"No."

"Yes," Sabina said with a big grin. "I think that's wonderful, don't you?"

"No. I'm not a brazen hussy. Oh, my God, how can I show my face in church tomorrow? And why are you grinning like that? I can't imagine that Reverend Lake would be interested in anyone who threw a chicken at him and then tried to mop up the grease on his lap with a napkin."

"You never know. And I'm thinking that a woman who does a thing like that is way more interesting than a mousy little thing who teaches math to disinterested kids."

"Well, you do have that." Jenny sat down with a sigh.

"Honestly, Jen, what happened?" Maryanne asked.

"I threw a chicken at the preacher," she said, because there was nothing else she could say.

"You did not."

"Did. He was being mean to Mr. Raintree, and I got annoyed at him."

Sabina and Maryanne stared at her as if she'd lost her mind.

"He accused Mr. Raintree of being some kind of, I don't know, evil person because he writes scary books with violence in them. If you really want to know, for all he's so handsome, Reverend Lake was being downright ugly."

"Honey, you can't throw chickens at people whose opinions you disagree with," Sabina said.

"I know. Something just must have snapped in my

brain. But I'll tell you one thing, Sabina, if Miriam Randall thinks I'm marrying that man, she's got another think coming."

Sabina picked up a throw pillow and hugged it. "I think Miriam is getting a little senile. She came into the store yesterday, and she was wearing her fuzzy slippers, and I don't think she knew where she was. I called Savannah, and she didn't even know Miriam had left the house."

"That's sad," Jenny said.

"Yeah, it is. Miriam was always someone you could count on, you know? I've been hoping for years that she'd have some advice for me."

"Sabina, you shouldn't be sitting around waiting for someday. You should just go live life to its fullest."

"By throwing chickens at ministers?"

Jenny shrugged.

Sabina gave her the evil eye. "You didn't throw that chicken on purpose, Jennifer Carpenter, and we both know it. What really happened?"

"It slipped. But I did try to mop up the grease. I don't even know why. It was just an immediate reaction to the disaster of seeing the chicken fly across the table and land on him. But when I started pressing on his thigh, you know to raise up the grease, he stood up and knocked over his chair, which knocked over a plant, which knocked over the china cabinet. Apparently the floor isn't level. That's what happened."

"Oh, you poor thing. We'll have to fix this. We'll have to make him understand you weren't actually trying to cop a feel. I'm sure he'll give you another chance to cook for him, and once he tastes your cooking, he'll be yours forever."

Jenny stifled the urge to roll her eyes. "Please don't

encourage him. It would be best if we just left things the way they are. I'm not interested in Reverend Lake. If you like him so much, you should make a play for him, instead of pining away for Ross Gardiner, who, I should point out, is your sister's boyfriend."

"Yeah, you're right. He's better looking than Ross, too."

"Good, so you invite him to dinner at your house."

"But I don't know how to cook."

"Well, that didn't seem to get in the way of Hettie Marshall and Bill Ellis, did it." Jenny crossed her arms and sat next to Sabina.

"Honey, let it go," Sabina said.

"Right. I should." But all Jenny could think about was how Gabe had allowed one of her apple pies to sit on a counter for something like twelve hours and hadn't once touched it.

Jenny ducked church on Sunday. The gossip about how she'd purposefully thrown the chicken was all over town. It was humiliating and embarrassing. Although Wilma Riley had called up late Saturday to congratulate her for seeing the light and recognizing that the last thing she needed was a husband.

Meanwhile, life settled into a routine of sorts at The Jonquil House. The ghost, if there really was one, had given up haunting her. He left her furniture alone. He didn't touch her alarm clock or cell phone. He stayed out of her kitchen.

She woke early every morning and made muffins or other sweet breads, testing out a variety of recipes for the future. Every morning at about seven-thirty, Mr. Raintree would emerge from his bedroom, looking sleepy-eyed and

tousled, bristling with dark stubble. And Jenny would find
some reason to be in the kitchen just to catch a glimpse of
him. She'd given up on telling her heart not to speed up
when she was in his presence.

He might, on occasion, mumble something unintelligible that resembled "good morning" before heading out
the back door with the dog. With each passing day, his
morning walk with the dog was longer, suggesting that his
ankle was healing.

After his walk, he'd wander back into the kitchen,
mumble a few more unintelligible words, ignore whatever
Jenny had baked that morning, and pour himself a bowl
of Cheerios with milk. He'd grab a mug of coffee and
head back into his room.

At noon, he came out of his cave and made himself a
sandwich. Zeph would show up shortly thereafter, bearing his own lunch box and cooler filled with orange Nehi.
He'd go to work on the furniture.

At about four o'clock, Gabe would wander into the living room, fire up the television, and play video games. He
would do this for at least two hours, after which he'd go
out to his car and leave the house until about eight.

The first night after the china cabinet incident, Jenny
cooked a big enough dinner for all of them. But she ended
up eating alone. Zeph always left precisely at five and told
her she didn't need to cook for him. And Gabe made it
clear that he didn't expect her to do the cooking, since she
refused to take any rent from him and since the inn wasn't
yet officially open for business.

In short, the ghost had eliminated her one and only
chance to actually cook for Mr. Raintree. And she kind
of resented it.

At the same time, she couldn't blame her boarder. He might have held her while she cried. He might have given her the tiniest little kiss, but that didn't mean anything. She knew this. And he knew it, too. But every morning she made muffins just the same in the vain hope that he might try one. And every morning she found some reason to be in the kitchen at seven-thirty, when he would go about his business and ignore her home-baked offering.

Aside from this singular and somewhat pathetic moment in the kitchen, Jenny spent her days with Bear in the office she'd set up in the Rose Room. She worked on the inn's web page and online registration system, checked on the delivery date for the Daisy Room's furniture, made appointments to have satellite television hooked up, and spoke with merchant service providers. When she needed a break, she surfed the web looking for ghost exterminators.

She had come to the conclusion that the ghostly world was divided into two sorts of people—clergy who seemed to believe that ghosts could be dispensed with by sprinkling holy water and praying, and psychics who claimed they could bring down vortexes of light into which the spirits would willingly go.

All in all both camps seemed crazier than loons. She had hoped the Internet would provide her the number of a real-life ghostbuster of the Bill Murray and Dan Aykroyd variety. She wanted guys in jumpsuits with ghost traps. Alas, it seemed that ridding oneself of pesky spirits was more difficult than she had expected.

So when Wednesday came around, she had to choose between the book club and the strange loneliness of The Jonquil House. A part of her wanted to duck the club meeting, too. After all, her friends would all be dying to know if she had really thrown that chicken. But how could she stay away? She was a member of the Library Committee now, and besides, they had chosen the book she wanted. It would be rude not to show up.

So she pulled up her big-girl panties and arrived at the library a few minutes early, bearing a big basket of blueberry scones she'd baked that morning that had, once again, gone begging. It wasn't even Jenny's day for refreshments, which made her offering all the more pitiful and obvious.

"I'm trying out recipes," she said brightly as she put the scones on the table.

She took a seat at one of the long library tables and tried to avoid talking to anyone. The Bill Ellis disaster had kept tongues wagging for weeks. She hoped the Timothy Lake incident wouldn't prove as long lasting.

Savannah Randall sat down next to her. "Honey, these scones are amazing. And no, I'm not going to ask for the recipe." She patted Jenny's hands, which were folded in front of her, on top of a paperback edition of *Jane Eyre*.

"Honey, don't give up," Savannah said.

Jenny fought the urge to grind her teeth, or to stand up and scream. "I haven't given up on anything that's important," she said. She didn't even care that her voice had come out kind of snooty and mean sounding. Sabina and Maryanne and a lot of her so-called friends were all trying to think of some way to snatch victory from the jaws of this disaster. It was as if the people who were certain she didn't throw the chicken were all in league to find a way for Jenny and Tim to find everlasting happiness together. And everyone else was hoping for round two, in which Jenny would progress to pie hurling.

Savannah patted her hand again. "Everything is going to work out just fine, you wait and see. And remember that there isn't any ill wind that doesn't blow some kind of good."

"Right, like throwing a chicken might discourage Tim Lake?"

Savannah smiled. "There is that."

Jenny turned. "You're not trying to find some way to salvage this disaster?"

She shook her head. "No. But I thought you might want to know that not everyone is focused on the flying chicken. There are a lot of folks who are wondering just how a big china cabinet falls over like that. And I'd say half of the gossips are buying into the idea that the floor wasn't level, and about twenty-five percent have a theory that it was the wind that night, coupled with the preacher making a sudden move to get away from your napkin. As you recall, it was a very windy night."

"And the remaining twenty-five percent?" Jenny couldn't resist asking.

Savannah laughed. "Well, those are folks who are convinced that you didn't throw the chicken at all. They're the ones who've experienced odd things out at The Jonquil House, and they're saying the ghost of Luke Raintree is responsible for everything. And just speaking one businesswoman to another, if I were in your shoes, I'd ride that horse. I mean, having a ghost is probably good for business."

Jenny stared at Savannah for a long moment. "Do you believe in ghosts?"

She shrugged. "I'm agnostic on the question."

"Savannah, if I did have a ghost, I wouldn't want one that threw china cabinets around when he was angry."

"I suppose you'd want to have a tame ghost, then?"

"Right." Jenny rolled her eyes. She hoped her dismissal of the ghost theory was convincing. She didn't want anyone to think she actually believed in ghosts. A real ghost wasn't nearly as much fun as a pretend one.

"I'm serious," Savannah said. "Having a haunted inn would be terrific for business in Last Chance. It would be a tourist attraction. You could do ghost tours on Halloween. You might give Golfing for God a run for its money."

"I doubt it," Jenny said. "Didn't I hear Rocky saying the other day that Elbert Rhodes is expanding Golfing for God?"

"Really?" Savannah said, "I hadn't heard that."

"Actually, I heard that he's adding another eighteen holes on some land that Lord Hugh owns. He's dedicating this new course entirely to angels."

"Wow, that's cool. But I don't see where a mini-golf trumps a haunted inn." Savannah's smile broadened. "Especially when the 'Dean of Horror' is living there."

"Yeah, well he's not particularly scary, except maybe in the morning before he's combed his hair."

Savannah gave her a knowing grin, and Jenny suddenly wished she hadn't said one word about Gabe Raintree. Her growing fascination with him was embarrassing and pitiful. "Uh, that came out all wrong. I mean he doesn't shave or comb his hair when he comes into the kitchen in the morning, and—"

"I bet he loves your scones."

Jenny's chest squeezed. Luckily she didn't have to admit that he hated her cooking because Nita chose that moment to call the meeting to order.

"I thought before we started our book discussion," Nita said, "that I'd let y'all know what the Library Committee has been up to. Hettie, do you want to fill folks in?"

Hettie was dressed in a winter white business suit, and as always, she looked way too well dressed to be a minister's wife. Jenny tamped down her resentment. She had no reason to dislike Hettie. Bill had chosen her because he loved her, even if it was a well-known fact that Hettie had never cooked for herself because she always had servants as a child. So Hettie couldn't even boil water. Apparently she had other talents that Bill admired.

"We had a meeting with Mr. Raintree last week." Hettie looked in Jenny's direction. "Thank you, Jenny, for giving him a place to stay. He's agreed to do a short talk about his writing and, in particular, the setting for *Black Water* and how he drew inspiration for it from our town. Savannah has agreed to hold the talk at The Kismet and make it a fund-raising dinner. She's going to use the theater's reservation system to take the donations. After Mr. Raintree talks, we'll show the movie version of the book. We've got it scheduled for Saturday, February fifteenth, which will give us time to publicize it.

"I've got flyers for it in the back of the room. If y'all would take some and hand them out at your churches and other places, that would be great. Nita has already posted the event on the library's Facebook page, and if any of you are on the Twitter, it would be great if you could get the word out. We want the county executive to know that there are people in this county who think there ought to be two branches of the public library."

A smattering of applause greeted Hettie's speech, and she turned the meeting back to Nita.

"All right, now let's get down to discussing the book. Does anyone want to start us off?"

"I do," said Lola May. "If any man had done me the way

Mr. Rochester does Jane, I would kick him in the family jewels, if you don't mind my saying so. I might take out my shotgun and put him out of his misery. I certainly wouldn't drag myself off to the middle of nowhere and wander the moors like a crazy woman. And I wouldn't go back to him either. Not that I'd ever marry a cold fish like St. John Rivers."

"Yes you would," said Cathy. "You'd marry any man who asked you, Lola May. In fact, you *have* married every man who ever asked you."

"Well, I never married a man who already had a wife, that's for darn sure."

"But Jane and Mr. Rochester were soulmates," Savannah said.

"Were they? I didn't notice that," Rocky said. "I mean he was nice to her and all, but he lied to her, and then when she found out he was already married, he asked her to be his mistress."

"But his wife was crazy," Jenny found herself saying. "I mean, if Mr. Rochester lived now, he'd be able to divorce his crazy wife and go for a happy life. He was trapped by the rules of the time, as much as Jane was trapped. And I agree with Savannah, the book makes it clear that they are soulmates. And he treats her like an equal, unlike anyone else in her life. Not to mention that he gives her a home and love and all the things she'd been denied. It broke my heart when she found out that they couldn't be married, but I understand that she had to learn to stand on her own two feet. In the end, that was a much more valuable lesson for Jane, wasn't it?"

When Jenny finished, everyone around the table was staring at her like she had egg on her face or something. "What?"

"Honey, I think we should talk about what happened last week with Reverend Lake," Rocky said. "I mean, having a china cabinet fall on your dinner table was just bad luck, you know?"

"And to tell you the truth," Cathy said, "I'm sure you just slipped with the carving knife and the chicken got away from you."

"And I know for certain," said Lola May, "that if I had inadvertently thrown a chicken at a handsome man, I wouldn't think twice about trying to wipe the grease off his lap."

"So none of us think this whole incident is an insurmountable impediment, like having a wife stashed in the attic. And I'm sure Reverend Lake would be happy to come to dinner another time. You just have to ask him," Rocky said.

"That's right," Cathy said. "And everyone in town knows that Miriam says you and Reverend Lake are made for each other. It would be wrong to let a simple thing like an inadvertently thrown chicken to get in the way of true love. You know Miriam is never wrong about these things."

Jenny pressed her lips together before she said something nasty about Miriam and her marital advice. The old lady was going senile. Everyone knew it. And she was flat-out wrong about Reverend Lake. He was a cold fish and a coward. He wasn't the guy she was thinking about night and day. He wasn't the one who made her pulse rate climb. He wasn't the one who had her tied up in knots.

In truth, she didn't give a rat's backside about Reverend Lake. If she was upset about anything right at the moment, it was the fact that Gabriel Raintree didn't care enough about her to *try* her muffins, much less *eat* one.

But she wasn't about to admit that to anyone, even her friends at the book club. So she pasted on a good-girl smile that was designed to mollify them. They were being helpful. Not a one of them believed that she'd actually thrown the chicken at Reverend Lake, and she appreciated that more than words could express.

"I'm so glad y'all don't believe I would actually throw poultry at anyone."

"Of course you wouldn't," Nita said. There was something more in Nita's look. Something that said she wasn't satisfied with the story that the chicken had slipped and the preacher had stood up and the china cabinet had fallen.

"I promise that once my furniture is repaired, I will ask Reverend Lake to dinner a second time, and I'll do all the poultry carving in the kitchen instead of at the table."

"Or you could just have him do it. Men love that kind of thing," Cathy said.

"Just don't give him one of those electric knives, honey," Lola May said. "My first husband nearly 'bout cut off his johnson one time with that thing."

And that comment ended any chance that the book club would ever return to their discussion of *Jane Eyre*.

"Jenny, do you have a moment?" Nita asked as the book club adjourned, and the members started heading for their cars.

"Sure, what is it?"

Nita took her by the arm and walked her to the children's nook, away from the other members of the club. "I'm worried about you."

"You don't think I really threw—"

"No, I don't. And I also don't for one minute buy the

story that the china cabinet toppled of its own accord. I saw you on Thursday morning, and you were a mess. You had scratches all over your face and your hand..." She reached down and pulled up Jenny's hand, which still had a Band-Aid covering the cut. "What really happened?"

"The china cabinet tipped over, and the china broke, and I cut my hand. That's what happened."

"There is no way that cabinet tipped over without some help."

Jenny stared at the librarian. What was she supposed to say? Savannah had blithely accepted the possibility of ghosts, but would Nita Wills? Jenny doubted it. And she didn't want to risk being called a fool or a liar. It was bad enough that everyone thought she was a poultry-hurling hussy.

Nita gave her hand a squeeze. "Look, Jenny, I feel responsible for what's going on here. I did some Internet surfing on Gabriel Raintree and I discovered that he's been in a couple of nasty public altercations. At least one of these was with his girlfriend at the time. He was arrested in Los Angeles, although no charges were ever brought. I think he might be violent. Did he go into a rage and start throwing stuff?"

"No." Jenny said this as firmly as she could. The idea that Gabe would hurt someone on purpose seemed wrong in every way. He might write dark stories, but his heroes were always people who triumphed over violence. They usually won the day by being smart and loyal and brave. She knew this because she'd downloaded every single one of his books into her e-reader and had kind of binged on Gabriel Raintree the last few days. The evil in his books was always conquered.

She stood there staring into Nita's concerned face, and she didn't know what to think. Something wasn't adding up, because for all his gruff attitude, Gabe didn't strike her as the kind of guy who would create a public spectacle. He seemed to be a man who was comfortable being solitary.

"Honey," Nita said, "you can tell me the truth. Don't be proud and don't be brave."

"Mr. Raintree is a little moody at times. But he's not violent and he didn't throw the china cabinet. In fact, the china cabinet almost fell on him. I cut my hand pulling him out of harm's way."

"I'm glad to hear it. And I want you to know that if you don't want Mr. Raintree to stay out at The Jonquil House, you can evict him. Don't you worry about the library, you hear?"

"I don't want to evict him. He's actually a pretty easy boarder, to tell you the truth. He doesn't expect me to cook for him, and he keeps mostly to himself." *Damn him.*

CHAPTER
14

Gabe left his room at about eight o'clock on Sunday morning, expecting to find Jenny waiting for him, as she always did, with a cup of coffee and something tempting and sweet and homemade that he couldn't eat.

But the kitchen was dark, and his morning went into a little tailspin until he remembered it was Sunday, the second day of February.

Jenny had gone to church.

He'd forgotten about that. She had skipped church last week because of the gossip. But it was exactly like her to go off this week. He could almost imagine her with her straight little backbone facing down the snickers and the smirks armed with a basket of muffins for the fellowship hour.

He'd been in town last week to see Doc Cooper, who'd removed the cast and put him in an air brace. He'd lunched at the Kountry Kitchen, so he knew what folks were saying about Jenny and that narrow-minded preacher. It was ridiculous, but there were idiots everywhere willing to believe anything.

Of course the same folks probably wouldn't believe that a ghost was responsible for the flying chicken and teetering china cabinet.

He hadn't believed it himself. But you could count him among the converts.

Luke was here in the house. He'd settled down with Gabe in the back bedroom.

Gabe pushed through the kitchen door and out into the thin February sunshine, which was warmer by far than the bedroom where he spent most of his days. He sucked in the fresh air and took Bear on a little walk in the woods. It wouldn't be long, now, before the jonquils bloomed. Already, the spear-like tops of their foliage were poking through the leaf litter and pine needles. Their tops looked so fresh and green.

So alive.

Gabe could use a little springtime, but he had a feeling that, even when the weather warmed, he'd still feel cold. This, more than any other thing, was the hardest part about being haunted.

He ought to run away. But how could he? The ghost was leading him out of his writer's block. He was making amazing progress on a book that was easily the best thing he'd ever written. He had to stay until it was finished. Because, to be honest, Luke was the book's co-author. And Gabe knew he wouldn't be able to finish it without the ghost.

Staying carried a lot of risk, though. He had the feeling that staying until the book was complete might mean he could never leave again. Of course, that wouldn't be all bad. It was peaceful here.

And there was Jenny every morning.

But the book's ending was a problem. Even though he didn't know exactly how to finish it, he was almost afraid of getting to the end.

The book wasn't even the story he'd set out to write. He had planned to write a ghost story with all the usual memes and tropes and clichés. But the ghost kept deleting that book. So he started another one on the night of the toppling china cabinet about a sweet little sociopath of an innkeeper.

But the next morning, instead of the files being deleted, they were changed—entirely rewritten. And now, almost two weeks later, he found himself writing a story about a middle-aged man who had come back to the old home place, prepared to tear it down and bury it, along with the painful memories of his youth.

But his hero was unable to carry out his goal. And the longer he stayed in the old house packing things up and selling them off, the more he became trapped by the past, haunted by something *inside* the house, and *inside* himself. At the heart of the book was the man's damaged relationship with his father. And the writing was leading Gabe to a place he didn't want it to go, filled with nightmares and the darkness that had always been right there in the middle of Gabe's soul.

To finish this book, he was going to have to go spelunking right into the heart of that dark place. And there was a real chance that the hero of his book was also its villain.

On Thursday morning, Jenny baked bran muffins from a recipe that didn't have all that much sugar in it. She test-tasted one and it was okay. Nothing to write home about, but it was healthier than some of her other recipes. She needed a few healthier choices on her menu since she was likely to have guests who wanted that sort of thing.

Not to mention that something healthier might lure Gabe. So when he came in from his morning walk and took out his box of Cheerios, she found herself saying, "I made these especially for you. They're loaded with bran and don't have a lot of sugar in them."

He looked up from the banana he was about to slice into his cereal. He looked tired. The skin around his eyes was bruised and dark.

"You're not sleeping well, are you?" she said.

He lifted one shoulder and the corner of his mouth. "I'm fine."

"Have a muffin. It won't kill you." She pushed the plate toward him. "Although I have to tell you that they are not my best effort. But I can attest that they have lots and lots of fiber in them and they're gluten-free."

He stared at the muffins as if he wanted one, but he shook his head and looked up. "Jenny, you know I stay away from food like that."

"But why? A little taste wouldn't hurt. I feel almost like you're being stoic or something. You want one of these. I can tell."

He leaned his fist on the counter, a muscle ticking in his cheek. "I should have told you this weeks ago. There's something about me that you don't know. You see I'm a—"

His big confession was interrupted by the newly installed doorbell, which was easily as loud as Big Ben itself. "Hold that thought. I'll be right back."

She hurried down the hallway and opened the door to

find a big man wearing a blue work shirt with the name "Buck" embroidered above his pocket.

"Ma'am." He actually touched the brim of his Atlanta Braves hat. "We've got your furniture, and we're all ready to unload."

"My bedroom furniture. Really! I've been waiting weeks. You can put it—"

"Uh, no, ma'am, I have a load of living room furniture."

"Living room furniture? I didn't order any living room furniture. Yet."

"Uh, well, we had an order to pick up some furniture at a place in Charleston yesterday and deliver it here."

"Charleston? Where in Charleston?"

"At a private home, ma'am. Oh, and there's also a piano."

"A piano?"

"Yes, ma'am."

"Wait right there."

She turned and marched down the hall to the kitchen, which was now abandoned. Apparently Gabe was a coward who didn't want to explain why he was rejecting her muffins. So she pounded on his door, ignoring the sticky note that was starting to lose some of its sticky and curling up at the edges. "Mr. Raintree, there is a man at the door who is trying to deliver furniture."

The door opened, and he had the tiniest of smiles at the corner of his mouth. The smile raised a few lines around his eyes and softened everything about his face. That smile didn't do one thing to slow Jenny's suddenly racing heart. "Good," he said. "I've been waiting for them to arrive."

"So you know about this?"

"I do. You need better living room furniture, and Luke is never going to stand for more sissy stuff with velvet and marble and crap like that. Believe me. You don't even want to try it."

"Luke?"

He shrugged.

"So you have accepted that we have a ghost?"

"I have. And I'm trying to appease him. So before you or Luke blows a gasket, why don't you let the men install the furniture in the living room? You might like it."

"But it's your furniture, not mine."

He shrugged. "If you want to be scrupulously honest, it's The Jonquil House's furniture."

"What?"

"When Grandma and Granddad shut up The Jonquil House, they put a lot of furniture into storage. And when I leased my first apartment, some of that furniture ended up in my possession." He brushed past her and headed down the hall. The wind of his passing seemed to have some odd, titillating effect on her skin.

She followed after him, intent on stopping him.

But when she got to the door, Gabe was smiling, his eyes twinkling. He seemed altogether another, younger, happier person. And she couldn't tell him to stop even though he was invading her space. Literally.

Wilma would tell her that to fully realize her potential as a free, independent woman she ought to be standing in the way of the moving men. But how could she step on Mr. Raintree's sudden happiness? It seemed a cruel thing to do, when he often seemed so unhappy. So haunted.

Which, now that he'd just admitted to it, was exactly what was happening to him. The ghost had been quiet as far as Jenny knew, but maybe Gabe was taking the brunt of it. That would sort of make sense. She wished there was something more she could do for him. Taking in his furniture seemed like a small thing. It could be changed once he moved out.

Although the thought of him leaving gave her a little pang. She had become fond of him. He'd become a part of her life in some odd way—a part of living in this house.

So when the moving men asked her what she wanted done with Mother's ancient furniture, she'd found herself telling them to haul it away someplace and get rid of it. The moment she gave that order, it was as if she'd jettisoned something important. Mother would be horrified by what she'd just allowed to happen. Not that Mother loved her living room—quite the opposite. But Mother would never have allowed some stranger to impose his furniture on her.

And until right at that moment, Jenny had never imagined doing any such thing either.

When the men finally hoisted the spinet piano into a spot by the front windows, she had to admit that Mr. Raintree's furniture, while not antebellum Victorian, seemed to belong in the room. The leather sofa was undeniably masculine and carried the patina of much use. The two facing chairs were so large and deep that Jenny thought she might drown in the burgundy tweed upholstery if she ever tried one. There wasn't an embellishment to be had in these straightforward pieces. Even the walnut end tables looked solid enough to take any abuse and still come back for more.

When the men were gone, Mr. Raintree lowered himself into one of the big armchairs and propped his injured foot on the ottoman. "Ah, this is more like home."

"I'm sure it is," Jenny said. "And it's very nice furniture, but when you move out, do you plan to take your furniture with you? I'm just asking because I've had Sabina and Lucy on the prowl looking for pieces for this room."

"The furniture belongs to the house. Like the bed in the back room."

"So you're giving it to me?"

"Why don't we just say that the furniture is in exchange for my rent and call it even?"

"Because the piano is worth more than any rent you might have owed up to this point."

"Yes, but it's Luke's piano."

That stopped her. Because she realized that the room, in fact the entire house, seemed warmer with this furniture in place. "He wanted the furniture back, didn't he?"

Gabe nodded.

"Have you thought that maybe giving in to him isn't helping him?"

"Helping him?"

"Or you, for that matter. You look very tired, Gabe. I'm a little worried about you. I'm thinking maybe we should get one of those crazy preachers out here and see if we can give the ghost a little nudge. He needs to go off to wherever spirits go. You know?"

"Heaven? You must believe in Heaven. You go to church regularly."

"Okay, so Heaven, then. Don't you think the ghost deserves Heaven?"

He looked away, out the front window, where a bright February sun was shining down, promising an early spring.

"What if he's supposed to go the other way?" he asked.

"Gabe, if the ghost is your brother I can't imagine why

he'd be going off to hell. He was only fifteen when he died. And from what I've heard, he was a sweet boy who loved animals."

"Yeah, he was. Everyone loved Luke."

"Well, he's become a bit of a pain in the butt in death. But I think it's only because he's confused. We should do something about sending him on to where he belongs."

Gabe shrugged, and a brooding look settled on his brow as he shifted his gaze to the piano. His entire being seemed to withdraw the more she talked about sending the ghost packing. All the joy he seemed to be feeling a minute ago had evaporated like summer rain after a shower.

He stared at the piano as if he were daring the ghost to sit down and play. Or send it hurling across the room like he'd done to Mother's china cabinet.

"Do you play?" Gabe asked after a long moment.

"A little. I learned as a girl, but Granny's piano was burned up in the fire that took the farmhouse. I haven't played in years."

"Please, don't hold back, although I'm sure it needs tuning. I've called the tuner, by the way. He's coming next Monday."

She was about to tell him he had lost his mind when the doorbell rang again.

"Goodness, it's as busy as a train station in here this morning." She headed back to the center hall.

When she opened the front door, she found a woman impeccably dressed in a black worsted suit and an animal-print silk blouse. Her chic, chin-length bob displayed her long neck and chunky jewelry. She was dark-haired, olive-skinned, and so thin she looked like she needed to stand up three times to make a shadow. She had a Louis Vuitton suitcase at her side and a matching purse slung over her shoulder.

"I'm sorry, but the inn isn't open yet," Jenny said.

"Oh? I was under the impression that Gabriel Raintree is staying here. I need to speak with him."

"I'm sorry, but—"

"Barbara? Is that you?" Gabe came limping out of the living room and into the foyer.

"Gabe. Thank God. I've been beside myself with worry." The woman named Barbara sailed through the door on her high heels and right into Mr. Raintree's arms. She gave him a kiss on the lips that lasted a bit longer than was necessary, followed by a big hug.

This public display of affection chilled Jenny like a gust of icy wind. She watched it and knew herself for the biggest fool that ever breathed. She had allowed herself to think that she mattered to Mr. Raintree, even if he wasn't pleased by her cooking, even though he was scrupulous about keeping his distance.

She had made this mistake before. And she wasn't going to make it again.

Barbara Ianelli was all over him like a bad paint job, and all Gabe could think was that Jenny was watching this display. His first instinct was to set his editor back a few feet. But he didn't do that. He let her rub her body up against him. He let her kiss linger. And he did it in the hope that this would discourage Jenny.

And discourage himself.

He needed to keep his distance from Jenny even though his sweet tooth and his libido were urging him in the other direction. He was wrong for her, and she was wrong for him. She was sweet and kind, and he was a failure at relationships. He didn't know how to commit, or even to love. And he had always been happier when the world left him alone.

Which the world rarely wanted to do.

He finally managed to disengage Barb's lips and set her away from him. "How did you find me?"

She gave him one of her sassy New York looks—the kind that involved an eye roll that pissed him off every time she did it. "C'mon, Gabe, you're all over Facebook. What's this business about giving a book talk on February fifteenth? You know the publisher doesn't like you to do things without letting us know beforehand. And I'm annoyed at you for changing your phone number. I've been trying to reach you for weeks. You're avoiding me."

"I didn't want to be reached."

She took his cheeks in her long, cool hands and tilted her head. It was a facsimile of a caring look. Barb wanted his latest book, and maybe a little fun between the sheets, but beyond that she didn't care. Not like Jenny.

"Oh, poor baby, are you still battling writer's block?"

He wasn't blocked anymore, but trying to explain how the ghost of his long-dead brother was helping him write a book would probably not go over well. Barb would think he'd gone crazy. And maybe he had. All in all, it was better to lie.

"I'm still blocked."

"But you spend all day in your room typing," Jenny said. "I can hear you. Aren't you making any progress?" She seemed so worried about him. Her concern warmed him to his core.

Barb let go of him and turned on his landlady. "And you are?"

"My landlady," Gabe said.

"Oh, good. I need a room."

Jenny's forehead wrinkled, and Gabe knew what Jenny was about to say. And as much as Gabe wished he could turn his editor away, tossing Barb out on her ass would just make more trouble. So he cut Jenny off before she could explain that the inn wasn't open for business.

"Jenny, this is my editor," he said. "You need to give her a room. I'm not going to let her stay at the Peach Blossom Motor Court."

Jenny put her hands on her hips and gave him a look that was one part angry and another part wounded. He was treading hard on her kindness. Hadn't he just imposed his furniture on her living room? And now he was imposing his editor. But it couldn't be helped. It would be better to humor Barb than to antagonize her and have her hanging around making a nuisance of herself. And besides, Barb was the best damn chaperone he could think of. Her presence would ensure that he didn't trip and make a big mistake.

"But I haven't yet—" Jenny began.

"She'll pay the going rate."

"But you don't understand, I have to get—"

"And she'll take the Iris Room." He picked up Barb's suitcase and headed up the stairs, leaving Jenny fuming in the foyer.

"Are you turning into an innkeeper instead of a writer?" Barb asked as they ascended the narrow staircase.

"No. I'm just humoring you so that you don't say something nasty to Jenny. The inn isn't even open."

"But you're staying here."

He briefly explained the situation, his broken ankle, the fact that the inn had once belonged to his family, and the deal he'd struck with Jenny and the Last Chance Book Club. He opened the door to the Iris Room.

"Oh, how beautiful," she said as she preceded him through the door.

"I'll let Jenny know you like it. I think it's a travesty. Granddad's probably spinning in his grave over the wallpaper. He used to have a deer head right there over the hearth." He put Barbara's suitcase on the floor by the bed.

"Gabe, you're babbling. How's it going, really? I need to have something to work with. You've already lost your slot for next September. That means you're missing the Halloween season, which is ideal for your book releases. I'm worried about you. You know how it is, out of sight, out of mind. You haven't had a new book in more than a year."

"I'm writing." He didn't elaborate. "And I'll write better and faster if you leave me alone."

"Absolutely not. I'm staying right here, and I want to read all the pages you've written so far. We'll work together as you write, and we'll get it done in half the time. I can easily manage things with my other authors from here for a while. Gabe, you're my star, and I'm not going to let you burn out." She cupped his cheek in her cool hand then raised up on tiptoes to give him another kiss.

He told himself that it was a good thing that she was here. She might actually help him salvage the ending of the book. She might also keep his mind off Jenny and help him convince his landlady that he was not the one for her. He felt nothing for Barb, except professional admiration. She could handle whatever the world dished out and not come away even slightly scratched. She was utterly heartless, infinitely shrewd, and wickedly smart. He didn't worry at all about breaking her heart, or even ruining their professional relationship.

So when Barb opened her mouth and added a little tongue to the kiss, he let her and tried to enjoy it. He also tried to feel not one iota of guilt when Jenny walked in carrying a stack of towels.

But he failed.

CHAPTER 15

Jenny didn't know what to do about Gabe's editor. It wasn't exactly legal for Barbara Ianelli to be staying at the inn, since Jenny had not yet had the fire department out to inspect and approve the building.

Not that she was out of compliance with fire codes. She had just installed smoke detectors and exit signs earlier that week. She had no doubt she'd pass inspection, but it wasn't legal to allow paying guests without that inspection certificate, and if anything should happen without that certificate, her insurance would be null and void.

She had spoken with Ross Gardiner, the fire chief, and was expecting his visit in a day or two. Now she'd have to talk with him about coming out sooner—like right now. And since Ross was the only paid member of the fire department, scheduling time might be difficult.

She headed into town, and God decided to smile on her because she found Ross hanging out with Matt Jasper and his new K-9 dog in the firehouse. She made arrangements for Ross to come out a day earlier. Then she swung by the day care center and dropped off her tasteless bran muffins for Saturday's bake sale. She didn't think they would be big sellers, and she promised herself that she'd stop trying to please Gabe with her baking skills. It was hopeless.

Her last stop was the BI-LO grocery store. If she was going to start taking in guests, she needed to stock up her pantry. And besides, in moments of high stress, cooking was Jenny's main way of coping. Tomorrow she'd make a big breakfast. Maybe an egg-and-cheese casserole. Although she was pretty sure that Mr. Health would bypass the eggs, and Ms. Skinny From New York probably didn't even eat breakfast.

She should let them starve. But she was not capable of allowing that to happen.

And besides, keeping busy was one way of stopping herself from throttling Mr. Raintree. The man seemed intent on taking over her life and her inn. She was tempted to tell him his furniture had to go, except that she actually liked his furniture more than she wanted to admit. And she kind of wanted to try out the piano.

But if she took his furniture, she had to take his editor, too. They had sort of arrived at the same moment, and in her mind, they were most definitely connected in some way that she couldn't quite explain.

She wanted to drop-kick Barbara Ianelli and her black designer suit right onto a patch of slimy red clay. But that would be unladylike. And ungrateful. And Mother, bless her heart, would be so ashamed of her if she let her emotions out like that.

But just for one moment, Jenny wanted to smash something up or let out a deep primal scream or otherwise express her pain.

She'd walked in on them kissing. And they seemed to be thoroughly enjoying each other's tonsils. She shouldn't have been surprised. This should not have hurt. Gabe had made things perfectly clear. He'd been kind the night of the china cabinet debacle, but that was all it was. Just kindness. And Jenny knew better than to mistake kindness for love.

Now she understood why he'd been keeping his distance. He was involved with someone else. And one look at Barbara and Jenny understood why. Why on earth would a man like Mr. Raintree look twice at a plain Jane like her when he could have someone like Barbara Ianelli?

She was being silly about the entire thing. Hadn't she decided that she was embracing the freedom of spinsterhood? In her liberated life, feeling jealous of another woman was a big waste of time and spirit.

By the time she pulled into the BI-LO's parking lot, she had brought her raging emotions under control. She was not going to be laughed at again. She was not going to be stupid again. She was going to be a self-sufficient innkeeper. That was her dream, and it was a good one.

She left her car and snagged a grocery cart and got two steps inside the front door before she came face-to-face with Lillian Bray, the blue-haired chairwoman of the Episcopalian Ladies' Auxiliary.

Lillian and a group of several other churchwomen, including Maybelle Radford, who was a member of the First Methodist choir and had been one of Mother's friends, had camped out right by the checkout counters. They were carrying hand-lettered oak-tag signs and having an argument with Floyd Eule, the store manager.

"Miz Lillian, you can picket and hand out flyers in the

parking lot until the cows come home, but you can't do that inside the store."

"But it's cold outside, Floyd. It's February."

Floyd didn't have the chance to respond because Maybelle interrupted. "Girls, look, it's Jenny. She's the one who can nip this in the bud right now."

Jenny suddenly found herself on the other end of Maybelle's rudely pointed finger. And then, before she could say Jack Robinson, she was surrounded by six large-bosomed churchwomen who shoved their homemade signs right in her face.

They all seemed to have the same message: "Good Christians!! Stop our library from leading our children into sin."

Lillian Bray pressed a black-and-white flyer into her hand. It had the same message in big type across the top with the subheading: "Boycott the Library fundraiser on February 15."

Below it was a badly reproduced image of *Black Water*'s cover and a photo of Mr. Raintree, obviously taken many years before, followed by a barely literate screed against the book and the devil worship it supposedly encouraged. The flyer concluded with a listing of Gabriel Raintree's so-called misdeeds—the same list of violent incidents that Nita had told her about a week ago.

"Jenny, that man you've opened your door to is a devil worshiper. You need to evict him." Lillian's double chins flapped as she shook her finger in Jenny's face.

Maybelle took up where Lillian left off. "Your mother would be so disappointed in you, reading those awful books and being a member of the Library Committee. Y'all can't be serious about using that man to promote contributions to the library. If this is what Nita Wills wants our children to read, it's just as well that the county wants to shut the library down." Maybelle's eyes gleamed with a feverish zeal that scared Jenny half to death.

Maybelle used to be a nice, quiet, reasonable woman, but ever since her husband left her, she'd gotten deeply fundamental. When she'd started a nasty rumor about Wilma Riley's sexual orientation, the entire sewing circle had voted to rescind her membership. Maybelle had become an ugly, troubled person.

Jenny straightened her spine. She wasn't about to kowtow to a bunch of zealots and hypocrites. "Mr. Raintree is not a devil worshiper. He's a writer," she said in as calm a voice as she could muster.

"I haven't seen him in church one time," Maybelle said.

"I don't think he's a Methodist."

"His family attended with us," Lillian said. "But I haven't seen him at our church either."

"I don't think he's a regular churchgoer. But that doesn't mean—"

"See, girls," Maybelle interrupted. "Jenny, I know you're a good Christian woman. But you've let that devil lead you astray. And if you want to know my thinking on this, there's a reason your china cabinet fell over when Pastor Tim was there."

Jenny's heart squeezed in her chest. Had the preacher said something to set this off? "Uh, Maybelle, the cabinet fell over because the floor was not level."

"Honey, I know your mother's china cabinet, and that piece of furniture is too heavy to just topple over. Either it was pushed by someone or there is another explanation."

"Like what?"

"Like Mr. Raintree wanted to keep a man of God out of that house where the two of you are living together without any chaperones."

"Uh, Maybelle, I'm thirty-six years old and a former schoolteacher. I am way beyond the need for a chaperone."

"You're living with that man, and you're not married to him."

"I'm an innkeeper. I'm going to be living with a lot of people."

"You should be married."

"Well, I'm not. Now, if you will excuse me, I have shopping to do."

"Maybe you would have a husband if you weren't so all-fired opinionated about everything. Jenny, men want sweet, obedient wives."

Jenny refrained from pointing out that Maybelle had spent thirty-five years being a sweet, obedient wife and her husband had cheated on her with his twenty-something secretary. In truth, Jenny felt sorry for Maybelle. She had substituted a zealous love of Jesus for the things she was missing in her life. She supposed it was nice that Jesus could give her comfort, but she doubted that Jesus would approve of what she was doing right this minute.

"I'm sorry, ladies. Gabriel Raintree is not a devil worshiper, or any such silly thing. Have you even read any of his books?"

"We don't have to," Lillian said, pointing her nose in the air.

There were times when living in a small town could be a royal pain in the backside. On at least half a dozen occasions during her teaching career at Davis High School, the good Christians of Allenberg County had tried to ban books, shut down sex education, and mess around with the science curricula. Thank Heaven, Davis High had a strong principled principal. And Jenny wasn't about to back down either.

"Ladies, you are mistaken. Mr. Raintree is a good, kind man. I've read a few of his books. They do have violence in them, but they all have optimistic endings. And his protagonists are all quite heroic. I think, perhaps, you should read *Black Water* before you judge it. Or if reading is too much for you, try watching the movie."

This speech did nothing to assuage the church ladies. They all started talking at the same time while Floyd tried to get them to leave the premises. Jenny attempted to wheel her cart around them, but the ladies continued to heckle her until Maybelle stepped over the line and took a swing at Jenny's head with her sign.

Luckily Maybelle missed, but the old lady lost her balance and fell down and injured herself. She started wailing like it was the end of the world. Jenny abandoned her cart and got down on her knees beside her mother's oldest friend.

"Maybelle, honey, where does it hurt?"

"My leg. I think I broke it," she sobbed, but she was moving the leg in question so Jenny relaxed a little bit. Maybelle had always been a drama queen.

"Honey, just keep still now," Jenny said as she looked up at Floyd, whose face had gone pale as a sheet. "Floyd's calling nine-one-one."

He swallowed hard, pulled his cell from his pocket, and called in the EMTs. When he was done, he turned to the circle of ladies and started yelling at them. "Y'all are crazy. See what happens when you start acting ugly? I've read those books you want to ban, and they're entertaining. There isn't anything in there that would encourage anyone to practice devil worship."

He might have continued yelling, but the Allenberg County Sheriff arrived on the scene, apparently called earlier by one of the other shoppers, who knew that if there was any soul on earth capable of imposing order on chaos, it was Sheriff Stone Rhodes.

Fifteen minutes later, Maybelle had been whisked off to the clinic with what appeared to be a contusion on her thigh and not much more. The rest of the protesting ladies had been threatened with jail time unless they took their protest out into the parking lot. That pretty much took the wind right out of their sails because it was now overcast outside, and it looked like it might rain.

They departed, much chastened, and Jenny found herself alone with the sheriff.

She handed him the flyer that Maybelle had given her. "Stone, I heard about some of this stuff from Nita, herself. She's concerned. And now I am. Is there any truth to this stuff about Mr. Raintree being arrested?"

He gazed down at the piece of paper. "I don't know, but I can find out. Has he been giving you any problems?"

She shook her head. "No, not at all. He's..." She couldn't finish the sentence because her eyes suddenly filled with tears.

The sheriff gave her shoulder a little squeeze. "It's all right, Jenny. What happened here was ugly, and I'm going to have a little chat with the pastors of the various churches in town. I don't like stuff like this happening here, and I dislike the fact that this was probably drummed up by a few outsiders intent on stirring up trouble."

"Outsiders?"

He nodded. "Dennis Hayden hired a political hack from up north to run his congressional campaign. And Dennis isn't above trying to make Nita look bad for this library effort. Remember that Nita is Mayor LaFlore's mother and Kamaria is thinking about running herself."

"That's despicable."

"Well, I don't know for certain. But I wouldn't be surprised if what's in this paper is a pack of lies designed to make Nita look bad, and by extension to smear Mayor LaFlore."

Jenny shook her head. "I'm really sorry to hear that. But I do hope that this stuff about Mr. Raintree isn't true. He's a good man. I mean, well, he's quiet and kind of reclusive and...But he's not evil, no matter what he writes about."

"I'm sure that's the case. So don't worry. I'll get back to you."

Gabe left Barb in her room, swearing like a sailor about the lack of cell phone and WiFi connection. In the face of this lack of connectivity, she was planning to drive up to Orangeburg for a few hours. While she was there, she also planned to buy a printer so she could read his pages as they were written.

He hoped the computer stores in Orangeburg were completely sold out of printers. And he thanked the swamp gods for making cell phone coverage so difficult. Barb wouldn't last more than two days out here.

Such was the beauty of living in the swamp, like Shrek.

Unfortunately, Barb didn't actually see the beauty of the swamp. She'd suggested no less than five times that

Gabe would do better renting a room at the Plaza Hotel in New York City, where he could write to his heart's content and email his pages on a daily basis, after which they could discuss them over dinner at a place that didn't chicken-fry steaks.

Barbara, it turned out, wasn't a big fan of hush puppies, corn bread, or okra, either.

But of course, Gabe couldn't leave. He doubted that the ghost could travel with him to New York. And he definitely needed the ghost's help with the book.

He retreated to Luke's bedroom, where it remained many degrees colder than any other spot in the house. He pulled on his sweatshirt, and a pair of fingerless gloves, and sat down at his laptop to read what the ghost had done to his pages today.

But he had a hard time concentrating. Jenny had left the house in something of a huff. He ought to be happy about that. But he wasn't. Whenever she left, the house felt empty, the air heavy and cold. He knew it was insane, but the house seemed to miss her when she was gone. Or maybe it was just Luke missing her.

"Do you have a jones for her, too?" he asked aloud. But of course the ghost never spoke to him directly.

Yeah, well, by the frigid air in this room, he had to believe that the ghost had a thing for Jenny. But neither one of them was going to pursue it. It didn't matter how many bran muffins she baked for him. He was going to refuse them. And he wasn't going to break down and tell her the reason. She didn't need to know, because she was merely his landlady.

Besides, he didn't like baring his weaknesses to people because he hated being pitied. And he could almost imagine the pity on Jenny's face when she discovered the truth. It was hard enough knowing that she was genuinely worried about him. He wasn't used to that. And her concern was seductive as hell.

He sat there in front of his computer screen brooding for more than an hour. Only the sound of Zeph opening the back door and heading off to the dining room pulled him out of his funk. Bear stood up from the place at his feet and crossed to the door. Zeph's arrival meant it was time to take a break, let Bear out, and make a sandwich.

After a short walk, he made himself a turkey sandwich and headed into the dining room, where Zeph was applying the final coat of varnish on the dining room table. It was amazing how he had managed to match the color of the undamaged wood.

Gabe leaned his shoulder into the doorway. "I never knew you had a talent for carpentry," he said, then took a bite of his lunch.

"I reckon not."

"I only remember you taking us out hunting." He spoke with his mouth half full.

Zeph said nothing. Gabe took another bite, chewed, and swallowed.

"I remember you weeding the garden. You were doing that the day Luke died."

Zeph quit applying the varnish and looked up at him. "I thought you didn't remember anything about that day."

Gabe shrugged. "I remember Granddad wanted Luke to turn off the video game and practice with his new gun. I remember watching y'all leave, and then getting my BB gun and tagging along after you. That's it."

"You're lucky, then. Don't go looking for sorrow, son."

"It seems to me that sorrow finds me even when I'm not looking. I need to know what happened."

"No, you don't. Trust me on this. You don't."

"Granddad said you were responsible. Did you shoot my brother? Is that what I can't remember?"

"Not intentionally." Zeph's words came out slow and careful as if he'd rehearsed them, and his eyes tracked to the left, a clear tell that he was lying.

"You're not telling the truth."

The old man shrugged and went back to applying varnish as if they'd been speaking about the weather and not the central mystery of Gabe's life.

"I need the truth."

And he did, for his book's sake. He wasn't stupid. He knew the ghost was making him write stuff that was intensely personal. And the ending of the story was heading toward a terrifying place that Gabe didn't want to go. But he had to go there. And it might be helpful if he knew what he had to face before it happened.

He stood there munching his sandwich while the old man painted until he couldn't stand Zeph's silence for another instant. "Zeph, did you hear me? I need the truth."

"All right, son, if you want the truth, here it is: I shot your brother right through the heart. He died instantly, and you saw it happen."

Gabe stared at Zeph. This time the old man's eyes hadn't tracked to the left, and his voice had gotten kind of cold and hard. He might be telling the truth. "But why?"

Zeph closed his eyes and took a deep breath. "I don't know why it happened. It was an accident. Son, you know this. I'm sure your granddaddy told you this."

Yes, he'd been told this story dozens of times. But it

never pierced that haze of amnesia that he carried around with him. Surely if this story were true, he'd remember something. Wouldn't he? "Why can't I remember?"

"Because watching your brother die wasn't pleasant. And you don't want to remember." Zeph turned back to brushing on varnish.

Gabe wasn't satisfied. Something didn't add up, and he couldn't put his finger on it. But before he could open his mouth, a car came up the gravel drive, its tires crunching. He walked down the hall to the front windows and looked out.

It was Jenny. And damned if it didn't feel like the house let go of a big sigh, as if it had been holding its breath, waiting for her return.

The Jonquil House wasn't the only one who felt that way.

Mr. Raintree and his editor had a shouting fight in the early afternoon. They each sulked in their rooms for about an hour, and then Ms. Ianelli came down to Mr. Raintree's room and apologized. They made up. She kissed him again. He seemed to enjoy it. And then they left the house around six-thirty with plans to have dinner at the Red Hot Pig Place.

Jenny had to hold her tongue when she saw the silk ensemble Ms. Ianelli wore. Boy, she was going to be in for a big surprise when she realized that they didn't use cloth napkins at the barbecue joint.

Jenny ate a salad for dinner, and then she wandered into the living room, drawn there by the piano. She opened the bench seat and was delighted to find sheet music. She found a book with easy practice pieces and sat down to refresh her memory.

The piano was slightly out of tune, but that didn't

diminish the joy she felt in moving her hands across the keys. Once, a long time ago, she had practiced regularly on Granny's piano. Mother had insisted that she learn hymns, but whenever she wasn't around, Grandpa would wink and hand her sheet music with old-time songs, like "Bicycle Built for Two." Gramps loved old songs like that. He used to whistle them when he worked his fields and the orchard.

She missed him with all her heart. And Granny, too. And even Mother, who had spent her whole life judging Jenny and finding her wanting. She was used to being alone, but sometimes it was hard not to feel lonely. Like right now. She'd gotten used to having people in the house with her, so when it was empty, she seemed to know it down in her bones.

She practiced for a long while and had almost lost herself in the music when Bear headed to the front door and started barking. A moment later, her doorbell rang. She checked her watch. It was almost eight o'clock, and her doorbell had been more than busy enough for one day.

She peered through the spy hole and was shocked to find Reverend Lake standing on her porch wearing a camel-hair coat and looking solemn and as handsome as ever.

"Hush, Bear," she said, but the dog refused to be quiet. Where was Mr. Raintree when you needed him?

"Just a minute," she called through the door and hauled the disobedient dog down the hall to the back bedroom. She shut the dog up, surprised to discover that the baseboard heating in the back room was on the fritz again. Mr. Raintree hadn't said one word about it. She closed the door behind her and noticed that Mr. Raintree's sticky note had fallen to the floor. She picked it up and pressed it to the door where it managed to stick, its edges curling.

She made a mental note that her guests would be needing "Do Not Disturb" doorknob hangers as she headed back down the hall and opened the door.

The preacher strode into the house like he owned the place, and for some reason, this bothered Jenny a great deal.

"What brings you to the swamp this evening?" she asked as she took his coat and hung it on the bentwood coat rack that stood in the foyer.

He pulled a piece of paper from his suit jacket and handed it to her. "I trust you've seen this?"

It was another one of those nasty flyers that Lillian and Maybelle had been handing out at the BI-LO.

"I have."

"Sheriff Rhodes came by to see me today. He told me about what happened at the store, and he practically demanded that I preach something from the pulpit this Sunday about tolerance. I can't tell you how deeply upset I was by this. I don't let anyone tell me what to preach, and in this instance, I can't preach tolerance, Jenny. I won't be goaded into doing the devil's work. You understand this, don't you?"

"Preaching tolerance is the devil's work?"

"You know good and well that's not what I mean. I'm happy to preach tolerance and kindness, but this is an altogether different situation. Your so-called guest is a threat to this community. Sheriff Rhodes is not a regular churchgoing man, so I don't expect him to see it the way I do. The way you should."

"How should I see this situation?"

"Goodness, you were there the night the china cabinet fell. You know what happened. It wasn't an accident. You didn't throw that chicken on purpose. You saw the claw marks on your wall. Gabriel Raintree was responsible for that with all that filth he writes."

"Uh, I hate to contradict you, but the china cabinet was aimed at Mr. Raintree's head. If I hadn't pushed him out of the way, he would have been seriously hurt. So, given that fact, how do I know that he's responsible? It could just as soon have been me hurling things around. Or maybe it was you."

"Jenny, your sarcasm is not appreciated."

She sucked in a deep breath and reached for calm. Mother would be so ashamed of her for speaking that way to a minister of God. But he was sanctimonious in the extreme. And it didn't matter how handsome he was on the outside. The stuff on the inside wasn't pretty at all.

"I think you should go," Jenny said.

He didn't budge. "Jenny, I fear we've gotten off on the wrong foot. We both know you have a demon here, and I want to help—"

He never finished his sentence because the demon, who seemed mostly benign except when Pastor Tim showed up, chose that moment to tip over the bentwood coat rack and send it, and the pastor's coat, toward Reverend Lake.

The preacher screamed and assumed a defensive position. The coat rack missed by a mile but his coat ended up draped over his head. He cowered there for the longest moment, before peeking out from under the camel hair and looking around like he was expecting the ceiling to fall or something. It was slightly comical, and Jenny had to suppress a laugh.

"Reverend Lake, I think the ghost of Jonquil House is letting you know that he would like you to leave."

"Ghost?" He straightened but didn't put on his coat.

"Yes, we have a ghost, not a demon."

"Jenny, I don't mean to be disrespectful, but I don't think you are qualified to know the difference. We need to schedule an exorcism right—"

The preacher couldn't finish that sentence either because he stumbled backward toward the door, which opened, even though it had been closed against the winter cold outside. He stumbled over the threshold and tripped, landing flat on his back on the front porch.

Jenny finally let go of big sigh and looked up at the ceiling. "Ghost, you need to stop acting out, now. The minister is well intentioned, and you might think about letting us know what you need so that you can cross over to the other side."

By this time, the preacher's eyes had grown as big as saucers. He scrambled to his feet. "You!" he said as if that meant something.

"Me?"

"You're the evil one." And with that, he turned and fled like a rabbit with a fox on his little white tail.

CHAPTER 16

Mozart's *Eine Kleine Nachtmusik* being played on an out-of-tune piano was audible from The Jonquil House's front porch. The music brought a smile to Gabe's lips, even though Jenny was playing the piece rather badly.

"Oh, my God," Barbara said in a loud, obnoxious voice as they entered the foyer. "Are we required to sit in the living room and endure recitals from your mousy landlady? Really, Gabe, in my opinion innkeepers should be neither seen nor heard. I mean, I want my linens clean and my coffee hot, but beyond that they have no other entertainment value."

Gabe had no doubt that Jenny had heard Barbara's unkind comment, because his editor had a loud, throaty, New York kind of voice. And she was forever expressing her opinions on everything.

The piano stopped in mid-arpeggio, and a moment later Gabe heard the hinges on the piano bench squeal as Jenny put away the score she'd been playing. He was helping Barbara out of her black cashmere coat when

Jenny wandered into the foyer, looking pale as a sheet of untouched paper. She was dressed as usual in a white turtleneck, her little blue cardigan, and a pair of baggy corduroys.

"There's coffee in the kitchen, and I put out some chocolate chip cookies in case you wanted a little after-dinner treat. I hope you don't mind my playing the piano. I know I play badly, but I haven't touched any piano keys in a good ten years."

"Maybe you should continue to avoid them," Barbara said before Gabe could tell Jenny that he'd brought the piano so that someone would play it. It had been sitting untouched for longer than he cared to admit.

And then Barbara continued in her clueless, rude fashion, "Jenny, I would love some coffee and cookies. Gabe and I are going to sit down and discuss his book, so bring them to the living room."

Barbara had obviously not gotten the message that this was a bed-and-*breakfast*.

And Jenny would have been entirely justified to tell her to go the kitchen and get the cookies for herself, but she didn't do that. She behaved just like the sweet, generous, hospitable southern woman that Gabe knew her to be. She turned and headed down the hall to the kitchen as if it were her job to serve Barb.

"Jenny, don't bother," Gabe said as he followed her down the hall. "I'll get the coffee and cookies."

Jenny didn't stop. He wasn't surprised. But he wasn't about to let her wait on him, either. In truth, he'd been putting Barb off all evening, and the last thing he wanted to discuss was his book.

When he got to the kitchen, Jenny was reaching into a

cabinet for a couple of coffee mugs. Her back was toward him. "You don't have to wait on us," he said.

She turned, mugs in hand. "Oh, it's all right."

He stepped farther into the room. "No, it's not. Let me do it."

"No, it's all right. I don't wish to disturb your book discussion with your editor."

"I wish you would. Have you played the piano all evening?"

She looked down, her face pale as the moon. "A little. I hope you don't mind."

"I don't."

"I play badly."

"You play better than I do. Are you all right? You look very pale tonight. You aren't coming down with something, are you?"

"No. I'm fine." She didn't look up.

"What's the matter? Has something happened?"

She looked up then, her eyes bright behind those big eyeglasses. "No. At least not something terribly important."

He knew she was lying. "What is it?"

"Nothing. You should go. Ms. Ianelli is waiting for you. I'll bring a tray with coffee and cookies."

"I don't want any cookies. What the hell is the matter, Jenny? You didn't let Barb's obnoxious comments bother you, did you? Because you don't have to listen to her endless opinions. Heck, I don't even listen to them, and she's paid to pass judgment on my work."

Jenny shrugged her shoulders in a gesture that was the opposite of nonchalance. She would not look him in the eye.

"Tell me, Jenny. You look depressed. What is it?"

"Nothing," she said with an emphatic shake of her head. She continued to stare off into space. "I'm not the least depressed."

But she was. And he knew why. He'd caused that look in her eyes, and he hated himself for it. It was easy to say that she'd be better off staying clear of him, but it was much, much harder to actually accomplish. He wanted to gather her up into his arms and hold her the way he'd done the night of her disastrous dinner party. He wanted another kiss. But a kiss was forbidden, for her sake. Of course, she didn't know that.

He took a step forward. "Look at me, Jenny." It was a command.

She looked up.

"You've got tears in your eyes. Why?"

She shook her head and put the mugs down on the counter with more force than was necessary. "I do not, Mr. Raintree. I'm not one of those weepy females, no matter what kind of impression I gave the other night when the china cabinet went flying. Please, help yourself to the coffee. I hope you enjoy my cookies. I'm going to bed."

She turned and fled the kitchen. He heard her steps sounding up the stairs, and he longed to follow after her.

But he didn't.

Jenny had another restless night filled with the same dream of canoeing on the Edisto and not making any headway against the vicious current. The house seemed as restless as her dreams. Perhaps the ghost knew that he'd bitten off more than he could chew with Reverend Lake. Jenny had no doubt that the preacher would be back, probably with buckets of holy water and crosses and hymns and prayers and whatever else one needed to exorcise a ghost.

Jenny wondered what the altar guild would think about this. She wondered what all the matchmakers in town would say. She didn't have to stretch her imagination. She *knew* they'd tell her that she'd blown another great chance with a handsome man. They'd say she was crazy to choose a ghost over a living, breathing guy.

But like Mrs. Muir in that old-time movie, she was ready to choose her ghost over the preacher. Of course, it wasn't exactly the ghost that she wanted, but that was her big secret. It was worth being humiliated by a ghost and a preacher just to make sure that no one discovered she was having hot flashes over Gabriel Raintree—a man who was entirely out of her league. He was rich. He was the grandson of a governor. He was a celebrity. And he obviously belonged to someone else.

To make it worse, Barbara Ianelli was beautiful and powerful, with great hair and a designer wardrobe. She also needed a personality transplant, but most men wouldn't even notice that. Gabe had probably learned to look beyond his editor's inner imperfections since he'd been working with her for so many years. And he obviously enjoyed kissing her.

Jenny brooded about that for hours while she tossed and turned. Finally, at about two in the morning, she gave up on the idea of sleeping. Her stomach was rumbling, and she needed a snack. And since she was up, she might as well do something useful, like getting a jump on breakfast. It took a while to make an egg-and-cheese casserole. And she could make some biscuits to go with it, too.

She didn't bother getting dressed. She padded downstairs in her fuzzy slippers and flannel PJs. She went into the kitchen and hit the light switch.

And screamed.

The moment Jenny screamed, Bear started barking like the house was on fire. There was no mistaking the absolute terror in that sound. Gabe bolted upright, immediately awake and alert.

He was out of his bed in a nanosecond and limping across the hallway as fast as his bad leg would allow him. He didn't take the time to put on his ankle brace. Or his clothes. He snagged a robe off the back of his door, and that was his one concession to modesty.

Bear beat him across the hall, only to be intercepted by Jenny who stood at the kitchen's threshold. She grabbed the dog's collar and yanked him back. "No, no, no, Bear, stay here. You can't go in the kitchen." Jenny's voice sounded strained.

Gabe hurried up behind her and took control of the dog's collar. "Sit," he ordered the dog, and he obeyed. "What is it?"

Jenny turned away from the kitchen and pressed her head against his chest. "It's horrible." He wrapped his left arm around her. His right hand still held the dog in place. Bear may have stopped barking, but he was still whining and agitated.

Gabe pressed Jenny's head into his chest as he simultaneously looked through the open archway to the kitchen.

The scene was horrific and eerily familiar because it had been ripped right from the pages of *Black Water*. A beheaded chicken, with all its feathers attached, sat on the counter, where it had been left to bleed. The meat cleaver that had done the deed sat right beside the bird in a pool of blood that had been there long enough to turn brown. Blood had dripped down the counter and onto the floor, leaving rusty trails. On the far wall, someone had used the blood to write a litany of foul words on every single one of Jenny's beautiful new cabinets.

The psychopathic killer in *Black Water* had done the exact same thing to the people living in the vacation house. The dead chicken had been his character's opening gambit—a sick, twisted curse his killer had conjured up for the purpose of terrorizing his victims.

Gabe pulled Jenny and Bear across the hall into his bedroom, where he shut the door. With the door closed and the dog safe, Gabe was free to use both arms to draw Jenny tight to his chest. She clutched the lapels of his robe.

"It's all right," he whispered into her ear, deeply conscious of the soft brush of her hair against his cheek. She was trembling all over, and he couldn't decide if she was cold or just scared to death. He choked back his fury and pressed her tighter to his chest. "Hush now. That was aimed at me, not you." He closed his eyes and inhaled her. She smelled like lavender.

He gave himself permission to hold her for a minute before he pushed her back at arm's length. Then he shucked out of his robe, leaving him standing there clad only in his boxers. He draped the robe around her shoulders. "Here, take my robe and go sit by the fire, it's the only heat that seems to work in this room." He gestured toward the old recliner he'd rescued from the moving men and placed near the hearth.

She didn't follow his command. Instead, she stood

right before him, her gaze traveling up his body, taking in his boxers and naked chest. What the baseboard heating failed to achieve in the back bedroom, Jenny managed just with her look. It seared him. It branded him. He needed to turn away before he embarrassed himself.

But she snared him before he could escape. She grabbed his right hand in both of hers, and her touch was as warm as the room was cold. Her eyes were liquid and kind behind the lenses of her glasses. He wanted to remove those frames and kiss her all over. Truly he had lost his mind.

So when she kissed his palm, his willpower broke. He pulled her closer, his left hand sliding down to the small of her back so he could draw her up along the length of his suddenly aroused body. He lowered his head and kissed her the way he'd been thinking about for days.

She opened for him, like the petals of a sweet flower. Her mouth responsive, her tongue dancing with his in a pattern that seemed familiar, as if she knew what he wanted, just as he instinctively knew how to please her. He devoured her and lost all sense of time and place and urgency, until she snaked her warm hands under the waistband of his boxers and cupped his ass.

That brazen exploration ignited a river of lust, but it also surprised the crap out of him.

This was Jenny. Not some groupie he picked up in some bar. This was sweet, tempting Jenny, who was unworldly and naive and cloistered. He might want to carry her across the room to his bed and lay down with her, but she deserved so much more.

And besides, he couldn't ignore the warning someone had left in her kitchen.

So he reluctantly lifted his head and set her back at arm's length. "I'm sorry," he said in a gruff voice. "I shouldn't have done that."

Jenny wanted to howl at him. She wanted to use some of the words that were painted on her kitchen cabinets. How could he just stop like that when it was just beginning to get interesting?

She was too confused to muster any words to hurl at him, though. She simply stood there feeling hot and cold and angry and frightened and aroused.

He turned away from her, hiding the obvious manifestation of his own arousal. He scooped up a pair of jeans lying on the floor and stepped into them, quickly adjusting himself and zipping his fly. His Harvard sweatshirt was similarly discovered in a heap by the bed and pulled on, hiding that beautiful expanse of chest that she'd not really had a chance to explore.

When he'd clothed himself he turned back to her.

"We should call the police."

His voice sounded low and gruff and filled with emotions she had no idea how to read. It took a moment before the content of his words registered in her fevered brain. The words edged their way past the lust and the anger and reminded her of what had instigated this moment of unguarded passion.

She let go of her anger, but releasing the pent-up desire was going to take a long, long time. She took a deep breath and blew it out, trying to find some shred of rationality.

"You stay here. I'll make the call and wait on the porch," he said. "Sit by the fire."

The reality of what had happened to her kitchen returned,

along with everything else that had occurred yesterday. "No," she said, before he could leave the room, "we can't call the police. I mean, if this gets out, it will create a huge sensation in the town that I'll never hear the end of. It will feed right in to the nastiness the church ladies have been spewing about you and your books."

"What? What nastiness? What church ladies?"

She wrapped his robe more tightly around her, like an embrace. "I didn't have a chance to tell you about this last night because you seemed to be otherwise engaged, but a couple of the more pious women in town—the ones who are always telling the rest of us how to live our lives— have mounted a boycott of the library program because they think your books aren't Christian."

"Oh boy, here we go."

"This has happened before?"

"My books are banned in dozens of high schools across the country. I'm not surprised that there are people here who think they're too violent. But what does that have to do with calling the police? Your house was broken into and vandalized, Jenny."

"Well, for starters, the church ladies could be the guilty parties."

"Sweetie, church ladies do not stage fake Hoodoo curses in people's kitchens."

"You've got a point." His scent escaped from the fabric of his robe. It clouded her mind a little. She had to fight the urge to run across the room and take up where they'd left off. But she didn't have the courage to do it. She'd already been rejected once. She wasn't going to be rejected twice, even if she was sure that, for a moment, he'd actually enjoyed the kiss, too.

"The church ladies might take advantage of what happened," she said. "And Reverend Lake might make a big deal out of this, especially after what happened last night."

"Something happened last night?"

"I had a little confrontation with the church ladies at the BI-LO in the morning. And Sheriff Rhodes read everyone the riot act. Then he apparently took it upon himself to visit the clergy in the county in an effort to head off any further problems. Reverend Lake took exception to the sheriff's meddling.

"So the preacher came by last night to tell me that he had no intention of downplaying community concerns about you and your books. He said it was because he knew The Jonquil House was infested with demons, and he was sure that you were the source of the trouble. He insisted that I let him perform an exorcism. And I'm afraid that when he got to that part, the ghost kicked him out on his backside."

"The ghost kicked him out?"

She nodded. "The ghost threw the coatrack at him and pushed him out the door. I'm afraid that the preacher believes I may be the source of the demonic infestation. Honestly, Gabe, we need to find a way to send the ghost into the light."

"And you didn't think that was important to tell me last night when I got back from dinner?"

She shrugged. "I'm sorry. I probably should have, but you were involved." She took a big breath. "So you see, we can't call Sheriff Rhodes. Because if we do, everyone in town is going to know what happened. And since the church ladies have been running around saying that you're in league with the devil . . . Oh, my God, this could get out of hand in the blink of an eye. And it would kill my business."

"I'm not worried about your business. I'm worried about your safety."

He was worried about her? Those words hit her chest and rattled around inside. She wanted to believe that his concern was a sign of something important. And maybe if it weren't for his editor upstairs, and the fact that Jenny had a history of mistaking kindness for something else, she might have let her emotions soar. But instead she hardened her heart. She mentally pulled on her armor and reminded herself that there was freedom and security in being alone.

"I'm trying to figure out how the perpetrator got into the house," he continued. "I checked the locks before I went to bed. The doors were secure. Who has keys?"

"As far as I know, only you, me, and Ms. Ianelli. Oh, and I gave Zeph a set."

"Zeph has keys?"

"You think he would do something like this?"

"He killed my brother."

His voice sounded flat and angry and wounded. The minute the words left his mouth, the temperature in the room plummeted, as if the ghost, himself, were trying to show his agreement.

"I always heard that your brother's death was an accident. Are you suggesting something else?"

Gabe started pacing the room. All that pent-up male energy made him look like a tiger prowling back and forth. "No. I think it was an accident, but I don't know."

"I thought you were there when it happened."

"I was. But I don't remember. And it's eating at me. It's been eating away at me for a long, long time. I think that's why the villain in *Black Water* is so much like Zeph. But it would be crazy for Zeph to stage something like that. Wouldn't it? I mean what would be the purpose of that? To get me back for turning him into a villain in one of my books? And why would he attack your kitchen in order to get to me?"

"He wouldn't. And neither would your editor." She paused for a moment, thinking. "I guess the ghost could have done it. But why?"

"No, not the ghost."

"You seem so sure."

"First of all, that scene in the kitchen doesn't look like the kind of thing a ghost *could* do. And second, if the ghost *is* my brother, then he would never ever harm a living creature, even a chicken."

"The only people left are you and me. Do you think I staged that?"

"Do you think I did?"

They simultaneously shook their heads.

"Then we have to conclude that someone got hold of your keys or picked the lock. You don't have dead bolts. I told you a few weeks ago that you needed them. First thing tomorrow, I want you to change all the locks again and upgrade to dead bolts."

"How would someone—"

"It can be done, Jenny."

"But this is Last Chance, South Carolina. Most folks don't even lock their doors at night here."

"Well, as of tonight, you aren't most folks."

CHAPTER 17

Gabe won the day, and the police were called. And since The Jonquil House was technically beyond the jurisdiction of the tiny Last Chance Police Department, the county dispatcher sent a deputy sheriff, who took one look at Jenny's kitchen and immediately called in the sheriff himself, even though it was almost four in the morning by that time.

The sheriff called in the crime scene people, who took control of Jenny's kitchen and showed no signs of being ready to give it back.

Ms. Ianelli had come downstairs at about seven o'clock, having slept through all the excitement. (Apparently, living in the big city had made her completely oblivious to barking dogs and legions of law enforcement. But the sight of blood definitely undid her.)

She pitched a full-out conniption fit and demanded a refund of her money, as if Jenny even cared about that at a moment like this. Of course, Gabe was completely solicitous of her, calming her down and then taking her out to breakfast somewhere far away from Last Chance, where, no doubt, people were beginning to wake up to the news.

Jenny stayed at the house. She had no desire to be a fifth wheel at breakfast, and besides the sheriff wanted her there even though she'd already answered dozens of questions. At around eight, someone brought in a carton filled with Styrofoam coffee cups from the doughnut shop. She sat in the living room, still wrapped in Gabe's robe, and sipped away at the warn drink. The coffee seemed to be melting her a little bit.

At eight-thirty, the crime scene people departed along with everyone except Sheriff Rhodes, who sat down beside her on Gabe's beautiful and comfortable leather sofa.

"There are a few things you should know," he said.

She looked up at him. His green eyes were as sober as the black coffee in her cup.

"The chicken wasn't killed on the scene."

"How can you tell?"

"Because there was an incident yesterday at the chicken processing plant. Someone pulled the fire alarm and stopped the processing line. There was a general evacuation, and the fire department was called, but there wasn't any fire. When they restarted the line, they discovered that a couple of chickens had been taken. We figured it was a prank. You'd be surprised how many times people try to steal dead chickens."

"Really?"

"It's like cow tipping. It happens all the time. In this instance, the chickens were taken after they'd been bled but before they'd been plucked."

"So the blood in the kitchen didn't come from the chicken?"

"Not unless it was a pretty amazing chicken. There was way too much of it for one bird, and the crime scene guys are pretty sure it's not even chicken blood. They're thinking it's pig blood, which is easy to come by considering how many people around here raise and slaughter hogs."

"So it would have been possible for someone to stage all that without making a lot of noise, huh?"

"I reckon. It's still amazing that it could be done with people and a dog in the house."

She looked away, through the windows at the front of the house. It looked like it was going to be a bright, sunny day. "Sheriff, do you have any ideas?"

"My first thought is that whoever did this had to have keys to the house. So I guess that makes you a suspect as much as your guests."

"And Zeph Gibbs."

"And Zeph." He paused for a moment. "Can you think of any reason why Zeph would do such a thing?"

"Not really. But I think there is some trouble between him and Mr. Raintree. Mr. Raintree thinks Zeph is responsible for his brother's death. And I guess he expressed his thoughts by making the villain in *Black Water* a lot like Zeph. But I don't know, Zeph is a little strange and different, but I just don't see him doing something like this. The only real reason I have my doubts is that Bear wouldn't have raised the alarm if Zeph came into the house, but he probably would have barked if it had been a stranger."

"Even if he was shut up in Mr. Raintree's room?"

"I don't know. Maybe not."

She drew in a deep breath and let it out. "Stone, this is going to cause big problems in town, you know."

He reached over and patted her knee. "I know it is. But

we'll get to the bottom of it. Oh, and by the way, I did a little fact checking on that flyer the ladies were handing out at the BI-LO yesterday. What's in it is halfway true."

"Gabe—I mean Mr. Raintree—was arrested?"

"Yes, he was arrested in Los Angeles, and then he was immediately released without any charges being brought. It was apparently some kind of domestic dispute."

"Domestic dispute?"

"All of the public altercations were domestic in nature. But no arrests or charges were ever made. That's all I know. But I think you need to be careful. Zeph isn't the only person on my short list."

"Are you saying Mr. Raintree may have staged this for some purpose? I don't believe that for a second."

"Maybe he's trying to scare you into selling him back the house. Have you thought of that?"

"No. Stone, he was writing all day yesterday. When would he have had time to go to the chicken plant and steal dead chickens?"

"You don't know that he was here all day. Seems to me you were in town in the morning, and the incident at Country Pride Chicken took place at about the same time you were having your run-in with Lillian Bray. Which, by the way, eliminates you from my short list of suspects."

She shook her head. "He didn't do this."

"Jenny, be careful, please." The sober look in Sheriff Rhodes's eyes was compelling. Stone Rhodes was an excellent lawman. She ought to listen to him, especially since the scene in the kitchen had resulted in another scene of an entirely different nature in Mr. Raintree's bedroom. She had to admit that, while her heart was telling her that Gabe was a good and honest man, her head was saying something else entirely. She had to be cautious around him for so many different reasons.

"I will be careful."

"Then you'll think about moving back to town, until I can figure out what's going on? I'm not comfortable with you living out here by yourself with only Gabe Raintree and Zeph Gibbs for company."

"But I'm not here alone. Gabe's editor is here now." And she had the ghost, but she wasn't about to tell the sheriff about that. He would probably rethink taking her off his short list.

"I don't think that New York woman is going to stay very long. I'd feel better if you moved back into town with Maryanne."

At that moment, Maryanne herself came barreling through the unlocked front door, toting Josh on her hip. "Oh, my God, are you all right? I just heard what happened. Why didn't you call me? Pack your things, I'm not letting you stay here another night until the police figure out what's going on. Ruby says she's got a roll-away bed that you can use, and she told me that she'd tan my hide if I didn't bring you back to town right this minute."

Sheriff Rhodes cracked the smallest of smiles. "Jenny, you don't want to mess around with my momma. She'll send all of her friends—and she has more friends in this town than just about anyone except maybe my brother— and those women will drag you back to the Cut 'n Curl kicking and screaming if they have to. Go stay there a couple of nights. And in the meantime, I'll beef up the nightly patrol out here. It won't be forever. I aim to find out who did this to you and put them behind bars, you hear? Oh, and change your locks. You need dead bolts."

• • •

Jenny didn't want to leave The Jonquil House. But when Sabina showed up, followed shortly thereafter by Wilma, Elsie, Lola May, and Nita Wills herself, she knew she was going to have to leave her home. Every single one of them was ready to blame Gabe for what had happened, especially since the vandalism had been pulled right from the pages of one of his books.

They all wanted to talk at the same time so she put every single one of them to work, helping her clean up the crime scene, walk the dog, and entertain Joshua. Nita was the last one to arrive. She came storming in the back door, the picture of outrage.

"Jenny," she announced to all assembled, "we're canceling the library event. I'm not going to give *that man* a platform."

Jenny looked up from the floor where she was trying to get chicken or hog's blood out from the grout between her beautiful floor tiles. "By *that man* I assume you mean Gabe Raintree."

"I do. It's clear he's trying to get you to sell out."

"No, it's not at all clear." Jenny stood up. "Gabe didn't do this. And more important, if you cancel the event, the people who want to shut down our library and ban Gabe's books win the day. Is that what you want?"

"No."

"Okay, then. If you ask me, this incident looks more like something the church ladies might have staged—or the political hacks who want to make you and the mayor look bad."

Nita stood there for a moment, clearly thinking things through. "You think that's possible? I mean Lillian Bray might be a narrow-minded woman, but I don't see her doing something like this."

"I don't either, but Sheriff Rhodes told me that Dennis Hayden has hired some outside political people. I could see them doing this. And the sheriff said that my locks were probably easy to pick."

"We should still cancel. I don't want you to be in danger."

"No, Nita. We are *not* canceling. I'm going to stay in town for a few days. I'll be fine."

"You really think Dennis Hayden might be behind this?"

"I do."

"Good Lord. I need to tell Kamaria about this." Nita turned on her heel and marched out of the door in the same hot hurry as she'd marched in.

Jenny sagged back against the counter, and Wilma gave her a little shoulder squeeze. "You're turning into quite a brave woman. I'm proud of you. I don't much like Mr. Raintree, but I like the way you're standing up for him and standing against those holy rollers. But you should do it from a distance, you hear?"

"Amen to that," said Lola May, putting away the mop. She gave the kitchen a once-over. "I think we've got the place almost back to rights. You'll need to get some industrial cleaner for that grout, but aside from that it doesn't look like anything bad happened here."

"Thank you all for being such good friends," Jenny said.

And she collected hugs from each and every one of them. And then they all departed except for Maryanne, who dragged Jenny up the stairs to the Rose Room.

"All right, I'll pack for you while you take a shower. You look like you need one."

"I don't really want to go."

"You're going." Maryanne gave her a determined look that reminded Jenny of her grandmother. There was no doubt that Maryanne was a Carpenter.

The expression on Maryanne's face relaxed into a little smile. "Please," she said in a pleading tone. "I just found you, and I don't want to lose you. I'm scared, Jenny. What happened in your kitchen was horrible, and Sheriff Rhodes is right—it won't hurt you to spend a couple of days away from here. Now, where's your suitcase"

Five minutes later, Jenny was standing under a stream of lovely hot water, wondering if she was crazy to have such faith in Gabe.

She had a miserable track record with men. She'd entirely misread the Bill Ellis situation. And years ago, when she'd been living in Chattanooga right after college, she'd made the mistake of a lifetime. She'd been looking for work as a teacher and filling in as a part-time secretary at a law firm when she'd fallen head-over-heels for one of the handsome associates. Jamie Kendrick had been young and ambitious and handsome as the devil. He'd also been interested in her, which made him irresistible.

She'd given him her virginity, and the two of them took to sneaking around having sex during their lunch hours. Jamie's *wife* interrupted them during one of those trysts. Jamie's *wife*. The one he'd neglected to mention.

Jenny hadn't especially regretted giving Jamie her virginity, but she was devastated by the fact that she'd given that gift to a man who wasn't interested in true love. She'd been so sure of Jamie's love. And she'd been so wrong.

The truth had been embarrassing and devastating. She'd run away from Chattanooga and come back to Last Chance. She'd told herself it was because Mother needed her, but she'd been lying to herself for years.

She'd confronted that truth when she'd decided to give up being a schoolteacher and do something important, like becoming an innkeeper in a town that desperately needed an inn. Bill's sudden marriage to Hettie had underscored the fact that Jenny had wasted half her life waiting for that nebulous "someday" when her prince would arrive.

But damn it, "someday" was right this minute.

She needed to quit waiting for it.

So she'd been wrong twice in her life. Did that mean she would always be wrong? No. Gabe had started something last night, and Jenny wanted to finish it. She wanted to finish it even if it turned out that he wasn't her prince.

If she kept staying out of the game because she was afraid to make mistakes, afraid to risk her heart, then she'd spend the rest of her life waiting instead of living.

And then it came to her. If she didn't care if Gabe Raintree had a wife, or a lover, or some other woman in his life. If she wasn't looking for forever . . . if all she wanted was another kiss that might lead to something else, well then, there wasn't anyone standing in her way except her own foolish self. She was running out of time to enjoy her own sexuality. And if she wanted to be a strong, independent woman, why on earth would she even care about a lifetime commitment?

The moment she allowed that thought into her brain, she became a changed woman. She wanted to seduce Gabe Raintree. She wanted him, even if it was only to share a few carnal moments. And why not? She wasn't interested in marriage anymore. She had embraced the freedom of spinsterhood. Like Wilma was always telling her, she was her own person. She was free. She could pursue a night with Gabe Raintree if she wanted to and not even feel guilty about it.

But if she planned to make a play for Gabe, then she needed to spruce herself up a little, or else he might do exactly what he'd done last night: Put her aside and treat her with emotional kid gloves. Sabina was right, she'd put all her effort into remaking The Jonquil House. It was time to remake herself.

When she emerged from the shower, she discovered that Maryanne had packed the biggest suitcase Jenny owned. She could probably live for a week and a half without doing laundry. "Jeez, I'm only leaving for a couple of days."

"You don't know that," Maryanne said.

"Look, Maryanne, I know you and the sheriff and half of Allenberg County have passed judgment on Gabe, but I haven't. I'm leaving only because I made a deal with you. And once the locks are changed, I'm moving back in. I'm tired of being afraid of life. Sometimes being safe and secure is stifling. Sometimes you just have to take risks. But I'm thinking a day away would be good, especially if we can talk Ruby Rhodes into giving me a makeover."

Maryanne blinked. "Honey, you're fine the way you are. I love you."

"I love you, too," she said, her voice wavering a little. Jenny opened her arms, and Maryanne came into them. They gave each other a fierce hug.

"I promise I'll be careful," Jenny said. "But this is just

like when you decided to throw caution to the wind and drive here without really knowing if you'd find your family. The Jonquil House is sort of like that for me. It's my statement or something. It's me telling the world that I'm strong, and I can deal with adversity, and that I'm free and independent. If I go running away at the first sign of trouble, then I'm just falling back into my safe and secure and boring life."

Maryanne nodded. "I get it, but, really, Jenny, safe and secure has a lot to recommend it. And what happened in your kitchen should scare the bejesus out of you."

"It did for a little while. I guess I still feel kind of violated. But I don't want to run away, okay? I've restored this house. And I'm not leaving it. I'm just starting to think that, before I open for business, I need to do a little work on myself. I'm going to do what Sabina has been telling me to do for a long while now. I'm going to cut my hair and update my wardrobe. I'm going to show the world that I'm a lioness, not a mouse. So let's go see what Ruby can do for me, and then maybe we should just take the weekend and go shopping down in Charleston or Hilton Head or Savannah."

"Uh, I can't go with you. Daniel and I have plans, but I'll bet you could talk Sabina into it. You could browse the antiques stores while you're there."

Jenny suppressed a momentary pang of jealousy. Maryanne deserved her happiness. She put on a brave smile. "I think I'm about to make Sabina's day."

Jenny set her suitcase by the door and headed into the living room, where Gabe and Ms. Ianelli were apparently having an argument about his book. Bear was lying with his giant head between his paws, watching the play-by-play like it was a tennis match.

Jenny hated to interrupt, but she needed to let them know that she was leaving for a few days.

Of course, the moment she set eyes on Gabe, looking a little worn and sleep-deprived with his hair falling over his forehead and his chin covered with stubble, her insides melted and her heart rate climbed.

She was going to seduce him. She just needed to work up the courage and get herself a new dress. She glanced at Ms. Ianelli's spike-heeled shoes. And maybe a pair of slutty shoes if she could figure out how to walk in heels that tall. Heck, if the town was going to think about her as a chicken-hurling hussy, she should have footwear to match.

But first she needed to tell him good-bye. Maybe her absence would make his heart grow fonder.

She jumped on that thought and expunged it from her brain. She was not interested in Gabe Raintree's heart. She was interested in other parts of his body, some of which she'd gotten a pretty good look at last night.

Ms. Ianelli cleared her throat and looked in Jenny's direction. "You wanted something?"

"I'm going away for a few days," she said.

Gabe grimaced and shot to his feet. "Why?" He took several steps in her direction, his dark eyes burning with more than fatigue. His display put her back a few steps. Could Sheriff Rhodes be right about him? No, surely not.

"I'm just going to Charleston for a little shopping." She waved her hand to indicate the living room. "You may have provided the furniture, but I need some accessories."

"You can't go," he said.

The words made her heart swell. He wasn't trying to get rid of her, even if he was trying to boss her around.

"I can and I will. I'll be back on Monday. In the meantime, please take care of Bear for me, will you? And be careful to lock the doors. The locksmith has promised to come early Monday morning to install more security. I should be back by then. If anything happens, you can reach me on my cell phone." She handed Gabe a yellow sticky note with her number on it.

"I'll go with you. I don't trust you to pick out accessories. You'll come back with china figurines or some other stupid, frilly stuff that the—" He bit off the rest of the sentence, but she knew what he meant to say. The ghost didn't like stupid frilly stuff. Of course, the ghost was a fifteen-year-old boy who was a bit spoiled. When she came back, she was going to have a serious talk with Gabe about trying to send the ghost on to the next world or wherever he needed to go.

But first she was going to go through with the seduction, and she wasn't about to have him come along on her shopping trip.

"No, you need to stay and write," she said in a no-nonsense voice.

Ms. Ianelli jumped to her feet. "That's right, Gabe. We've lost an entire morning, thanks to the events of last night. You need to stay here and fix this story. What you've given me is too dark and has very little action in it. We'll need major revisions." His editor turned toward Jenny. "You should stay and take care of us like the innkeeper you're supposed to be. And you shouldn't be foisting the care of your giant of a dog off on Mr. Raintree."

Jenny chomped down on the guilt Ms. Ianelli's words

raised. "I guess I shouldn't. Mr. Raintree, should I take Bear with me? I'm sure I can board him for a couple of days at the—"

"Don't be ridiculous. I feel safer with Bear here," Gabe said.

Jenny turned toward Ms. Ianelli. "I know you think you are entitled to breakfast, but the fact is, I'm still getting ready for business, and I haven't run your credit card because I don't even have my merchant services set up. I'm *letting* you stay here because Mr. Raintree is here, and I promised the book club that I'd give him a place to stay until the library program. I keep my promises."

"You know what I think?" Ms. Ianelli said. "I think you staged that mess in the kitchen. I'm glad to see you cleaned it up."

"Barbara, please, Jenny wouldn't have done that to her kitchen." Gabe turned his back on Ms. Ianelli and spoke again in a near whisper. "You're running away, aren't you?" His black eyes burned with emotions Jenny could only guess at.

"No, I'm going shopping."

His mouth twitched. "Is this like that old T-shirt about when the going gets tough, the tough hit the malls?"

"Exactly. Look, I promised Sheriff Rhodes a few days to hunt down the dirt bag who trashed my kitchen. He was concerned about my safety, and he communicated that to half the female population of Allenberg County. Honestly, I have no choice. I'll give him a couple of days, and I'll be back."

"You promise?"

"Of course I do. This is *my* house, not yours. And besides, I haven't given up on wooing Bear away from you. Please remember to feed him. Sometimes you forget."

He nodded, and his lips twitched a little, as if he was amused.

"But there is one bit of business that I need to talk with you about," she said.

"Business? What?"

"It's about Ms. Ianelli. You see, I've been working on the assumption that you're planning to stay here for a total of three months. That's what you told me the first day you came banging on the door. I need to know if Ms. Ianelli will be staying that long. I really do need a checkout date. I'm about to launch my website and reservation system, and right now, between you and her, I only have one room to let, and that's the one that has no furniture. I'm assuming that you and Ms. Ianelli will be leaving together."

His brow lowered into a scowl. "What makes you say that?" His voice took on a keen edge.

"I just assumed that you and she were—"

"Well, don't assume anything."

Her heart took flight. Maybe Ms. Ianelli would be leaving sooner rather than later. Perfect.

"All right," she said in her best schoolteacher voice. "We'll discuss her departure date when I return." She turned her back on him and headed into the foyer.

He followed her. "Good God, it looks like you packed for a month, not a weekend," he said.

She turned to find him staring at her with color in his cheeks. Was his heart beating as fast as hers? She thought maybe it was.

"I'll be back on Monday."

"You won't let the sheriff or the church ladies change your mind?" One of his dark brows rose in question.

"No, I'll be back."

She bent to pick up her suitcase, but he snagged her hand. He held it in his for the longest moment, his fingers strong and warm. "Good-bye, Jenny. Come back to me." And then he raised her hand to his lips and pressed a single kiss to her palm. It was no less and no more than what she'd done to him last night.

The breath caught in her throat, and she might have melted right there in the foyer but Ms. Ianelli called to him from the other room in a slightly panicked voice.

"Gabe, help, that gigantic dog of yours is all over me with... Yuck! Down, you smelly thing!"

"Go, rescue Bear," Jenny said. "I'll be back in a few days."

CHAPTER 18

Zeph sat in his favorite rocking chair, reading *Great Expectations* for the umpteenth time. He had a view of the river out his living room window, and his driveway wasn't much more than a dirt track leading up to the highway. He never had visitors out here, so he had plenty of time to escape into books. And now that the ghost had left him to haunt Gabe, he was feeling a little bit lonely.

For the last twenty-five years, since Luke died, Zeph had been living down here on the patch of bottomland that his daddy had purchased back in the mid-1950s. He'd torn down his daddy's tin-roofed shack and replaced it with a four-room house built entirely from deadwood that he'd had milled into lumber. The house was an eclectic mix of swamp chestnut oak, loblolly pine, and red cedar. Hand fitting the cabinets and making the furniture had kept Zeph busy for a long, long time. He'd learned a lot about woodworking by building his own house from the ground up.

He was entirely off the grid. His water was pumped up from the river. His electricity came from a microturbine hydroelectric system he'd installed a few years ago. His sewage went into a septic tank that was pumped every year or so. He didn't have TV or Internet.

For entertainment, he had books. Lots and lots of books that he bought at the Goodwill store for pennies apiece. And of course, there was hunting and fishing. He worked some, too. He had a part-time job for Mr. Randall at the Painted Corner Stables, and he'd helped Dash's wife restore the theater in town. He took in jobs repairing furniture from time to time. But his life was pretty simple compared with a lot of other folks'.

He was comfortable here. He didn't have to say much to anyone. And that was always good, because he'd never been good with words. Not even before Vietnam or Luke's death.

So he was pretty well blown away on Friday when Nita's familiar Toyota Camry came bumping down his dirt road.

He got up and peered through the front windows the minute he heard her engine. He stood there staring like an idiot or something when she got out of the car, wearing a pair of blue jeans, those big, puffy suede boots the ladies seemed to like, and a winter jacket. She looked like she'd come out here for a winter hike.

She stood by her car for a long moment, studying his house. His heart started pounding in his chest because he couldn't tell if Nita thought his place was a shack or something else. He'd been working hard to make it something special, something unique. But he knew folks in town continued to refer to his place as a shack in the woods. Mostly he didn't care what people thought. But he cared about Nita.

More than he should.

She crossed the little clearing and stepped up onto his porch. She knocked on the door like a woman on a mission.

He thought about playing possum and not answering, but Nita destroyed that plan by shouting, "I know you're in there, Zeph Gibbs. So don't you pretend otherwise."

He had to smile. Nita had been a little bossy when she was in elementary school, and she had evidently not outgrown the tendency.

He put his book down on the rocking chair's seat and answered the door.

The woman didn't wait for an invitation. She barreled right through the door, forcing Zeph to take a step back.

And then she stopped, and her eyes grew round, and she kind of spun around as she studied the wooden walls of his front room.

"Good God almighty, Zeph, you must have a thousand books on these shelves."

Every wall in his house had built-in shelves. And every shelf had books on it. "All told I have eight hundred and fifty-nine books. All of them are paperbacks, though, and out here they don't last so good. The damp gets to them."

"You know how many there are?"

"Yes, ma'am. I have them sorted and cataloged. But I don't use the Dewey system." He managed a little smile.

"Good heavens. I could teach it to you if you were interested in working part-time at the library."

"Miz Nita, unless we do something, no one's going to be working at the library."

She folded her arms across her chest. "Exactly, Zeph. And that's why I'm here. I need to talk to you about Gabe Raintree."

This was, of course, the last thing on earth that Zeph wanted to talk about. So he stalled. "Uh, can I get you a cup of coffee or something?"

"Yes, that would be very nice."

"Come on back, then."

Nita followed him into his little kitchen. "Oh my goodness." She practically breathed the words.

"Ma'am?"

"Zeph, this is beautiful." She gestured at his hand-built cabinetry and the stove and oven that he'd just installed. The appliances weren't exactly new; they were each slightly damaged, and he'd gotten them from a salvage company for much less than retail. "You've been keeping secrets. Folks in town believe you live in a shack."

"I know. That's probably because my daddy lived in one, and that's where I came up. But I decided a long time ago that I didn't ever want to live in one again."

"You built this place?" She sank down into a one-of-a-kind chair, at his one-of-a-kind kitchen table.

"I did. It kept me busy. Kept my mind off things I didn't want to think about."

He pulled down two mismatched coffee mugs and poured some coffee from an old-fashioned, on-the-stovetop percolator.

"It's pretty strong, ma'am. Do you want milk or sugar or something?"

"No, Zeph. Just sit down. We need to talk."

He sat and put his hands around his cup but he didn't look up. Never in his wildest imagination had he ever envisioned Nita sitting at his kitchen table. And if he had fantasized about it, he would have had her staring out the window at the view of the river, not staring at him like she was seeing him for the first time.

"Zeph, did you hear about what happened at The Jonquil House last night?"

He nodded. "Yes, ma'am. I spoke with Sheriff Rhodes over the phone this morning."

"You didn't do that to Jenny, did you?"

He gripped his cup a little tighter. "Do you think I'm the kind of man who would do something like that?"

She shook her head, her dark eyes big and kind, the way they always were. "No, Zeph, I don't. But I reckon there are people in town who've read *Black Water* and who can't help but see parallels between you and the crazy man in that book. Folks are saying you did that thing to Jenny just to get her and Gabe to move out."

He nodded. "I reckon I'm not surprised. I reckon it's mostly white folks saying that."

"That's true, I'm sorry to say. I wanted to come out here and tell you that I don't for one minute believe you'd do something like that. But it looks bad, Zeph. Real bad."

He shrugged. "There isn't anything I can do about it."

"Yes, there is. I'm convinced that Gabe Raintree is not what he appears to be. And we both know there's more to his history than folks realize. I'm worried about Jenny. I'm worried about you. And I don't know what to think about Gabe. You need to tell Sheriff Rhodes what happened when Luke died. He needs to know all the facts."

"I promised I would never do that."

"Why?"

"Because Gabe deserved a chance to live a normal life. He was only ten, and the gun misfired. It was an accident, pure and simple. But it was one of those accidents that could have been avoided if I had been paying attention. I knew Gabe wanted to try that gun. I knew his granddaddy had forbidden it until he was twelve. I should never have taken my eye off him. I tell you, Nita, it's just a blessing that Gabe doesn't remember what happened. Telling him now would rip him apart, especially since—" He drew himself up short before he could say one word about the ghost.

"Especially since what?"

"Nothing."

She put her mug down and gave him a stare like the one his old granny used to give him when he'd been up to no good. "What, Zeph? The time for secrets is over. If Gabe is unbalanced, we need to get him out of that house and into some place where he can get help. I'm not going to sit by and let Jenny Carpenter get hurt because of something I asked her to do. Do you understand me?"

"Yes, ma'am, but Gabe isn't a threat to her, unless you're thinking about him breaking her heart."

"What?"

He shrugged. "They're falling for each other. Any fool can see it. And I think..."

"You think what?"

He laid his hands palms-down on the table. Maybe it was time to tell the truth, the whole truth. He took a breath and let it out slowly. Then he looked up. "Nita, I'm going to tell you the whole truth. And when I'm finished, I'm going to ask you not to blab it all over town, or run to Doc Cooper, and try to get me help. Because I'm not crazy. I'm not disturbed. I just like being alone, is that clear?"

She reached out and put her hand over his, and he immediately knew that, while he liked his solitude, he wouldn't mind Nita coming out here from time to time just to break the monotony. "I don't think you're crazy, Zeph. What's eating you?"

"Nita, I'm about to tell you a ghost story."

• • •

Friday wasn't nearly as busy at the Cut 'n Curl as Saturday, but it was busy enough. When Jenny walked through the front door, Ruby Rhodes was juggling two of her best clients, Lillian Bray and Thelma Hanks, while Jane Rhodes was giving Savannah Randall a manicure.

Ruby looked up from the body wave she was putting into Lillian's hair with a big, wide smile. "Stone called this morning, honey. We've all heard about the horrible thing that happened out at The Jonquil House. Don't you worry, now, Clay promised that he'd bring the roll-away bed from my place up to the apartment on his lunch hour."

"Thank you, but, I'm not here about the bed. I was..." Her mouth went dry. She wanted to be made over in the worst way, but saying it out loud felt like a betrayal of her own principles. Why should she have to get herself all dolled up to catch a man?

Not that she was trying to catch a man, exactly. She just wanted to...

Well, what she wanted was scandalous. But a woman her age needed to look things squarely in the eye and get on with it. The Jonquil House had needed a makeover. And if she wanted to be the in-charge innkeeper, she needed to upgrade as well.

"What, honey?" Ruby asked.

"I was wondering if you could squeeze me in today?"

Every head in the place swiveled, even Lillian's. Good Lord, Lillian was liable to blab all over town that the chicken-hurling hussy had come down here and demanded a brand-new look.

"Hallelujah!" Jane said from her manicure station.

"Amen to that," Savannah seconded with a grin.

"It's that nice young preacher, isn't it?" Thelma said. Eugene Hanks's wife was having her roots attended to, and she looked a little bit like Phyllis Diller or maybe the bride of Frankenstein. Seeing her hair all covered in tinfoil and standing on end was almost terrifying.

"I declare," Thelma continued, "that preacher is as handsome as the day is long."

"He certainly is. And he's a pious man as well. I like that about him," Lillian said with a sniff and turned away as if dismissing Jenny's chances with the preacher. Which kind of rankled even if Jenny didn't much like Reverend Lake in the first place.

Jane popped up from her place and crossed the room with a big smile on her face. "You come right on in. Ruby is busier than a one-armed paper hanger today, but Savannah is my last manicure for a while. I'll do your hair."

Jane took her gently by the crook of her arm and guided her across the room and into one of the salon chairs. "So, tell me what you had in mind while I finish up Savannah's mani."

"Uh, well, uh…" All coherent speech fled Jenny's mind. Now that she was here, surrounded by pink walls and the ammonia smell of Lillian's permanent solution, she was completely flummoxed. She had no idea how she wanted to look, except that she wanted it to be natural. And she wasn't sure she was ready for weekly visits to Ruby.

She just wanted to look better, sexier… something.

She was saved by the bell over the front door. Sabina came charging in, her cheeks pink from the chilly temperatures outside. "Is she really here?"

And everyone in the shop said yes in unison, which was even more embarrassing.

"Praise the Lord and tipsy china cabinets," Sabina said, crossing the room. "I never thought I'd see the day."

She sat down in one of the pink vinyl hair-dryer chairs. "So, I think we need to spruce up the color and cut it to chin length. What do y'all think?" Sabina asked Ruby and Jane.

"I wouldn't do anything drastic to the color," Ruby said. "Just a few highlights."

"I was thinking the same thing," Savannah said. "And, honey, if you really want to change your look, you need to think about contact lenses."

"Or a least a pair of frames that don't make you look like an owl," Jane said.

"Honey, I'd go whole hog," Ruby said, "and get that Lasik treatment. Alma Newberry did that last summer, and it just changed her life."

"You also need some clothes that fit you better," Savannah said. "You're hiding your figure under a bushel basket."

"Oh don't you worry, Savannah, just as soon as Jane and Ruby work their magic on her hair, I'm taking her to Charleston for some shopping. I have an auction down there on Monday, anyway."

"I need to be back by Monday."

"No, you don't. You need to stay away and let Sheriff Rhodes do his thing. And then when we get back, we're going to have a big bonfire and burn every sweater and turtleneck in your closet."

"But I like sweaters," Jenny protested, suddenly uncertain of all these changes.

"Of course you do. But there are floppy, shapeless sweaters and then there are tight-fitting twin sets that display your assets. Once you try one of them, you'll see that you can be comfy and sexy at the same time."

"Really," Lillian said in an unpleasant voice, "I doubt that Reverend Lake would be terribly impressed by a woman who dressed like a slut."

Everyone glowered at Lillian. "No one is dressing her like a slut," Sabina said.

"Jenny," Lillian said, "it seems to me you'd do better to worry about your character instead of your wardrobe. In my mind, you deserved what happened to you last night for harboring that devil Gabriel Raintree."

"Lillian," Ruby said in a voice that was as unfriendly as Jenny had ever heard from the hairdresser, "that was an ugly thing to say. Stone told me what happened. It was horrible and malicious. And I won't have anyone saying that she deserved something like that. And furthermore, Mr. Raintree is the grandson of a governor from a well-respected family, who has written many entertaining books. I don't think he's a demon, and I won't have people saying such ugly things in my shop, is that clear?"

"I'm sorry." Lillian managed to sound contrite until she added her next little dig. "But it seems to me that Reverend Lake will be more interested in Jenny's character than her looks."

"Okay, let's get something clear right now," Jenny said. "I'm not interested in the preacher. I know y'all think he's the man who is going to sweep me off my feet. But here's the thing: I don't want to be swept off my feet. In fact, I don't even want to get married."

"What?" Five voices spoke in unison.

"It's true. I just want to be a strong, independent woman, like Wilma Riley, or Arlene Whitaker now that

Pete has passed. And Wilma and Arlene come to the beauty shop, and no one gets on their cases."

"Honey, you have a point," Ruby said.

"But don't give up on finding your soulmate," Savannah said, her dark eyes gleaming as if she knew something.

"Savannah, I know everyone says your aunt is trying to match me up with Reverend Lake. But I don't love him."

Savannah grinned. "I don't think Aunt Miriam ever said that you and the preacher were soulmates. But here's the thing, when you meet your soulmate, you'll know him, because he'll make it hard for you to think or breathe. And everything you ever tried on any other man is just not going to work on him. He'll be different, and you'll know it almost from the start."

Thelma gave Savannah the oddest look. "Did Miriam tell you that?"

Savannah blushed right to the roots of her naturally blond hair. "Well, y'all, no, not exactly."

"Honey, are you saying that you and your aunt have the same gift?" Ruby said.

"Well, uh, it would be presumptuous of me to say that I have Miriam's knack. After all, she's been matching people up for decades."

"But . . . ," Jane said.

"But I sometimes see things other people don't."

"And you're saying that Jenny is not fated to be with the new Methodist preacher?" Thelma asked.

"No, Thelma, Reverend Lake is not Jenny's soulmate." She smiled at Jenny. "So I think you can pour your assets into as many sexy twin sets as Sabina can talk you into, because I don't think your soulmate will judge you for it."

Sabina folded her arms across her chest with a disappointed frown on her face. "Oh, that's a shame. When Miriam said she was going to have a handsome man, well, Reverend Lake is like a movie star, and so I naturally thought... Besides, most of the single men in town aren't all that much."

"Oh I don't know about that, Dr. Dave the Vet is nice looking," Jane said.

"And don't forget the Canaday twins. They're young yet, but I see real promise there, and Pat told me that Beau's cancer is in remission," Ruby added.

"And there's always Ross Gardiner over at the fire station," Savannah said, giving Sabina the oddest look.

"Ross isn't exactly single. He's my sister's boyfriend," Sabina said.

"That boy needs to get off his backside and pop the question, if you ask me," Ruby said. "And until he does, he still technically qualifies as one of the town's good-looking bachelors."

"Goodness, there are so many bachelors that I feel like I've fallen right into an episode of *The Dating Game*," said Thelma. "If Jenny isn't going to be matched up with Reverend Lake, then who is it going to be, Savannah?"

Savannah smiled like the Mona Lisa. "Aunt Miriam has already spoken on this point. Jenny is destined to have a very handsome soulmate. So Jenny, don't you be settling on anyone who's ugly, you hear me?"

"Ugly inside or out?" Jenny asked.

Savannah blinked. "Honey, you don't need me to answer that. You already know the answer."

Jenny's shopping trip to Charleston lasted a week, instead of a weekend. Not only did Sabina ensure that she bought new clothing, but the two of them attended no less than two auctions and then spent several days wandering the back roads of South Carolina picking through barns, looking for antiques for Sabina to sell at her store.

Jenny scored a box of Blue Willow china to replace the pieces that had been broken in the china cabinet debacle. She also found assorted stemware and side pieces that would make her breakfast table special, as well as a few knickknacks that would probably make Mr. Raintree hurl. She didn't care. She had a weakness for china figurines, and she wasn't giving that up for anyone, not even Mr. Raintree.

Between them, Sabina and Jenny managed to fill up the back of the van Sabina used for her business.

At night, they stayed at other inns and B and Bs, which allowed Jenny to check out the competition and talk shop with other innkeepers. She learned a lot, and she was looking forward to the day, only two weeks away, when she would be officially open for business.

While she was away, she checked back with Sheriff Rhodes on a regular basis, but he didn't seem to be making much headway in solving the mystery of the trashed kitchen. And the farther away she got from that night in time and distance, the less worried she became. The prank, which is how she'd come to view it, had been organized by some of Dennis Hayden's hacks. It had been intended to stir up the church ladies, and it had succeeded.

According to emails from the Library Committee, Lillian Bray's protest of the event had sparked a great deal of statewide publicity, which translated into brisk ticket sales. The event was sold out. But the organizers worried that attendees might have to cross a picket line of mobilized Christians in order to come.

Poor Gabe. He'd come to Last Chance looking for solitude and quiet, and the library had handed him something else altogether. Which, although it was ironic, still seemed like a bad bargain. It couldn't be easy to become the eye of a storm like that.

She also exchanged a few texts with Gabe, who assured her that he was fully capable of making sure that the locksmith did a good job of installing dead bolts on all the exterior doors at The Jonquil House. He also informed her that the much-delayed furniture for the Daisy Room had arrived and been installed.

Their communiqués had been terse, which didn't surprise her either. Now that she'd been away for a while, she was starting to wonder if the idea of seducing him had been a by-product of the fear she'd experienced the night her kitchen had been vandalized. Maybe this time away was a good thing after all.

She had a new wardrobe, a new pair of glasses, a new hairdo, and a new attitude. She was going to be strong and independent. If, upon her return, she still had feelings for Gabe, then she would make a play for him, provided, of course, that he and Barbara Ianelli weren't shacked up together in the Iris Room.

On Friday afternoon, she picked up her Fiesta where she'd left it at the Cut 'n Curl, loaded it with shopping bags and boxes of china, and headed out of town toward Bluff Road and home.

Home. She hadn't felt this way about any place since the old farmhouse burned. The Jonquil House might be haunted and have a troubled past, but to her heart it had become home. She wasn't going to let anyone—living or dead—drive her away.

Her spirits were high when she turned up the driveway. It was an unseasonably warm day in February, and the landscape offered the hope of an early spring. Tiny buds on the wild dogwoods had swelled, promising blossoms. And everywhere in the woods on either side of the house, jonquils peeked above the leaf litter and pine needles, giving the forest floor a haze of green. It was Valentine's Day—a long time until the first day of spring. But here in South Carolina, the jonquils would bloom in early March, a couple of weeks away.

She was grinning like a fool when she marched up the porch steps, keys in hand. But one look at the two locks on her front door reminded her that, while she owned The Jonquil House, she didn't have a set of keys to the place.

She pressed the doorbell. Bear started barking, and her heart took flight.

The door opened a moment later, and Bear rushed out and jumped up on her, lavishing kisses on her face. "Did you miss me, Bear-y boy?" she said on a laugh that sprang from deep inside. It had been a long, long time since she'd been welcomed home with such love.

"Down!" Gabe said, and the dog obeyed. But Jenny could tell that Bear still wanted to get up and do a Snoopy dance.

Jenny looked up at the man in the doorway, and she lost the ability to breathe. He wore his old blue jeans and tattered Harvard sweatshirt, his face rough with stubble, his eyes sparked with something that made Jenny's heart run away with her.

She struggled to appear calm and not to fall right into him and cover his grim face with kisses. If she behaved that way, she ran the risk of him saying something like,

"Down girl." And that would be humiliating. Of course, she didn't have to obey him. She was, after all, a chicken-hurling hussy. She could do what she wanted.

His stare stopped her, though. No doubt he was surprised by the shorter, lighter hair, the new glasses, the sweater set, and the stretchy jeans that hugged her butt. But, oddly, his gaze seemed locked on her eyes and nothing else.

"There you are," he said in a low voice. "You're back." His brows lowered into a scowl. "You told me it was just for a weekend, and you left for a whole week." He sounded peeved. If she didn't know him better, she might have been intimidated by his words. She might have mistaken them for a complaint about her abilities as an innkeeper. But she didn't read them that way.

He had missed her.

His words brought a smile to her lips despite her efforts to play it cool.

His gaze slid down to take in her new clothes. "Maybe this isn't Jenny Carpenter," he said. "Maybe this is some changeling she sent back to me."

"I let Sabina pick out a new wardrobe fit for an innkeeper. And I went antiquing and bought a bunch of things that you'll probably hate. I have a couple of boxes in the car."

That brought a smile to his lips. His gaze moved to her Fiesta, with its still-open hatch. "Let me help you bring in your treasures."

He brushed past her, and her skin prickled from head to toe. His limp was entirely gone.

"You've been to the doctor," she said inanely.

"I have," he answered.

A moment later, they stood in the kitchen, where she noted that the bloodstain on the grout had been scrubbed clean. He put a box of dishes on the counter.

"Thank you, for your kindness," she said in a voice that was barely a whisper. "I'm strangely glad to get back again...to you."

Time hung suspended as their gazes met and held. She wanted to wrap him in her arms but she didn't know how to start. Maybe he would make the first move and carry her off to his bedroom. And maybe she was an idiot.

"Is Ms. Ianelli still here?" she asked. It was lame. She didn't care about his editor. She didn't care if he loved her or lusted after her or whatever. She was liberated.

Not.

His mouth twitched. "I sent her back to New York. We argued about the book. She's not happy with it, and it may be that I've lost my publisher for good. I'm not worried, though."

And yet the skin around his eyes looked bruised and his brow was wrinkled and he appeared in every respect to look like a man who was worried. Or maybe "haunted" was a better word for it.

"Are you still blocked?"

He shook his head. "No. Can I tell you something?"

"Of course."

"The ghost is helping me write this book. And I think it's better than my others. But Barbara says it's not. I think I may be losing my mind."

She lifted her hand to his cheek. It was warm. "No. But I think maybe living with a ghost has been hard on you. And now I feel guilty because I left you."

For an instant Gabe leaned into her touch. Then he

stepped away from her. "I hate to say this, Jenny, but I think it might have been better if you hadn't come back. I don't think it's safe for you to be living here."

Was he talking about the kitchen vandal or the literary ghost? It didn't matter. She pasted a smile on her face. "I'm not afraid," she said. "And it looks as if you need a good, warm meal. Please, let me cook for you. We can have a nice homecoming meal on the new china and the repaired table."

"You should go, Jenny."

"Don't be ridiculous." It was now or never. If the man wouldn't let her seduce him with her cooking, then she was going to have to use her body. Since she was not exactly sexually liberated or experienced, this was going to be a real challenge.

But she was ready.

And it sure did look like Gabe needed a distraction.

So she did exactly what Barbara Ianelli had done a week ago. She wrapped her arms around his neck, rose up on tiptoes, and kissed his mouth.

For an instant, she thought Gabe would succumb to her kiss. His arms briefly came around her middle, and their tongues touched for a fraction of a second. An insatiable hunger burned up her middle, but in the next minute he retreated.

He set her back on her heels and took three steps in the opposite direction.

"No." His voice was rusty.

"But—"

"No. Jenny, no. You're a beautiful, warm, lovely woman. But no."

He turned, stalked to his room, and slammed the door

behind him. The sad little "Do Not Disturb" sticky note let go of his door and fluttered to the ground like a falling leaf.

She'd ignored that note many times before, but she wasn't going to ignore it this time. He'd made his preferences clear and, really, it was better this way. At least he hadn't led her on. They'd had one crazy moment, but that was all it was ever going to be.

She stood there breathing hard and telling herself that she was better without this experience. But her throat closed up, and tears threatened anyway.

She refused to cry. There was no reason to cry. She'd spent many a Valentine's Day alone. This one would be no different.

Gabe didn't sleep much that night, knowing that Jenny was upstairs in the Rose Room. At least Bear was with her. The dog had defected, which came as no surprise. If he were Bear and had the choice of sleeping down here with him in Luke's frigid bedroom or upstairs with Jenny, he'd do the same thing.

That thought raised a bark of laughter, because he did have that choice. If he went upstairs and knocked on her door, she'd willingly let him in. Her new clothes and her kiss had told him as much.

God knew he wanted to go there. But he wasn't going to be that selfish.

Tomorrow was the library fund-raiser, and once he'd fulfilled his obligation he was going to leave town and never come back. He understood why Zeph had warned him about staying. It was hard to be haunted.

He sat in the folding chair staring at his computer

screen. His novel was almost finished. He just needed to write the ending. If he stayed here, the ghost would make him write something that would wrench his soul. If he left, he could avoid that and maybe salvage his relationship with his publisher.

He knew how hauntings worked in ghost stories. You got out before it was too late.

And he was perilously close to being trapped.

He was falling in love, which was more frightening and dangerous than being haunted. The first, last, and only time he'd fallen in love, he'd ignored every misgiving. He'd thrown himself into it with his whole being. And he'd paid a gigantic price.

Love was blind.

Not that he thought Jenny lacked for anything. She actually seemed perfect in every way. But how could he be sure?

And if she was, indeed, the sweet, wonderful, kind woman that she appeared to be, then loving her would be the most selfish thing Gabe could do. He couldn't subject Jenny to his life. It would be unfair. It would be dangerous.

He hadn't even told her the truth about his diabetes—or the truth about anything else that was important, for that matter.

No, it was better to run away. Running was a good option sometimes. So he'd hit the road and go to Columbia or someplace where they didn't know his name, where they didn't expect anything from him. Someplace where he could hide out and finish this story the way he wanted to, without the damn ghost constantly kibitzing, and without his libido being tweaked by his pretty innkeeper.

The ghost could go back to haunting Zeph. Or maybe

Jenny could figure out a way to send the ghost packing, or turn him into a tourist attraction. He wasn't a scary ghost, in any case. He was just an emotionally exhausting one.

And Jenny could be the free, independent innkeeper she wanted to be.

So, he'd go. The ghost would deal. Jenny would deal. And everything in the sleepy town of Last Chance would return to normal.

CHAPTER
19

Gabe's determination to leave Allenberg County was reinforced the minute he turned his Lexus onto Palmetto Avenue and caught sight of the mayhem the library fundraiser had created.

Last Chance didn't look anything like a sleepy southern town. There had to be half a dozen county deputies directing foot and vehicular traffic in front of The Kismet. On one side of the street, people were queuing up by the theater's doors. These people, by and large, were not locals, unless Allenberg County had a colony of Goths living nearby. The people in line were wearing black, with lots of tats and body piercings. A few of them had dressed up like his characters and victims. All in all, they looked like they'd come out for a Halloween party.

No doubt the Library Committee had underestimated the reach of Facebook and Twitter. And so had he. If he had known what would happen, he never would have agreed to this presentation. He'd expected a small local event. Not this. He'd come here to the middle of nowhere to avoid this.

And now, unfortunately, his throngs of followers would realize that the locale in *Black Water* was based on Last Chance. And that probably meant Last Chance would be dealing with these crazies for some time to come.

Obviously this wasn't going to endear him to the locals, some of whom had gathered on the other side of the street in front of the Knit & Stitch and the Wash-O-Rama. This group consisted of mostly blue-haired ladies who were marching back and forth carrying signs that pretty much called his Christian values into question. Which, actually, was fair game because Gabe didn't have any values that were strictly Christian. He'd given up going to church when he'd moved out of his grandfather's house. He'd had his fill of Granddad's hypocrisy.

Sheriff Rhodes was in the middle of the street, directing his deputies who were directing traffic. And good thing, too, because the sheriff was able to spot Gabe's car before he ended up in the middle of this fracas. Sheriff Rhodes waved him forward to an area in front of the theater that had been roped off.

Gabe lowered his window to speak with Stone. "I'm really sorry about this."

Stone shrugged. "Not your fault. I've saved you a parking spot. And I'll escort you into the building."

"You know the fans may look weird, but they are mostly harmless."

Stone gave him a solemn look. "Are they? We've had about a dozen complaints from Garnet Willoughby down at the Peach Blossom Motor Court. Apparently every room is sold out, and your fans are a rowdy bunch. Of course Lillian Bray is beside herself. It's bad enough that she spies on people who go to the Peach Blossom for sex, but having it overrun by a bunch of Goths has put her into a self-righteous hissy fit."

"I'm sorry."

"Yeah, well, I don't blame you. To be honest, Gabe, I pity you. And don't worry. I've got my eye on every single one of those people staying at the motel. I don't let people get hurt in my town, especially people who've lived here all their lives, like Jenny Carpenter."

Gabe decided that Stone Rhodes might be a perfect model for one of his traditional heroes. It was funny how a small-town cop took Gabe's security way more seriously than the cops in the big cities. "Thank you."

"It's my job."

Gabe pulled his car to the curb. When he stepped out of it, the ladies across the street started chanting something nasty about him worshiping the devil. The people in line clapped and cheered.

Stone took him by the arm, hurried him inside, and left him in the lobby without so much as a word. Gabe stood there for a moment bowled over by memories. He and Luke had come to this theater every summer. They had bought candy at that counter. His mouth almost watered at the thought of the Milk Duds he'd consumed as a boy.

It had been decades since he'd allowed himself the luxury of eating a whole box of Milk Duds.

Just then a wave of frigid air enveloped him and chilled him from the inside out. He knew this feeling well. The ghost was right behind him.

Damn. Weren't ghosts supposed to be attached to the places they haunted? How was he going to ditch the ghost if the ghost planned to follow him? The thought made the hairs on the back of his neck stand up.

Nita Wills, the town librarian, came through the double doors that led to the auditorium. "Oh, thank goodness you made it all right. We were worried. Jenny has been trying to get you on the phone for half an hour. She was going to run back to the house, drive you here, and smuggle you in by the side door."

He reached into the pocket of his dress slacks and pulled out his smartphone. It was set on mute. He didn't remember muting it, but this wouldn't be the first time something odd had happened with his phone. The ghost loved to play with his electronics, and Gabe had the feeling that Luke was a little jealous he hadn't lived long enough to truly enjoy the information age.

He slipped the phone back in his pocket and looked up at the librarian. "Sorry. I guess it was on mute. Sheriff Rhodes walked me in."

"I'm glad you're okay. And I'm sorry this has turned into a circus."

"I should have warned you that it might. People seem to either love me or hate me."

"Come on back. We've got a place for you at the reserved table, and there are some folks who would like to say hey." She took him by the arm and guided him through the doors into the theater.

The Kismet wasn't exactly the same theater as the one he remembered. The traditional auditorium chairs had been removed. The sloping floor had been terraced, and dining tables had been set up on each level. The tables were set with white cloths and standard restaurant silverware. On each table was a floral display of daffodils. Apparently the organizers were hoping he would celebrate the restoration of The Jonquil House, which, of

course, had been the setting for *Black Water* as much as
the town and the swamp had been.

He looked up. The old ceiling, which once had sparkled with twinkling lights like a starry night sky, was
gone. He swallowed his disappointment. He'd heard
something about how the theater had almost burned
down. If the ceiling was all that had been lost, then he was
grateful. He'd been happy here as a child, watching movies with his older brother. Luke had liked Goobers better
than Milk Duds. It was a strange and random thought. But
it brought a warming smile to his lips.

He followed Nita down to the front of the auditorium
where a group of people had gathered. These people wore
suits and dresses and looked pretty mainstream. Jenny
was there, wearing a green dress made of some kind of
knit material that clung to her body. This dress didn't button up to her chin, and it exposed a lot of leg. She was
wearing a pair of heels, too. Lust percolated through him.
This craving was deeper and more intense than any desire
for sweets.

And it was just as dangerous.

"I want to introduce you to members of the Last
Chance Book Club who have done such a terrific job
publicizing this event. We're all very thankful that you
agreed to do it. We've raised more money than we ever
thought we could."

He chuckled darkly. "But I imagine the fuss outside
isn't helping your efforts to save the library, is it?"

Nita gave him a gentle smile. "It's hard when the church
ladies get all riled up. But that's not your fault. Come on,
now, don't be negative. We do appreciate your help."

He forced a smile to his face and let Nita lead him to the

group of people. He met five or six women whose names went through his brain like water, and then suddenly he was standing face-to-face with someone he remembered.

"Simon?" He almost whispered the name because something cold and heavy seemed to press down on him the moment he shook the man's hand. He was tall and thin with dark hair threaded with strands of gray. He was impeccably dressed, as if he bought his clothes in Savannah or Charleston, and he was standing beside a woman who was much younger than him and easily nine months' pregnant.

"It's me," he said.

Simon and Luke had been inseparable friends during the summers Gabe spent in Last Chance. Random memories of Simon rushed back through him. Simon had always played the peacemaker. How had he forgotten that? For all Gabe adored his brother, the two of them had squabbled over a lot of things. Like brothers do.

Simon hadn't changed much in twenty-five years. "I've been meaning to stop by The Jonquil House for a couple of weeks, but I've been a little busy," he said. His voice sounded tense, and his eyes tracked left. He was lying. Why would he lie about that?

Gabe's brain seemed to be moving in slow motion. Simon was always at Luke's side, almost every day. They were inseparable friends.

The monster at the bottom of the black hole that was Gabe's memory shifted and writhed, while the cold became almost unbearable. The ghost was making himself known. Luke wanted Gabe to pay attention to Simon.

"Hi, I'm Molly, Simon's wife," the pregnant woman said, drawing her knitted shawl closer around her shoulders, as if she also felt the drop in temperature. In fact, everyone in the room seemed to be hunching down in their jackets and shawls. "I don't reckon you and I ever met," Simon's wife continued, "But I've heard about you. I'm the reason he's been so busy. I've been running Simon ragged getting ready for the baby." She snaked her arm through Simon's in a gesture that was protective. She was lying, too.

"Goodness gracious," Nita said, tugging him away from the couple, "I need to tell Savannah to turn up the heat."

Gabe allowed himself to be pulled away, but he looked over his shoulder and discovered that Simon was staring at him as if he were evil incarnate.

Zeph stayed at the back of The Kismet's dining room, feeling constricted in his new dress shirt and blue blazer. He shouldn't be here. He felt strange and out of place.

But Nita had insisted. In fact, she'd come visiting this afternoon bearing chocolate chip cookies, a VIP ticket to the fund-raiser, and this suit of new clothes for him to wear.

And when he'd told her that he wouldn't accept any of it, she'd scowled at him and told him to get down off his high horse. She'd also made it clear that she wasn't pushing charity at him.

Like every member of the Library Committee, she'd been given one VIP ticket to the fund-raiser. For some reason, Nita had chosen him as her guest. And she'd told him that she had no objections to his overalls, but that she didn't want people staring at him if he chose to wear them.

She'd told him that he didn't even have to wear the clothes again, which was a good thing because the shirt's neck was too small, and he hated wearing ties.

But it wasn't the clothes or the VIP ticket that had gotten him here. Nita had impressed upon him that Gabe was going to be standing up in public talking to a bunch of strangers about how *Black Water* was influenced by the summers he'd spent in Last Chance, and everyone in attendance was going to figure out that Zebulon Stroud, the villain in the book, was loosely based on him.

"I do not want strangers to think you're some kind of crazy man ready to commit murder," she'd said pushing the clothes at him.

"Would it be all right if I was just a crazy man?"

She looked him in the eye. "Zeph Gibbs, you are no more crazy than I am. I told you that I believe you have been haunted by the ghost of Luke Raintree."

"Yes, ma'am, but there is believing and *believing*. You think I've been haunted by the past, but I'm telling you I've been haunted by a real, dead ghost."

"Either way, it's time to lay that ghost to rest. And there is only one way to make that happen, and that's to tell the truth and expose the lie."

"It will tear Gabe apart."

"It might. But I don't care about Gabe Raintree. Oh, well, I *do* care, but I don't care about him the way I care about you."

The idea that Nita Wills cared about him was what did him in. And now he was standing here in the back of the auditorium with his eyes glued to Nita, who circulated around the crowd of VIPs like a honeybee, wearing a yellow dress that made him want to do things that weren't right.

Man, that woman was hotter than Louisiana Hot Sauce, and she had no clue.

And then Gabe arrived, and the temperature in the room fell to near freezing because the ghost came walking in right behind him. Of course, Zeph couldn't see the ghost any more than Gabe or Nita could. But he knew. The cold was a giveaway.

And when it got this cold, it meant the ghost was agitated—ready to do something like throw furniture across the room.

Zeph watched Gabe as Nita introduced him to the VIPs. And then Gabe came face-to-face with Simon. For the first time in twenty-five years, Zeph's boys, or what was left of them, were reunited. Based on Simon's stiff posture, Gabe's confused look, Luke's cold rage, and Zeph's guilty conscience, it looked as if disaster was about to strike.

Nita seated Jenny at the head table. The seating arrangement was so awkward that Jenny felt like a hippo wearing a tutu.

For starters, Bill Ellis was at her right hand, and he kept giving her glances like he couldn't believe what she was wearing. The green Calvin Klein dress draped over her body in a way that revealed and concealed at the same time. The neckline was the most revealing part of the dress. It showed off her cleavage. Which was something, because Jenny had no cleavage to speak of until she put on the little black bra that Sabina had talked her into. It was truly amazing what a little bit of padding and spandex could do for a girl's boobs.

Five people had come up to her already and told her she looked amazing and beautiful. But sitting next to Bill and his disapproving glances kind of popped her bubble. Along with the fact that Gabe Raintree seemed impervious to the green-dress kryptonite she was aiming in his direction. He was, apparently, not Superman.

She needed to remember that. He'd told her no, and she ought to accept that and move on. But as the auditorium filled up with paying customers, both in-towners and out-of-towners, she only had eyes for him.

He looked good enough to eat tonight. He'd gotten a haircut, and he'd shaved and almost looked clean-cut, except for the all-black outfit and the tailored leather sport coat. All in all, he conveyed an impression of a brooding, badass author who was slightly tortured.

And she wanted desperately to cook for him, not to mention the other stuff that Lillian Bray wouldn't approve of.

Of course the whole Bill/Gabe thing wasn't the only negative dynamic playing itself out at the head table. For some reason, Nita had seated Simon and Molly Wolfe at the table, even though Molly was not a member of the Library Committee. And Simon was staring at Gabe as if he were some kind of ax murderer.

To round it all out, Zeph Gibbs was there wearing a sport jacket and a tie. And he kept looking at Gabe and Simon like he expected the two of them to call each other out at any moment. She'd never seen Zeph so antsy, but maybe that made some sense, given that Gabe was about to get up and talk about how Last Chance was the setting that inspired *Black Water*. And you couldn't talk about that novel without talking about its villain, who was possibly one of the most memorable psychopaths ever portrayed.

Of course, Zeph wasn't crazy like Zebulon Stroud. Everyone in town knew that. But still, it was mighty uncomfortable to be sitting at this table with Zeph there.

"So," Nita said, jumping into the conversational lull

right after everyone took their seats and the chicken dish was being served, "Simon, I'll bet you remember Mr. Raintree when he was just a little boy. You were friends with his brother, weren't you? Got any juicy secrets to share?"

Icy cold prickled the back of Jenny's skull. She'd had the same sensation right before the chicken took flight and landed in Reverend Lake's lap.

Good heavens. The ghost was here. He wasn't tied to The Jonquil House. And he didn't like Nita's question.

Her pulse rate zoomed, and she had to bite her lip to keep from standing up and warning everyone to leave the auditorium immediately via the emergency exits. What the heck was Nita up to? That question had been loaded, and there was an avid spark in her dark eyes.

To make it worse, Simon looked like he'd been trapped in a spider's web, with no way out.

Jenny needed to stop Nita before the evening got out of hand or the ghost did something heinous. No doubt, Zeph had been living this reality for decades. And one look in his direction confirmed Jenny's suspicions. Both Zeph and Gabe sat with rigid shoulders and wide, dark eyes. They knew the ghost was here. And neither of them seemed to know what to do about it.

It was up to Jenny to head off a disaster.

"So, Savannah," she said, throwing herself into the breach. "You've done a wonderful job with The Kismet. And you too Zeph, the lobby restoration is incredible."

Savannah grinned from ear to ear and started talking about everything that had gone into the restoration of the old movie theater. And of course Savannah could go on and on and on like a broken record on this topic, which made it precisely the right one for the moment. Hettie, Dash, Bill, and Molly all joined in the table discussion, apparently oblivious to the cold and the crisis that had just been averted.

Simon, Zeph, and Gabe remained silent, their heads down, pushing food around their plates, acting like they were eating, when clearly all of them had lost their appetites.

Gabe thought he might vomit. His stomach roiled and twisted. His face went clammy and cold. In a minute, he was going to have to stand up and talk to an auditorium about *Black Water*. Normally this wouldn't have bothered him.

But the ghost was right there at his back, practically breathing ectoplasm, or whatever it was that ghosts were made of, down his back.

Meanwhile Nita was looking at him, speculation in her eyes. And Simon was trying not to look at him at all. Gabe got the feeling Simon wished he were anywhere except sitting at this table with Molly between them.

"Excuse me," Gabe said as he pushed up from the table and headed toward the restrooms. If he didn't know better, he'd say he was suffering from low blood sugar. But he wasn't about to take out his monitor and do a blood test with nine pairs of eyes watching him. His diabetes was something he preferred to keep quiet.

And low blood sugar seemed unlikely, since he'd eaten a good lunch and had choked down a few bites of the chicken dinner. Stage fright had never been a problem before. But suddenly, the last thing he wanted was to stand up and give an introduction to the movie version of *Black Water*.

He headed into one of the stalls, took out his meter, and checked his blood glucose level. He was fine. His rapid pulse and clammy hands had nothing to do with his diabetes. Which made sense, because he had his illness under control.

He stood in the stall for a few minutes before someone else entered. His heart rate climbed even higher. What an idiot. He'd allowed himself to be cornered in the men's room. He knew better. The house was filled with crazy fans.

"Gabe, it's Simon. You've been in here awhile, and Nita is getting restless."

Shit. Having to face Simon seemed worse than being cornered by one of his rabid readers. But either way, there was only one exit to this room, and he'd have to face Simon or someone else.

He came out of the stall.

"You okay?" Simon asked.

He needed an excuse so he pulled the meter out of his pocket. He hated using the diabetes this way, but he needed the fig leaf tonight. What the hell was wrong with him? "Just needed to run a quick blood test," he said, stepping to the sink and washing his hands, trying to avoid the accusation in Simon's dark eyes.

He pulled a few paper towels out of the dispenser and dried his hands. The silence was growing heavier by the minute.

"Gabe," Simon said, "I think we need to talk. Clear the air, you know?"

He turned. There was such a look on Simon's face.

"Clear the air about what?" he said. Sweat was trickling down his back, and he was starting to wonder if his blood tester was faulty.

"About Luke."

"What about him?"

"About what happened the day he died."

Gabe stood there riveted to the floor. "You know what happened?"

"I was there. Don't you remember?"

Gabe was going to be sick. He was going to faint.

"Hey, man, are you okay?" Simon asked.

"You were there?" Gabe's voice sounded far away to his own ears.

Simon blinked a few times. "Oh, shit, you *don't* remember."

Gabe shook his head. "I don't remember anything except that I tagged along after Luke and Zeph with my BB gun. Granddad told me to weed the front garden, but I didn't do as I was told."

"Holy shit." Simon turned his back and slapped the wall with an open hand. "Shit, shit, shit."

"Tell me what happened? I've been trying to get Zeph to tell me, but he won't. I have a feeling I'm not going to like the truth." He leaned up against the wall, but for some odd reason his heart rate was beginning to slow. He'd wanted the truth for ages. He'd wanted to understand that dark hollow place inside.

Simon turned. "I can't tell you now, you have to—"

"I don't give a rat's ass about the library or the speech I'm supposed to give. I want the truth. I want to know why you're looking at me like I'm evil. Why I've always had this feeling that down deep, I was the monster, not Zeph."

"Zeph isn't a monster, and you know it."

"Yeah, I do. And if he's not and you're not, then that leaves me."

Simon shook his head. "No, it makes you human. You were a kid and you were jealous of Luke. All your grandfather ever did was sing Luke's praises and hold him up to you. I remember. You were never good enough for him. And I know how that feels, believe me. I didn't have the greatest relationship with my parents either. So you were envious of that stupid rifle..." He paused.

"Yeah, and..."

"So Zeph turned his back and was watching the river and talking about fishing later in the afternoon. He knew Luke hated target shooting. The gun had already been fired a couple of times so that your grandfather would hear it and know that Luke had done as he was told. But Luke was more interested in watching the great blue heron that was feeding by the riverside. And I was bird-watching, too."

"Which means I was left alone."

"You were left alone. You don't remember any of this?"

Gabe stood up straight and wrapped his arms around his chest. His whole body had started to tremble as Simon spoke. It was as if Luke's boyhood friend had switched on a light, revealing the gruesome reality that Gabe had been running from since he was ten. Gabe closed his eyes and let the horror in.

He remembered the rifle, leaning up against a tree. He remembered his small, fat hand reaching for it. He remembered the weight of the gun in his hands.

"I shot him." He breathed the words.

"The heron flew off, and Luke turned and saw you with the gun," Simon said, apparently needing his own catharsis. "I guess he was scared you'd hurt yourself. Or maybe it was just a continuation of the bickering you two used to get into. I don't know. As a boy I thought it was just Luke being possessive of something that was his, the way he sometimes was. But as a man, I like to think Luke was worried about you hurting yourself. I don't know, Gabe, honestly. All I know is that he turned and ran toward you and told you to quit playing with his gun, and those were his last words."

Gabe knew what Simon was going to say before the words left his mouth. The memory of that horrible day tumbled back into his head. His synapses reconnected, and he could almost hear the sound of the gun going off, could almost feel the horrible recoil that knocked him right on his ass. And then the sound of Luke trying to breathe through the horrible hole the gun had made in his chest. He remembered that sound and how it ended in a sigh. He remembered the silence after that.

And then Zeph was crying a little and yelling at Luke. And then Zeph turning toward Gabe, who was still sitting there on his backside trying not to think about what he'd just done.

"Did you take the safety off?" Zeph yelled at him.

And Gabe just sat there, because he hadn't done anything to the gun except pick it up. He didn't even remember putting his finger on the trigger. "You listen, boy, and you listen good. You didn't do this, you hear?" Zeph was right in his face.

And then Zeph was talking to Simon, who was standing there looking at Luke's bloody dead body. Luke's face was pale, and his lips were blue. And then Simon started crying, and Zeph told him to keep his mouth shut. And then Simon took off into the woods, and Zeph let him go.

And they were alone with Luke, who was dead.

Gabe opened his eyes onto the utilitarian scene of the men's room at The Kismet. "You never told anyone the truth?" he asked Simon.

"I told Molly. I think Molly told Nita. And I think Nita set this up so that you'd learn the truth tonight. As far as I know, no one else knows this secret."

Gabe stepped to the bank of sinks and put his hands under the faucet. He let the water run for a few moments before cupping a handful and splashing it over his face. He rubbed his eyes and then straightened. He found the paper towel dispenser and dried his face.

Then he turned his back on Simon and left the bathroom. He had a book talk to give, and he didn't plan on disappointing anyone.

CHAPTER
20

Jenny watched Gabe cross the auditorium as he returned from the restroom. He stopped along the way to greet some of his readers and fans. But he looked like a zombie. His face was deathly pale, his eyes bruised, the skin across his cheeks tight. He was paying too high a price for allowing the ghost to haunt him.

The ghost was sucking him dry. Anyone with any heart would see it.

When he got back to the table, he apologized to Nita and then allowed her to kick off the program. He took his place at a podium on the theater's raised stage.

"I've been asked to talk about the link between Last Chance and the setting I used in *Black Water*," he started.

"But setting is a funny thing. An author uses more than geography to create a setting. The setting of a story is mostly about the people. And I fear that I did a grave disservice to a few people who live here in Last Chance when I wrote *Black Water*.

"I'm going to keep my remarks more than brief. I'm

simply going to make an apology to a person I owe more to than I can ever express." He stopped and looked down at Zeph. "We have a lot of folks here who aren't locals, but for those of you who are, y'all know Zeph Gibbs. He's the man who restored the woodwork in this beautiful auditorium. He's the man who taught me how to bait a hook and cast a line. He's a man who used to give me great books to read during the summertime, and I think I never would have thought about becoming an author without his insistence that reading a book could take a person to someplace he'd never been. A better place, usually.

"And I repaid this kindness by turning him into the villain of *Black Water*, when in truth…" His voice quivered, and Jenny suddenly realized that Gabe was about to fall apart. He took several deep breaths. "When in truth…the villain has always been me." And then he turned and walked off the stage and headed in the direction of the side exit.

Jenny and Zeph stood up in unison. But Simon grabbed Zeph by the arm and said, "He needs to be alone to process it all."

And Zeph scowled. "You told him the truth? You're an idiot."

And it looked for an instant like Zeph might punch Simon, but Nita got in the way. "Yes, he did. I asked him to."

"You what?" Zeph said. Jenny had never seen Zeph so upset or animated.

"What the hell is going on here?" Jenny said out loud.

And that's when Savannah stood up, grabbed her by the shoulders, and shoved her toward the side door. "Honey, it's now or never. Go on and get that man."

"What?"

Savannah rolled her eyes. "Go. You have my blessing."

"What? Oh. Oh!" She turned, took off her stupid shoes, and ran like a barefooted fool.

A filthy curse fell from Gabe's mouth when he ran down the street toward Palmetto Avenue and the spot in front of the theater where he'd parked his car. Why the hell hadn't Sheriff Rhodes created a space here on the side street where he could make a quick getaway?

As he rounded the corner, the crazy women on the opposite side of the street took up their sign waving and chanting. The hate in their voices hit him like bullets right to the chest. He stopped, unable to breathe, unable to think, unable to go on.

They pointed fingers at him and called him evil.

And they were right.

He might have stood there frozen for all eternity if it hadn't been for Jenny, who materialized right behind him. She must have followed him. But why?

She took his hand and pulled him back from the corner. "My car is back here. No one will follow us. Come on, we're going home."

"Home?" he said as she pulled him away from the scene on the sidewalk and back into the dark side street. "I have no home."

She had the good sense not to argue with him. She merely pulled him down the street, her hand impossibly warm in his. It wasn't until they'd reached her tiny Fiesta that he realized she was barefoot in the middle of February.

"Where are your shoes?" he asked. The question was inane.

"I couldn't run in the heels." She opened the door for him, and he got inside.

When she'd gotten into the driver's side, she handed him her shoes. They had insanely high heels. "I bought those for you," she said.

He blinked down at them. Then up at her. She smiled. "Not to wear. To admire."

"Oh." He let go of a long, deep breath. "Uh, look, Jenny, I need to go. I need to get out of here and—"

"We're going home."

"No, you don't understand. I packed all my things. They're in my car. I was planning to leave after the speech. And after what I just said, I better get going."

She'd been about to start the car, but she stopped. Her face was hidden in darkness, which was good because he couldn't see the impact of his words. Also, he could hide in the dark.

"Where are you planning to go?" she asked.

"I don't know." He paused a beat, the silence heavy and cold. "Someplace far away," he added as an afterthought.

"Far away from me? Or the past?" Her voice sounded tight.

"Not you. God, not you. Jenny, sometimes I have this feeling that you and I are connected in some way. As if there were a string from your heart to mine. And I'm pretty sure the string will break when I leave. I'm sure it will hurt a lot to go. But it doesn't matter. I'm leaving. I have to. But you? You're stronger than I am. And I'm sure you'll forget me in time."

"Never."

"I have to go."

"No, you don't. I don't know what Simon said to you, but it doesn't matter. You don't have to leave."

"Jenny, I killed Luke. Simon told me what happened."

That stopped her. Her shoulders squared, and he was sure she was giving him one of her somber looks. Thank God it was dark in the car because he didn't think he could bear to see censure in her eyes. "Simon was there when Luke was shot?"

"Yeah."

"What happened, tell me?"

He sat there like an automaton and told her the full, unadulterated story from beginning to end. While he spoke a numbness crept over him, but the moment he was finished, a bubble of emotion, stirred by sorrow and love and guilt, lodged in his throat.

"I don't see why this means you have to leave. It was an accident."

"I don't want to go," he said through the knot in his throat. "I love The Jonquil House. And for the last few weeks, even with the ghost haunting me, I've seen a glimpse of how my life might be full and happy. And I've known you, Jenny. I guess the ghost is going to haunt me for the rest of my life. He doesn't seem tied to the house. I'll be taking him with me."

"Wrong," Jenny said. "Just as soon as we can, we're going to send Luke back to wherever he needs to go. Ghosts are not supposed to hang around after death. It's sort of a rule, and your brother has outworn his welcome. I think he knows it, too."

"Jenny, I told you. I'm going." He started to reach for the door lever, but her voice called him back.

"Coward. You're running away because of a senseless accident that happened twenty-five years ago? You need to get over it."

"How do you know it was an accident?"

She leaned toward him and cupped his cheek with her hand. The touch was so gentle she might have been an angel. "Because you just told me that you didn't even pull the trigger."

He closed his eyes and sank into her touch. "The gun just went off. At least that's the way I remember it. But obviously I must have touched the trigger."

"Maybe not. And by Zeph's reaction, someone, probably Luke, forgot to put the safety on. And—"

"But if I'd never touched that gun, Luke would never have—" She put her fingers across his lips.

"Hush. Zeph could say the same thing. If he hadn't turned his back on y'all. And your grandfather could also blame himself, and probably did. I'll bet he kept blaming himself for telling Luke to go out and practice. I'm sure he wished that he'd let y'all stay inside and play video games. But all those things happened. And like every accident, it always comes down to a bunch of things, not just one. Honey, time goes in only one direction. You need to forgive yourself."

"I have to go."

"I know what you're thinking: No one could possibly love someone like you, because you're a monster. You as much as said it tonight in front of the whole town. But here's the thing, Gabe, *I'm* strong enough.

"I've watched you for weeks now. I've seen that way you look at me sometimes, as if you're afraid to let me see too deeply inside. But here's the thing, I'm ready to meet you in your darkest place. I'm ready to turn on the lights. I'm ready to love you in spite of it all.

"Maybe I'm too plain and small for you. Maybe you'd rather have someone glamorous like Ms. Ianelli, but I'm here and I have a heart that's big enough to love you. All of you. Even the dark parts. Even the moody parts. Because those parts are balanced by the Gabe who writes about heroes who always win against evil. The Gabe who made me change my locks two times because he was worried about me. The Gabe who has a big, fat, soft spot in his heart for one gigantic pain-in-the-behind dog.

"I love all those Gabes. I love you even though you don't like my pie, and that's saying something."

"Jenny, you don't know me. I have so many secrets I haven't told you. For instance, I haven't touched your sweets because I'm a diabetic, not because I don't like pies. Not eating your muffins in the morning required an enormous amount of willpower. And that's just one secret. I have a whole graveyard of skeletons in my closet."

"You're a diabetic?"

"I was diagnosed when I was twelve. Granddad blamed me for that, too." His voice wavered. He needed to go now and never come back.

"We have plenty of time for you to tell me your secrets. And I can tell you mine. You don't have to bear every burden all by yourself, you know."

He wanted to believe that most of all, so he didn't move. He didn't try to leave her. He didn't open the door and walk away. He sat there and let her seal the deal with a kiss. She leaned over the console and touched her soft lips to his. The kiss started out tentatively, as if she was testing him to see what he might do.

He should have pushed her away like the other times.

But her kiss was like a healing balm. It seemed to work its way into all the endlessly aching places in his soul. It filled him up with something golden and pure, like some miraculous elixir. And so he fell into the kiss as hard as he'd ever fallen into a kiss. He opened his mouth and she moved in and blew all his good intentions and deep fears to smithereens.

Jenny unlocked the two locks on The Jonquil House's front door. Her heart was pounding so hard she couldn't breathe. This was it. She was taking charge, but holy God she didn't have the first idea how to actually do that.

It was still kind of amazing that Gabe was here, coming back to the inn knowing that they were not going to say good night and go to their separate bedrooms. And really, she was starting to have a tiny bit of performance anxiety. It had been one hell of a long time since she'd gotten intimate with a man.

More important, if she was crazy enough to buy into what Savannah Randall had suggested earlier in the evening, then there was a boatload riding on this moment. Like her heart and her future. Which explained why her hands were shaking so badly that she was fumbling with the keys.

It seemed to take an eternity to get the door open. She was running out of time to think of something hot and sultry to say that would get him up to her bedroom.

Then, as the door swung inward, Bear came flying down the hall and knocked her back into Gabe's waiting arms. The dog was probably ruining her green dress with his paws up on her chest, but he was giving her lots and lots of sloppy dog kisses, and somehow that seemed exactly right for the moment.

Because it made Gabe laugh. He was right behind her, holding her up. And he'd used the moment to sneak his big manly hands around her waist while he propped her up against his sturdy chest and hips, where she discovered that Gabe was turned on.

Evidently, he didn't need any sultry lines. The kisses they'd shared in the car had done the trick. They were some first-class kisses.

His heat penetrated her being and wormed its way into every cell of her body, melting her so that she kind of settled back into him with a vocal sigh.

"Bear. Down. Now." Gabe could be commanding when he chose to be.

The dog obeyed. And she found herself back on her own two feet while Gabe shut and locked the door.

"He needs to be walked," she said, suddenly realizing that a dog complicated things. And then something else occurred to her. "You were going to leave Bear behind? With me?"

He turned away from the door and aimed his gaze on her. His eyes seemed even darker, and his look lit a fire in her. "He's your dog," he said.

She shook her head. "No, I think he's *our* dog."

The corner of his mouth twitched. She wanted to kiss it and wondered why the heck she was holding back. She needed to break free of these restraints that she'd imposed on herself for all these years.

But before she could act on the impulse, he was striding down the hall toward the kitchen.

"Wait." She followed after him.

He pulled the dog's leash down from the hook by the back door. "I'll walk the dog."

She didn't want him to leave her. If he did, she'd lose her nerve. Or maybe he'd talk himself out of it.

She shook her head. "No, we'll walk the dog after." And she took a couple of steps toward him, snaked her arms around his neck, and pulled him down for the kiss she'd wanted to give him a moment before.

His mouth met hers, his lips firm and moist and gentle. When he opened the seam of her lips, his tongue proved to be exceptionally talented.

She ran her fingers up into his hair, and he made a noise that made her feel powerful in a way she had never felt before.

His mouth left hers and trailed a string of kisses and half bites along her jaw and down into the hollow of her neck.

Her insides melted, as if some warm being had breathed spring into the desolate, cold places that she'd been guarding. The walls came down. She stopped worrying. She stopped thinking.

She simply was. Alive.

Gabe knew the minute Jenny lost her reserve. She threw her head back and let him have complete access to that soft, warm, tender spot at the hollow of her neck. He sucked her in, he tasted, he breathed her. And something inside him answered back. She had unlocked a place inside him that he didn't even know existed.

That place wasn't evil, but it was primordial and kind of wild. He wanted to expose it. He wanted to lose control. But finding the release point was so hard.

He was afraid.

She seemed to know that, because she backed away a little and looked up at him, her hazel eyes wide and dark and full of a deep, soul-wrenching kindness. "I have a whole heart," she said. "I can love all of you."

And just like that, kissing and touching her through her amazing dress wasn't nearly enough. He didn't want to distance himself from her anymore. He wanted to inhale her. He wanted to be a part of her. He needed to be with her. He put his mouth on hers and lost himself.

He pulled her hard against him just as she ran her hands down to his butt. It was a relief to be that close, but still it wasn't close enough. He wanted to feel her skin against his. He wanted...everything.

So he did the only reasonable thing he could think of. He picked her up. She didn't weigh hardly anything, and he carried her right into Luke's old bedroom. She squeaked in surprise and then she laid her head on his shoulder. And that made him feel potent and strong and male in a hot and wicked way.

"I'm liking this. I'm glad your ankle is better."

"Me too."

She ran her fingertips over his ear. "Oh, God," he breathed as the heat climbed up his neck.

"You like that?"

"Yeah."

"Oh good. I intend to find more places like that. I'm going to winnow out all of your secrets."

"Yeah." It was the only word he could think of to say. He was, for an author, surprisingly empty of words at the moment.

"I want to get naked. You can undress me," she said, as he put her down by the edge of the bed. She put her arms around his neck again. "The dress has a zipper on the side."

Wow, his little bird was taking charge and apparently wasn't having any problems with words. He followed her directions. But just for fun, he took his own sweet time getting her out of that amazing dress, not to mention her black underwear. By the time he'd accomplished all this, both of them were panting.

And while it might have been a complete turn-on to let her undress him, he didn't think he could stand it. He wanted to feel his skin against hers. Right now. So he batted her hands away and shucked his clothes in a matter of seconds.

And then the fun began in earnest.

And that was amazing, because being with her *was* fun. And mind blowing, too.

CHAPTER 21

Zeph didn't rightly know what he should do. He stood up, feeling like the walls of the old theater were closing in on him. Gabe's fans were all looking at him like he was some kind of freak show. Meanwhile, Savannah Randall remained standing as she watched Jenny run from the theater on bare feet.

And Nita...was on her way up the stairs to the podium.

"Well. I reckon that was a little surprising," Nita said into the mic. "But y'all already know that Mr. Raintree is a funny man. So, without further ado, why don't y'all sit back and enjoy *Black Water*. Your servers will be coming around to take your dessert and drink orders."

The house lights dimmed, and the opening credits of the movie started, while a slow confused murmur spread through the crowd. Clearly they felt they'd been cheated in some way.

Of course, the local folks didn't feel cheated at all. They were stunned.

And Zeph was furious. He'd tried to leave his anger in the past. He'd given it up after Vietnam, but here it was right front and center.

He'd never been so angry.

So when Nita came down those stairs, he was waiting for her in the darkness, and he grabbed her by the arm, and he pulled her out through the same side door that Gabe had escaped through.

She didn't fight him, which only registered when they got to the sidewalk. And suddenly he was ashamed. He'd manhandled her, and she was a fine lady, and he was, well, he wasn't much of anything.

And just like that his anger disappeared. And he was grateful for his self-control. His daddy had had a terrible temper, and Zeph had spent an entire lifetime trying not to be his daddy.

"I know you're upset," Nita said.

He took a deep breath and blew it out. "I was a minute ago. But I'm getting over it."

She laughed. "You always were like that."

"What?"

She shrugged. "I remember you from grade school and high school. You were the one who watched out for the little kids. You were the one who stood up to the bullies, but you never took a swing. You just used words. And I admired that so much. You were a peacemaker. How on earth does a peacemaker end up in Vietnam?"

He couldn't speak a word.

"What?" she said. "Cat got your tongue."

"You watched me?"

"I did."

"I watched you."

"Did you? I had no idea. I might have been happy to know."

"Me too."

She took a big breath and hugged herself. She was cold. He took off his jacket and draped it across her shoulders.

"My library program has raised a lot of money," she said, "but I don't think it's going to be a success in the way I intended. Still, if it got you and Gabriel Raintree to acknowledge the truth, then I'm pleased."

"The truth hurt him. I've been trying to save him from that hurt."

"Just like on the playground." She turned and looked at him. "Zeph Gibbs, sometimes you can't save people from being hurt. Sometimes life is just hurtful, and you have to deal with it and move on. Lord knows I've been hurt a few times, but it's made me stronger. It's made me know what I value and what I don't.

"Gabe will be better for knowing the truth. He'll find his peace one day. And if you believe the silly match-makers in this town, it's possible that Jenny Carpenter is exactly the medicine Gabe needs. Do you have faith in the matchmakers, Zeph?"

He felt the corner of his mouth tip. "I reckon I do."

"Zeph, the matchmakers in this town have given up on me."

"They've given up on me, too."

She turned all the way around and pointed a finger at his chest. "You know, sometimes you can go searching for something you think you've lost, or something that you think you'll only find in some far-off place, and then one day you take a little trip down the local road and make a left turn down to the river, and there it is, plain as day:

The thing you thought you'd lost forever. The thing you thought you'd never be able to find unless you went on some big-ass search."

"Nita, what are you saying?"

She reached up and put her hand on his cheek. "I'm saying, Zeph, that I had the worst crush on you when I was fifteen. And somehow I never had the courage to tell you. I reckon it was because of the way your folks lived. I was prejudiced about that. And I guess I've been kind of uppity for all these years, until I walked into your home and realized that you were the same person I admired so much at school."

Zeph didn't know what to do but the one thing he thought he'd never, ever have a chance to do. He took Nita Wills in his arms, and he kissed her. And he put his whole, big heart into that kiss. To his utter surprise, the librarian kissed him right back.

Gabe woke up sometime around two o'clock and slipped from the bed. He threw on his slacks and shirt and took the dog out for a little walk. Then he got some wood and built a small fire in the hearth.

It wasn't cold, but the fire would be kind of romantic. And he laughed at himself as he took off his clothes and climbed back into the bed. For once, his sheets weren't freezing cold.

He propped himself on the pillow and watched Jenny sleep. Her hair was all tumbled across the pillow. In the fire's glow it danced with red highlights. She was breathing deeply with a contented smile on her lips.

Strange and tender emotions rushed through him. She was changing him in some elemental way. She'd told him that she would meet him in his darkest place, and she'd pretty well done it.

She'd faced that place with no fear and only love. And last night she'd told him that she thought he was kind and good. He didn't see it. He knew she had put on her rose-colored glasses. But he wanted to be kind and good. He wanted to be that man because she loved him as if he were.

What would happen when one day she woke up from this dream and realized she'd made a mistake?

He couldn't bear to think about what that would do to him. But there was a chance it would happen. He hadn't told her all his secrets. He'd only just told her about his illness. There were others secrets, some of them pretty hard to swallow. So he had to be prepared for it.

But he had time. He had the opportunity to become a better man. He could give her his heart. Hell, who was he kidding? She already had his heart.

And that was pretty scary because, the last time he'd fallen in love, his heart had been crushed.

He couldn't bear thinking about that. So he pushed it all away and leaned over his love and kissed her right in the place he'd discovered at the base of her throat. Yeah, that spot.

She sighed, and then she groaned, and then she opened her eyes. Without her glasses, that gaze was slightly myopic, which was sexy as hell.

"You built a fire."

"I did. I also walked the dog."

"Oh good. I forgot." She smiled and snuggled against him.

And he spent the next thirty minutes waking her up.

Dawn lit the windows in the back bedroom. Jenny lay in the curl of Gabe's arms, her body warm as she watched the day break. It was Sunday. She should be getting up and heading for church. If she didn't show up, there would be gossip.

She didn't care.

Gabe pulled her a little closer, the stubble on his chin abrading her temple. She wanted to stay like this forever.

But Bear had other ideas. He must have sensed that she was awake because he got up from his place by the now-cold fire and trotted over to her side of the bed. He put his snout up where she could give him a pet if she was of a mind to.

He had adorable, pleading, deep, puppy-dog eyes. And he let go of a little whine.

She glanced at her watch. It was just after seven o'clock. He needed a walk. And then maybe she could make a nice breakfast for Gabe. Something without a lot of carbohydrates.

She wiggled out of Gabe's arms, reluctant to leave that warmth for the cold February morning. But she also needed to visit the loo.

She tiptoed out of the room, gathering clothes as she went, then skedaddled up to the Rose Room, washed her face, and dressed in jeans and a sweater and a pair of sneakers. She pulled on her big, puffy coat.

"C'mon boy," she said, getting the leash from its hook by the door. "We'll let your master sleep in this morning. He had kind of a rough day yesterday and a busy night last night. So this morning, it's just you and me on a walk down by the river."

They headed out the back door and took the path by the rhododendrons that eventually led to the public boat launch. Somewhere along this path had been the target range where Luke had been killed. You wouldn't know it today; the woods and the kudzu had taken the clearing back, and that was probably a good thing.

She started to whistle one of Grandpa's silly songs. She was as light as a feather. The world was a beautiful place.

Bear stopped to investigate all the interesting scents along the trail. She didn't hurry him up, even though she was anxious to get back to Gabe. She realized, as the sun crept higher, promising another unseasonably warm February day, that she had all the time in the world. Gabe wasn't going anywhere. They had found each other.

Savannah had told her to go after him.

She smiled at that. He was the handsome man that Miriam had promised her. Handsome on the inside, and really, he was pretty darn hot on the outside, too. She couldn't imagine why she hadn't seen it at first.

They reached the public pier. The brown water of the Edisto River gurgled past with little swirls and eddies and bubbles marring its surface. The current was usually strong this time of year, and the water was always cold.

She and Bear walked out onto the pier and watched the sun rising. There wasn't a clear view to the horizon, but the dawn light filtered through bare branches and painted the clumps of Spanish moss in gold. Her mind was a million miles away, lost in the beauty of the moment and the peace in her heart.

The first clue that she wasn't alone was the sound of a step on the boards behind her, and then Bear growled and tugged on his leash.

She was just turning around when someone taller and stronger grabbed her from behind, placing an ice-cold hand across her mouth. A husky voice said, "I tried to warn you. But no, you didn't listen. You can't have him. He's mine."

Bear started barking, and she instinctively let go of his leash as she tried to break the hold of her attacker. She didn't know what Bear was up to, only that he was barking and growling. She wanted to tell Bear to run away and get Gabe or Zeph or anyone, but the dog wasn't leaving her.

Maybe the dog could bite her attacker, maybe—

The person behind her gave a mighty shove, and Jenny toppled over the edge of the pier and into the river. Her clothes dragged her under, the current took her, and the icy water paralyzed her.

Gabe awoke with a start. Something wasn't right. The room was bitterly cold. Jenny and Bear were gone, and he didn't have to guess that the ghost was agitated.

He rolled out of bed and reached for his dress pants. "Jenny," he called, but got no answer. He scooped his shirt and jacket from the floor where he'd tossed them last night. His heart was galloping.

"Jenny?"

No answer. He ran into the kitchen. The leash was gone. She'd taken the dog for a walk. It was okay.

Only it wasn't. The ghost was almost in a frenzy, and for the first time, he nudged at Gabe's mind. He needed to find Jenny, now. Gabe tore out of the back door because that seemed like the only reasonable thing to do.

And that's when he heard Bear. The noise was terrible. Barks and growls and then yelps, as if he'd been hurt in some way.

Terror of the kind he'd never known seized him as he ran down the path toward the public boat pier. The barking and yelping ended before he'd taken more than ten steps but he continued down the path, sliding and slipping in his haste.

When he reached the pier, poor Bear was lying on his side, bloodied but still alive. He raised his head and gave a weak bark. Gabe fell to his knees, tears streaming down his face.

"Oh, Bear, who did this to you? Where's Jenny?" His voice broke.

Something pushed him from behind.

He turned, but no one was there, just the oppressive feeling that he wasn't alone. The ghost poked him again. Gabe scrambled to his feet.

A wind sprang up that blew so hard he almost lost his breath, and yet the trees remained perfectly still on this mild winter day. Gabe couldn't stand against the force that pushed him downriver. He turned his back to the wind and started walking past the boat launch and the small parking lot, and into the weedy, wild riverbank, the habitat of water moccasins.

The banks were steep here, and he had to wade in the shallows, his dress shoes filling with icy water. And then he saw her, snagged on a log, her face white as death.

He reached Jenny a moment later and managed to get her waterlogged body into his arms. He carried her upriver and to the parking lot, where he lay her down on the winter-brown grass, leaned over her, and listened to see if she was breathing.

Thank God. But she was unconscious and pale and cold as death. He took off his jacket and draped it over her body. Then he pulled his cell phone out of the pocket and dialed 911.

• • •

Jenny huddled under an electric blanket. She was dressed in a hospital gown and was resting in one of the beds at the Last Chance clinic. Annie Jasper was checking her vital signs. "You gave us all a real scare," Annie said patting her arm. "How's your head?"

"All right," she lied. She had a splitting headache but she wasn't about to whine about it. The river had apparently washed her right into a cypress knee or a fallen log or something, and she'd hit her noggin. Doc Cooper said it was a lucky thing that she came to rest faceup; otherwise she might have drowned. As it was, the doc was worried about a concussion and hypothermia.

Jenny was worried about Bear. She'd regained consciousness in the parking lot, shivering under Gabe's leather coat as he tried to keep her warm. She'd heard Bear's whines.

"Do you know how bad the dog is hurt?"

Annie shook her head. "No, I don't. I heard Gabe talking to Charlene Polk on the phone, though. I think he needs surgery. Something about a broken back."

Tears leaked from her eyes. Damn. He should have run away when she let go of the leash. But no, he had to play hero.

Annie patted her shoulder. "Honey, I don't want you to worry, you hear. The sheriff is all over this like a cheap suit. And the doc said it was okay for him to come ask you a few questions. Are you up to it?"

She nodded, but her head was on fire. And her heart was breaking over the dog.

A minute later Sheriff Rhodes came striding into the cubicle where she was recovering. He filled up the small space with his large presence.

"Where's Gabe?" she asked.

"He's fine. He'll be in when I'm finished. We like to interview witnesses individually. It helps get the story right."

"Okay."

"So how did you end up in the river?"

"Someone pushed me."

"Did you see who it was?"

"No. But she said something to me."

"*She?*"

"I'm pretty sure it was a woman. She was tall though. Much bigger than me. Maybe five-ten and really strong."

"What did she say?"

"She said something about having warned me but that I hadn't paid attention. And then she said something about how I couldn't have something. I don't remember."

"All right, Jenny, I'm going to be blunt. You are moving into the apartment above the Cut 'n Curl until I can bring this person to justice. I'm pretty sure that the person who stole the chickens and vandalized your kitchen is the same one who attacked you and the dog. And I'm practically certain that I know who it is, but proving it is another thing altogether. I've got exactly no evidence, and you and the dog are not exactly good witnesses since you didn't see her and the dog can't talk."

"You know who did this?"

He nodded, his face as sober as a judge's.

"It's not someone from Dennis Hayden's campaign, is it. They wouldn't have attacked a dog or pushed me in the river."

He shook his head.

"Who then?"

"Gabe Raintree's wife."

CHAPTER 22

Gabe's gratitude to God and the Last Chance emergency rescue team—and yes, even his brother's ghost—knew no limits. Jenny was sitting up in bed, her cheeks pink, her hair all tumbled. She was alive. And she was pissed off. And she had every reason to be.

"You have a wife?"

"We're estranged," he said. Boy, *there* was a euphemism.

"When, exactly, were you going to tell me this?" She looked away, her mouth narrowing with her fury. "I am such an idiot. I do this all the time. It's like the minute I think I'm interested in someone, I put on the rose-colored glasses." She shook her head, but her eyes were filling with tears.

"Jenny, listen to me. I'm sorry I disappointed you. But it was bound to happen. I'm not nearly as good or as kind as you think I am. You don't know me very well. I wish I could be the man you want, but I'm not. I'll never be."

"Because you're married. That might have been nice to know before we got naked."

"I haven't lived with Delilah in more than eight years, but we are still technically man and wife. More important, I made a promise to keep her in sickness and in health. And I try to keep my promises."

"Right. That's what they all say."

He reached for her hand, and she pulled it away. "My wife is mentally ill. I have tried for a long time to get her help, but she refuses my efforts. I've set up a trust fund for her, with a large chunk of the money I inherited from my grandfather. It's hers no matter what, to take care of her for the rest of her life. I have filed for divorce on the grounds that we've been separated for more than a year, but she won't sign the papers, and the more I insist, the more unstable she becomes. I was pretty sure the minute I saw that dead chicken in your kitchen that it was her doing. She's committed countless similar acts of vandalism."

"Why didn't you say anything?"

"I did. I told the sheriff right away. But you were off in Charleston, and that seemed like a good, safe place for you while the sheriff tried to figure out if Delilah was lurking about somewhere. And while I missed you when you were gone, I was glad that Sabina kept you away for a week. I knew that I would have to leave after the library fund-raiser. And if you remember, we weren't involved when you left. I tried so hard not to make that mistake. But last night..."

"You think it was a mistake?"

He closed his eyes and hauled in a huge breath. His heart was breaking. "Yeah, I do. Not for the reasons you think. I don't want to remain Delilah's husband. But by allowing myself to become your lover, I put you in danger. I'm willing to bet she's been watching us for days. She knew we came home together last night. Heck, she probably watched us kissing through the kitchen windows. And if I'd been in my right mind last night, none of this would have happened.

"I can't do this anymore. I'm responsible for the death of one person I loved, and won't be responsible for another. As it is, Bear is badly hurt, and I don't know if I can forgive myself for not keeping him safe. And it's all my fault. I was selfish last night. And I was selfish the day I picked up Luke's gun."

Jenny pressed her lips together. She was fighting tears, and that made him feel like total crap, but a little part of him needed her to understand. Last night she'd said she'd meet him in his darkest place. Well, here it was.

"Do you know how hard it is for a man to deal with a crazy female stalker?" he asked. "Probably not. But take my word on it, until Sheriff Rhodes, no one in authority has taken me seriously. Everyone thinks a man should be able to control his wife. But if his wife is mentally ill, it's not so easy. What the hell am I supposed to do when Delilah starts screaming obscenities at me or trying to attack me in the middle of a public place? You think it would be okay for me to hit her back?"

"No," Jenny whispered.

"Right. So I'm stuck. And she is relentless. A couple of months ago, it got so bad that I couldn't write. I couldn't think. She was disrupting my life on a daily basis. So I came here to escape. And I fooled her for a while, until the Library Committee advertised the fund-raiser on Facebook and Twitter. And then all my troubles followed me."

He leaned down and kissed Jenny on the temple, even though she had her arms folded and a scowl on her face.

He was glad that she was angry. It would help her move on. And he thanked the Lord that he hadn't paid too high a price for his momentary lapse of judgment. As it was, Bear was not likely to survive. And the thought of losing the dog was almost more than he could endure.

He needed to go. He'd brought nothing but conflict and misery to the one place and the one person who had brought him happiness.

He was not fit to live here in Last Chance, South Carolina. He was not worthy of Jennifer Carpenter.

Gabe left Jenny and headed south on Palmetto Avenue, half a mile past the Peach Blossom Motor Court to the Creature Comforts Animal Hospital. He pulled his Lexus into the almost deserted parking lot.

It was ten o'clock on a Sunday morning. Everyone was in church, except for Dr. David Underhill, the chief veterinary surgeon in the area, and his associate doctor, Charlene Polk.

He parked his car and entered the building. The docs, who both looked way too young to inspire confidence, were waiting for him. He sat in Dr. Underhill's office and listened as Bear's injuries were cataloged. He got the feeling that Dr. Dave, as he wanted to be called, was not entirely convinced that it was worth trying to save Bear.

The doc's attitude infuriated the ghost, who had attached himself to Gabe's backside like a shadow no one could see. It infuriated Gabe, too.

"It's possible he might not have the use of his back legs," Dr. Dave said. "So you do have to consider the dog's quality of life."

"Then we'll build him a goddamn wheelchair. I'm not putting him down. You understand." Gabe's voice broke.

Dr. Polk, who'd been quiet up to that point, stood up and gave his shoulder a squeeze. "We'll do everything we can for him."

"Thank you. I'll be hanging out in the waiting room." He took a deep cleansing breath. He needed to get a grip on his emotions.

"Uh, Mr. Raintree, the surgery is going to take hours, and then there may be days of recovery time. You need to go home, and we'll call you, okay?" Dr. Polk's voice was kind.

There was just one problem: He didn't have a home to go back to.

The adrenaline of the last few hours was wearing off. He felt heavy and exhausted. The omnipresent weight of the ghost was more than he could endure. And adding to that, his face was a little clammy, like he might be experiencing low blood sugar, which wasn't surprising seeing as he'd been running around like a crazy person and had yet to eat breakfast.

The prospect of getting in his car and driving to Columbia or Atlanta or Charlotte suddenly seemed more than he could manage. Besides, he didn't think the ghost would let him go until Bear was out of danger.

"Okay, you have my cell number. Call me when you know something. I'll be spending the night at the Peach Blossom Motor Court."

An hour later, he had a key to a room at the seedy motel, and he was almost finished scarfing down the Kountry Kitchen's two-egg breakfast. His blood sugar was back in check. The churches of Last Chance were letting out, creating a traffic jam on Palmetto Avenue. Pretty soon the Kountry Kitchen was going to be crowded with a bunch of holier-than-thou people giving him dirty looks.

He gulped down the last of his coffee, intent on making a quick getaway, when Zeph and Nita came walking into the diner. Zeph was still wearing his dress slacks and shirt from the night before, only without the tie. The old guy had a smile on his face and a light in his eyes.

There was no escape. A moment later Zeph sat down in the chair next to Gabe, while Nita continued on to a booth at the back of the diner.

"What you doing here, boy?" Zeph said, "I thought sure you'd be back at the house letting Miz Jenny cook your breakfast."

"That didn't work out," he said, taking a ten-dollar bill out of his wallet and slapping it on the counter. He had no desire to rehash the events of the morning with Zeph. He wanted to be left alone. "I gotta go."

"Wait. Son, you need to know something."

"Yeah?" He finally looked up into Zeph's face.

"The safety was on."

"What?"

"The gun. When I looked at that gun afterward, the safety was on. And I showed that to old Sheriff Bennett, and he had the county ballistics experts examine that gun. It was defective. Sooner or later, someone was going to get hurt with that thing. It could just have easily been you, or me, or Simon, or your granddaddy. But I knew your granddaddy would blame you if he knew the truth. That man was hardhearted when it came to you boys. He wanted you both to be extensions of himself. And I guess he figured Luke was more likely to succeed than you. He just couldn't get past the fact that you were a little overweight as a child."

"That was the diabetes."

"Yeah, I heard about that last night. Why'd you keep it a secret from Miz Jenny, making her bake all those sweet things for you and you turning them down? Didn't you know that was breaking her heart?"

"No."

"Then you're a fool."

"Look, Zeph, I gotta go." He pushed up from the table, but the old man grabbed his arm and pulled him back down.

"Listen, you need to know something, seeing as the ghost has decided to haunt you and not me. I guess he was just waiting on you to come home. And I'm sorry about that. But to be honest, I'm glad my penance is done."

Gabe blinked at him in surprise. "Penance?"

"Yeah, that's what it is. And you need to prepare yourself. Every stray animal in all of creation is going to darken your door. And the ghost is going to help you find homes for them."

"What? Animals hate ghosts."

"I don't know about that. In my experience that hasn't been the case. You got experience with ghosts?"

Gave shook his head. "No, I just mean that in every ghost story—"

"Right, like those authors know anything about ghosts the way we do."

"You have a point."

"Look, son, I been thinking on this for a while. And I'm thinking that taking care of critters is the reason Luke stays here instead of going where he needs to go. You remember how he loved critters."

"I do."

"Well, he still does. And if he haunts you like he

haunted me, then you're going to be busy finding homes for the strays that come your way. And you'll have to do it, or he makes you cold. But if you take care of the animals, the ghost stays happy and you can live, sort of."

"Thanks. That's encouraging." His voice was laced with sarcasm.

"Course, Nita says that we should try to find some way to send Luke on to wherever he needs to go. But I don't have a clue how to do that."

"Nita knows about the ghost?"

"Uh-huh. And she doesn't think I'm crazy. It's kind of a relief if you want to know. There were times when I thought maybe I *was* crazy."

"You're not. Trust me. I do have experience in dealing with crazy people. I think that's why all of my stories have wackos in them."

"In that case, you might want to think about figuring out how to send Luke on to Heaven or whatever."

"Jenny suggested that we find a ghost exterminator."

"Exterminator? I don't like the sound of that."

"Now that I've gotten to know the ghost, neither do I."

"Maybe we should talk to that preacher man."

Gabe gnashed his teeth. No way was he inviting Timothy Lake to send the ghost on to the next world. That had disaster written all over it.

"Thanks for the advice, but I gotta go," Gabe said, breaking Zeph's hold on his forearm.

This time the old man let him leave. Ten minutes later, Gabe pulled into the parking lot of the Creature Comforts Animal Hospital. The door was locked, so he camped out in his car, listening to Bach cantatas and praying for the docs and the dog and the ghost and himself.

• • •

Jenny moved into the apartment above the Cut 'n Curl that afternoon. Well, it was more accurate to say that Maryanne went out to The Jonquil House, packed a suitcase, and hauled it over to her apartment. Doc Cooper kept Jenny under observation until Maryanne came and got her and forced her up the fire stairs into the tiny apartment.

With Jenny, Maryanne, and the baby all occupying space in the little flat above the beauty shop, there was absolutely no privacy. But it was sweet of Maryanne to make dinner. And Jenny's cousin had the good sense not to pry too deeply into what had happened.

At least until the baby was put to bed. Then Maryanne flopped down on the daybed and said, "So, are you going to talk about it?"

"About what?"

"You know good and well what I'm talking about. Gabe Raintree."

"No."

"For the record, I think he's a lying sack of you-know-what. Annie told me that she heard Sheriff Rhodes tell you that he's already married. It's exactly like the way that Rochester guy treated Jane in that book you lent me. Sometimes men can be total bastards. So if you want to cry and scream and gnash your teeth, I'm here. And I even have some wine up in the cabinet if you want to drown your sorrows, although Doc Cooper said you probably shouldn't touch any alcohol."

"Thanks for the support," Jenny said with a half-hearted smile. Still, as hard as she tried, she couldn't wrap her concussed brain around the idea that Gabe had lied to her in the same way Jamie Kendrick had.

Of course, Jamie had taken her to any number of no-tell motels for afternoon trysts with absolutely no intentions of leaving his wife. Her one-night fling with Gabe had been entirely different.

And now that her headache had subsided and the shock of what had almost happened to her was fading, she could clearly and rationally see the difference. For one thing, she had seduced Gabe, not the other way around. And she had gone further than that. She'd made all kinds of bold statements last night about being strong enough to love him come hell or high water.

Yes, she had. And then the minute the going got tough, she got squirrelly, and fell right back into that inflexible mold of the upright Christian woman. The mold her mother had tried to jam her into all her life.

What the heck happened to the liberated woman she had proclaimed herself to be?

That question made her head hurt worse. So she pulled out her cell phone and changed the subject. "I'm calling Charlene," she said as she dialed the emergency number for Creature Comforts.

"Hello," Charlene's voice came over the line.

"Hi, it's Jenny Carpenter, I'm checking up on Bear."

"Oh, hi. How are *you*? It's all over town about what happened to you. People are kind of freaking out about the possibility that we have a real stalker-slash-murderer here in town. And Mandy told me that the phones at WLST are ringing off the hook with people who want the radio station to broadcast hourly updates from the sheriff. And I heard from Arlene Whitaker that there's been a run on dead bolts at the hardware store. She's all sold out."

Jenny wanted to talk about her brush with death about

as much as she wanted to talk about her feelings for Gabe Raintree. "How's Bear?" she asked, sticking to the main point of her call.

"I'm afraid that Bear is in bad shape. Dr. Dave operated on his spine, and we'll have to see how he comes through. There are likely to be profound implications for him, like the loss of bladder control. I can't even promise that he'll be able to walk again. And he's got months of recovery ahead of him. Honestly, hon, you have to ask yourself about his quality of life. And I'm afraid Mr. Raintree isn't listening to reason about this."

"Mr. Raintree is still here?"

"Oh, yes, he's been in a couple of times. I think he's staying at the Peach Blossom Motor Court, but I swear he sat in his car outside the clinic for hours this afternoon waiting on word that the surgery was finished. He's devoted to the dog. But I'm worried about him because I don't think Bear is going to survive the night. And I know you don't want to hear this, but I kind of think it might be better if he didn't."

Gabe startled awake. He lay in the dark on the hard mattress and watched the faint pink from the Peach Blossom's neon sign leak through the thin curtains at the window. The clock on the bedside table said it was only eight o'clock.

He must have dozed off while he'd been reclining here on the bed, brooding about Bear and Jenny and Luke and Zeph.

He let go of a sigh. He should get up and eat. But he stayed put, watching the blinking pink light.

Until the light cast a silhouette on his curtains.

He sat up. Someone was trying to look through his windows. The spying lasted for about half a minute before the shadow moved away.

He got up and went to the bathroom, where he pulled out his cell and called Sheriff Rhodes. "It's Gabe. I've got a prowler by my room. Number Twenty-Seven at the motor court." He kept his voice low, almost a whisper just in case it was Delilah out there listening in.

"I'll be out there in two minutes."

You had to like Sheriff Rhodes. He hadn't laughed once about Gabe's predicament. It was like he totally understood that a man had few options when he was being stalked by a crazy woman.

Gabe returned to the bedroom, but he didn't turn on the lights. He continued to watch the front window. So he was almost prepared when it suddenly shattered into a hail of flying glass.

He ducked, and the next minute his worst nightmare propelled herself through the jagged remnants of the window.

"You thought you could leave me?" she screamed at him as he straightened up. "You thought you could cheat on me? You fornicator."

He said nothing. Nothing he could say would stop her ranting about how he was evil incarnate. So he stayed still and waited for the sheriff to arrive. Maybe the two of them could subdue her and get her into custody before any more private property was destroyed.

She advanced toward him. "There's only one place for you. With the other sinners."

He backed up. It was probably a cowardly reaction, but what was he supposed to do? She had something in her hand that looked like one of those hiker's canteens made out of aluminum.

She raised the can with clear intent. She was planning to throw the contents of that canister right at him. What the hell? Was it acid?

He ducked as she threw, and the liquid landed on the bed, except for a splash that soaked through his shirtsleeve. The liquid felt cold on his skin.

Not acid.

The acrid odor of lighter fluid or some other kind of petrochemical filled the room.

Oh shit. He scrambled away from the bed just as she threw a match or a lighter at him.

The sheets, blanket, and bedspread went up in a whoosh that heated the side of Gabe's face as he tried to get away. But he wasn't fast enough. His sleeve was on fire.

Oh shit, shit, shit. Panic hit.

He wanted to run, to tear the shirt from his body. But something stopped him and pushed him down on the carpet. And then he heard his brother's voice telling him to stop, drop, roll.

He obeyed, rolling onto his side, feeling the heat on his injured skin, but knowing that the fire had been small and it was out now. He still wanted to tear the shirt from his body, but he didn't have time.

Delilah was coming at him, and she probably had more matches.

He rolled over and regained his feet just in time to charge at her. He connected with a thud that carried her to the floor.

He landed hard on top of her, but the floor was carpeted,

so the fall didn't stun her in the least. Instead she fed on the violence. She scratched his face and bit his hand and spit profanity at him.

"You're going to burn in hell," she said. Then she called him a monster and a beast, and he had no doubt that in her twisted mind he was all those things. He'd been hearing this crap for the last eight years.

Meanwhile the mattress was fully engulfed in fire now, filling the room with noxious fumes that were making it hard to breathe. Thank God the window was already broken out because the smoke might have overcome them both.

The situation was getting dire and he had no choice, so he pulled back his fist and popped her one right in the face. He hit her so hard that her teeth cut his knuckles. She went limp and the shame hit him.

He picked her up and carried her from the room, just as the sheriff rolled into the parking lot with the bubble-gum lights on his cruiser going at full tilt.

CHAPTER
23

Jenny had just pressed the disconnect button on her phone call with Dr. Polk when the Last Chance Volunteer Fire Department siren began to wail. And since the Cut 'n Curl was only about a block away from the firehouse, the sound was practically deafening.

"What the heck is that?" Maryanne, a newcomer to town, asked.

"It's the signal for the volunteer firefighters to head to the station." Jenny didn't tell her that the siren always raised her hackles. She remembered that sound from the night the farmhouse burned. And since the farm was a ways outside of town, the house had been fully engulfed by the time the volunteer firefighters had arrived.

Now, every time she heard that noise, she prayed for the people who were involved. There wasn't anything sadder than a fire. It destroyed everything of value.

Jenny closed her eyes and prayed for the people in danger tonight. And while she was at it, she prayed for Bear. And pretty soon she was praying for Gabe, too.

She was going to lose Gabe and Bear both. And while it wasn't entirely her fault, she also shared some of the blame.

She wondered if maybe she should go down to the Peach Blossom, find Gabe, and apologize for her behavior earlier in the day. How could she blame him for keeping secrets? He was a solitary man. And it seemed like every time he revealed a little piece of himself, someone judged him. And hadn't she done that earlier in the morning? Jenny didn't need a marriage license to validate her feelings for Gabe. She loved him. And she had no doubt that he loved her back.

So what if he was still technically married to someone? If that wife of his was the one who had beaten Bear and pushed Jenny into the river, then he deserved better. And she didn't care if Reverend Lake and the altar guild kicked her out for being a brazen hussy. She was going to go and get her man.

"Holy God," Maryanne shouted. "Jenny come quick."

Jenny opened her eyes. The front door was open, letting in a cold draft. Maryanne was out on the landing, probably watching the fire department right down the street.

"What is it?" Jenny said as she got to her feet.

Maryanne's face appeared around the corner of the door. "I think the Peach Blossom Motor Court is on fire. And it's lighting up the night like fireworks."

Someone pressed an oxygen mask to Gabe's face. He didn't think he needed it, but he let the EMTs fuss over him. He was shirtless, wrapped in a blanket, and sitting on one of the motel's rusty metal chairs feeling kind of numb and shaky. The EMTs had seen his medical alert bracelet and checked his glucose levels. They'd given him a sugar tablet. And they'd checked the burns on his arm.

His injuries weren't all that bad, considering. But he had ice strapped to his upper arm, and they were debating whether to transport him to the clinic or the hospital in Orangeburg. He wasn't sure which.

He didn't care, either. It was the other kind of hurt that had him stunned.

He'd lost Bear and Jenny and Luke, and he couldn't ever get any of them back again.

Meanwhile, the motel was burning like a collection of matchsticks. Thank goodness all of his fans who'd come for the program last night had checked out this morning. The place was empty, except for himself.

He had the strange thought that the demise of the Peach Blossom Motor Court would probably mean more business for Jenny. Not that her three rooms would ever be rented out by the hour.

He also had no idea where Delilah was. The sheriff had taken her out of his arms, and that was the last he'd seen of her. He didn't care anymore. And he refused to feel any shame for having punched her in the face.

He flexed his hand. His knuckles were sore.

"Where is he? Let me through." The voice pierced the fog that had settled into his head.

He blinked his stinging eyes and turned his head. And there was Jenny, wearing her old blue sweater and her new, tight jeans. Her shorter hair was up in some kind of clip that left tendrils escaping around her face.

"Thank God," she said as she came at him full-tilt. She ended up on her knees in front of him, with her arms around his middle and her head buried in his chest.

"I saw the light in the sky, and I knew you had checked in here," she said. "Oh, God, I thought I'd lost you. And that made me mad, because I was just beginning to realize what an idiot I'd been this morning. The truth is, I had an affair once a long time ago, and the guy turned out to be married. He lied to me and broke my heart. And I confused you with him."

She looked up at him and then ran her cool hand over his hot face. "But you never lied to me, did you? You told me you had secrets. And I told you there was time for you to tell me all of them. But the thing is, I already *know* the important things. Like the fact that you sat all day in your car at the vet's because you're worried about Bear.

"So I don't care if you're married. I'm perfectly happy to live in blissful sin with you, and if the altar guild has a problem with that, they can get their muffins elsewhere."

Pushing Jenny away was the hardest thing he'd ever done, but he did it anyway. He put both of his hands on her shoulders and set her back onto her heels. "No, Jenny. It's not going to work. Delilah will never give us any peace." He felt used up. He didn't have the energy to fight this fight anymore.

"So what? We'll just put more locks on the door, and we'll wear flak jackets when we walk the dog. I'm not going to let that woman make you miserable."

"Look." He pointed. "She started that fire."

"You saw her do this?"

He nodded.

"Well then, that changes everything." She turned and yelled at Sheriff Rhodes, who stopped talking on his walkie-talkie and strode over to her.

"You need me?" he asked.

"Yeah," Jenny said. "Gabe just told me that Delilah started the fire. If that's true, how many years can we send her away for?"

"At least thirty," the sheriff said. "But we've got her on several other counts. Starting with two counts of attempted murder, and one count of animal cruelty." The sheriff looked somber and kind of pissed off that anyone had the temerity to come into his county and cause trouble. "Gabe, I know she's mentally ill, but I intend to send her away for a long, long time."

"But you don't have evidence." Gabe's throat hurt from sucking in too much smoke.

"Oh, yes, I do. Delilah has a nasty bite on her calf that looks exactly like something a dog would do. Forensics are going to take photos of that bite and if it matches Bear, then he's going to become our star witness. Besides, Gabe, you survived this fire. And you don't get to decide whether charges are brought. This was arson, pure and simple, with a little attempted murder on the side. I'm sure the prosecutor will subpoena you as a witness. That's if it ever actually gets to trial."

The sheriff's radio squawked, and he turned away.

"You gotta love that guy," Jenny said as she got up from her knees and sat herself right down in Gabe's lap. "You're burned," she said noticing the ice strapped to his bicep.

"It's minor. The EMT said I probably wouldn't even have a scar. But they want to take me to the clinic or the hospital."

"Maybe if I give you a kiss, it will make it all better." And then she removed his oxygen mask and gave him one of her incredible kisses. And damn if it didn't actually make everything much, much better.

• • •

It was early on Monday morning, before the sun was up, when Dr. Dave called Gabe's cell phone. He and Jenny were tangled together in the iron bed that had once belonged to Luke.

They'd come here after Doc Cooper had released him from the clinic. And they'd talked for hours. And made love. And discussed what should be done about the ghost.

Gabe came awake slowly and groped for the phone. It was bad news.

Something of his emotions must have shown on his face because Jenny sat up in bed, a frown on her beautiful face, her eyes unfocused without her glasses. "What is it?" she asked.

"It's Bear. Dr. Dave says he's losing ground. He wants me to give the okay to put him down." His voice wavered.

"Maybe it's best."

"He says the rib injury is more serious than he thought. His lungs are compromised. He's having trouble breathing." He could barely push the words past the constriction in his throat.

Jenny wrapped him in her warm arms and held him tight. "Maybe we aren't being kind to him," she whispered. She seemed so much stronger than he was. He didn't want to lose Bear a second time and he knew that was kind of crazy because this wasn't Luke's Bear, even if he was a lot like him.

"We should let him go," she said. "He's suffering for no purpose."

"I need to be there," he said. "I don't want him to be alone."

"All right."

They got dressed in the dark and took Gabe's Lexus

down to the veterinary hospital. The sky was getting light but it was going to be a cold, gray day. And the cold in the car settled down into his bones.

The ghost was with them, and he wasn't happy about what was happening.

"He doesn't want us to do this," Gabe said as he pulled into the parking lot.

Jenny knew exactly who Gabe was referring to. "I know."

"Zeph said that my penance is going to be helping the ghost find homes for strays. Zeph said that, if I didn't do what the ghost wanted, the ghost would make things difficult. And I've seen just how difficult the ghost can be."

"Yeah, well, it's the ghost of a fifteen-year-old boy," Jenny said. "I've been a teacher for decades, and sometimes fifteen-year-old boys need to be disciplined or they go completely out of control."

"Jenny, it's not like that. I don't think we should put Bear down," Gabe said. "You know what they say, where there's life there's hope?"

"Yeah, I guess. But if he's suffering..."

"Maybe he's not suffering. The ghost might know better. He's been through it, you know?"

They headed inside. Dr. Polk was waiting for them because Dr. Dave had been up all night with Bear and had just left to get some sleep. Charlene ushered them into one of the examining rooms, where poor Bear was lying on the table, clearly struggling to draw breath. He'd been shaved along his backbone. An incision bisected the spot where his spine had been fractured.

He looked beaten and exhausted, and Gabe couldn't stanch the flow of tears streaming out of his eyes.

"He's suffering, Gabe," Jenny whispered.

She was right, but the room was getting colder by degrees. Luke was more than agitated. This freezing temperature had preceded his temper tantrum over the wallpaper in the dining room. God only knew what kind of disaster the ghost could wreak here in a vet's clinic.

"Gosh, there must be something wrong with the heat," Dr. Polk said. "It's cold in here. I'm sorry. Let me go check the thermostat. In the meantime, you can say your good-byes."

She left the room, and Gabe pulled up a rolling stool so he could be right at the dog's head. "Are you there, Bear?" Gabe petted the dog's head. "I love you," he said.

The dog showed no sign that he was conscious. They probably already had him sedated. So maybe he wasn't suffering.

Except that you'd have to be a fool to believe that. Every breath took all of the dog's effort. It seemed obvious that this couldn't go on for much longer.

Gabe looked up at the ceiling, even though he knew Luke wasn't there. The ghost was behind him, like a shadow. "I love you, too, Luke. And I know you want to save this dog, but maybe it can't be done. Dr. Dave is one heck of a surgeon, but he's not God. Maybe God wants something else from Bear."

The cold was seeping into Gabe's fingers and toes, but Jenny stood behind him, too, her warm hands on his shoulders. She gave him a little squeeze as if she understood what he'd decided. As if she already knew and approved. It was kind of strange the way she seemed to be able to know his heart even better than he knew it himself.

"Luke, listen to me," he said aloud. "I've been carrying around this lonely place inside me for years and years.

It's the hole that was made in me when you left. And I figure maybe you feel it, too, and that's why you're still here. Not because you're mad at me or Zeph and want us to pay some penalty for still being alive when you're not.

"But just because you're lonely. Maybe you miss Bear.

"I know you loved him more than me, probably. And I don't know what happened to your dog, Luke. Zeph kept him until he was real old and had to be put down. Maybe you got mad at Zeph for doing that to the first Bear and you missed your opportunity to go on.

"Maybe you couldn't go on because I needed to come back and remember what happened and tell you how sorry I am for doing such a stupid thing. But I was just a kid. I was ten. I wish it hadn't happened, 'cause I miss you. But it feels better, somehow, to know what really happened than to have nightmares about it. I can live with what I did. I guess God will judge me when it's my time."

Jenny gave him another squeeze on the shoulder.

"So here's the thing. This Bear is in trouble. He's a hero, but he's hurt bad, and he's not going to get better. He's going to come and join you soon, whether Doc Polk sends him there or we just wait for God to do it. And I'm going to ask you to take care of him."

The temperature in the room was starting to rise.

"And I've got this feeling that if you just let Bear run and follow him, you know, like we used to do when we went hunting with Zeph's old hound, he might lead you where you need to go."

The doctor returned. "I didn't see anything wrong with the heat. I guess it's just getting cold outside. They say we might have snow. Can you believe it? The daffodils are almost in bloom."

Dr. Polk was obviously trying to put them at ease. She looked from Jenny to Gabe. "So, y'all are ready?"

Gabe nodded.

"He's already asleep, you know," Dr. Polk said. "We've got him sedated. So I'm going to give him something and he'll just drift off."

Gabe stood up and Jenny wrapped her arms around his middle. He closed his eyes and rested his chin on her head. She was warm, and she smelled like flowers.

The doc gave the injection. And it was over in just a few minutes.

And then something strange happened. Something let go inside him. Like grace shining down from someplace. Like forgiveness washing over him.

And he knew. Bear was gone, but he hadn't gone alone. He'd taken Luke with him.

EPILOGUE

Jenny stood in the middle of the driveway with her camera on a bright March afternoon, the golden sun pouring down onto a thousand blooming jonquils.

She had snapped off dozens of photos of the restored house nestled in the woods, and it was just as she had imagined: the beautiful, white house against the backdrop of the dark Carolina woods, gray Spanish moss, and bright yellow daffodils.

Tonight she'd go through all of the photos and post them on the inn's webpage.

And tomorrow, her first guests, a couple who wanted to canoe and fish on the Edisto River, would be checking in.

Now, if she could just find the dog . . .

"Pilot," she called, and was rewarded by a rustling in the rhododendrons. "Come on, boy. I've got food for you. Please. Come on." She got down on her knees to make sure the dog was in the bushes. He was. He was hiding.

She sighed. Pilot had been living there for exactly

three days. He was a rescue mutt of unknown parentage and breeding who had been abused by his previous owners. He liked to hide in the rhodos.

"Hey there, sweetie. I've got lots of treats and toys for you. Come on, now."

"Did you let him off the leash, again?" This question came from Gabe, who sauntered through the front door and onto the porch. He was wearing his usual everyday outfit—a ratty Harvard sweatshirt and a pair of ancient jeans. He was drinking coffee out of one of the new Jonquil House coffee mugs she'd ordered. Somehow he didn't look right holding a cup with all those flowers on it. She knew right then that Gabe was going to win the great wallpaper debate. She wanted to put up jonquils in the back bedroom, but he'd pretty much said over his dead body. And since she liked him alive and warm (and sleeping in the bed in the back bedroom with her), she was going to have to give in on this.

"He's terrified of the leash," she said. "And it breaks my heart to see the way he cringes and whines when I snap it on. He's not going to wander away. He's pretty much scared of his own shadow." She turned back to look at the dog. "Come on, boy, we love you. It's fine. I've got chew toys for you."

The next instant Gabe was beside her, the dog leash in his hands. He gave the dog one of his masterful looks. "Pilot. Come." he said.

And damned if the dog didn't get up and come right to him.

"Clearly he's your dog," she said, getting to her feet.

He stood up, too, and snagged her by the arm. "He's *our* dog. And how about my midmorning smooch?"

"How about it?" she asked.

"I want it. It's my reward for having written a thousand

words this morning. And it doesn't mess with my blood sugar."

"Your reward?"

"Uh-huh."

"So what do I get out of this, huh?"

He stepped a little closer. "You know that thing I do to your neck that makes you scream?"

"Uh-huh."

He gave her a smarmy and utterly adorable smile.

She giggled and fell right into his chest and cocked her head a little. "You may proceed."

And then his mouth was on her neck, and she was sort of screaming right there in the middle of the driveway, with the spring sun shining down on them.

Mother and the altar guild would be scandalized.

In fact, the altar guild *was* scandalized that she was living in sin with Gabriel Raintree who was still, sort of, married. But maybe not for long. Delilah's daddy had swooped in and cut a deal with the Allenberg County authorities. Gabe's soon-to-be-ex-wife was going to spend the next thirty years in a mental hospital—one that Gabe was going to pay for out of the trust he'd created for her years ago. And in return, she was going to sign his divorce papers.

So maybe, in a month or a couple, Jenny might be able to marry him. If she wanted to.

But in the meantime, she didn't give a rat's behind what anyone thought. He was hers and she was his and that's all either one of them needed.

READING GROUP GUIDE

Discussion Questions for
Inn at Last Chance

1. *Inn at Last Chance* begins in the middle of winter during an ice storm and ends at the beginning of spring. Discuss how the season change and moving into the warmth of spring is reflected in the characters arcs of Jenny and Gabe.

2. There are several characters in the story who keep important secrets. Who are they? How do the secrets that they keep affect the story? Have you ever been like Nita, keeping a secret that you thought should be told? Did you pay a price for keeping that secret?

3. Do you think Zeph was right to lie about what happened when Luke was killed? Talk about the positive aspects of Zeph's lie. Talk about the negative aspects. Have you ever told a white lie in order to protect someone? How did that turn out?

4. Do you believe in ghosts? Have you ever had a ghostly encounter? How is the ghost in the story the same as or different from ghosts in other stories or ghosts you may have encountered?

5. Which is more important to Gabe's development as a character: his eventual acceptance of and belief in ghosts or remembering what happened on the day Luke died?

6. Scattered throughout the novel are several scenes that mirror *Jane Eyre*. Can you find them? Email your answers to hope@hoperamsay.com for prizes and swag.

7. How is Gabriel Raintree similar to Edward Rochester in *Jane Eyre*? How is he different? How is Jenny Carpenter similar to or different from Jane? How is Reverend Lake similar to or different from St. John Rivers?

8. Jenny and Gabe have serious differences of opinion about decorating the house. Have you ever had this problem with your spouse or significant other? Did you fight about it? Who do you think usually wins the fight over the wallpaper in the bedroom?

9. Jenny is unmarried, and while she is often lonely, she also recognizes that being unmarried has its own rewards. Do you think there are real advantages to remaining unmarried? What are they? Does a woman have to give up those advantages when she marries? Do you think that trade-off is worth it in the end?

10. Discuss Jenny's obsession with her mother's old things and her desire to have china pieces that match perfectly. How does this mirror Jenny's personality at the beginning of the book? Does the ghost do her a favor when he smashes her mother's dishware? How so?

See the next page for an excerpt from

Last Chance Book Club.

CHAPTER 5

Savannah pulled the biscuits out of the oven and began transferring them to a basket lined with a red-and-white-checked napkin. She loved cooking in this kitchen where she had learned at the elbow of her grandmother. It almost felt as if Granny were standing right beside her telling her how to roll the dough and cut each biscuit.

"Good gracious, that smells good," Miriam said as she shuffled into the room. She was leaning heavily on her cane today.

"Did you have a good nap?"

"I rested." Miriam sat down at the small kitchen table. "I declare, when I opened my eyes I thought, for just one minute, that Sally was still alive."

Savannah looked over her shoulder. "I was just thinking about how close I feel to Granny when I'm cooking in this kitchen. I wish I had a kitchen this big in Baltimore. Of course, a big kitchen would be wasted, since it's just me and Todd most nights. But still."

"Sugar, I thought we'd decided you were staying and reviving The Kismet."

"Bringing The Kismet back to life is more than I know how to do. It's a mess, and I have no money. I don't know what I was thinking. I guess I was just dreaming."

"And when you came here as a child making gravy and biscuits was more than you knew how to do. But you learned. My nose is saying that Sally taught you everything she knew about cooking and, she sure knew more than any other cook in Allenberg County."

"Learning how to cook and reviving The Kismet are different things. The Kismet is beyond my abilities and my means. Dash helped me to see that quite clearly."

"You call that help? So you're just going to give up?"

"What other choice do I have?"

"You could learn what you need to learn. You take it from me, when you stop learning stuff, that's when you get old."

"But I need more than knowledge. I need money."

"That's just your fear talking. Tomorrow I think we need to get Todd registered for school. And then you need to visit Miz Ruby. Once she's done with you, you'll start seeing things straight."

"Miz Ruby? Is she, like, the local banker or something?"

"No, of course not. She's Rocky's momma. You know, the beautician who owns the Cut 'n Curl. I go there every Friday for a manicure, but you need more than that, sugar. Rocky called me this morning, and we both agreed. Ruby will fix you right up. And believe me, when she's done, you'll have a spring in your step. And I'm sure you'll figure something out for The Kismet."

Savannah stifled a laugh. If only it were that easy. "I don't need a makeover."

"Don't you? You're sitting in this kitchen pining away because you don't have a crowd to cook for like your granny did. Sugar, the only way to get a crowd for dinner every night is to find a new husband and have more babies. And believe me, you aren't going to catch that hero you've been searching for if you don't take care of yourself first."

"What hero? What are you talking about?"

Savannah turned away from the pots on the stove and sat down facing her aunt, suddenly concerned. Miriam had a gleam in her eye that hadn't been there before. Savannah took Miriam's knobby hand in hers. The thin, cold feel of Miriam's skin was a little alarming. She was getting up there in years. Was she getting senile now that Harry had passed?

"I'm fine. And I'm not senile," Miriam said as if reading Savannah's mind. "All I'm saying is that you need to be looking for a man with an appetite. Just like your grandmother did."

"But I've sworn off men altogether. Greg was a huge mistake. And my recent past is littered with men who were commitment-phobic workaholics, and not very interested in kids."

"Well, I'm sure none of those men was your soulmate. So don't give them any more thought than they deserve."

"Soulmate? Really?"

"Now, sugar, you listen. You want a man like your granddaddy was."

Savannah stroked Miriam's hand. "Men like Granddaddy are hard to find. I thought Greg was like him, but I was wrong." She let go of a frustrated breath. What she really wanted was a man like George Bailey, the protagonist in *It's a Wonderful Life*. And she knew that was impossible, because George Bailey wasn't a real person. Real people were not like the ones in those old black-and-white movies that Granddaddy had taught her to appreciate.

"Savannah, I know you've been hurt. But I also *know* that you're going to find the kind of man you've been searching for. I know it in my bones. It's just not going to be easy to find him. You're going to have to delve beneath the surface."

Savannah stood up and crossed back to the stove to check on the gravy. Miriam was too old to understand. Her great-aunt had been married to one man for more than forty years. Marriages like that were rare. Savannah's marriage had failed in its third year. And Savannah's mother had been unable to keep three different husbands. All in all, it seemed wiser to figure out a way to be independent.

Her cell phone rang. Savannah checked the caller ID. It was Mom. She had been expecting this call for at least a day. She had told everyone in Baltimore that she'd be home by now. So of course, Mom was checking in.

Savannah pushed the talk button and put the phone to her ear.

"Savannah Elizabeth Reynolds, are you insane?"

Uh-oh. When Mom used her full maiden name, it was always a tip-off that one of Mom's rants was headed Savannah's way.

"Hi, Mom, how are you?" Savannah said carefully.

"I'm not good. What's this nonsense about you staying in Last Chance and trying to renovate The Kismet?"

"Who told you this?"

"Todd called me earlier. He apparently borrowed your cell phone when you were in the shower. Savannah, what about Greg? He has a right to see his son, you know."

Great. Her son had tattled on her. It wouldn't be the first time.

She took a deep, calming breath. "Mom, you know and I know that Greg couldn't care less about visitation. It's been months since he's paid any attention to Todd. And then it was just to give him that infernal PSP that he plays all the time. Maybe coming to South Carolina will wake Greg up. I would be happy if that happened. Of course, we both know that Greg is sort of like Dad, and that is probably not going to happen."

"Okay," Mom said on a long sigh. "I'll concede that point. But you don't want to live in Last Chance, and you sure don't want to subject your son to that. I know, I grew up there, and aside from church and football games there wasn't much to do."

"There was the movie theater."

"Right, like that's the height of culture." Mom's voice rose in pitch. "I knew I should have put my foot down when Daddy started filling your head with all those silly ideas about reopening that place. That was *his* dream, not yours. How are you going to pay for a thing like that? And have you any idea about the quality of the schools in that little town? This is a huge mistake you're making. Don't be an idiot."

Savannah looked through the kitchen window at the Spanish-moss-laden oak in the side yard. She remembered the tree house Granddaddy had built for her. It was gone now, but the memory remained steadfast and true. Why couldn't Todd have a father like that? Why couldn't she have had a father like that? Or a mother who encouraged her to follow her dreams instead of pointing out how hollow they were.

"You know, Mom," she said in a shaky voice, "it would be nice if just once you would support me in the things I want to do."

"I certainly *would* support you if you were opening a business you knew something about, in a city where you might get customers. My goodness, Savannah, you can't be successful in a place like Last Chance."

"When was the last time you came down here?"

"I don't know. Decades. I avoid the place. I don't want you bringing up Todd in that one-horse town."

Before Savannah could counter, Mom rolled on. "And Todd said Dash was there. He told me Dash destroyed his PSP. Really, I can't believe you're letting Todd have anything to do with that man. My God, Savannah, don't you remember the way he treated you as a girl? He's fully capable of abusing Todd. Or worse."

Mom was silent for a moment, obviously letting her arguments take their toll, before she continued, "And I don't think Greg will be wild about the situation after I explain it to him. And you should know that Claire is fit to be tied. How could you turn down her offer to pay Todd's tuition to the Gilman School?"

Something deep inside Savannah snapped. "I turned her down because she wants to turn Todd into a big snob, just like you've become. Just like Greg is. I'm sorry, Mom, but I'm going to stay in Last Chance. Miriam needs a cook. Todd needs the fresh air. And Dash is not a child molester. I may not have approved of his methods, but he did me a huge favor by breaking that idiotic game. Besides, this is *my* life, not yours or Claire's or Greg's. It's mine, and if I want to come live here with Aunt Miriam and Cousin Dash, well then, that's what I'm going to do."

She pulled the phone from her ear and pressed the disconnect button.

"Bravo."

She looked up to find Dash leaning in the kitchen doorway clapping his hands. His fitted cowboy shirt accentuated his broad shoulders and narrow hips. He looked tanned and healthy and incredibly male. The puppy Todd found stood beside him looking up with total adoration on his face.

"I take it that was Aunt Katie Lynne on the phone telling you how to run your life?"

Savannah nodded, suddenly unable to get a word out. How much had he heard of her rant?

"Thanks for telling her off on my account. I've been wanting to do that since I was thirteen, when she called me a bad seed."

Savannah's eyes began to itch. She'd heard her mother's opinion about Dash. In fact, she'd *repeated* her mother's opinion. Everywhere. To everyone. And now that she thought about it, repeating her mother's ugly words had set off the infamous snake incident.

Guilt slammed into her. She hadn't really understood when she was ten. But now, suddenly, it all came back in a rush. She'd been cruel and mean-spirited.

Sort of like Mom.

Savannah took a deep breath and turned back toward her gravy. She needed to get dinner on the table and not think about what had happened in the past or what might happen in the future. Either way it was bad.

She squeezed her eyes shut and prayed for courage—and maybe an investor with a really, really deep pocket.

"Princess, I've changed my mind about The Kismet," Dash said.

She looked over her shoulder. "What?"

"Last Chance needs a movie theater. So I reckon I'm going into business with you."

Dash took one look at the frown on Savannah's face and decided he didn't want to hang around long enough for her to refuse his help. He hadn't considered the complexity of what he'd promised Hettie. It was irksome, to say the least, that Cousin Savannah could stand in the way of his plan to win Hettie back.

He turned and stalked down the hall and out to the front porch, where he found the kid sitting on the front step looking pitiful. His annoyance at Savannah disappeared, replaced by deep empathy for the boy.

"Bad move, calling your grandmother and having her call your mother."

The kid looked up over his shoulder. "Who asked for your opinion?"

"No one. Just sayin'. Your momma got all riled up and told your granny that there was no way in hell she's going back to Baltimore. And I think Aunt Miriam plans to get you registered down at the school tomorrow. So it looks like you're here for a while."

"My father's going to come and get me, just as soon as he has a free weekend where he's not playing in a pool tournament."

Dash felt for the kid. How many times had Dash told himself the same thing? Dash's daddy had been a rodeo rider always promising to come home after the next rodeo on the circuit. It sounded like Todd's daddy loved pool more than his boy. Dash prayed the man wasn't some kind of hustler or gambler.

The puppy crawled into Todd's lap and started washing his face with a darting pink tongue. The kid's lips quivered. "I can't even keep him," he said, stroking the dog's floppy ears.

"Well now, that can be arranged," Dash said as he sat on the porch railing. "Aunt Mim has no objections to the puppy. I have no objections either. And your momma is a guest in this house until she can fix up the apartment above the theater. So she doesn't have much to say about it. I reckon the dog can stay. Which means we need to find him a name. I've been calling him Boulder Head. What do you think of that?"

The corner of the boy's mouth lifted just a little. "That's a stupid name."

"Yeah, but it describes him. It's like someone stuck a head as big as a boxer's on a frankfurter's body. That is one weird-looking dog you got there."

The kid sniffled and stared down at the dog's face for a long time. "He's not weird looking. We should call him Champ."

"Champ?"

"Yeah. He's got a head as big as a boxer's, right?"

"Yeah, I guess. Champ it is, then." Dash paused for a long moment. "And, uh, I went up to Orangeburg this afternoon, and I got you something."

The kid raised his head.

"It's in my car." Dash nodded toward the Cadillac in the drive. "Go on and get it."

The kid hopped down from the steps and ran to the car. He opened the passenger's side door and found the PSP Dash had bought that afternoon.

"You bought me a new one?" The kid looked really confused.

"Yeah I did. See, I probably shouldn't have destroyed your property like that. But I reckon it worked out because, if I hadn't, we might not have found Champ."

"Yeah, I guess."

"And there's another thing. If you're going to be living in this house, you're going to have to do some chores. I was twelve when I came to live in this house, and I was required to mow the lawn. And Uncle Ernest—that would be your great-grandfather—insisted that I work at the movie theater and that I go to church and a bunch of things that I wasn't all that wild about. But there were some good things. I got to help out at Mr. Nelson's stables, and I like horses. And I got to play baseball."

"I hate sports. I'm not any good."

"Have you ever played football?"

He shook his head. "My dad did in college. He was an offensive lineman. He's always talking about how he almost made it to the NFL."

Dash had to stifle a snort of laughter, because the boy was built like an offensive lineman. He might only be twelve, but he was one big child. Dash couldn't wait to introduce him to Red Canaday, the Davis High football coach and one of Allenberg's Pop Warner football commissioners. Dash made a mental note to run up to Orangeburg tomorrow and buy a football.

"Well, maybe you just haven't had much chance to play anything but that video game. So here's the deal. You can play that game in the evening after you finish your homework and walk the dog. I also need your help with some repairs around the house."

He didn't mention anything about tossing a football.

He would try to ease into that one slowly, like Aunt Mim had suggested.

"You're kidding, right?"

"Nope. It's all that stuff in order for you to keep the dog and the game. Deal?"

Champ stood at Todd's feet wagging his tail and looking up at the boy like he hung the moon. The dog was more eloquent than Dash could ever be. Todd left the game on the front seat of Dash's car and got down on his knee and petted the dog. Champ responded by wagging his tail and giving the kid a bunch of sloppy puppy kisses.

Dash tried not to smile, but he couldn't help it. He said a quiet prayer of thanksgiving to the angels who looked out for lost kids and abandoned dogs.

Just then a tornado hit the front porch. It came down the hall with fists clenched and blond hair bouncing. "You know I've been standing in the kitchen stirring the gravy, trying to control my temper and figure you out. I give up. What do you mean, I'll have to go into business with you?" Savannah put her fists on her cute little jean-clad hips.

She'd lost the apron she'd been wearing in the kitchen, but her cheeks looked pink, and there was a little smidgen of flour on her navy T-shirt that kind of accentuated her assets, so to speak. Oh, boy, homemade biscuits for dinner. His mouth started watering.

"Well now," he said, leaning his backside into the porch railing and folding his arms over his chest, "I think the words are self-explanatory. You're going into business with me. Actually, I think it's more accurate to say that I'm going into business with you." He smiled.

She gave him her imperious-princess look. "I am *not* going into business with you."

Well, that was predictable. But he wasn't going to give up. Hettie had asked him for his help, and he regarded it as a test. Besides, if Hettie had asked him to swim the English Channel in his birthday suit, he'd have done it with a smile. "Princess, I hate to disagree, but you and I are about to become partners."

"Over my dead body." She turned and stalked back into the house.

"Mom really hates you, doesn't she?" Todd said in a snarky tone.

Yes, she did. And Dash had the feeling that once Savannah made up her mind about something, she wasn't ever going to change it.

THE DISH

Where Authors Give You the Inside Scoop

❤ ❤ ❤ ❤ ❤ ❤ ❤ ❤ ❤ ❤ ❤ ❤ ❤ ❤

From the desk of Lily Dalton

Dear Reader,

Some people are heroic by nature. They act to help others without thinking. Sometimes at the expense of their own safety. Sometimes without ever considering the consequences. That's just who they are. Especially when it's a friend in need.

We associate these traits with soldiers who risk their lives on a dangerous battlefield to save a fallen comrade. Not because it's their job, but because it's their brother. Or a parent who runs into a busy street to save a child who's wandered into the path of an oncoming car. Or an ocean life activist who places himself in a tiny boat between a whale and the harpoons of a whaling ship.

Is it so hard to believe that Daphne Bevington, a London debutante and the earl of Wolverton's granddaughter, could be such a hero? When her dearest friend, Kate, needs her help, she does what's necessary to save her. In her mind, no other choice will do. After all, she knows without a doubt that Kate would do the same for her if she needed help. It doesn't matter one fig to her that their circumstances are disparate, that Kate is her lady's maid.

But Daphne finds herself in over her head. In a moment, everything falls apart, throwing not only her reputation and her future into doubt, but her life into danger. Yet in that moment when all seems hopelessly lost...another hero comes out of nowhere and saves her. A mysterious stranger who acts without thinking, at the expense of his own safety, without considering the consequences. A hero on a quest of his own. A man she will never see again...

Only, of course...she does. And he's not at all the hero she remembers him to be.

Or is he? I hope you will enjoy reading NEVER ENTICE AN EARL and finding out.

Best wishes, and happy reading!

Lily Dalton

LilyDalton.com
Twitter @LilyDalton
Facebook.com/LilyDaltonAuthor

♥ ♥ ♥ ♥ ♥ ♥ ♥ ♥ ♥ ♥ ♥ ♥ ♥ ♥ ♥

From the desk of Shelley Coriell

Dear Reader,

Story ideas come from everywhere. Snippets of conversation. Dreams. The hunky guy at the office supply store with eyes the color of faded denim. THE BROKEN, the first book in my new romantic suspense series, The Apostles, was born and bred as I sat at the bedside of my dying father.

In 2007 my dad, who lived on a mountain in northern Nevada, checked himself into his small town's hospital after having what appeared to be a stroke. "A mild one," he assured the family. "Nothing to get worked up about." That afternoon, this independent, strong-willed man (aka stubborn and borderline cantankerous) checked himself out of the hospital. The next day he hopped on his quad and accidentally drove off the side of his beloved mountain. The ATV landed on him, crushing his chest, breaking ribs, and collapsing a lung.

The hospital staff told us they could do nothing for him, that he would die. Refusing to accept the prognosis, we had him Life-Flighted to Salt Lake City. After a touch-and-go forty-eight hours, he pulled through, and that's when we learned the full extent of his injuries.

He'd had *multiple* strokes. The not-so-mild kind. The kind that meant he, at age sixty-three, would be forever dependent on others. His spirit was broken.

For the next week, the family gathered at the hospital. My sister, the oldest and the family nurturer, massaged his feet and swabbed his mouth. My brother, Mr. Finance Guy, talked with insurance types and made arrangements for post-release therapy. The quiet, bookish middle child, I had little to offer but prayers. I'd never felt so helpless.

As my dad's health improved, his spirits worsened. He was mad at his body, mad at the world. After a particularly difficult morning, he told us he wished he'd died on that mountain. A horrible, heavy silence followed. Which is when I decided to use the one thing I did have.

I dragged the chair in his hospital room—you know the kind, the heavy, wooden contraption that folds out into a bed—to his bedside and took out the notebook I carry everywhere.

"You know, Dad," I said. "I've been tinkering with this story idea. Can I bounce some stuff off you?"

Silence.

"I have this heroine. A news broadcaster who gets stabbed by a serial killer. She's scarred, physically and emotionally."

More silence.

"And I have a Good Guy. Don't know much about him, but he also has a past that left him scarred. He carries a gun. Maybe an FBI badge." That's it. Two hazy characters hanging out in the back of my brain.

Dad turned toward the window.

"The scarred journalist ends up working as an aide to an old man who lives on a mountain," I continued on the fly. "Oh-oh! The old guy is blind and can't see her scars. His name is . . . Smokey Joe, and like everyone else in this story, he's a little broken."

Dad glared. I saw it. He wanted me to see it.

"And, you know what, Dad? Smokey Joe can be a real pain in the ass."

My father's lips twitched. He tried not to smile, but I saw that, too.

I opened my notebook. "So tell me about Smokey Joe. Tell me about his mountain. Tell me about his *story*."

For the next two hours, Dad and I talked about an old man on a mountain and brainstormed the book that eventually became THE BROKEN, the story of Kate Johnson, an on-the-run broadcast journalist whose broken past holds the secret to catching a serial killer, and Hayden Reed, the tenacious FBI profiler who sees past her scars and vows to find a way into her head, but to his surprise, heads straight for her heart.

"Hey, Sissy," Dad said as I tucked away my notebook after what became the first of many Apostle brainstorming sessions. "Smokey Joe knows how to use C-4. We need to have a scene where he blows something up."

And "we" did.

So with a boom from old Smokey Joe, I'm thrilled to introduce you to Kate Johnson, Hayden Reed, and the Apostles, an elite group of FBI agents who aren't afraid to work outside the box and, at times, outside the law. FBI legend Parker Lord on his team: "Apostles? There's nothing holy about us. We're a little maverick and a lot broken, but in the end we get justice right."

Joy & Peace!

Shelley Coriell

♥ ♥ ♥ ♥ ♥ ♥ ♥ ♥ ♥ ♥ ♥ ♥ ♥ ♥ ♥

From the desk of Hope Ramsay

Dear Reader,

Jane Eyre may have been the first romance novel I ever read. I know it made an enormous impression on me when I was in seventh grade and it undoubtedly turned me into an avid reader. I simply got lost in the love story between Jane Eyre and Edward Fairfax Rochester.

In other words, I fell in love with Rochester when I was thirteen, and I've never gotten over it. I re-read *Jane Eyre* every year or so, and I have every screen adaptation ever made of the book. (The BBC version is the best by far, even if they took liberties with the story.)

So it was only a matter of time before I tried to write a hero like Rochester. You know the kind: brooding, passionate, tortured...(sigh). Enter Gabriel Raintree, the hero of INN AT LAST CHANCE. He's got all the classic traits of the gothic hero.

His heroine is Jennifer Carpenter, a plucky and self-reliant former schoolteacher turned innkeeper who is exactly the kind of no-nonsense woman Gabe needs. (Does this sound vaguely familiar?)

In all fairness, I should point out that I substituted the swamps of South Carolina for the moors of England and a bed and breakfast for Thornfield Hall. I also have an inordinate number of busybodies and matchmakers popping in and out for comic relief. But it is fair to say that I borrowed a few things from Charlotte Brontë, and I had such fun doing it.

I hope you enjoy INN AT LAST CHANCE. It's a contemporary, gothic-inspired tale involving a brooding hero, a plucky heroine, a haunted house, and a secret that's been kept for years.

Hope Ramsay

♥ ♥ ♥ ♥ ♥ ♥ ♥ ♥ ♥ ♥ ♥ ♥ ♥ ♥ ♥ ♥

From the desk of Molly Cannon

Dear Reader,

Weddings! I love them. The ceremony, the traditions, the romance, the flowers, the music, and of course the food. Face it. I embrace anything when cake is involved. When I got married many moons ago, there was a short ceremony and then cake and punch were served in the next room. That was it. Simple and easy and really lovely. But possibilities for weddings have expanded since then.

In FLIRTING WITH FOREVER, Irene Cornwell decides to become a wedding planner, and she has to meet the challenge of giving brides what they want within their budget. And it can be a challenge! I have planned a couple of weddings, and it was a lot of work, but it was also a whole lot of fun. Finding the venue, booking the caterer, deciding on the decorating theme. It is so satisfying to watch a million details come together to launch the happy couple into their new life together.

In one wedding I planned we opted for using mismatched dishes found at thrift stores on the buffet table. We found a bride selling tablecloths from her wedding and used different swaths of cloth as overlays. We made a canopy for the dance floor using pickle buckets and PFC pipe covered in vines and flowers, and then strung it with lights. We spray-painted cheap glass vases and filled them with flowers to match the color palette. And then, as Irene discovered, the hardest part is cleaning up after the celebration is over. But I wouldn't trade the experience for anything.

Another important theme in FLIRTING WITH FOREVER is second-chance love. My heart gets all aflutter when I think about true love emerging victorious after years of separation, heartbreak, and misunderstanding. Irene and Theo fell in love as teenagers, but it didn't last. Now older and wiser they reunite and fall in love all over again. Sigh.

I hope you'll join Irene and Theo on their journey. I promise it's even better the second time around.

Happy Reading!

Molly Cannon

Mollycannon.com
Twitter @CannonMolly
Facebook.com

♥ ♥ ♥ ♥ ♥ ♥ ♥ ♥ ♥ ♥ ♥ ♥ ♥ ♥ ♥ ♥

From the desk of Laura London

Dear Reader,

The spark to write THE WINDFLOWER came when Sharon read a three-hundred-year-old list of pirates who were executed by hanging. The majority of the pirates were teens, some as young as fourteen. Sharon felt so sad about these young lives cut short that it made her want to write a book to give the young pirates a happier ending.

For my part, I had much enjoyed the tales of Robert Lewis Stevenson as a boy. I had spent many happy hours playing the pirate with my cousins using wooden swords, cardboard hats, and rubber band guns.

Sharon and I threw ourselves into writing THE WIND-FLOWER with the full force of our creative absorption. We were young and in love, and existed in our imaginations on a pirate ship. We are proud that we created a novel that is in print on its thirty-year anniversary and has been printed in multiple languages around the world.

Fondly yours,

Sharon
&
Tom Curtis

Writing as Laura London

♥ ♥ ♥ ♥ ♥ ♥ ♥ ♥ ♥ ♥ ♥ ♥ ♥ ♥ ♥

From the desk of
Sue-Ellen Welfonder

Dear Reader,

At a recent gathering, someone asked about my upcoming releases. I revealed that I'd just launched a new Scottish medieval series, Scandalous Scots, with an e-novella, *Once Upon a Highland Christmas*, and that TO LOVE A HIGHLANDER would soon follow.

As happens so often, this person asked why I set my books in Scotland. My first reaction to this question is always to come back with, "Where else?" To me, there is nowhere else.

Sorley, the hero of TO LOVE A HIGHLANDER, would agree. Where better to celebrate romance than a land famed for men as fierce and wild as the soaring, mist-drenched hills that bred them? A place where the women are prized for their strength and beauty, the fiery passion known to heat a man's blood on cold, dark nights when chill winds raced through the glens? No land is more awe-inspiring, no people more proud. Scots have a powerful bond with their land. Haven't they fought for it for centuries? Kept their heathery hills always in their hearts, yearning for home when exiled, the distance of oceans and time unable to quench the pull to return?

That's a perfect blend for romance.

Sorley has such a bond with his homeland. Since he

was a lad, he's been drawn to the Highlands. Longing for wild places of rugged, wind-blown heights and high moors where the heather rolls on forever, so glorious it hurt the eyes to behold such grandeur. But Sorley's attachment to the Highlands also annoys him and poses one of his greatest problems. He suspects his father might have also been a Highlander—a ruthless, cold-hearted chieftain, to be exact. He doesn't know for sure because he's a bastard, raised at Stirling's glittering royal court.

In TO LOVE A HIGHLANDER, Sorley discovers the truth of his birth. Making Sorley unaware of his birthright as a Highlander was a twist I've always wanted to explore. I'm fascinated by how many people love Scotland and burn to go there, many drawn back because their ancestors were Scottish. I love that centuries and even thousands of miles can't touch the powerful pull Scotland exerts on its own.

Sorley's heritage explains a lot, for he's also a notorious rogue, a master of seduction. His prowess in bed is legend and he ignites passion in all the women he meets. Only one has ever shunned him. She's Mirabelle MacLaren and when she returns to his life, appearing in his bedchamber with an outrageous request, he's torn.

Mirabelle wants him to scandalize her reputation.

He'd love to oblige, especially as doing so will destroy his enemy.

But touching Mirabelle will rip open scars best left alone. Unfortunately, Sorley can't resist Mirabelle. Together, they learn that when the heart warms, all things are possible. Yet there's always a price. Theirs will be surrendering everything they've ever believed in and accepting that true love does indeed heal all wounds.

I hope you enjoy reading TO LOVE A HIGHLANDER! I know I loved unraveling Sorley and Mirabelle's story.

Highland Blessings!

Sue-Ellen Welfonder

www.welfonder.com